FOREWORD

A Prize for Princes is the first Rex Stout novel to broach three subjects associated with Nero Wolfe: the country where he spent his youth, how his marriage ended, and his feelings in general toward women.

Set in 1914, *A Prize for Princes* concerns Balkan intrigue. Nero Wolfe was from that neck of the woods, growing up in Lovchen, Montenegro, and he was named after Monte Nero, located there.

Aline Solini, the title subject of *A Prize for Princes,* tried to end her marriage to Vasili Petrovich by poisoning him, which Nero Wolfe had mentioned was the crowning touch of his.

Referred to as "that most dangerous thing in the world—a woman with the face of an angel and the heart of a demon," Aline Solini further becomes the example in the extreme of Nero Wolfe's thoughts on women: "the vocations for which they are best adapted [are] chicanery, sophistry, self-advertisement, cajolery, mystification, and incubation . . . astonishing and successful animals."

A Prize
for
Princes

Rex Stout

CARROLL & GRAF PUBLISHERS, INC.
NEW YORK

Copyright © 2001 by Carroll & Graf Publishers, Inc.
(2nd edition)

Foreword copyright © 1994
by Carroll & Graf Publishers, Inc.

First Carroll & Graf mass market edition 1994
Second Carroll & Graf mass market edition 2001

Carroll & Graf Publishers, Inc.
A Division of Avalon Publishing Group
19 West 21st Street
New York, NY 10010-6805

Library of Congress Cataloging-in-Publication Data
is available.
ISBN: 0-7867-0882-4

Manufactured in the United States of America

CHAPTER I.

THE CONVENT.

Richard Stetton stopped at the first turn into the main street and gazed down its length, lit by the soft brilliance of the moon.

What he had seen in the last hour made him regret that he had come to Fasilica; he cursed the insatiable and morbid curiosity of youth that had brought him there.

Gutters running with blood; wild-eyed Turks, drunk with victory, striking down men, women, and children and looting their pockets and homes; the pitiful cowardice of the small garrison of soldiers whose duty it was to protect the little town with their lives; all this filled him with a revolting disgust and made him long to flee somewhere, anywhere, away from the sights and sounds of this night of horror.

Suddenly, as he stood wondering which way to turn, surrounded on every side by the terrible din and confusion of the stricken city, he was startled by hearing a new sound that rose above all the others.

It was the ringing of a bell, in wild, irregular strokes that seemed to epitomize the cries of suffering and despair which filled the streets from one end of the town to the other.

Stetton looked up; there could be no doubt of it—the sound of the bell came from the air directly above; and there, before his eyes, he saw the form of a belfry in the shape of a cross appearing dimly in the moonlight, at the top of a low, rambling building of dark stone, against which he was at that moment leaning.

The significance of the cross did not escape the young man; his face went white as he murmured: "A convent! God pity them!"

He turned and started to retrace his steps down the little street through which he had reached the center of the town.

As he turned he was jostled roughly by three or four Turks who were rushing past with drawn bayonets, and he again sought the shelter of the wall. Other soldiers came, until a group of thirty or more were gathered on the street in front of the stone building.

"This is the place," they were calling to one another. "How do we get in?"

They were searching along the wall for an entrance to the convent.

From round the corner there came a great shout of triumph and exultation from many gruff throats.

"Come, they have found it!" called the soldiers, as they disappeared in the direction whence the cries came.

Stetton, following them round the corner, saw in one glance that the convent and its occupants were doomed. A hundred or more soldiers were banging away with stones and paving-blocks at a little iron gate set between two pillars at the foot of a short flight of steps.

Others were approaching at a run down the street

from either direction, having left their victims to a short respite at the scent of this larger and richer prey. The bell above continued to ring in a wild and vain cry to Heaven for assistance.

The gate trembled, hung crazily on one hinge, and fell. For an instant the soldiers hung back, then swept toward the opening in a mad rush.

Stetton saw, just within the door, the figure of a woman, bent and gray-haired, standing in the path of the invaders with uplifted arm. A stone hurled by the foremost soldier struck her in the face, and she sank to the ground, while the soldiers surged through the gateway over her body.

Stetton, feeling himself grow faint, again turned the corner to escape the fearful scene. Then, possessed of a sudden hot anger against these men whom war had turned into wild beasts, he halted and looked round as though for some magic wand or brand from Heaven with which to annihilate them.

His eye, roving about thus in helpless fury, fell on an open window set in the wall of the convent, not three feet above his head. It was protected by iron bars, through which the dim light of a candle escaped to meet that of the moon outside.

Without stopping to consider the reason or rashness of his action, Stetton rushed into the street, picked up a heavy stone and hurled it with all his force at the window. It struck squarely in the center, bending two of the bars aside for a space of a foot or more.

In another second the young man had leaped up and caught one of the bars, and, pulling his body up and squeezing it through the space left by the stone, found himself within the convent.

He stood in a small room with a low ceiling, entirely bare and unoccupied. At one end was a narrow door; he crossed to it, and, stopping on the threshold, stood transfixed with astonishment.

Before him was a room exactly similar to the other.

Two wooden chairs were placed against the wall at the right. A closet stood on the opposite side, and in the center was a wooden table holding some scattered papers, a Bible, and a crucifix. Near the left wall was a *prie-dieu*; and before it, on the bare stone floor, knelt the figures of a young woman and a girl.

It was the sight of the young woman that had halted Stetton and rendered him speechless. At the noise of his entrance she had turned her head to face him without moving from her position, and it was not strange that he was startled by the beauty of her face even in that moment of excitement.

Her hair, magnificently golden, flowed over the folds of her gray dress and covered the ground behind; her eyes, whose deep, blue-gray color could be perceived even in the dim candle light, gazed compellingly straight into the face of the intruder. He remained silent, returning the gaze.

The girl who knelt beside the young woman—a small, slender creature with black hair and olive skin—suddenly sprang to her feet and crossed to the center of the room, while her black eyes snapped viciously at the young man in the doorway.

"Coward!" she said in a low tone of hatred and fear. "Strike! Are you afraid, because we are two to one? Strike!"

"Vivi!"

It was the young woman who called. She had risen to her feet and made a step forward.

"You are not—with them?" she continued, as her eyes again found Stetton's and seemed to take in every detail of his face and clothing. "You are of the town—you will save us?"

The young man found his voice.

"I am an American. I came through the window. I will save you if I can. They have already entered the convent—listen!"

From the corridors without came the sound of tramping feet and shouting voices.

"There is no time to be lost."

The girl and the young woman gazed about in terror, crying: "What shall we do? Save us!"

Stetton tried to collect his wits.

"Is there no way out—no secret passage?"

"None."

"The rear entrance?"

"It can be reached only by the main corridor," replied the young woman.

"The roof?"

"There is no way to reach it."

"But where are the others? Surely you are not alone here? Have they escaped?"

The young woman opened her lips to reply, but the answer came from another quarter. As Stetton spoke, the oaths and ejaculations of the soldiers in the corridors without were redoubled, and a series of frightful screams sounded throughout the convent. The shrieks of distress and despair rose even above the hoarse cries of the soldiers; they came evidently from the room on the other side of the wall. The face of the girl was white as she looked at Stetton and stammered:

"They are in the chapel. They were hiding there. God pity them!"

She approached the young man with trembling knees and an eloquent gesture of appeal; he stood as though paralyzed by the cries from beyond.

The cries grew louder. Footsteps and the gruff voices of soldiers were heard approaching down the corridor outside; another moment and they would be discovered.

Feeling a hand on his arm, Stetton turned to find the young woman gazing at him with eyes that held impatience and resolution, but nothing of fear.

"Could we not escape through the window?" Her voice was firm and calm.

"The window?" Stetton repeated stupidly.

Suddenly roused, he turned and ran swiftly into the next room and glanced through the barred window by which he had entered. The street without was deserted.

With a word to the others, who had followed and stood at his side, he squeezed his way through the bars and dropped to the ground below, falling to his knees. He got to his feet in time to catch the girl as she was pushed through the window by her companion. The young woman followed, disdaining any assistance as she came down lightly as a bird, and they stood together in the dimly lighted street.

Knowing that, close as they were to the main thoroughfare, they were apt to be discovered at any moment, Stetton lost no time in discussion of a route.

"Run!" he whispered, pointing down the narrow street by which he had approached the center of the town.

The young woman hesitated.

"But you?"

"I'll follow. Go!"

As they ran the shouts of the drunken soldiers and the cries of their victims assailed their ears from behind, urging them forward. The street which they were following—crooked and narrow, and saved from darkness only by the fading light of the moon—appeared to be completely deserted and the houses on either side were closed and shuttered and without lights.

Here and there a head appeared, thrust through a door or window, but at their approach was hastily withdrawn. It was evident that this street had not yet been invaded; their escape seemed a certainty—but where to find a safe retreat? Stetton overtook his companions and spoke as they ran:

"Do you know the town? Do you know any place to go?"

The young woman shook her head.

"No."

"Then follow this street. We must take to the country. If I could find General Nirzann—I know him—"

This suggestion—a somewhat foolish one under the circumstances—brought no response, and they continued their rapid flight. They had already passed three or four cross streets, and Stetton was beginning to think they were well beyond danger, when, as they reached the next crossing, they were suddenly confronted by a band of Turks who pounced on them from behind a little wooden building on the corner.

At the same moment, glancing to the left, Stetton was dimly aware of a fresh burst of shouts and outcries as the soldiers came rushing into the street from the other end and began a furious assault on the doors and windows of the houses and shops.

As the group of six or seven soldiers stopped directly in the path of the fugitives, they appeared to hesitate momentarily. Stetton heard one of them cry, "Come on, they have nothing! To the stores!"

Then, catching sight of the face of the young woman as she stood clinging to Stetton's arm, the speaker jerked himself forward and stared at her with a drunken leer.

"Allah! A beauty!" he laughed, and grasped her roughly by the shoulder.

Even as he acted, Stetton cursed himself for his folly. He knew that the little slip of paper in his breast-pocket, signed by General Nirzann, would permit him to pass unmolested, though it would be useless to protect his companions.

With a rapid glance he counted the group of soldiers—there were seven of them. Against such odds what could he do? He was a man of caution; he thrust his hand into his pocket and brought forth the slip of paper.

As he did so the leader of the band jerked the young woman violently forward and caught her in his arms.

It was then that Stetton acted, cursing his own folly.

11

Leaping forward, he struck the soldier a savage blow in the face with his fist.

The soldier staggered back with a cry of surprise and pain, releasing his hold on his intended victim.

"Pig!" he screamed, rushing at Stetton. His comrades sprang to his assistance with upraised bayonets and pistols.

Before they could reach him Stetton had thrust the young woman and the girl to one side, calling to them to run. Then he himself leaped aside, barely missing the point of the foremost bayonet. Dashing off to the right he had joined his companions before the soldiers had time to turn, and was racing down the street at the top of his speed.

The girl who had been called Vivi caught his hand as he came up to them, saying, "Are you hurt?" Stetton shook his head and urged them forward.

The sound of pistol shots came from behind, and bullets whistled past their ears. Then the shouts of the soldiers as they started in wild pursuit, shooting as they ran.

There came a sudden, sharp cry from the young woman.

"Are you hurt?" panted Stetton. "In the arm. It is nothing," she answered, without slackening her pace.

Glancing behind, Stetton muttered an oath as he saw that the soldiers were gaining on them. The street ran straight ahead as far as he could see in the moonlight, and he knew that a turn to the right or left would probably land them in the arms of another of the bands of marauding soldiers.

To escape by flight appeared impossible. With a hasty glance toward either side of the narrow street, in search of a possible refuge, he saw, some distance ahead and to the right, a house, through the window of which appeared the feeble light of a candle. It was removed somewhat from the street; reaching it, Stetton dashed suddenly onto the gravel walk in front, pulling his companions after him.

The door was locked; he rattled the knob and pounded frantically on the panels with his fists; the soldiers had turned into the path were now but a short distance away.

"In Heaven's name, open!" shouted the young man.

His companions had crouched against the door, locked in each other's arms. There was the sound of bolts drawn back, the door flew open, and the fugitives tumbled within.

Stetton heard a man's voice calling to the young woman and the girl to go to the rear of the house, to escape the bullets that were coming through the door. He turned to face the speaker—a giant of a man with a bushy black beard who was relocking and bolting the door.

"How many are there?" asked the man with the beard, pulling Stetton aside, out of range from the door.

"Seven."

"Turks?"

"Yes."

The man with the beard muttered an oath and ran to a window. Soon he called out:

"They seem to be out of ammunition. The drunken devils! Come here!"

Stetton joined him and looked through the window. The soldiers had halted a dozen paces from the door, and the one who had felt Stetton's fist appeared to be urging the others to make an attack.

Suddenly the man with the beard pulled a revolver from his pocket, thrust it through the glass of the window, and fired into their midst. One of the soldiers fell; the others, without stopping to look after their comrade, took to their heels and disappeared down the moonlit street.

"Cowards!" the man grunted contemptuously, pocketing his revolver. Then he turned to Stetton:

"You had better look after your companions—I'll stay here."

"But how—I don't know where—"

"You must remain for the night. By morning the officers will get these brutes under control, and you can return home. There are two rooms with beds in the rear. If you need me, you will find me in there," he finished, pointing to a room on the right.

"But, pardon me, are you alone?"

The man with the beard gazed at Stetton with piercing eyes. "Young man, you talk too much. But then—no wonder—it is your confounded English impertinence."

"American," Stetton smiled.

"It is all the same."

"We do not think so."

"Well—leave me." Black eyes flashed above the black beard. "Anyway, all this," he made a circle with his arm to encompass the war-devastated city of Fasilica, "this is all the result of your impudent interference. These mountains were made for us to rest our feet on. And if the Turks did not have your favor to rely upon—if you would leave it to us—"

Stetton had started to leave the room, but turned at the door.

"Us?"

The man with the beard scowled unpleasantly.

"Yes, us. I am a Russian, sir."

The scowl deepened; and Stetton, thinking that this was a strange host indeed, turned without making any reply and went in search of the young woman and the girl. He found them in a room in the rear, crouched on a bed in the corner. At his entrance they sprang to the floor and advanced to meet him with an eager question:

"The soldiers?"

"They have gone," said Stetton. "You are safe."

His eyes were fastened on the face of the young

woman; now that they had leisure for the feast, they could not leave it.

Wondrously beautiful she was, indeed; almost supernaturally so; what with the whiteness of her velvet skin, her glorious golden crown of hair, and the bright glitter of her gray-blue eyes. But even in that moment, when Stetton felt for the first time her compelling fascination, he beheld those gray-blue eyes with something like a shudder as they grazed boldly into his own.

"Our host frightened the soldiers away," he said, recovering himself with an effort. "We are safe for the night—we can sleep here—and by morning the trouble will be over."

"Oh, but you are good to us!" cried Vivi, advancing with outstretched hand.

She was a girl of seventeen or eighteen; while her companion was perhaps five years older. Her modest attractions, though by no means contemptible, were completely eclipsed by the other's bold beauty.

"You are so good to us!" Vivi repeated.

The young woman smiled.

"Indeed, you have earned our gratitude," she said. "If it had not been for you—but it is too horrible to think about. It would be absurd to try to thank you—*monsieur*—"

"My name is Stetton—Richard Stetton."

"And mine is Aline Solini. My little friend is Vivi Janvour—French, as you can see. There is nothing to tell about ourselves; when one has entered a convent the past is dead."

"And the future?" asked Stetton, wondering if he meant anything by the question."

"That, too."

"Still, it seems a shame to bury a flower."

"When it is withered?" Aline Solini smiled.

"I was about to add, when it is yet fresh and beautiful."

"You are bold, M. Stetton."

"Pardon me—I have eyes, and my tongue speaks for them—" Stetton stopped suddenly and cried: "But I forgot! You are wounded and need immediate attention."

Aline shrugged her shoulders.

"It is nothing."

But Stetton insisted, and finally she uncovered her arm for his inspection. The wound was by no means serious—scarcely painful—but the white skin was torn apart for a space of an inch or more, and an ugly red line extended below the elbow. With an exclamation of concern Stetton disappeared, and soon returned with a basin of water and some strips of cloth.

Noting Vivi's smile at his clumsy efforts to bathe and bandage the wound, he allowed her deft fingers to take the place of his awkward ones, watching her in silence from a seat on the edge of the bed.

Now that the danger was past, Stetton was congratulating himself on having met with so interesting an adventure. And, he added complacently, in his thoughts, it was apt to become more interesting still. If it did not, it would be no fault of his.

He looked at Aline, wondering how so glorious a creature had persuaded herself to abjure the world and its pleasures; in the usual total ignorance of the American Protestant concerning the Roman Church, he supposed that no one ever entered a convent without taking the veil.

Well, nun or Ninon, she was perfect, he was reflecting, when he was suddenly startled by the sound of her voice:

"You are staring at me, M. Stetton."

"Forgive me," stammered the young man. "I was thinking."

"I admire boldness," said Aline, and though her tone was playful, her eyes were cold. She turned and spoke to the girl.

"Thank you, Vivi; the bandage is perfect. Do we sleep in this room, *monsieur*?"

"There is another," said Stetton. "Perhaps it is more comfortable. Shall I find it?"

"No; this will do very well. We will leave the other for you."

Stetton shook his head, pointing to the door.

"I shall lie there."

"It is unnecessary."

"But if you will permit me—I should not forgive myself if any harm came to you—"

"Very well." Aline smiled, extending her hand. "Then we will say good night."

Stetton advanced and took the hand in his own. It was white and soft; he could feel the warmth of her blood through the delicate skin. There was a pressure of the fingers—or did he imagine it?

Raising his head, he saw her regarding him with a strange smile at once cold and friendly, and her eyes held an invitation that was at the same a challenge. Stetton felt a thrill run throughout his body—he could not have told whether it was pleasure or fear; still looking into her eyes, he lifted her hand and touched it with his lips deliberately.

Then he turned and left the room without paying any attention to Vivi, who had advanced to his side; nor did he reply to the scarcely audible good night that came from her lips.

Half an hour later, having seen the light of the candle disappear from the transom above their door, he approached and knocked lightly and cautiously.

"Well?" came Aline's voice.

"Do you wish anything?"

"Nothing, thank you."

"All right, good night."

Stetton, having wrapped himself in blankets obtained from the adjoining room, lay down on the floor across the doorway to dream of golden hair and piercing gray-blue eyes.

CHAPTER II.

THE MAN WITH THE BEARD.

On the following morning the streets of Fasilica bore mute evidence of the havoc wrought by the looting soldiers the night before. Well it was that the commanding officer of the Turkish forces had halted his victorious troops in their career of plunder with sternness and resolution, or the little city would have been leveled to the ground.

Everywhere doors and windows hung in splinters; the streets were strewn with rubbish and articles of clothing or household goods which the soldiers had thrown away in their haste to escape the punishment of their general; great brownish splotches appeared here and there on the pavement, a testimonial to the misfortune or unhappy resistance of some citizen; and in the business section of the town many of the buildings had been destroyed or damaged by fire.

One of these latter was the convent, which had been totally denuded of all its contents. What remained was a mere skeleton of stone, with its empty gloominess accentuated by the rays of the morning sun.

But the sight appeared to strike Richard Stetton as a joyful one rather than a sorrowful. He stood at the corner of the narrow street at the side, exactly opposite the barred window through which he had entered and escaped the night before.

Half an hour previous he had left Aline Solini and Vivi Janvour in the house where they had found refuge from the soldiers, with the object of ascertaining if the convent was in a condition to admit of their return. Obviously, it was not; hence Stetton's smile of satisfaction. His adventure, he was telling himself, was not to end with the excitement of the night.

On his way back to the house he tried to find something to take to his companions for breakfast, but no shops were open; besides, the soldiers had appropriated nearly everything eatable for their own use.

Aline met him at the door of the room in which she said Vivi had slept.

In a few words Stetton told her of the destruction of the convent, and of the impossibility of their finding shelter there. She received the news quite calmly, giving him her hand with a smile and inviting him within the room. Vivi, who had been sitting in a chair by the window, rose as he entered, with a timid nod of greeting.

"The convent is gone," said Aline, turning to her. "We cannot return there."

"Gone!" cried the girl, her face turning pale. "But what—are you sure?"

"I have been there," said Stetton. "It is nothing but an empty ruin."

"Then what are we to do?" faltered Vivi, looking at Aline. "Where can I go? I have no friends, no home—nothing."

"You have me."

Stetton tried, with a sidelong glance, to include Aline in this offer, but felt that the attempt was somehow a failure. She had crossed to the girl and put her arm around her shoulder.

"Don't be alarmed, Vivi," she said. "I shall take care of you."

"And you—have you a home?" asked Stetton.

"I? None." The tone was hard.

"Nor friends?"

"I have never had any."

"Then—if you will permit me—I would be only too happy—"

"Wait a moment." Aline had taken her arm from Vivi's shoulder and crossed half-way to Stetton's side. "You are about to offer us your protection, *monsieur*?"

"I am," Stetton nodded.

"Then before you continue I have something to say. Vivi, leave the room!"

The girl looked up in astonishment, then, as her eyes met those of the speaker, she crossed to the door without a word and disappeared in the hall outside, closing the door behind her. Stetton, left alone with Aline, sat waiting for her to speak.

For a moment the young woman was silent, regarding Stetton with a gaze of speculation, then she said abruptly:

"I thought it best we should be alone."

"But why?" he stammered, frankly puzzled. "What I have to say—"

"I know what you would say, but you think something very different. Let us be frank."

"I have no reason to be otherwise."

"Well, then—what would you say?"

"Merely this, that I place myself at your disposal. You are alone, without friends, with no place to go. I could be of service to you. I will do whatever you say."

"And why?"

"Need I give a reason?" Stetton began to be a little exasperated. "You are a woman, and in trouble. I am a man."

Aline, smiling, came closer to him.

"Do not be angry with me. If I ask questions, it is because my experience has taught me that they are necessary. You are, then, completely disinterested?"

"Yes, I assure you—"

Aline Solini came closer, still smiling. Her eyes looked full into Stetton's, filled, as on the night before, with something that might have been either an invitation or a challenge. There was something in their depths that frightened the young man and made him want to look away from them, but he could not. The woman stood close beside him as she murmured:

"Quite disinterested?"

"No!" Stetton exploded suddenly, and he grasped her hand in his own and held it firmly. "No!"

"Ah! You have spirit, then. I had begun to doubt it. Perhaps, after all— But what do you expect?"

"What you will give," replied Stetton, emboldened by her tone. He still held her hand.

"I do not give," said Aline, still smiling. "I pay—always."

She was quite close to him now; he could almost feel her breath on his face. Her lips were parted in a smile, but the beautiful eyes were cold, and Stetton was conscious of an overmastering desire to see them filled with warm surrender. At the same time, he felt a vague uneasiness; there was something terrifying about that unwavering gaze that seemed to be weighing him in some secret scale.

"You may believe it," he said in answer to her question, while his voice trembled, "for it is so."

He raised her hand to his lips.

She drew away from him and sat down on the edge of the bed.

"Well—we can talk of that later, when you have earned the right. I have something to say to you, Mr. Stetton."

There was a pause. Presently she continued:

"When you offer me your protection, *monsieur*, you invite danger. You found me in a convent. I had gone there not to escape the world, but a man. No matter why, he is my enemy—and I am his."

The gray-blue eyes flashed, brilliant and merciless.

"If you help me, he will be yours as well, and he is not one to be despised. For more than a year he has been searching for me, and though I fancied myself securely hidden in the convent, I was wrong. In some way he has traced me to Fasilica; two weeks ago, as I looked through the window of my room, I saw him pass below in the street.

"That is why I am willing to accept your aid; I must leave Fasilica at once. If he finds me he will kill me, unless—"

She stopped, looking at the young man significantly.

"But who is this man?" asked Stetton with dry lips. This was rather more than he had bargained for.

"As for that, I cannot tell you. Is it not enough that I hate him?" Aline eyed him narrowly "If it is not, that is well, you may leave me."

"But who is he?" repeated Stetton, who, like all men except heroes of romance, detested mystery. Besides, his caution was pulling at his coattails. "If he finds us—"

The gray-blue eyes flashed scornfully. "Oh, if I am not worth the trouble—" Then she leaned toward him, softening. "What, *monsieur*? But there, I thought you brave. It was a mistake, then?"

She smiled.

Stetton looked at her and his caution vanished.

"Tell me what to do," he said.

"You will help me?"

"Yes."

"It is dangerous."

"I accept the danger."

"Oh," Aline cried, suddenly, springing to her feet, "if you kill him, Stetton, I will love you! But yet—wait—let us understand each other. I must know what you expect."

"My eyes should tell you that."

"They do—but they say too little."

"It is love that is in them."

"That is not enough."

These words had passed rapidly, and Stetton did not understand them—or would not, had it not been for Aline's significant tone and glance. It was the meaning of these that made him hesitate and bring himself up sharply.

22

At his decision you will wonder; but not more so than he did himself.

To hear Aline Solini's words—their bluntness, their sharp precision—and to hear and see nothing else, was to lose all the charm of her, which lay in her electric glance, her soft velvety tones, her little movements of arms and shoulders, provocative, alluring, calculated to fire the blood of any man beyond any thought of caution or price.

It was not with words that Cleopatra persuaded Antony to throw away an empire to remain at her side. Words are never the weapon of a beautiful woman, nor should be. Aline Solini understood this—she knew full well the power she held and its source.

Richard Stetton looked at her. Young, vain, impressionable, he met her glance of fire and was lost. It has been said that her meaning was clear to him, and for a moment, creditable to his caution, he hesitated.

But some few things there are which appear to us, even at a first glance, to be so transcendently priceless that whatever the value set upon them they seem to be cheap indeed; and thus it was with Stetton. Besides, he did not take the time to consider consequences—a habit begun in the cradle. He said:

"It is not enough that I love you?"

"Not—No." This with a smile.

"Not—with all it means?"

"That is what I do not know." Aline raised a hand toward him, then let it fall again. "There can be no double meaning here, *monsieur*. You think I have offered myself to you? Perhaps; but first I must know what you ask."

Stetton looked at her, and thought of nothing but what he saw. He burst forth impetuously:

"I am asking you to marry me, *mademoiselle*."

"Akh!"

This cry, Russian in accent, tender and provocative in tone, was all that was needed to complete the young man's madness. He grasped her hand, standing in front of her, close, and looking into her eyes. Their glances melted into each other like a passionate embrace.

He whispered:

"Say yes—I ask you to marry me—say yes. Anything—anything! Ah! Speak to me!"

"Yes—yes—yes!"

It was a caress and a promise at once, tender and yielding. Sudden tears came to Stetton's eyes as he folded her gently in his arms and held her so for a long time. To look at her was music; to touch her a song of love.

He could not speak; for two minutes he remained silent, feeling himself overwhelmed by a rush of emotion, strange and sweet, but somehow—not satisfying. He moved a little back from her, suddenly demanding:

"When?"

Aline's lips were parted in a little smile at this display of eagerness.

"You must wait," she said.

"Wait?"

"Yes. Have I not said I have an enemy? You have said you love me; you have asked me to marry you; well, we cannot do everything at once. You must realize that I am in danger, that I must first escape—"

"Your fortunes are mine."

Aline flashed a glance at him.

"Thank you for that. Then—we are in danger. But you must make no mistake. I have not said I love you—though—perhaps in time— You have offered me your protection; I have agreed to marry you; that is all—it is a bargain. It must wait; we must first consider our safety."

"Well—" Stetton released her, stepping back a pace—"What are we to do?"

"We must leave Fasilica."

"Where do you want to go?"

"Anywhere—stay—" Aline stopped and appeared to reflect—"To Warsaw. Yes, Warsaw. That is best."

"But how are we to get there?" objected Stetton. "The whole country beyond here is nothing but a battlefield—indeed"—the young man interrupted himself, struck by a sudden thought—"it is most likely that you will not be allowed to leave Fasilica."

"Why should they detain us?"

"The policy of the Turk. Any one who once falls under his authority remains there. But, of course, with the Allies—and yes, by Heaven, that is it! I shall see General Nirzann. He is in command of the Frasars who combined with the Turks in the siege. He will get me passports—I am sure of it."

"Do you know him?"

"Yes—that is, slightly. I came in, you know, with the army."

"Ah! You are a soldier?"

"No."

"A journalist?"

"No. I am merely a curiosity-seeker. I looked for excitement, and I found you. Aline! You will let me call you that?"

"As you please," said the young woman indifferently. "But what of General Nirzann? When will you see him?"

"Today—now—at once."

"That is well. Vivi and I shall wait here."

Stetton turned quickly.

"Ah, I had forgotten her! Who is she? Is she to go with us?"

"She is an orphan. Her parents were French—Janvour was a minor diplomat, I believe, who died somewhere in the Balkans and left Vivi to be cared for by the Church. I met her in the convent. She loves me; we shall take her with us. And now, go."

"Yes."

Stetton hesitated a moment, then bent over Aline to

kiss her. But she held him back, saying, "Not yet, you must wait," in so cold a tone that he drew away from her half in anger.

Then, looking into her wonderful eyes and thinking of the future, so rich in promise, he turned without another word and left the room to go in search of General Nirzann. As he passed Vivi in the hall he heard Aline's voice calling to her to return.

On his way to the street Stetton stopped for a moment in the front of the house to look for the man with the beard, their strange host, but he was not to be found.

Once outside, he turned his steps rapidly toward the center of the town, which was gradually resuming its normal appearance as the citizens, reassured by a proclamation of the Turkish commander, came forth to clear away the debris of the night of pillage.

At the first corner, where he turned, Stetton approached a soldier standing on guard and obtained directions to the headquarters of General Nirzann.

As he walked down the narrow sunlit street, his mind was working rapidly, revolving the incidents of the night's adventure and their probable consequences to himself.

He did not know what to think of Aline Solini. What was the truth about this enemy whom she seemed to fear so greatly? Was she an adventuress? A political refugee? Perhaps, even, a fugitive from justice?

He did not know. What he did know was that he was afraid of her. Those eyes, whose beauty was eclipsed by the cold light of some implacable hatred of secret design, were not the eyes of innocence in distress.

"I would do well to be rid of her," muttered Stetton as he turned into the main street. Nevertheless, he continued to follow the route given by the soldier.

Having looked into Aline Solini's face and felt the quick pressure of her velvety fingers, he was held by them in spite of his native caution that amounted at times to cowardice.

"I would do well to be rid of her," he muttered again. Then he remembered the intoxicating promise of her lips and eyes as she had said: "You must wait."

As for time, he had plenty of it for any adventure. His father—a manufacturer of food products, with a plant in Cincinnati and offices in New York—was wealthy and somewhat of a fool, both of which facts were evidenced by his having furnished the necessary funds for a two years' tour of the world by his unpromising son, Richard.

Richard had been sojourning *à la Soudaine* at Budapest, when, on hearing that the mountains to the east were being invaded by the Turks and Frasars, he had betaken himself thither in search of sensation.

At Marisi he had introduced himself into the camp of the Frasars with letters of introduction from Paris and Vienna, and had followed them through their filibustering campaign till they had joined the Turks in the taking of Fasilica.

Then the entry into the town and the adventure of the night before. He was telling himself that he had found the sensation he sought, and, by dint of dwelling on the face and figure of Aline Solini, he became filled with a resolve that amounted almost to heroism.

He would take her away from Fasilica—away from the mysterious enemy whom she so evidently feared, to Moscow, or Berlin, or perhaps even St. Petersburg.

He went up the steps of a large stone building surrounded by a guard of soldiers for the protection and dignity of the general whose temporary headquarters were within.

In the first room off the hall on the right Stetton found General Nirzann seated before a large wooden table on which were spread maps and papers in apparent confusion. Near a window at the farther end stood a small group of young officers, with swords at their sides, conversing together in low tones.

In the rear of the room a telegraph instrument clicked noisily at intervals. The orderly who had conducted Stetton into the room stood at attention, waiting for the general to look up from his papers.

General Nirzann sat with lowered head, evidently lost in thought. He was a medium-sized man of about forty-two or three years. Beneath his bristling brows a long, thin nose extended in a straight line, and under that, in turn, appeared a dark brown mustache, turned up at the ends after the manner of Berlin.

His dark, rather small eyes, as he raised them to address the orderly, were filled with impatience and irritation. At his nod the orderly turned and left the room.

"What can I do for you?" said the general, looking sharply at Stetton.

The young man approached a step nearer the table.

"I have come to ask a favor, sir."

"A little more and you would have been too late. What is it?"

Stetton, who did not understand the remark, but thought he observed a grin on the face of one of the young officers who had approached, began to tell in as few words as possible of having found the young woman and the girl in the convent, without, however, mentioning the encounter with the soldiers.

The general waited in silence till he had finished; then he said:

"But what do you want of me?"

"Passports, sir, to leave the city."

"Who are these women—residents?"

"No, sir; that is, they were in the convent; one is French, the other, I think, Polish. They wish to go to Warsaw."

For a moment the general was silent, dropping his

eyes on the papers before him; then he looked up at Stetton:

"You know, this is none of your affair, *monsieur*. Because you had letters from friends of the prince, you were allowed to accompany us, but only on condition that you would stand on your own responsibility and cause us no trouble. You have annoyed me on several occasions; you are annoying me now. Besides, I do not know that my protection would be of any use; I leave Fasilica tonight. You say you intend to accompany these women to Warsaw. I am sorry for that. I should prefer that you remain here to torment my successor."

"I am sorry, sir—" Stetton began, but the general interrupted him:

"I know, I know; that will do. You shall have your passports. What are their names?"

"Aline Solini and Vivi Janvour," said Stetton.

General Nirzann had picked up a pen and begun to write on a pad of paper, but suddenly threw the pen down and said:

"After all, that will not do. I shall have to see these women and question them. Confound it, Stetton, you are more trouble than a dozen armies! Can you bring them here at once?"

The young man hesitated, thinking rapidly. Aline had said her enemy was in Fasilica; would it not be dangerous for her to appear on the streets in the daytime? But the passports must be obtained; it was necessary to take the risk. Stetton answered:

"Yes, sir; I can bring them."

"Very well, do so." And the general turned again to his papers, indicating that the interview was ended.

On his way out of the building Stetton, meeting a young lieutenant whom he knew, stopped him to ask why General Nirzann was leaving Fasilica.

"You haven't heard?" said the officer, smiling. "The prince has recalled him to Marisi and sent old Norbert in his place. He's in for a picking."

"Well," thought Stetton, "that means that we must get our passports as soon as possible," and he set out down the street at a rapid walk.

He found Aline and Vivi, especially the latter, in a fever of impatience and anxiety. As soon as he told them that it would be necessary for them to go with him to General Nirzann for their passports, this gave way to genuine alarm, in spite of his assurances that no harm would come to them.

"I do not like it," said Aline, frowning. "Besides—you know—it is scarcely safe for me to appear in the streets."

"But what are we to do?" demanded Stetton.

"Are the passports necessary?"

"Positively. Every road out of the city is guarded."

"Then we must make the best of it." The young woman turned to Stetton suddenly: "It is well you returned when you did; Vivi was frightened. Someone has been tramping up and down in the room in front as though he would tear the house down. Where are we? Who was it that let us in last night? I did not see him."

"Russian, he said he was," replied Stetton. "By the way, we must thank him before we leave. I have not seen him this morning. We owe him our lives, perhaps."

They made ready to depart. Vivi was clinging to Aline's arm, evidently completely dazed at her sudden contact with the whirl of life, for she had spent most of her years in the convent. As they passed into the hall and toward the front of the house, she kept muttering a prayer to herself under her breath.

At the end of the hall, Stetton, who was in front, stopped and knocked on a door leading to a room on the left. After a moment's wait a gruff voice sounded:

"Come in."

Stetton looked at Aline. She nodded, and all three of them passed inside.

The man with the beard was seated in a chair by the

window, holding in his hand what appeared to be a photograph. As the newcomers entered and he caught sight of the women he rose to his feet and bowed.

"We stopped to give you our thanks and to say good-by," said Stetton. "I assure you, sir—"

"You! *Mon Dieu!*"

The cry came from Aline.

At the same moment that it reached his ears Stetton saw the face of the man with the beard grow livid with violent emotion, and his eyes flashed fire. The next instant, before Stetton had time to move, the man with the beard had leaped past him to the door, which he locked, putting the key in his pocket.

Aline had at first started for the door, but, intercepted in that attempt, had retreated to the other side of the room, where she stood behind a heavy table at a safe distance; and when the man with the beard turned after locking the door he found himself looking straight into the muzzle of a revolver, held firmly in her small, white hand.

Stetton and Vivi stood speechless with astonishment, unable to speak or move.

"Stand where you are, Vasili." It was Aline's voice, calm and terrible. "If you move I shall shoot!"

"Bah!" said the man with the beard, with supreme contempt. Nevertheless, he stood still. "You may shoot if you like; you will not hit me, and you will not escape me. Fate will see to that.

"It has sent you to me, daughter of hell that you are! I am coming; you know my strength, Marie; I am going to choke the life out of your lying throat with these fingers."

As he moved a step forward he extended his hands in a terrible gesture of menace and hate.

"Look out, Vasili—not a step!"

Disregarding the warning, he leaped forward with incredible agility for his ponderous frame.

As he did so the report of the revolver sounded loud

and deafening in the small room, and the man with the beard, halted midway in his leap for vengeance, dropped to the floor with a bullet in his side.

Aline stood motionless, with the smoking barrel leveled at the prostrate form. "See if he is dead, Stetton," she said calmly.

The young man jerked himself forward, crying. "Good Heavens! Aline, what have you done?"

"Fool!" she exclaimed, "does the sound of a pistol frighten you?" Then, moving round the table and looking at the form on the floor: "And so, Vasili, you found me. So much the worse for you."

Suddenly the form moved, and, muttering a dreadful curse, the man tried to rise to his knees, but sank back helpless.

"So? You are not dead?" said Aline in a tone indescribable.

She raised the revolver and pointed it at the head of the wounded man. But Stetton sprang across and, snatching the revolver from her hand, threw it out of the window before she could pull the trigger. Then he shrank back before Aline's furious glance.

"Aline! Aline!" Vivi was crying. "Aline!"

"Silence, Vivi!" The young woman turned to Stetton. "We are ready now to go."

"But he may be dying! We cannot leave him—"

"Let us hope so. But for you I would have finished him. Take us to General Nirzann's."

Stetton, completely subdued by the tone of her voice and the imperious look of her eyes, opened the door, taking the key from the pocket of the man with the beard, not without a shudder, and let them pass out before him.

Aline had her arm around the shoulder of Vivi, whose face was deadly pale.

Stetton followed, after a last hasty glance at the prostrate form on the floor, and a moment later they were making their way down the street toward the headquarters of the general.

CHAPTER III.

MARISI.

Often, unwittingly, the shepherd leads his flock, or a member of it, straight into the jaws of the wolf. Similarly Stetton conducted Aline and Vivi before the gaze of General Paul Nirzann.

If he had been only partially acquainted with the fashionable gossip of Marisi he would have taken them to sleep in the fields in preference.

They found the general in the room where Stetton had had his interview an hour before.

By this time the group of officers had increased to a dozen or more, and the building was filled with an air of bustle and activity, incident, no doubt, to the transfer of the command which was to take place at noon. Orderlies were hurrying to and fro, and the telegraph instrument clicked continuously, while the low hum of voices was heard on every side.

An orderly approached the general:

"Richard Stetton asks to see you, sir."

The general looked up. "Is he alone?"

"No, sir; two women are with him."

"Show them in."

A minute passed, while General Nirzann busied himself with the inventory of ordnance to be handed over to his successor. Then, hearing an ejaculation of astonishment from the officers near the door, he looked up sharply.

Aline Solini had entered the room, followed by Vivi and Stetton.

The eyes of General Paul Nirzann widened in an involuntary stare as they rested on the face of the young woman, while the officers crowded together near the table with murmurs of admiration, which caused a flush of resentment to mount to Stetton's brow, and Vivi shrank closer to him, trembling.

Aline stood perfectly composed, though her face was slightly pale.

"Are these the women who desire the passports?" asked the general, looking at Stetton.

"Yes, sir."

The general regarded them for a moment in silence, then spoke to Aline:

"What is your name?"

"Solini—Aline Solini."

"And yours?"

But Vivi could not utter a syllable, and Aline answered for her:

"Mlle. Vivi Janvour."

"Where do you wish to go?"

"Warsaw."

"You were residing, I believe, in the convent. Are you citizens of Fasilica?"

"No, sir."

"Where do you come from?"

Aline hesitated perceptibly before she answered:

"I am from Odessa."

"And Mlle. Janvour?"

"She is from Paris. Her father, now dead, was Pierre Janvour, a French diplomat."

"You say you are from Odessa?"

"Yes, sir."

"Are you married?"

"No—that is—I am not."

The eyes of the general narrowed.

"You seem to be in doubt on the question," he observed dryly.

"I beg your pardon, sir"—Aline's eyes flashed with resentment—"I said I am not married."

"Very well, very well," The general was silent for a moment, then he continued: "I think, *mademoiselle,* I

34

should like to question you further—alone. Gentlemen, leave us."

The officers went out in a body, with backward glances at Aline; then the general rang for an orderly and told him to conduct Stetton and Vivi to another room. Stetton opened his mouth to protest, but was stopped by a glance from Aline, which said plainly: "Be easy; I can handle him."

As he waited with Vivi in a room at the further end of the hall, Stetton was consumed with impatience at the delay. He had before his eyes a picture of the man with the beard lying wounded on the floor, and he wanted only one thing now: to get out of Fasilica, and that as soon as possible.

What if he had been only slightly injured—what if he had followed them and was even now entering the headquarters of the general? He went to the door of the room and looked down the hall; no one was to be seen but the guard at the entrance.

"After all, Aline was right; I was a fool to interfere," he muttered.

"I beg your pardon; what did you say?"

It was Vivi's voice; he had forgotten her presence.

"Nothing," he answered, turning. "I was thinking aloud."

Presently the girl spoke again:

"Do you know who that—that man was, M. Stetton?"

"What man?" Stetton affected not to understand.

"The one—we left—back there."

"No." Stetton looked at her. "Do you?"

"No. I know nothing. How could Aline do it? You heard—she would not allow me to speak to her on the way here. She has been so good—I have always loved her so!"

"Did you know her before she came to the convent?" asked Stetton.

"No. I saw her first there. I was not allowed to be with her, and she used to come to my room at night

35

to talk. She was there last night when the soldiers came—and you.''

There was something in the last two words that sounded pleasantly in Stetton's ears. He looked at the girl.

"So that was your room?"

"Yes. I have lived there ever since I could remember. It was so pleasant after Aline came, and now—" Vivi shuddered and turned away.

"Now it will be pleasanter still," declared Stetton, "as soon as we get away from Fasilica. You will see. You know nothing of pleasure, child."

He was surprised to hear her cry:

"But I do! And I am not a child!"

"No?" he said, amused. "Pardon me, Mlle. Janvour."

He walked to the door again and looked down the hall. It remained empty.

"What the deuce can they be doing?" he muttered, and took to pacing up and down the room.

Vivi had seated herself in a chair, and her face betrayed an anxiety as keen as his own. For twenty minutes or more they continued to wait thus in silence, and Stetton had about decided to investigate for himself when the orderly appeared at the door to announce that General Nirzann requested his presence.

Vivi accompanied him. They found the general still seated at the table, while Aline occupied a chair at one end. As they entered, the general rose to his feet and bowed politely, while Aline sent a reassuring smile to Vivi.

"I beg your pardon, *mademoiselle*," said General Nirzann, "for having subjected you to an inconvenience that you perhaps regarded as a discourtesy. Believe me, it was not so intended. Mlle. Solini has explained everything satisfactorily."

Setton sighed with relief.

"And the passports?"

"They will not be necessary, M. Stetton. Mlle. Solini has changed her mind—the privilege of every woman. She is going to Marisi; and, since I myself leave for that place this afternoon, she has done me the honor to accept the protection of my escort."

Stetton started with anger.

"So that is what—" he began violently, but was interrupted by Aline's voice:

"We shall expect you to accompany us, M. Stetton. Vivi, too, of course."

"But I thought you wanted to go to Warsaw!" the young man protested; then, catching a significant glance from Aline, he checked himself and said: "Of course, as the general says, you have a right to change your mind. And, since I have nothing else to do, I shall be glad to go with you."

This apparently did not please General Nirzann; he frowned at Stetton with evident hostility, saying: "It is not necessary." Whereupon the young man smiled provokingly.

"Nevertheless, as Mlle. Solini invites me, I shall go. And now, sir, we must leave you; the ladies have not breakfasted."

"They can breakfast here," said the general.

"Nor I."

"Well—and you, too."

Stetton hesitated. He wanted to refuse, but caution advised otherwise. At this moment, he reflected, the man with the beard, breathing vengeance, might be searching the streets for its object; decidedly they were safer where they were, especially under the protection of the general. He ended by accepting.

Breakfast was served to them in a room on the floor above by General Nirzann's personal steward—fruit and eggs and rich, yellow cream from some neighboring farm.

They ate in silence; once or twice Stetton started to speak, but was halted by a glance from Aline, with a nod at the steward. Then, when they were finished and the dishes had been cleared away, she sent Vivi to the other end of the room and turned to him with a smile.

"You look angry, *monsieur*—and full of words. Now you may talk."

"Have I not reason to be?"

"Angry?"

"Yes."

"What is it?"

"Good Heavens!" Stetton burst out. "Have I not seen you mur—"

"Stop!" Aline's eyes flashed. "You are not happy in your choice of terms. It was in self-defense. He would have killed me."

"Not when he was lying on the floor helpless," retorted Stetton. "I cannot help my choice of terms. You would have murdered him."

"I do not deny it," said Aline calmly. "And I do not regret it. He is not fit to live."

"Who is he?"

"Did I not say I had an enemy?"

"Oh," said Stetton slowly, "it was—the one you told me of?" Aline nodded, and he continued: "But I might have guessed it. Then—of course I cannot know—nor can I blame you."

A smile appeared on Aline's lips, and she stretched out her hand and placed it on his as it lay on the arm of his chair.

"You trust me, do you not?" she whispered; and Stetton, gazing into her eyes, forgot to look for a meaning in her words.

Presently he said:

"Still, I failed you. You must laugh at me when you remember that I offered you my protection. It was a sorry bargain you made, *mademoiselle*."

"I do not think so," said Aline, with her inscrutable smile. "I know why you say that—because I accepted the protection of General Nirzann. But was it not best?

Our bargain still holds; I—I do not wish to forget it"—
Stetton seized her hand—"and you may still fulfil your
part. Did you not say you are an American?"

Stetton nodded, wondering.

"Then," Aline continued, "perhaps it will soon be
necessary that you return to your own country?"

"No," said Stetton.

"I suppose you are rich, like all Americans?"

"I am worth ten millions," said the young man impressively. His caution did not extend to his father's
money.

"Francs, of course?"

"No, dollars," said Stetton.

"Well, that is not what I wish to talk of," said Aline,
who had found out what she wanted to know. "It is
this: I have accepted General Nirzann's escort because
he declares that without it we would be unable to get
ten miles from Fasilica. The country is devastated, and
the railroad runs no farther than Tsevor. We must leave
Fasilica, so what could I do?"

"It is best, I suppose," muttered Stetton.

"There was another reason," Aline continued, re-
garding the young man speculatively, "why I accepted
General Nirzann's offer. You will be surprised—so was
I. He is my cousin."

Stetton turned quickly.

"Your cousin!"

"Yes, a distant one. He is a cousin of my mother.
We discovered it quite by accident, while he was questioning me in your absence. I had never seen him before, but he established the fact."

Aline smiled.

"So you see I have a relative, after all."

Stetton looked at her curiously. The truth was, he
doubted her, and he was searching for a corroboration
of his doubt in her face.

She met his gaze unfalteringly. He ended by be-
lieving, and made some remark concerning the strange-

ness of the coincidence by which she had found this unknown relative.

"Yes," said Aline composedly, "it had been so long since I had heard of him that I had forgotten his very existence.

"But," she added, "notwithstanding the fact that he is my cousin, I do not trust him. He said—it is not necessary to repeat his words, but I want you near me till we arrive safely at Marisi. You see, I trust you."

Stetton, who had not completely lost his reason, tried to tell himself that the timidity of this speech fitted ill with the resolute and terrible action of Aline Solini but two hours before; but what could he do?

Her eyes were now gazing into his with an expression at once tender and appealing, and her hand again sought his and pressed it gently.

"Then it is settled," she said, crossing to the window and looking down into the street. "We leave with General Nirzann this afternoon. Vivi! Come here, child. We must make up a list of things we will need for the journey."

Stetton started up from his chair, exclaiming: "I was a fool not to have thought of that! Of course, you will need—here is my purse. Take what you want."

"Thank you, General Nirzann has already come to our rescue," said Aline. "An orderly is coming at noon for my list."

"And you accepted!" Stetton exclaimed angrily.

"Why not? It was kind of him."

The two women began to write down the names of the articles they desired, and Stetton turned away. A vague sense of uneasiness and danger was within him; he did not know why exactly, but he began to ask himself questions.

This Aline Solini, who and what was she? Why did he feel, as though it were a natural law of his being, that he must follow her and await her pleasure? Young as he was, and cautious, he had not been without affairs of love, but he had always congratulated himself that no woman had ever made a fool of him. And, he had added, never would.

It was evident to him that General Nirzann, too, had been fascinated by her. This increased his uneasiness. Clearly, he would be a fool to have anything more to do with her; he saw before him the form of the man with the beard lying on the floor, with the revolver pointed at his head, and he shuddered.

Then he thought of what she had just said—of her abrupt question concerning his fortune. "She is a schemer, an adventuress," he thought, "and she is too much for me. I will not go to Marisi."

But, looking at Aline, and meeting her eyes, he felt his resolution waver within him. He crossed the room to her side and began to discuss arrangements for the journey.

Three o'clock that afternoon found them ready to depart. They were to travel on horseback to Tsevor, thirty miles away, where they would take train for Marisi. A hundred troopers were to conduct them; a precaution rendered necessary by the wildness of the country and the hostility of its inhabitants to those who had allied themselves with the Turks.

Aline and Vivi, attired in coarse black suits, the best costume obtainable in Fasilica, were mounted on ponies from the mountains—raw, hungry-looking animals, while Stetton had been given an old black troop-horse. General Nirzann rode a magnificent white Arabian.

The formalities were few: a salute from some five hundred soldiers drawn up at attention, and they were off down the main street of Fasilica. As they passed the convent, Stetton saw tears in Vivi's eyes as she gave a last, long look at the ruins of what had sheltered her for so many years.

Aline's face was set straight ahead, without so much as a farewell glance.

Half of the escort of troopers rode ahead as a vanguard, while the remainder brought up the rear, riding in fours. This until they reached the mountains; then they were forced to ride in single file by the narrowness of the trail, which at times hung to the side of a steep precipice, hardly more than a shelf.

Two hours it took them to pass the range, and then they found themselves again in a level, winding valley—the valley of the Schino River, which has so often been the scene of bloody conflicts in that war-infested region.

It was a little past seven o'clock when they clattered on to the pavement of the main street of Tsevor. Vivi, who rode at Stetton's side, was greatly fatigued by the unusual and violent exercise, and was barely able to keep her seat in the saddle.

Stetton himself was angry and in ill humor, for General Nirzann had monopolized Aline's company throughout the journey. As he alighted at the railroad station and helped Vivi to dismount, he tried to persuade himself once more to end the matter by returning with the troopers to Fasilica; but he heard the general's little speech of farewell and saw the men turn and ride off, without hinting at any such intention.

A courier had been sent ahead in the morning to arrange for a private car, and they found everything in readiness. They entered it at once and in haste, for a good-sized crowd had collected on the platform at their arrival, and were amusing themselves by hurling insults and epithets at the head of General Nirzann, who took his seat in his compartment with a scowl, muttering something about "revenge on the scurvy rascals."

Aline and Vivi had a compartment together toward the front of the car; Stetton's was in the rear. A few minutes after they had arrived the train pulled out.

Stetton sank back in the seat of his compartment with a feeling of utter dejection and depression. Something indefinable seemed to weigh upon his heart with a suffocating pressure; something seemed to be saying to him, "Do not go to Marisi."

He tried to shake this feeling off, but it would not leave. He raised the window and allowed the cool night air to rush in against his face, but the desolate blackness without seemed to bring with it a voice that said: "Do not go to Marisi."

He closed the window with a bang, muttering: "This is ridiculous. Am I a weak fool, to allow myself to be afraid of nothing? One might think that Marisi was the home of the devil himself. If it gets too hot for me I can get to Berlin in eighteen hours."

He composed himself with an effort and began to doze, and finally fell sound asleep.

Six hours later he was awakened by some one opening the door of his compartment. It was Vivi. She watched him with a little smile on her face as he opened his eyes.

"What is it—what is it?" asked Stetton, rubbing his eyes

Vivi replied:

"Aline sent me to wake you. She is the only one who did not sleep. We have reached Marisi."

CHAPTER IV.

THE WHEEL STARTS SLOWLY.

It was late in the morning of the following day when Stetton awoke after four hours' sleep in a luxurious room of the Hotel Walderin, Marisi, and, rising, walked to an open window which looked out on an open court of the hotel.

All his depression of the night before was gone; he felt buoyant, confident, and he was humming a lively popular tune as he thrust his head into a basin of cold water with a little shiver of pleasure.

At Fasilica and Tsevor he had felt more or less out of the world, away from the safeguards and conventions of civilization; now he was in a fashionable hotel in Walderin Place, as much a part of European life as Hyde Park or the Bois de Boulogne.

This fact drove away his nonsensical fears; he laughed aloud at them. And, he was reflecting, on the floor immediately above was sleeping a young and beautiful woman, as his guest.

He laughed aloud again, in great good humor with himself and the world, and began to dress. What a divine creature! Was she not worth any price? He asked himself this question with an air of bravado to frighten away what doubt remained.

Marry her? Gad! Who would not? Such an opportunity comes only by miraculous luck. This was his thought.

An hour later he presented himself before Aline and Vivi in the drawing-room of their apartment.

"We breakfasted here," said Aline in answer to his question. "How could we go downstairs? We have no clothes."

"I forgot—of course," said Stetton, a little embarrassed. Then he added with a touch of malice: "But what of the general's list?"

Aline laughed at his tone, then said with a smile:

"You are wrong to be angry with me; we needed his help, and it was necessary to humor him."

"Well, as for the clothes—I shall send someone from Morel's. Will that do?"

"That will do excellently."

"And you, *mademoiselle,* is there anything else you require?"

"Nothing," said Vivi quietly.

She was standing by Aline's chair, with her large, dark eyes passing from one to the other as they spoke.

There was an air of watchfulness about her; Stetton

had noticed it before, but it appeared to be the result merely of childish and innocent curiosity.

He wished that she would leave the room; he felt constrained in her presence, and there were several questions he wanted to ask Aline. He lingered a while longer, making observations on nothing in particular, then left to perform the errand at Morel's, saying that he would return in the afternoon. As he went out he laid a bank-note on a small pedestal near the door.

As soon as the door had closed behind him Aline crossed the room with quick steps and picked up the bank-note. It was for five thousand francs. Smiling, she placed it in her dress.

"What is that?" asked Vivi curiously.

Aline told her. She looked puzzled.

"But why should he give us so much money? What can we do with it?"

"You little goose," said Aline, and there was genuine affection in her tone; "you are no longer in a convent. Wait; you will see. Luck is with me now; it is all I needed. Ah, Vasili—" her eyes became cold and her tone hardened—"you taught me—others will pay for you."

"All the same, we should not take that money," said the girl stubbornly.

"Listen, Vivi." Aline looked at her speculatively, as though trying to decide what to say. Then she continued: "You know I love you."

"I know," said Vivi, taking her hand.

"You know I would do only what I think best. I am wiser than you."

"I know," Vivi repeated.

"And you do not think I did wrong when—last night."

"No, I no longer think you did wrong; but it was horrible."

"Well, you must trust me." Aline patted the girl's hand gently. "You must not ask me to explain things.

As for M. Stetton's money—I will tell you about that. But it is a great secret. You must not mention it."

"How could I? I know no one."

"You know General Nirzann; and you must not speak of it to M. Stetton. He does not wish it to be known. I accept his money because I am going to marry him."

Vivi hastily drew her hand away and looked up with startled eyes.

"You are going to marry him?" she said slowly.

Aline answered: "Yes. Does it surprise you? What is the matter, child?"

Vivi's face had grown pale and she seemed to be trembling. But she soon controlled her emotion and said:

"I am so glad, Aline. Do you love him?"

"Yes," replied the woman with her peculiar, inscrutable smile. "But, remember, you must say nothing of what I told you."

"No; I promise," said Vivi. Her face was still pale and she seemed to be forcing her voice to be calm.

At that moment a servant appeared to announce that a messenger from Morel's asked to see Mlle. Solini. He was admitted at once, and they were soon busily examining samples of dresses, suits, cloaks, and lingerie.

Vivi held back at first, but it was not long before she had entered the performance with as great delight as Aline herself.

In the meantime Stetton, having called at Morel's and performed two or three errands on his own account, was walking along the sunny side of the fashionable drive which stretches away to the north from Walderin Place.

On this side was the park, on the other a long line of sumptuous dwellings, the most important of which was the white marble palace of the Prince of Marisi.

It was too early for anyone to be seen; the Drive was practically deserted.

"Hang it all," Stetton was saying to himself as he walked along, "that little Vivi is not at all bad-looking, but she is in the way. Something must be done with her. I wonder if Naumann is in town."

On his way back to the hotel he stopped at the German legation and asked for Frederick Naumann. He was told that his friend would not be in till late in the afternoon, and he resumed his walk along the Drive, now impatient for the time when he should see Aline again.

A little after one o'clock found him in her apartment.

She and Vivi were both quite transformed by their purchases of the morning—so much so that Stetton felt a thrill of joy and pride run through him as he advanced to take the hand of this wondrously beautiful woman who had accept his protection and his money.

He wanted everyone to see her; he wanted to tell people that she belonged to him. Above all, he wanted her; though always he felt a curious sense of uneasiness in her presence.

Instinct was trying to do for him what reason would have done for a wiser man, who, looking at Aline Solini, would have said: "She is that most dangerous thing in the world—a woman with the face of an angel and the heart of a demon. Beware!"

Stetton approached her, saying:

"Now, indeed, you are irresistible."

"The least I could do was my best for you," replied Aline.

"And Vivi, too!" said Stetton. "*Mademoiselle*, allow me to say that you are charming."

The girl bowed without replying as she retreated to a seat at the farther end of the room.

Stetton cast a meaning glance at her, saying to Aline:

"I want to talk with you."

She smiled, reading him with her eyes.

"Yes," she agreed; "it is necessary that we come to an understanding."

She sent Vivi away on some pretext or other and again turned to Stetton:

"Well, *monsieur*?"

But, despite his firm resolution of the morning, the young man could find nothing to say, now that he found himself alone with her. He hesitated, seeming to search for words, and finally ended by stammering out:

"You know—you know—"

Aline laughed outright:

"You are an awkward lover, Stetton!"

This brought Stetton to a standstill and left him without anything to say. He burst out brutally:

"Well, you promised to marry me, and I can't wait. You promised me."

Aline said coolly:

"If you can't wait, really I am sorry. I see that you have greatly misjudged me. I will not detain you longer. Good-by, *monsieur*."

"What do you mean?" cried Stetton, frightened at the thought of losing her.

"You are too impatient. You approach me like a savage with a club; you have no tact, no finesse; in a word, I am disappointed in you, and we had best part while we are friends."

"But that is impossible!"

"Impossible?"

"Yes, it is indeed!" The young man's anxiety made him eloquent—that, and her exquisite face so close to his own. "Good Heavens, I love you! How can I leave you? I see plainly I have made a mistake, but you will forgive me—you must forgive me. I will be patient—I swear it! Tell me you will not send me away!"

"You love me, then?"

"You know it! Devotedly!"

Aline smiled and he seized her hand.

"I may stay?" he cried.

48

"I don't know," said Aline, assuming a tone of doubt, for she was now sure of him. "I did not wish to forget our bargain—you may believe that, Stetton. But I must have my own time."

"You will see—I shall be patient."

"Then—"

Aline extended her hand, and he pressed it to his lips, kissing the fingers and palm over and over.

She continued slowly, as though picking her words: "It is only fair you should know why I desire a delay. I mean the particular reason—it is Vivi."

"Vivi?"

"Yes. I love her, and I feel that I am responsible for her welfare, which means in the case of a young girl like her, her marriage. I will never have another opportunity like the present.

"General Nirzann"—Stetton started slightly at the name—"has promised to introduce me into the best circles of Marisi, and it will be strange if I cannot find a match for her. Then I shall be ready to leave Marisi—with you, if you still desire it."

"But General Nirzann—why should he do this?" demanded Stetton in astonishment.

"I have made a friend of him. Besides, is he not my cousin? Be easy; you have no reason to be jealous; he is an old fool. I can manage him."

"I don't like it," Stetton muttered.

Aline laughed.

"Surely you have not so poor an opinion of yourself as to fear an old fossil like the general? You should know better—if I did not prefer you to any other—but there, I shall confess too much."

She glanced into his eyes and then quickly away, as though afraid of betraying her thoughts.

"Confess!" cried Stetton. "Ah, tell me!"

"What can I say?" She pretended to hesitate, and actually succeeded in bringing a pink flush to her face.

"Tell me you love me!"

"Well, then—I do—a little."

Stetton clasped her in his arms. She submitted to the embrace for a moment, then drew herself away.

"But there—you know you must be patient."

"I cannot promise that," said Stetton, breathing quickly. "But I shall not annoy you. You are worth waiting for a lifetime; you will see if I mean what I say. In the meantime I must see you every day—you cannot deny me that—and I can help you."

"Yes, you can help, now that you are sensible," said Aline with a tender and provoking smile.

"No other pleasure is worth a thought," said Stetton, completely bewitched. "Tell me, what can I do?"

Aline had been waiting for that question. She glanced at him narrowly through her eyelashes, saying:

"There are so many things I don't know where to begin. Of course, it is all a matter of money."

"Of course," Stetton agreed, kissing her fingers.

"In the first place," Aline continued, "If my plans for Vivi are to be successful, we cannot live in a hotel, even the Walderin. We must have a house on the Drive, with a carriage and servants."

Stetton looked up quickly, frowning. He had not thought of beginning on such a scale. The rent alone would amount to fifty thousand francs. "But I don't see why—" he began.

"Luckily, that difficulty is settled," Aline interrupted quickly, noting his frown. "General Nirzann has offered me the use of his house, since he expects to occupy rooms in Marisi Palace for some time. He is a bachelor, you know. It is very good of him."

The fact was, General Nirzann was so far from being the owner of a house on the Drive that he was a pauper, but Stetton did not know that. What he thought was that under no circumstances should Aline live in a house belonging to the general. He said sarcastically:

"Yes, I have no doubt it was a very kind offer. But you must not accept it."

"I have already done so," said Aline.

"Then you must reconsider and decline."

"Stetton, you are positively childish. Besides, I must have the house."

There was a slight pause before the young man said:

"Then I will rent one."

Aline lowered her eyes, that he might not see the light of triumph in them, saying:

"It will be expensive."

"I can afford it," replied Stetton.

"It must be furnished."

"Of course."

"And we shall need a carriage and servants."

"Certainly."

"Then it is settled?"

For reply, Stetton kissed her hand. They talked a while longer, discussing the details of this new arrangement; then the young man made ready to go. At the door he turned, saying:

"By the way, I have a friend or two in Marisi; you will allow me to introduce them to you?"

Then, as Aline answered in the affirmative, he went away to his room on the floor below. There he sat down to write a letter to his father in New York, containing a request for a fifty-thousand-dollar draft.

An hour later, as Aline sat revolving her plans in her mind, with a smile that meant danger for anyone who got in the way of them, a servant entered with the card of General Paul Nirzann. Aline took the card, while the smile became deeper. Then she said:

"Show him up."

In a few moments the general entered. Though he held himself erect as he walked across the room to bend over Aline's hand, his bearing was more that of a beau than a soldier. His gait was mincing and he wore a smirk on his face.

After greeting him, Aline said:

"Have you made your peace with the prince?"

"Perfectly," replied General Nirzann with a wave of the hand. "The prince read me a lecture on the brutalities of the campaign, and then opened his arms to me. It is impossible to avoid cruelty when you are allied with the Turks, and I told him so. You may believe he did not like it, but I crammed the truth down his throat."

Aline smiled at the idea of this popinjay cramming anything down another man's throat. She said:

"Why didn't he return you to the command?"

"He preferred to keep me in Marisi," replied the general. "The fact is, he can hardly do without me. When I am not at the palace everything goes wrong. He admits it."

"I see."

"And besides," he continued, "I preferred to stay. He was a little surprised at that, but he has never seen you, *mademoiselle*. He does not know the attraction that Marisi holds for me."

"But he will," thought Aline to herself. She said aloud: "It is good of you to say so, my dear general."

"Tut!" said the general. "There is no sense in that. Nor is there any goodness in me. Ask the ladies of Marisi—they could tell things that would astonish you. You know very well I love you, *mademoiselle*."

"Yes; you have told me so," said Aline, trying not to appear impatient.

This was the general's side of the question, and she wanted to talk on her own. After a short pause she added:

"I suppose you did not mention my name to the prince?"

"Good Heavens, no!"

"I presume that will come later?"

"Much later," said the general emphatically. "We must proceed with caution."

"It is just as well. It will take a week or so, at least,

to obtain a house and make the necessary preparations. After that—''

''Have you hooked the American?'' the general interrupted.

Aline shrugged her shoulders.

''Of course. And paid him with promises. He is at this moment searching for a house.''

The general cackled with amusement.

''The young fool!'' he snorted gleefully. ''He doesn't know women, that's sure. The way with them is, pay first and maybe afterward. Eh, *mademoiselle*?''

''It is evident that you do know women,'' said Aline.

She was wondering to herself when the old fool would stop his chatter and allow her to gain some information. After a short pause she said abruptly:

''And now, what of our conspiracy?''

The general looked puzzled as he repeated: ''Our conspiracy?''

''Yes. When is my first dinner party?''

''Tomorrow, if you wish.'' The general bowed gallantly. ''You may count on me.''

''Thank you,'' said Aline with a touch of irritation. ''But you know very well what I mean.''

''Yes, I know what you mean. But are you not pushing things a little, *mademoiselle*?''

''Why delay?''

''Because it is necessary.''

''I do not understand that. The season has begun; the sooner we take advantage of it the better.''

The general looked at her with something between a simper and a frown; then he said:

''You seem to forget something.''

''What is that?''

''My happiness.''

''But, my dear general, that is absurd.''

The general sighed. *''Chère amie,''* he said, ''will you come to dinner with me this evening?''

''I have no clothes.''

53

"That is true. Then I suppose I must wait."

Aline whispered:

"Wait until I am mistress in my own house, and you will see, my brave soldier."

"Divine creature!" the general reiterated, trying to give himself the appearance of one dying for love.

"Still, you try to bargain with me," said Aline.

"Who would not bargain where possible to gain heaven?" exclaimed the general.

"Really, you are in danger of making me think you love me."

"Do I not?"

Aline smiled. "Perhaps."

"But it is certain!" cried General Nirzann fiercely. "You think I bargain with you—well, that is because I love you. Do not think I have been idle in your behalf. As I was coming to the hotel I met Mme. Chébe on the Drive, and I spoke to her of you. You will probably receive her card within the first week at your house, and she is one of the six most important women in Marisi."

"My dear general," cried Aline.

The general was unable to meet her flashing eyes.

"You intoxicate me!" he murmured, half dazzled.

And when five minutes later, General Paul Nirzann left the Hotel Walderin he was hardly able to walk straight for the dizzy exaltation in his brain.

As for Aline, she remained in the chair where the general had left her, with her chin resting on the palm of her hand. Her eyes were narrowed in deep speculation and a peculiar smile appeared on her lips.

But her thoughts were not of Richard Stetton, who at that moment had just finished the last paragraph of a six-page letter to New York, nor of General Nirzann, who was strolling along with an erect figure and a satisfied smile.

No; they had traveled down the fashionable drive to the white marble palace of the Prince of Marisi.

CHAPTER V.

NAUMANN TELLS A TALE.

The following morning found Stetton running from one end of Marisi to the other in search of a house suitable as a setting for his jewel. So he phrased it to himself.

Owing to the fact that the fashionable season had begun two weeks before, he found his task by no means an easy one. All day he searched and the better part of the day following; then quite by chance he ran across an old rugged stone structure at one end of the town, in the worst possible repair and filled with musty furniture. He hastened to the hotel to report to Aline.

"But that will not do at all," said she when he told her where the house was. "It would be much better to stay here. We must positively be on the Drive."

Stetton declared that to be impossible, saying that a house on the Drive could not be procured for love or money.

"Nevertheless, we must have it," was her calm reply.

"But I tell you we can't get it!" cried Stetton with pardonable irritation, as he thought of his weary two days' search.

"Then," said Aline, "it will be necessary to accept General Nirzann's offer. It would have been better to do that in the first place."

But Stetton would not hear of it.

"He is too much in evidence already," he muttered angrily, pacing the length of the room. "I don't like it."

"Nevertheless," Aline insisted, "we must have the house."

"Very well," said Stetton, stopping in front of her, "then we'll get it. Give me one more day. If there's

55

no other way, I'll rent the blooming palace itself. I understand the prince is hard up for cash.''

"Now, I admire you!'' cried Aline. "I could never love a man without spirit.''

She allowed him to kiss her hand.

The following morning he set out again. He would have enlisted the services of his friend Frederick Naumann, of the German legation, but for the fact that he had been told the day before that Naumann was spending a week in Berlin. He had inquired at every possible source, and now took to wandering about more or less at random. By noon he had found nothing, and began to fear that he must perforce allow Aline to accept the hospitality of General Nirzann.

Early in the afternoon, at the Hotel Humbert, he was told by some one that there was a possibility of obtaining for the season the house of M. Henri Duroy, at 341 the Drive.

Stetton hastened to the address as fast as a six-cylinder motor-car could take him. He was shown in to M. Duroy himself. Yes, M. Duroy would let his house—he had been called to Paris by the sudden death of his brother. Of course, M. Stetton could furnish the proper references? Very good. The rent would be seventy-five thousand francs.

Stetton made a rapid calculation.

"Fifteen thousand dollars!'' he muttered to himself—he was able to think only in dollars. "Good Heavens! It's robbery!''

But he paid it—to keep Aline from accepting an offer that had never been made to live in a house that did not exist.

Four days later—for they had to wait for M. Duroy to depart for Paris—Stetton took Aline and Vivi to inspect their new home.

It was a three-story structure of blue granite, somewhat imposing, and in the very best locality. On the ground floor were a reception-hall, drawing-room, library, and dining-room; the floors above held the sleeping apartments and servants' quarters.

Aline was frankly delighted, sending Stetton eloquent looks and words of gratitude that drove all thought of the seventy-five thousand francs from his mind.

"These rooms," he observed—they were in the chambers on the second floor—"are exactly the thing for you and Vivi. I shall take the one in the rear. It is not large, but that is of no importance."

Aline looked at him in genuine astonishment.

"But that is impossible!" she cried. "Surely you did not imagine you are to live here with us!"

It was Stetton's turn to be astonished.

"Not live with you!" he exclaimed. "Where, then, should I live?"

"I suppose at the hotel."

They began to argue the matter; Stetton with a bluntness that caused Aline to send Vivi from the room. He was stubborn; Aline was persistent; finally she declared she would abandon everything.

"Very well," said Stetton sulkily. "There is no good arguing the matter. I shall live at the hotel."

Frowning, he moved to a window, gazing out on the Drive with his back turned.

Aline crossed to him, smiling.

"You must not be angry with me," she said in a low voice softly.

Then she placed her arms around his neck and kissed him on the back of the head.

Turning, Stetton clasped her roughly in his arms and held her close.

"Would you care?" he demanded.

Aline whispered: "You know I would."

"Do you know something?" said Stetton between his teeth. "It makes me crazy just to look at you—and to feel you—like this—"

"I know—ah, do I not?" Aline drew herself gently away. "But there—I shall confess too much."

"Confess!" cried Stetton. "Tell me you love me!"

There was a noise from behind; Vivi was returning.

"Well, then—I do—a little," Aline whispered. Then, moving away, she went with Vivi to explore the room above.

"Vivi—always Vivi!" Stetton muttered.

Three days later found Aline and Vivi in possession of the house of M. Duroy. Stetton had kept his room at the Hotel Walderin. As for the expenses of the household on the Drive, he had settled that question in what he would have called a businesslike manner.

"I have arranged for a limousine and an open carriage," he told Aline, "and will pay the chauffeur and coachman myself. The other servants will be six hundred francs a month. The table fifteen hundred francs—for you will want good dinners; dress, a thousand; and incidentals, a thousand more. The first of each month I will give you five thousand francs; that will more than cover everything."

Aline thanked him with a kiss; but when he had gone she laughed scornfully. Then she said: "But I suppose I am wrong to blame him; it is the American way, but how detestable!"

She was alone in the library—a tasteful, quiet room, with its low, ebony cases, rich, dark carpets and paintings of the eighteenth century.

"At last," she said to herself, "I have room; I can breathe—and act."

She moved to the dining-room and stood gazing from the doorway with the eye of a general contemplating a field of battle. A smile of anticipatory triumph was on her lips as she walked to the reception-hall and began to mount the stairs to the rooms above.

She had not followed Stetton's suggestion concerning the arrangement of the sleeping chambers. With the exception of the little room in the rear, shut off from the others, which had been given to Vivi, she had taken the entire second floor for herself. A little manipulation of furniture and the result was a bedroom, a dressing-room, and a reception-boudoir. But Vivi had declared herself perfectly satisfied, saying that she had lived so long in the convent that even her one little room appeared frightfully large to her.

Late in the afternoon of the second day at their new home Aline and Vivi went for a drive in the open carriage. Never was toilet more carefully planned and executed than that of Mlle. Solini on this occasion, though she really had little need of it.

Her appearance on the Drive created a sensation that bade fair to become a triumph. Every one was staring at her; every one asked: "Who is she?" Vivi could not have served better as a foil if she had been selected for the purpose.

But the one carriage that Aline was looking for—the carriage of the Prince of Marisi—did not appear; and she ordered the coachman to drive home long before the line had begun to thin.

They had met Stetton, driving alone in his motor-car, and General Nirzann, who was seated by the side of a large, haughty-looking woman with enormous ear-rings and a wart on her nose.

Aline had returned the general's salutation with the merest inclination of her head; at Stetton's bow she had smiled pleasantly.

That evening General Nirzann called. When the servant entered with his card Aline turned to Vivi and said:

"Remember, Vivi, do not leave the room."

So the general was unable to make much progress in his own interests, and was forced to discuss the plans for Aline's assault on the society of Marisi. She got little satisfaction out of that; the general was cautious, and whenever she asked a leading question he would reply with a knowing smile that seemed to say: "Softly, *mademoiselle,* softly."

Aline said to herself after he had gone:

"Really, that little general is more astute than foolish. Is it possible that he is going to force my hand? Well, if I must, I must; but he shall pay dearly for it after." And her eyes flashed ominously.

In the meantime Stetton, not to be outdone in the business of intrigue, had concocted a little scheme of his own, though an inglorious one. He believed that it was the presence of Vivi that stood in the way of the fulfilment of his desires. His plan led to the removal of this difficulty.

Within an hour after Frederick Naumann's return to Marisi he received a call from Richard Stetton.

Naumann was a young and aspiring diplomat who counted on winning position with his wealth and talents. Stetton had met him a year before in Berlin, and had renewed the acquaintance during his short stay in Marisi previous to the departure of the army.

"But what are you doing here?" asked Naumann, after greetings had been exchanged. "Did the dogs of war bite you?"

"Not exactly," Stetton replied with a laugh. "The fact is, I have found the most beautiful woman in Europe."

"Indeed?" said the other skeptically. "But there is nothing wonderful about that—there are thousands of her. May I ask, has the lady found you?"

"Yes—and no. She is living in a house I have rented—the house of M. Duroy, at 341 the Drive. I have taken it for the season—perhaps longer."

Naumann whistled. "Lucky dog! But is she as beautiful as you say?"

"Ask any one in Marisi. The entire promenade stopped yesterday in confusion when she appeared. And I—well, the fact is, I am going to marry her."

"No."

"Yes. When you see her you will not blame me. She is wonderful. Nothing short of it. But it is to remain a secret for the present—our engagement, I mean. No one is to know of it. I count on your discretion."

"You may."

"And, besides that, I count on your help. She has a girl with her—a pretty little thing, about eighteen. Her name is Vivi Janvour. Aline has what she calls plans for Vivi's welfare, and I am supposed to linger in hope till they are accomplished."

Naumann smiled. "But why?"

"On account of General Nirzann. You know him, I believe. He is her cousin; at least, so she says. He is to stand sponsor for her in Marisi, and she is afraid that if he knows of her engagement to me he will decline the office. Besides, she talks some silly rot about not wanting Vivi along on the honeymoon, and that sort of thing. In short, she wants me to wait, and I don't feel like it."

"But what can I do?"

There was a pause while Stetton seemed to be searching for words. Finally he said:

"Well—the fact is—this little Vivi is not bad-looking."

"Ho!" Naumann's eyebrows lifted.

"And you, I believe, are not blind to the charms of the fair. What might come of it I do not pretend to say. Talk to her, drive with her, amuse her; at any rate, I want you to meet her; then we shall see."

"What kind of a girl is she?"

"The quiet, timid sort—lived all her life in a convent. But she is really pretty."

"My dear fellow, I really believe you expect me to marry this creature."

"By no means. I expect nothing. But, at any rate, you can see her—introduce your friends to her, start the ball rolling—I would consider it a great favor."

"I'll see her, of course," replied Naumann.

"Thåt's all I ask of you—now. Dine with me to-night at the Walderin and we'll talk it over."

So much for Stetton's plan, crude and simple indeed, but nevertheless with a fair chance of success. Naumann was a good-looking young fellow, polished and graceful, with an air of cynicism that had made him a great favorite with young ladies under twenty.

The following morning Stetton called at No. 341. Aline received him graciously; she knew that his love must have something to feed on, even if it were only crumbs. Besides, she had an additional favor to obtain from him.

"I have a friend I would like to introduce," said Stetton. "Naumann—Frederick Naumann—secretary of the German legation. He knows every one in Marisi—that is, every one who counts—and he might be of some use to you."

"Bring him to see me," said Aline.

"Tomorrow?"

"Certainly."

They chatted for an hour or so, and Stetton stayed to lunch.

"This is delightful," he said, sitting down with Aline and Vivi; and he felt a thrill of pride and satisfied vanity as he thought that this was his house, these his servants, and that this beautiful woman had promised herself to him.

His was one of those natures that live as much on appearances as on realities. He was so filled with a sense of his royal power and generosity that Aline talked him out of another twenty thousand francs with comparative ease, pleading the poverty of her wardrobe.

On the following day, accordingly, Stetton conducted his friend Naumann to the house on the Drive.

Naumann went with a certain reluctance; but Stetton had befriended him—no matter how—on a certain occasion in Berlin, and for that reason he at least pretended to acquiesce.

After they had waited in the drawing-room for a quarter of an hour the ladies entered.

Aline was ravishing; she was never otherwise; but Stetton himself was struck by the appearance of Vivi, perhaps because he had never before taken the trouble to give her any particular notice.

Her dress was light blue, of some soft material that set off her slender figure to perfection; her face was filled with color and her eyes glowed.

"By Jove," Stetton thought to himself, "Naumann could certainly do worse!"

His friend was thinking the same thing as he heard Vivi's soft voice acknowledging Stetton's introduction.

But within fifteen minutes Stetton was telling himself that he had made a mistake; and, indeed, so it appeared; for as they sat chatting together, Naumann, seeming to forget that the declared object of his attack was Mlle. Janvour, kept his gaze riveted on the face of Mlle. Solini.

"I ought to have known better," said Stetton to himself. "Who could look at any one else when Aline is there?"

He tried to catch Naumann's eye, but the young diplomat took no notice of him.

Aline rang for tea.

"It is too early, I know," she said with a smile; "but we shall be driving at tea-time. Besides, this may be quite correct in Marisi." She turned to Naumann: "You know, I am a stranger here."

"Yes; otherwise I should have seen you," Naumann replied. "Are you to be with us long?"

"For the season, at least."

"And then I suppose you will leave, like everyone else who is worthwhile? You should see Marisi in August! Silent as the grave and hotter than an oven. It is intolerable."

Vivi put in:

"You are here all the year, M. Naumann?"

"Yes, worse luck. For no conceivable reason. The prince invariably goes to Switzerland, and we swelter for nothing."

Tea arrived and Aline poured.

Still Naumann seemed unable to take his eyes from her face, but an acute observer might have thought that it was with an air of intense curiosity, as though he were trying to recall where he had seen her before, rather than one of fascination. This distinction Stetton was incapable of making; he thought only that his friend was succumbing to the irresistible charm of Mlle. Solini, and he grew nervous with fear and displeasure.

"Come," he said to Vivi when tea was finished; "play something."

She walked obediently to the piano.

Naumann left his seat and joined Stetton, who stood near Vivi as she skipped lightly through a tragic piece of Tschaikowsky. It was ludicrous; the girl felt absolutely nothing of the music.

Naumann whispered to Stetton:

"Who is she?"

Stetton looked up.

"I told you. Her father was Pierre Janvour, a Frenchman."

"No; I mean Mlle. Solini. Where is she from?"

"I don't know. Fasilica."

"You don't know?"

"My dear fellow," said Stetton dryly, "I know nothing whatever about her except that you seem to be uncommonly interested in her. Why do you ask?"

"Don't be an ass," said Naumann, moving away and across the room to Aline.

When Stetton and Vivi, tiring of the piano, joined them, a few minutes later, they found them again discussing the disadvantage of being forced to remain in Marisi throughout the summer.

"Really, it is awful," Naumann was saying. "Cheap park concerts, empty hotels, every house on the Drive closed up. Of course, the boss has to stand it with the rest of us, but he is an old elephant with a wife to cool his beer."

"The boss?" Aline looked at him inquiringly.

"Von Krantz, the minister," Naumann explained.

"Oh! Why don't you follow his example and get married yourself?"

"No, thank you," said Naumann with feeling. "I shall never be such a fool."

Aline lifted her eyebrows.

"That is hardly complimentary to us, M. Naumann."

Naumann looked at her.

"I speak from experience, *mademoiselle*. Or, at least, from observation of the experience of others. One thing alone that I have seen was enough to convince me—the experience of a friend of mine, who was also a friend of my father's."

"Indeed?" said Aline. "Tell us about it."

"It is unpleasant."

"That makes it all the more interesting."

Naumann looked at Vivi.

"And you, *mademoiselle*?"

"I should love to hear it," she declared.

The young diplomat seated himself that he might look into Aline's eyes and began:

"This friend of mine—as I say, he was also a friend of my father—was about ten, perhaps fifteen, years older than myself. He was a Russian landowner of noble birth—a man almost without education and yet with a certain strength of intellect that compelled respect and admiration."

"Like all Russians," said Aline contemptuously.

Naumann continued, without noticing the interruption:

"Whenever this man came to Germany on business,

which was at least once every year, he paid us a visit. Thus we came to know him well, and to appreciate his finer qualities.

"I used often to have long talks with him. His thoughts were simple and direct as those of a child, and yet his brain was remarkably keen, as was proved by his considerable material success. In my boyhood he was one of my heroes; I used to look forward to his visits with the utmost interest and pleasure."

Naumann paused, glancing round the little circle of his audience. Stetton was listening with ill-concealed irritation, Vivi in frank interest; Aline had on her face the expression of the hostess who wishes to do her duty by her guest.

Naumann kept his eye on her as he resumed:

"One summer—four years ago it was—his first words on entering our house were to the effect that he had found a wife. He gave us all the details; I remember yet with what eager enthusiasm he recounted the incomparable charms and goodness of his wife.

"He had married the daughter of a peasant on one of his neighbor's estates. When my father spoke to him of the danger of a man marrying out of his own class in society, he replied: 'You are right, Herr Naumann; she is not of my class; she is an angel from heaven.'

"Two years passed, during which our friend visited us two or three times. He had, in fact, become rather a bore; he would talk of nothing but his wife. Then—this was about eighteen months ago, and we had not seen our friend for about a year—I was sent on a diplomatic mission to St. Petersburg.

"On my way back, having some leisure at my command, I suddenly decided to pay a visit to our friend's estate, which I had never seen. I felt sure of a welcome, for he had often invited me to visit him.

"If I had been twelve hours later I should not have seen him, for when I arrived he was making the last preparations for a prolonged journey. I was so shocked at the change in his appearance that I could not suppress a cry of amazement at sight of him.

"His face was sunken and deathly pale; his eyes gleamed like two coals of fire, as though he were being consumed by some burning hatred or undying grief. At first he would not tell me the nature of his trouble or the goal of his intended journey; but when I expressed a desire to meet his wife he broke down completely and told me everything."

The narrator paused.

He held the interest of his audience now; Vivi and Stetton moved a little closer that they might not miss a word. But Naumann did not look at them; he kept his eyes fastened on the face of Mlle. Solini, who still listened as though with an effort at politeness.

"Two months before, so our friend told me, he had learned of his wife's affection for another man—a young Jew, who had wriggled himself into the position of manager of the estate. He had shot and killed the Jew; but his wife had pleaded for forgiveness with so wild remorse and sincere repentance that he had taken her back. But, naturally, he was suspicious and began to watch her, and soon he discovered—no matter how—that she was slowly poisoning him."

Vivi gasped with horror; Stetton muttered an ejaculation.

Aline had looked away, and was tapping the floor gently with her foot.

"Somehow she became aware of his discovery," Naumann finished, "and made her escape. Our friend's journey was a search for vengeance. I shall never be able to forget the expression on his face as he swore to kill the woman who had broken his heart and ruined his life."

Vivi burst out:

"Did he find her?"

"I don't know. I have never heard from him." Naumann turned to Aline: "Is not that enough to cause a man to forswear marriage?"

"Perhaps; it is a matter of opinion, M. Naumann."

She was still tapping the floor with her foot.

"I call it a deuced unpleasant tale," said Stetton. "Come, Vivi; for Heaven's sake, play something lively and get the taste out of our mouths."

He and Vivi moved together to the piano.

Naumann turned round in his chair to make sure they could not hear, then leaned forward and spoke in a low tone to Mlle. Solini:

"I forgot to tell you the name of my friend, did I not, *mademoiselle*? It was Vasili Petrovich, of Warsaw. Every one in that part of Russia knows him—a huge fellow with a black beard and black eyes."

Aline turned and looked him squarely in the eye.

"Indeed?" she said; and though her face was perhaps a little white, her voice was well under control. "He must be a very interesting man, this friend of yours. It is really too bad you did not get to see his wife; she is, if anything, even more interesting."

"Yes," said Naumann, leaning close to her; "but I know that she is a beautiful woman, for Vasili Petrovich showed me her photograph, and I would recognize her among a million."

Aline started suddenly, then sank back into her chair.

"Ah!" she breathed, looking into Naumann's face with eyes that gleamed ominously. Then, controlling herself with a visibly extreme effort of will, she rose abruptly to her feet and called to Vivi:

"Come, child; it is time for our drive."

CHAPTER VI.

THREE SIDES TO A TRIANGLE.

It soon became evident that General Nirzann, in spite of his cox-combry, had given Aline no promises which he was unable to fulfil. Once assured that he was not being played with—which assurance he duly received—he undertook immediately the introduction of Mlle. Solini into the select society of Marisi.

As a beginning, she received a card for a reception at the home of Mme. Chébe.

The affair was anything but exclusive, for everybody in Marisi was there whose name appeared on the biggest list, headed "possible"; still, it served as the point of the wedge.

A week later she and Vivi attended a ball given at the Hotel Walderin by the French minister.

Early in the game Aline began to make her selections of those whom she could most easily use, quite disregarding General Nirzann's advice and substituting her own judgment. This was natural, since the general had no knowledge of her real goal.

"Mme. Nimenyi is perhaps the most important of all," the general would say. "Hers is the richest and oldest family in Marisi. Once she sits at your dinner-table you are made."

"Is she in favor at the palace?" Aline would ask.

"No; a year ago M. Nimenyi refused a loan to the prince, and they are no longer seen at court, as we say. But that is a minor disadvantage. She is almost as important as the prince himself."

"Well, we shall see," said Aline. But she no longer paid any attention to Mme. Nimenyi.

She perceived that her own remarkable beauty was the greatest obstacle she would have to encounter.

Women are always the guardians to the doors of society, and they seem to have found a limit to the physical charms of their own sex beyond which respectability ceases. Whether this is the result of a deep law of nature, or of the instinct of self-preservation, or merely of common envy, no one knows except the women themselves; however, we may be allowed to suspect that they are not disinterested in the matter or they would divulge the secret.

For a week the beauty of the unknown *mademoiselle* who had taken Duroy's house for the season was the chief topic of conversation in Marisi drawing-rooms. Strange things were averred of her; still stranger were hinted. She was a spy in the service of the Sultan; she was a rich American who had killed her husband; she was a courtezan who had fascinated the young King of Spain, and had been paid a million francs by the Spanish government to leave the country.

Then it began to be whispered about that she was a distant relative of General Paul Nirzann, from somewhere in Russia, and that the general intended to introduce her into Marisi society whether they would or no. Society got out its little knives and sharpened them up.

In the meantime Aline appeared daily in her open carriage on the drive with Vivi at her side. Her carriage always appeared early and remained late, for two reasons. One, which she told General Nirzann, was that a face becomes less hateful and less beautiful to people as it becomes more familiar. The other reason she kept to herself.

The young men were eager to meet her, and Aline was willing, but General Nirzann entered a firm negative.

"You must ignore them," he declared, "at least for a time. Everyone is inventing lies about your past. You must make them ridiculous by an irreproachable present. It is a field of battle whose victory will lie with the one who exhibits superior wit and strategy. You have been introduced; it is now a waiting game."

Then came the reception at the house of Mme. Chébe and the ball of the French minister. By that time everyone knew who Mlle. Solini was—a cousin of General Nirzann, Russian by birth, and by inheritance the owner of vast estates in her native land. Vivi, the daughter of a French diplomat, was her ward.

Impecunious young men and their mothers began to look with favorable eyes on Mlle. Solini; not to mention a dozen or so of the old beaus who had stuck to their guns for so many years that they deserved to be called professionals. Such are to be found in every European capital.

The date arrived for Mme. Nimenyi's annual ball. The best of Marisi attended; and one of the minor surprises of the evening was the absence of Mlle. Solini. Questions were asked, and though Mme. Nimenyi did her best to keep the thing secret, it leaked out that the beautiful Russian had indeed received an invitation, but had returned a polite refusal.

It was the sensation of the evening. Knowing Mme. Nimenyi's power, everyone said: "The Russian has killed herself; she is buried. All the same, it is a great joke on Mme. N."

But by this action, seemingly suicidal, Aline had unwittingly made for herself a devoted friend in the person of the Countess Potacci, Mme. Nimenyi's strongest rival for the leadership.

Within three days she was invited to a select musicale at the home of the countess. This was followed by a party call and an intimate chat. Aline had arrived; discretion only was needed to make her position secure.

"Let me tell you, Vivi," said Aline, on her return from the Countess Potacci's, "within a year these people will all be there." She pointed to the ground at her feet. "But—bah! What does that amount to? They are merely so many stepping-stones."

"To what?" asked the girl. "Why do you not tell me anything?"

"Have I not?" Aline smiled.

"No; you only tell me what to tell others."

"Is not that sufficient, since it is the truth?"

"Is it the truth?" It was a question.

"Certainly, dear."

Vivi hesitated while a little frown appeared on her clear, white brow, then she said:

"But if you are so wealthy, why do you take money from M. Stetton?"

For a moment Aline, with all her cleverness, was taken aback by this simple, direct question.

"You do not understand," she said finally. "I have my reasons; you must believe me, Vivi, and trust me."

She smiled with genuine affection; the girl seemed to hesitate a moment longer, then she sprang forward and threw her arms around Aline's neck.

"I do believe you," she cried, "and I love you! You are so good to me!"

And, in fact, she was.

During this month of preliminary maneuvers Stetton was restraining his impatience with difficulty. He told himself that he was paying all the bills and getting nothing to show for it. But still Aline had little difficulty to keep him within bounds; and now that he saw how highly her charms were regarded by the critical cosmopolites of Marisi, he felt that his reward was all the more worth waiting for.

He had abandoned his own little scheme with regard to Vivi and his friend Naumann; he had dropped it as one does a match that has burned one's fingers. He could not understand his friend's conduct in the matter; Naumann had seemed to be completely fascinated by Aline, and yet he evinced no desire to pursue the acquaintance, and indeed refused absolutely to discuss Mlle. Solini in any way.

Aline appeared to be equally desirous of forgetting

M. Naumann. Stetton felt vaguely that there must be some reason for this apparent antagonism, but he could make only the wildest guesses as to its nature.

One morning General Nirzann announced to Aline:

"It is time to begin now; you are safe."

Aline's eyes sparkled. She had been waiting for this word from him, for she knew that in this case the old warhorse could give her instruction to be obtained in no other way. She said:

"Are you sure? Is it not too soon?"

"No, we are timed to the minute," he replied. "The question is, shall it be a reception or a dinner? There is more to be gained by the reception; but the dinner is much safer, for you can make sure of your guests before you send them cards."

"Then it shall be the dinner," said Aline without hesitation, for this question had long before been decided in her own mind. "Come, my dear Paul, you must help me with my list."

The general arranged himself before her in an attitude intended to express mad ecstasy.

"Ah!" he exclaimed, "you call me Paul! Angel!"

"Did I really?" Aline smiled. "But it is not surprising. I call all of my servants by their first names."

General Nirzann stared at her for a moment, then burst into laughter.

"Ha, ha! I see. What a joke! Very good!" Then his face was suddenly filled with portentous gravity and an expression of utter devotion. "All the same, I am your servant in reality. I adore you! I worship you!"

It was quite fifteen minutes before Aline could get him started on the list.

A week later the day of the dinner arrived. It promised to be a complete success; the gathering was small and quite select, and there were no disappointments. Present: the Count and Countess Potacci, M. and Mme. Chébe, Nirzann, Stetton, Naumann, and two or three young fellows whom Aline had added to the list against the advice of the general.

It may seem necessary to account for the presence of Naumann, but only Aline herself could do that. It may have been that she wished to have him under her eye; at any rate, she put the thing so strongly to Stetton that he absolutely insisted on his friend's acceptance. Naumann finally gave in, and he and Stetton went together.

The evening was spoiled for Stetton at the very beginning. He understood, of course, that the Count Potacci would have the honor of taking in Mlle. Solini, but he had counted on the seat at her right. General Nirzann, too, had had his eye on that coveted position; and, behold, it was assigned to one Jules Chavot, a young Frenchman from Munich, who possessed nothing except a fashionable wardrobe, and a somewhat sinister reputation as a duelist.

Stetton sulked and refused to open his mouth, except for the entrance of food; General Nirzann muttered, "What the deuce does she want with that blockhead?" as he glared at M. Chavot with a gaze intended to frighten him off the earth.

The dinner itself was excellent, and Aline performed the duties of a hostess to perfection.

"This is just what Marisi needed," said Mme. Chébe to the general, who had taken her in.

"I beg your pardon?" said the general, removing his ferocious glare from the lucky Chavot.

"Are you getting deaf, little one?" asked Mme. Chébe. Her tongue was the heaviest in Marisi. "I would advise you to be polite to me, or where will you go of an afternoon? I said, this is just what Marisi needed—a woman like Mlle. Solini to give us new life; another dinner-table at which—"

"At which all the homeless puppies can get a square meal," interrupted the general, still thinking of the Frenchmen.

74

"—one may expect to hear something besides a discussion of Lehar's latest waltz," finished Mme. Chébe serenely, ignoring the interruption.

The voice of the Count Potacci came from across the table.

"How is the prince today, general?"

At these words Aline, who had been chatting with M. Chavot, raised her head quickly, looking at the speaker.

"He is better; much better," replied General Nirzann. "He will probably appear on the drive tomorrow; the doctor has promised it."

Aline turned to Chavot:

"Has the prince been ill?"

"Only indisposed, I believe," replied the young man. "Why—are you concerned, *mademoiselle*?"

"Indifferently so."

"If you would only confess even so slight an interest in myself!"

"M. Chavot, be quiet."

He sighed, and, lifting his eyes, encountered the ferocious glare of General Nirzann, which he immediately proceeded to return in kind.

When the dinner was over, and the gentlemen had smoked their cigars, they rejoined the ladies in the drawing-room. M. and Mme. Chébe left to attend the opera, taking with them two of the young men; the others remained.

The Count and Countess Potacci, with General Nirzann, began a discussion of Marisi politics in general and the alliance with the Turks in particular; Chavot, Stetton, and a M. Franck gathered round Mlle. Solini; and Naumann and Vivi strolled toward the piano in a corner of the room.

"Do you play?" asked Vivi, looking up at him. Her pretty lips were parted and her eyes glowed with the unwonted excitement of the evening.

"No; I used to, but I am out of practice."

"I am glad; I hate music," Vivi declared.

"You hate music!" he exclaimed in amused surprise.

"Yes. I think it is because at the convent they kept me at dreary, dull compositions until I felt like knocking the piano to pieces."

"Quite naturally," said Naumann. "How long were you at the convent?"

"All my life. That is, until Mlle. Solini—" The girl seemed confused.

"You need not guard your tongue with me," said Naumann, looking at her.

"Need not guard my tongue—what do you mean?"

"Nothing." said Naumann hastily, regretting his words. "Except that I am a very discreet person, and am therefore an excellent repository for itching secrets."

"That is really too bad," said Vivi, smiling, "for I haven't any to divulge."

"A pretty girl without secrets! Impossible!" cried the young man.

"That is the second," observed the girl with apparent irrelevance.

"The second—"

"Yes. That makes twice that someone has called me pretty since we came to Marisi. It is delightful to be told so, even when they say it only to be amusing."

"Who was the other man?" Naumann hadn't the slightest idea why he asked.

"The other man?"

"The one who told you you are pretty!"

"Oh! M. Chavot. Aline laughed when I told her of it. She said that M. Chavot was the kind of man who possesses just a certain number of words, and considers it necessary to use all of them every day. I thought it was scarcely nice of her."

They chatted thus for an hour or more without being joined by any of the others, who had formed an animated group round Mlle. Solini. Naumann had no desire to join the circle, and as for Vivi, she found M. Naumann quite the nicest man she had met.

He got her to talking of her life in the convent, then of her future, and she was surprised to find herself revealing thoughts and desires which she had hitherto considered too intimate to discuss even with Aline.

Then Naumann told her a little of life in Paris and Berlin, while she listened with eager ears, declaring when he had finished that her greatest desire was to travel.

"Paris especially," said she. "I was born in Paris, you know. Aline has promised to take me there next winter."

"Have you relatives there?"

"None. None anywhere. I have no one except Aline, but she is so good to me! I want you to know it—you particularly."

"May I ask why?"

"I want you to. Because when I asked her the other day why you did not come to see us"—Vivi seemed unconscious of the fact that she was betraying a special interest in the young man before her—"she said that you had taken a dislike to her. Why should that be, *monsieur*?"

Naumann looked at her: every feature of her face, as well as her words and tone, betokened the most absolute sincerity. He hardly knew what to say, and ended by declaring that he did not dislike Mlle. Solini, but that he had not felt sure of a welcome at her house.

"But she invited you tonight!" cried Vivi. "You are completely in the wrong, M. Naumann. Acknowledge it, and I will forgive you."

At this moment Jules Chavot approached. The group at the other end of the room had broken up; the Count and Countess Potacci were preparing to leave. General Nirzann had taken himself away half an hour before, saying that his presence was required at the palace.

At parting he had pressed Aline's hand affectionately

before the assembled company, calling her "dear cousin," and sending a last glance toward Jules Chavot, which was intended to utterly annihilate that young gentleman.

The departure of the count and countess was taken by the others as the signal that the evening was ended. There was an expression of triumph on the face of Mlle. Solini as she bade her guests good night, which carried with it a hint of defiance as she acknowledged the bow of M. Naumann. Stetton and Naumann left together, to walk together down the drive to Walderin Place, where the young diplomat's rooms were situated.

Stetton chatted for an hour in his friend's rooms, then left to return to the hotel. He was in the worst possible humor; he had that evening, for the first time, begun to fear—as he expressed it to himself—that he "was being worked for a sucker." He was filled with anger at Aline, at Nirzann, at Chavot, at himself. He decided at one moment to leave Marisi the following morning; then he laughed aloud in scorn at his own weakness.

He reached the hotel and went to his room. But he did not go to bed; he felt that he could not sleep. All his anger had left—he was now thinking of Aline—the promise of her eyes, the whiteness of her skin, the intoxication of her caress. He allowed his thoughts to dwell on her until his blood was heated and his brain feverish, and he felt that he could no longer contain himself.

He went to the window and opened it, allowing the cool night air to rush across his face. A clock on the church on the side of the square struck twelve.

"I'll do it," Stetton muttered aloud; "by Jove, I'll do it."

He put on his hat and coat, left the hotel, and started afoot at a rapid pace down the drive. It was quiet and deserted, save occasionally when a limousine or closed carriage whizzed rapidly past with those returning from the theater or opera.

Stetton walked with long strides, face set straight ahead, like a man who knows his destination and intends to reach it. As he arrived in front of No. 341 he took out his watch and looked at it by the light of a street lamp. It was twenty-five minutes past midnight.

He ascended the stoop and rang the bell. After a wait of a minute or so he rang again. Almost immediately the door was opened the space of a few inches, and the face of Czean, Aline's butler, appeared.

"It is I—Stetton," said the young man. "Let me in." He was saying to himself, "I'll show them whose house this is."

"But—M. Stetton—" the butler stammered. "Mlle. Solini has retired—"

"What does that matter?" demanded Stetton and, as Czean did not move, he pushed the door open and stepped inside.

He was in the reception hall. The drawing-room, on the right, was dark, but a light appeared through the transom of the door of the library at the further end of the hall. He started toward it.

From behind came the voice of the butler in frightened tones:

"Mademoiselle! Mademoiselle!"

Stetton had nearly reached the door of the library when it opened and Aline appeared on the threshold.

"What is it, Czean?" she asked impatiently; then, catching sight of Stetton, she stepped back with a start of surprise.

Stetton moved inside the room before she had time to speak. The library was flooded with light from a chandelier over the table in the center of the room. At one end two or three logs were blazing merrily in a large open fireplace.

In an easy chair placed before the fire, with his back turned to the door, sat the figure of a man. Stetton crossed to his side with an ejaculation. It was General Paul Nirzann.

The general sprang to his feet.

"Ah! M. Stetton!" said he with a weak attempt at a smile.

Aline had crossed the room.

"I did not expect to see you again so soon," she said to Stetton in an easy tone. "Won't you sit down?"

She was perfectly composed.

The young man remained standing.

"I seem to be intruding," he observed with heavy sarcasm, looking at General Nirzann. "I did not know your house was open to visitors at all hours of the night, *mademoiselle*."

"Then why did you come?" said Aline, still smiling.

The general broke in with great indignation:

"Do you mean, *monsieur*, to dictate to me the time when I shall be allowed to visit my cousin?"

"Bah!" Stetton exploded in contempt for the little warrior. He turned to Aline: "Listen to me. I am in earnest. Send this man away—at once. I want to talk to you."

"But, M. Stetton—"

"I say send him away! Can't you see I mean it? Otherwise, you leave this house tomorrow."

Aline lowered her lids to cover the glance of hatred she could not keep from her eyes.

"You had better go, general," she said quietly, turning to Nirzann.

"But—" the general began furiously.

"No; you must go."

The general found his hat and coat and crossed to the door, while Stetton followed him with his eyes. There he turned.

"Good night, M. Stetton." This ironically. "Good night, dear cousin."

He was gone.

Aline waited until she had heard the outer door open and close, then she turned to Stetton, who had not moved from where he stood near the fireplace.

"Now, *monsieur*," she said in a freezing tone. "I shall ask you to explain yourself."

The young man looked at her with eyes as cold as her own.

"Am I the one to explain?" he demanded quietly.

"You seem to forget that I pay the rent here, *mademoiselle*. Surely I have the right at least to come and bid you good night, and what do I find?"

"Well, then—yes—what do you find? If I am not angry with you, Stetton, it is only because you are such a fool. You know perfectly well that General Nirzann has been of use to us, and that we are not yet through with him. But because you find him sitting in my library, boring me to death with his silly chatter, you insult me and make me ridiculous! Yes, decidedly, it is you who have to explain."

"It is my house. I pay the rent," said Stetton stubbornly, feeling that he was somehow being placed in the wrong and sticking to his one idea.

"That no longer interests me," said Aline coldly. "I shall leave here tomorrow."

"Leave! But how—you cannot!"

"You are mistaken; what I cannot do is stay here and be insulted by you."

"But hang it all, what could I do? How could I help it when I saw—"

"You saw nothing."

That was all she would say, and Stetton had to make the best of it. Aline stuck to her intention of leaving on the morrow; Stetton, in despair, acknowledged himself in the wrong and begged forgiveness.

In the future he would leave her completely free; he would not presume to dictate to her; he would wait for her own pleasure. Aline appeared to hesitate; he fell on his knees and pleaded with her not to leave him.

"You said you loved me!" he cried. "So I do, Stetton. You know it." She allowed a little tenderness to creep into her tone.

He clasped her in his arms, crying: "You would not be angry with me if you knew how I loved you. These delays are driving me mad—it is more than flesh and blood can stand. Must I wait forever?"

He was completely conquered. She allowed him to

embrace her again, then she gently disengaged herself, saying that it was late—she must retire—he must go.

"As for General Nirzann, do not think of him," she said. "He is an old idiot whom I shall discard when he is no longer useful; in the meantime, I shall give you no reason to be jealous of him."

With that promise in his ears, and her kiss on his lips, Stetton walked back to the hotel.

CHAPTER VII.

LOYALTY FOR TWO.

Mr. Richard Stetton had enough to worry about in Marisi—nobody will deny that; and hence the piece of good fortune that befell him on the morning following the events narrated in the last chapter will not be begrudged to him.

It arrived in the morning mail, and took the form of a draft for five hundred thousand francs from his father in New York. Business was good, it appeared, and Stetton senior wished his son Richard to miss nothing. He wrote: "In another year or so I shall be ready to retire, and then you will be tied down here for the rest of your life. Have a good time; you are old enough to take care of yourself."

"He's a good sort," said Stetton junior, gazing lovingly at the draft.

The unpleasant scene of the night before, while it had not allayed his impatience, had increased his infatuation for Mlle. Solini, and, curiously enough, his trust in her. He was so far from being jealous of General Nirzann that he laughed at him.

"Aline is working him prettily," he said aloud as he made his toilet. "Gad! Won't he be surprised when we go off together?"

After breakfast he wandered into the street, and crossing Walderin Place, began to stroll idly past the shops on the other side. It was nearly noon; the sidewalks were crowded with smartly dressed women and hurrying men.

Stetton paused in front of a jeweler's shop and began to look at the trinkets displayed in the window. His eye was caught by a necklace of pearls reposing in a box of black velvet.

"Deuced pretty," muttered the young man, assuming the air of a connoisseur. "Quite elegant."

He thought how well the pearls would look round the white neck of Aline, and he pictured to himself her delight and gratitude at being surprised with such a gift; also, he thought of the draft from New York tucked away in his breast pocket.

He walked inside the shop and asked the price of the necklace. The clerk told him it was seventy-five thousand francs.

"Ridiculous!" said Stetton—this was premeditated. "At Lampourde's, in Paris, I got one exactly similar— only I believe the pearls were a little larger—for forty thousand."

The clerk raised his hands in horror.

"Forty thousand! Impossible" he exclaimed. "This necklace is worth at least three times that amount. But wait, *monsieur*, I will call the proprietor."

When the proprietor arrived Stetton again expressed his astonishment and indignation at the absurd price asked for such an inferior trinket.

The proprietor, in his turn, jumped up and down with excitement and declared himself to be perfectly insulted. It was all a part of the game.

They compromised on sixty thousand francs. Stetton ordered the necklace delivered at his hotel that afternoon and left the shop, feeling himself beaten.

"Hang it all, I should have got it for fifty thousand," he said to himself. "The little man is a sharp one."

That evening after dinner he walked down to No. 341, the Drive. He found Aline and Vivi alone—a fact which added to his good nature and ease of mind. Vivi stayed only long enough to exchange greetings with the visitor, then excused herself and went upstairs.

Stetton, finding himself alone with Mlle. Solini, was a little embarrassed. He wondered if she had entirely forgiven him for his conduct of the night before. They were in the library, before an open fire; Stetton was seated in the very chair which he had found occupied by General Nirzann.

"We did not see you on the Drive this afternoon," said Aline.

"No, I was writing letters at the hotel," Stetton replied. After a short pause he continued: "Also, I had a little business at my banker's. Money must be scarce in Marisi. Really, the fellow nearly fell on my neck when I announced my intention of depositing a draft for half a million francs."

Aline glanced at him. "But that is a great deal of money."

"To some people, perhaps; not to me," said the young man grandly. "I shall probably run through it in a couple of months. By the way, I have spent part of it already on a little surprise for you."

"A surprise for me?"

"Yes." Stetton rose and took from the table a small package which he had laid there when he entered. "A little peace offering," he continued, opening the package. "I don't know if you will like it."

He pressed the spring, displaying the pearl necklace, and handed the box to Aline.

She drew a quick breath with an exclamation of surprised delight, and taking the necklace from its velvet cushion, clasped it about her throat.

"Oh!" she cried ecstatically, unable to say anything. Then she threw her arms round Stetton's neck and pressed her lips to his. "There!" she whispered in his ear. "I owe you so much now that I must begin to repay you at once."

Never had she been so gracious to him as she was that evening. She allowed him to hold her in his arms as long as he wished, and he got a kiss whenever he asked for it. She expressed a hope that they would be ready to be married and leave Marisi soon—very soon.

In this new tenderness Stetton found her irresistibly intoxicating; he could hardly bring himself to leave, and when he did go he walked on air and sang to the stars.

A few days later Aline informed him that she did not care for any more jewelry. She said that she was afraid to keep it with her in the house, and that otherwise it would be useless.

Nevertheless, she added quickly, she was so in love with the necklace that nothing could make her part with it—it was made doubly dear by the fact that Stetton had given it to her with his own hand. Her reason for bringing up the subject was that, knowing Stetton's princely generosity, she wished to forestall such another gift.

"But hang it all, you do not refuse to accept my presents?" said Ştetton, whose ears were ringing with her phrase, "princely generosity."

The controversy ended three days later by her acceptance of a gift of one hundred thousand francs. The poor fellow was actually worked up to the point where he brought it to her in cash and forced it into her hands.

As he walked up the drive after leaving her house he was haunted by a feeling that he had made a fool of himself, but the memory of her caresses and her assurance of love drove it back into the unexplored recesses of his brain—in his case, a not inconsiderable area.

He reached Walderin Place, and turning to the east, entered the door of No. 18. It was one of those old-fashioned residences, abandoned when society moved to the drive, now divided into apartments for bachelors.

Stetton ascended a flight of stairs and knocked on a door at the end of the long, narrow hall. A voice said:

"Come in."

He entered. The room was filled with tobacco smoke and an odor of beer. Frederick Naumann rose from his seat in a large, easy chair by the window and extended his hand to the visitor. Stetton sniffed disagreeably.

"Whew! This smells more like a cheap saloon than the aristocratic apartments of a rising young diplomat. For Heaven's sake open a window."

"Can't help it," said Naumann cheerfully. "This is the proper atmosphere. I am indulging in profound thought. Keep away from that window!"

Stetton pounced on the book his friend had laid on the table at his entrance. It was "Bel Ami."

"Very profound," said he with sarcastic emphasis. "You're nothing but an immoral and morbid devotee of the flesh—that is, your own flesh. Why the deuce don't you show your face once in a while?"

"I've been busy," Naumann declared; "very busy."

"Of course. You forget that I've just caught you in the act. Every one in Marisi thinks you are dead. Come on out and look at the sun."

He ended by dragging Naumann into the street almost by force. They strolled about for an hour or so, then went to Stetton's hotel for dinner.

Naumann was still grumbling that he had been dragged out into a world which no longer interested him, declaring that his entire evening had been wasted, and that he would visit dire vengeance on Stetton's head. He wanted to know why he should not be allowed to sit quietly in his own room when that had come to hold for him the greatest pleasure in life.

"You'll die of dry rot, that's what you'll do," said Stetton in a tone of conviction. "Besides, I have not pulled you out of your hole for nothing. I have a purpose."

"Aha! A plot!" cried Naumann.

"Be quiet and listen. This afternoon I was with Mlle. Solini." A frown appeared on Naumann's face. "Vivi was present, of course—she always is. Well, all she would talk about was M. Naumann. Why didn't he come with me? Where was he? Didn't I think he had pretty eyes? It was pitiful. Why the deuce don't you meander down there once in a while and let the poor girl look at you?"

"I told you the other day I couldn't help you," said Naumann, who appeared to be considerably moved by what the other had said.

"I'm not talking about that. This is a matter of common charity."

"Rot. The girl has forgotten I exist. For the twentieth time I tell you I sha'n't go to Mlle. Solini's."

"And for the twentieth time," Stetton retorted half angrily, "I ask you why?"

"That is my own affair."

"Of course. I suppose it has nothing to do with me. Only, as a friend, it seems to me that you owe me some sort of explanation."

"It would do no good."

"Nevertheless, I want to hear it."

Naumann looked at him and made a sudden decision.

"Very well; you shall. I do not want to go to Mlle. Solini's house, because she is a dangerous and detestable woman; worse, a criminal."

"What the deuce—"

"Wait. Let me finish. You remember the first day you took me there. I told a story concerning a friend of mine, whose wife betrayed him, and after being forgiven for that tried to poison him. Well, Aline Solini is that woman."

Stetton stared at him in amazement. "How do you know this?"

"My friend showed me a photograph of his wife. I cannot possibly be mistaken; the likeness was perfect, in spite of her cleverness. Have you not seen that she hates me? It is because she is aware that I know her secret."

"But why have you not written to your friend—her husband?"

"I did so. I sent a letter to his estate. It was returned by the manager with the information that he had not heard from his employer for nearly a year."

"Then all your proof consists of her similarity to the photograph?"

"Is not that enough? I tell you I cannot be mistaken."

There was a silence, while on Stetton's face appeared a reflection of the struggle between reason and desire. Finally he said, in the tone of a man who has made up his mind:

"I do not believe it."

And nothing that Naumann could say was capable of shaking him. He repeated merely, "I do not believe it," to every argument. When Naumann insisted on knowing how he had met Mlle. Solini, he told of the rescue from the convent at Fasilica, but for some reason or other undefined even to himself he did not mention the episode of the man with the black beard.

"But it is absurd!" cried Naumann exasperated. "She is certainly the same. I would inform the police—I would, positively—but what charge could be preferred against her? There is no evidence. Let me tell you this, Stetton—for I am your friend, though you seem to think otherwise—beware of her!"

"I do not believe it," said Stetton stubbornly. "She loves me."

"She is deceiving you."

"I do not believe it."

In the end. Naumann, perceiving that his friend was immovable, gave it up and departed for his rooms. He

88

had not before admitted to himself the reason for his excessive interest in Mlle. Solini, but now he was forced to self-confession. Only partly was it owing to love for his friend, Vasili Petrovich, and a desire to see him avenged. He was concerned about Vivi.

"Though why, I don't know," he muttered to himself as he paced up and down the length of his room. "It isn't possible that I am really interested in her. Any man would be moved by the thought of a young and innocent girl like her under the influence of that woman. It's an infernal outrage."

He got into bed, but the turmoil of his thoughts kept him awake for several hours.

The following day, early in the afternoon, he called at No. 341, the Drive. He hardly knew what he intended to do or say; he thought that he knew Mlle. Solini too well to expect her to be moved by mere threats, but still he felt himself carried forward by an irresistible impulse to action. At the very door he weakened and turned to beat a retreat; then he turned again and resolutely pressed the bell button.

After all, he was not compelled to face Mlle. Solini, for he found Vivi alone. She said that Aline had gone driving with Jules Chavot.

"And why did you not go along?" asked Naumann, as she led him to a seat in the library. "Have you tired of the promenade so soon?"

"On the contrary. I am more in love with it than ever," said Vivi. "But I do not like M. Chavot."

"That is jealousy," said Naumann, laughing at her frankness. "I have not forgotten that he began by telling you you were pretty, and now he has deserted you."

Vivi began to protest earnestly that she was not the least bit jealous, then, seeing the smile on Naumann's lips, stopped in confusion. "M. Naumann, I really believe you are taking advantage of my inexperience to make fun of me."

It was the young man's turn to protest. He declared that under no circumstances would he make fun of her.

"But yes," Vivi insisted, "it is evident. I need not say that I am offended."

"I assure you, *mademoiselle,* you wrong me," said Naumann earnestly. "I had no such intention. I would not—" He stopped, catching sight of a little provoking smile on Vivi's face. "Now you are making fun of me!" he exclaimed.

Vivi's smile became a rippling laugh. "Well," she cried, "then now we are quits, *monsieur.*"

"What the deuce!" thought Naumann to himself. "She is not so simple as I thought."

He began to speak of Aline. Soon he discovered that Vivi knew absolutely nothing of the woman who was supposed to be her guardian; he knew no more, after half an hour of careful questioning, than he had already learned from Stetton.

But of one thing there could be no doubt: the girl's unbounded affection for Mlle. Solini. She sang her praises in the key of hyperbole; Aline had been both father and mother to her; Aline had opened her heart to her and found a home for her when she was absolutely alone in the world—alone and friendless.

Naumann saw that here again, as with Stetton, his task was next to hopeless, but he decided to venture. He began:

"But what would you say, *mademoiselle*, if you were told that all your confidence and love were misplaced?"

Vivi looked at him. "I don't know what you mean."

"What if you discovered that Mlle. Solini is a bad woman, heartless and criminal—a faithless wife and a murderess?"

Vivi shuddered in horror at the mere force of the words. "I do not know why you say that, unless you wish to frighten me. Of course, it is impossible."

Naumann said impressively, looking into her eyes:

"On the contrary, it is true."

Then, as Vivi sat in silent amazement, he continued: "I repeat, it is true. Mlle. Solini was faithless to her husband, and if she did not murder him it was only because he discovered her villainy barely in time." Then he told her everything that he had told Stetton, arguing with the eloquence of a prosecutor in court, hoping to save the sweet young girl.

When he had finished Vivi said quietly, using the very words that he had heard from Stetton's lips the night before:

"I do not believe it."

He opened his mouth to speak, but she interrupted him:

"M. Naumann, there is some mistake; I am sure of it; I do not know why I am not angry with you; I ought to be. You do not know Aline. She is the best and sweetest woman in the world.

"She has been as kind to me as my own mother could have been. I may not know much of the world, but I am not a silly or thoughtless girl, and I know that what you tell me is impossible."

"But I tell you she betrayed herself to me by her own actions when I told her I had seen the photograph."

Vivi shook her head. "That was your imagination. You wished to convict her." The girl paused for a moment, then she continued in a voice that trembled a little: "You see, *monsieur*, I love her. I cannot listen to you. If you persist I must ask you to—I must say farewell."

"I am sorry—my intentions were good," said Naumann stiffly, rising from his chair.

The girl replied:

"I do not doubt it; but you are unjust to her."

Naumann, standing before her, said in a voice that he tried to keep even:

"Then—since you desire it—farewell, *mademoiselle.*"

He waited for a moment, but she did not speak, and he moved to the door. He was crossing the threshold into the hall when he heard her voice behind him, so low that it barely reached his ears:

"Do not go."

He turned; Vivi had risen from her chair and stood facing him. He crossed to her side.

"Did you speak, *mademoiselle?*"

She spoke quickly, looking into his eyes:

"Yes. Why must you go? Can we not be friends? That is, if you care to."

"But you told me—you said I offended you."

"Well, am I not allowed to forgive?"

Naumann wanted to take her sweet, serious face in his two hands and kiss the pretty, trembling lips. Instead, he lifted her hand and kissed it lightly, saying:

"That is the privilege of every woman."

Vivi smiled—a serious smile. "But you must not say anything more about Aline."

Naumann frowned. "It is hard to promise that."

"But you must. You see, you must be very careful not to make me angry again, since I have just forgiven you."

She stood smiling at him with a new air, half of coquetry, while the young man gazed at her in silence. What was there about the face of this girl, barely pretty, that seemed to interest him in spite of himself? Her freshness and youth? Impossible; he had known a thousand like her. Her naive frankness? But he had always disliked that in a woman. He gave it up, and presently said:

"Then we will talk no more of Mlle. Solini—at least, for the present."

Vivi answered calmly, as though nothing less was to be expected of him:

"That is sweet of you. Now we can amuse each other."

They did so with astonishing success of nearly two hours. It was Naumann who did most of the talking, while Vivi listened to everything from adventures in school to philosophical egotisms with an absorbed interest that was immensely flattering. It appeared that their views on general questions coincided wonderfully, since she agreed to every proposition he honored with his support.

Once, however—probably just to show him that she did have a mind of her own—she undertook to disprove his assertion that Schopenhauer had destroyed Christianity for all thinkers; and (let this be whispered low) he avoided utter annihilation only by demanding, in the middle of the argument, that he be served with tea.

By that time they were as old friends, and the ceremony of tea was exceedingly informal. She remembered, from his previous visit, that he took lemon and two lumps—a circumstance which gave him an unmistakable thrill of pleasure.

The maid announced apologetically that there were no muffins. Vivi looked inquiringly at Naumann.

"Bread and butter?" he suggested.

Vivi nodded.

"And tarts," she added, as the maid disappeared.

The young man declared that the tarts, of apricot, were delicious.

"Of course they are," said Vivi with an air. "I made them myself."

"No! Really? Give me another."

He ate four of them, while Vivi laughed at him.

"You'll be sick—very sick," she declared, shaking a warning finger at him. "Stuffing yourself is no proof of friendship, even if the tarts are my handiwork. It is clumsy flattery."

"You are right," said Naumann. It is a proof of love—" a pause, then he added, "for the tarts."

He stayed half an hour longer, then rose to go. Evening had arrived; it was so dark in the little library that they could barely see each other's faces. Vivi rang for lights.

"Good Heavens! exclaimed Naumann suddenly, "it's after five o'clock, and I had an appointment at the legation at four!" This statement appeared to have no particular meaning for Vivi, but she was plainly puzzled at the lapse in his regard for duty. He prepared to leave hurriedly.

"Then we are friends?" asked Vivi at the door. "You are not going to forget me, as you have done?"

"I am more your friend than you think," he replied. "As for my forgetting you—you will see. *Au revoir.*"

She watched him through the glass of the door as he ran swiftly down the steps and started up the drive.

As she turned slowly to return to the library she heard a carriage stop without, and she hastened back to her chair by the fireplace. Soon the outer door opened and closed, and she heard Aline's voice in the hall.

"No; do not thank me, *monsieur.* I sought merely my own pleasure."

Then the voice of Jules Chavot, more than a murmur:

"Ah, you make me hope for happiness."

Vivi, buried deep in her chair, gazing at the fire, smiled as she murmured to herself:

"Happiness? I really believe that I begin to know what it means."

CHAPTER VIII.

M. STETTON ISSUES AN ULTIMATUM.

That evening at dinner Aline said to Vivi:

"We saw the prince today on the drive."

Mlle. Solini uttered this speech quite in her ordinary tone, and how was Vivi to guess at all that was contained in it?

She knew nothing of Aline's far-reaching and ambitious plans; she did not know that this casual appearance on the drive was the signal for the beginning of the great campaign. And what did she care about this Prince of Marisi, whom she guessed to be gouty and tottering with age? She had her own prince to think about.

In fact, Mlle. Solini had stated only one side of the case of Vivi, and that the least important. She had not only seen the prince, but the prince had also seen her, as she sat beside Jules Chavot in her open carriage, radiant, smiling.

The prince was accompanied by General Nirzann, and as the two carriages came abreast of each other Aline had seen the great man address a sudden question to his companion. She had no doubt that the question had to do with the identity of the golden-haired beauty with M. Chavot; the prince had noticed her. The question in her own mind then was, what answer to the prince had been made by the general?

On that point she received information the following morning when General Nirzann called at No. 341. Almost his first words after greeting her were:

"*Mademoiselle,* you are irresistible. You have caught the eye of the Prince of Marisi."

Aline sent him a quick, searching glance; but her tone was calm to indifference as she said:

"Indeed?"

"Yes, I assure you. He insisted on knowing who you are."

"And you told him—"

The little general raised his penciled eyebrows to show that he considered the question superfluous. "What I have told every one else, of course."

Aline, satisfied for the present, changed the subject abruptly. General Nirzann needed careful handling.

But every day thereafter, for a week, her carriage met that of the prince on the drive, and each day she fancied she noted a growing interest in his gaze. Then came a tea at the Countess Potacci's, which the prince attended. Surrounded as he was by the entire company, he had little opportunity for any speech with Mlle. Solini, but Aline, with her penetrating eye, read the wish on his face. She was satisfied.

The following evening at the opera the prince paid a visit to the box of Mme. Chébe, in which Aline was a guest. Here, again, the conversation was exasperatingly general, but the prince found opportunity to say in an undertone:

"I understand, *mademoiselle,* that you have taken a house in Marisi for the season."

Aline replied:

"Yes; that of Mr. Duroy, at No. 341."

"It certainly must be a very pleasant place if it is as charming as its occupant."

"Your highness is pleased to be kind."

"Not at all; merely sincere."

"If you should find it so in reality, it would make me happy."

At that interesting point they were interrupted by the American Miss Ford, whom Aline thenceforward hated.

But that, as if subsequently appeared, had been enough, for two days later General Nirzann brought to Aline the information that an invitation from Mlle. Solini would be considered acceptable at the palace of the

Prince of Marisi. Curiously enough, this commission of the general's appeared to be pleasing to him; Aline could not understand that. She had not yet discovered General Nirzann's one genuine attachment.

"That is my message, *mademoiselle*—a formal one, and so have I delivered it. Now we can talk it over."

"But is this usual?" asked Aline, successfully concealing the drill of triumph that was pounding in her veins.

"You mean this message from the prince?" asked the general. "My dear Aline, it is not only usual, it is necessary. No one would dare send a card to the Prince of Marisi without a previous intimation that it would meet with acceptance."

"Indeed? You know why I ask, Paul. I am ignorant about these things, and a single false step would ruin me."

"Trust to me."

"Do I not?"

"Ah, yes. I am doubly glad now that I have been able to help you. Since the princess died, five years ago, the prince has been interested in only one woman, and that little devil of a De Mide had the blind luck to find her. But she did not last long, while you—ah, we shall show them!"

Aline did not quite like this speech, but she kept her own counsel about it. If General Nirzann were really willing to turn her over to his prince, it meant that she would have so much more freedom in the furtherance of her own plans. At the same time, she hated the little warrior for this hint of his attitude toward her; it was one of the things she laid up against him for the day of reckoning.

Having been informed that a week would be the proper interval before the issuance of the "acceptable" invitations, Aline waited out the prescribed period with ill-concealed impatience. Then she arranged a dinner-party, inviting only those of whose friendliness she was absolutely certain, and who would be pleasing to the guest of honor.

Imagine the surprise of Marisi when it found that Mlle. Solini had already reached that exclusive circle whose houses the prince graciously honored, now and then, with his presence! Why, the woman had not been heard of two months before! When an echo of the tumult reached Aline's ears through her good friend, the Countess Potacci, her only comment was a contemptuous smile.

The evening of the dinner-party arrived. Aline had spent the day with an appearance of outward calm, but with feverish anticipation within her bosom. She had given her personal supervision to every detail of the dinner; she had spent a quarter of Stetton's hundred thousand francs on the decorations and favors.

The gown she wore had been ordered especially from Paris two weeks before, for she had foreseen this occasion and prepared for it. In its selection she had displayed the depth of her shrewdness. She had guessed intuitively that this great man was not to be impressed by the frivolities and impudences of fashion; simplicity, nobility, real elegance were for him. This she achieved.

Jules Chavot, Richard Stetton, and Mrs. and Miss Ford were in the drawing-room when she entered, and she noted with pleasure that her costume failed to impress any but Mr. Chavot, who was in the way of being a man of taste. (As for the Fords, the latest Marisi loan had been negotiated through Papa Ford's New York bank.) A little later the Count and Countess Potacci arrived breathless.

"We were so afraid we should be the last," said the countess, "and that, you know, is frowned upon by *him*. Thank Heaven, he hasn't arrived!"

Ten minutes more and still the guest of honor did not appear. Aline began to be a little uneasy; there was no sign of it, however, as she chatted gaily with Vivi and Mrs. Ford. She heard the countess, some distance away, saying to Stetton and Jules Chavot: "It would not be surprising, you know—he has not been well for several months."

Aline forced a smile to her lips and put down her desire to rush to the window like an impatient school-girl. It was twenty minutes past the dinner hour—she was filled with despair.

Then a bell rang, the outer door was opened and closed, and Czean's voice was heard pompously announcing:

"The Prince of Marisi and General Paul Nirzann."

They halted a moment on the threshold—the prince a little in advance.

He was a man in the early fifties, tall and slightly stooped. His brown hair was a a little gray round the temples; his keen, commanding eyes, in which the fire subdued all color, looked out from a face habitually pale; added to this, his sharp aquiline nose and firm though sensitive mouth gave him almost the appearance of an ascetic.

Above all, there was something indefinable about both the face and figure that would have seemed more or less to justify, a century or more before, that exploded doctrine of the divine right. (In passing, you are invited to consider what sort of a figure the prince's little general made at his side.)

Mlle. Solini advanced to greet her guest; he met her in the middle of the room. Her conduct, as General Nirzann told her afterward, was perfection.

"I am afraid we have discommoded you," said the prince in his low, agreeable voice. "It was unavoidable—I am sorry."

Then, after a bow to the remainder of the company assembled in his honor, he offered his arm to his hostess, to conduct her to the dining-room.

The prince, of course, had the place of honor; at his right was Aline. On her other side was the Count Potacci, who had taken in Miss Ford; beyond them, M. Chavot with Vivi and Stetton with his fat countrywoman—Mrs. Ford. The table was rounded out by General Nirzann and the Countess Potacci, who sat on the left of the prince. Thus, it will be seen, Aline had given herself as free a field as possible under the circumstances.

She felt that this one evening was more important than all the rest that might follow; here what was needed was not so much fascination—the lure of provoking lips and inviting eyes—as an impression of distinction, of aloofness. The rest could come later.

In this, of course, she was mistaken, and it was just as well for her that she found herself unable to adhere to her prearranged plan of attack. Finding that the Prince of Marisi talked much like ordinary men, she shifted her forces and began to use her ordinary weapons. The result was, that before the roast had been served the prince was saying to her:

"You see, *mademoiselle,* I was right. The house is pleasant—quite the pleasantest in Marisi."

Aline replied merely with a glance, much less incautious, and far more effective, than words.

"You are from Warsaw, I believe," observed the prince, stopping in the act of wielding his knife and fork to look at her. "I have been wondering why you selected Marisi for the winter, instead of going to Paris or Italy, as all Russians do."

"But I am only half Russian," replied Aline. "Perhaps that is why I go only half as far. I am tired of Paris—and you know Paul is my cousin. It was he who recommended Marisi."

This was safe—she and the general had rehearsed their little story well.

"Then it is to General Nirzann I owe my present happiness?"

"If your highness considers it so, he is the one to receive your thanks."

"I shall give him another decoration tomorrow; he likes nothing better," the prince replied with a smile.

Aline looked across the table at her "cousin," the breast of whose coat was completely covered with ribbons and medals in five mathematical rows. Then, knowing that a thoroughbred must be driven with a tight rein, she turned the conversation to the military exploits of General Paul Nirzann and kept it there.

The natural result was that when, an hour later, the time came for the ladies to withdraw, the prince felt that he had not said the tenth part of what he had wished to say to his charming hostess.

But this slight disappointment of the Prince of Marisi was as nothing compared to the savage-mingled emotions that were tumbling about in the breasts of two of the other gentlemen at the table. M. Jules Chavot and Mr. Richard Stetton were genuinely disturbed by the vulgar sensations of jealousy, anger, and helplessness.

Chavot was thinking: "She is playing for the prince—well! If she succeeds, there is no hope for me."

Stetton was saying to himself: "Here I am in my own house, with my own servants—and what do I get? I'll show her—I pay the rent here—I'll show her!"

This thought was uppermost and came from the depths of the man. "I'll show her!" It appeared even on his face, and caused Vivi to remark to him: "M. Stetton, you are positively gloomy. Indeed, you look at every one as though you hate them."

Stetton merely grumbled in reply; it was all he could do to keep himself from uttering a decidedly unpleasant remark that rose to his lips as he thought that but for this Vivi he would long before have achieved his desire.

He continued morose and sulky over his cigar, and

when the men rejoined the ladies in the drawing-room he thought for a moment of going home instead; but he ended by following the others. He got little satisfaction out of that. The Prince of Marisi continued to keep his beautiful hostess to himself, while the others were allowed to amuse themselves as best they could.

Stetton, Mrs. Ford, and the Count Potacci were conversing together in a corner when Vivi approached and said abruptly in an undertone:

"Have you seen anything of M. Naumann lately, M. Stetton?"

"I see him every day," Stetton replied shortly.

"Has he dragged himself into his hole again? He has not been anywhere for a week."

"Not that I know of."

"Is he ill?"

"No."

Stetton turned his back rudely on the girl. He was beginning to hate her, merely because the stock of the emotion that was gathering in his breast had to be bestowed somewhere.

He wandered off by himself and, placing himself where he could not be seen, stood watching Aline and the prince. They were seated side by side on a divan at the further end of the room, engaged in a conversation evidently both animated and amusing. The sight caused Stetton's anger to rise till he could scarcely contain himself.

He made a sudden involuntary gesture of decision, muttering to myself, "I'll show her. I'll not be made a fool of any longer!"

And having thus made up his mind, he walked back to the count and Miss Ford, whom he found discussing the undoubted success of Mlle. Solini's assault on the highest circle of Marisi society. Stetton smiled grimly to himself, wondering what they would say if they knew the truth about her.

At ten o'clock the prince rose to go, beckoning to General Nirzann, who had been cornered for the past hour by the fat Mrs. Ford, and was therefore hugely relieved at the sign for departure. The prince spoke to the Countess Potacci and Mrs. Ford, bowed to the others, and then said good night to his hostess.

This operation required some five minutes, during which time the room was respectfully quiet, but no one heard any of the prince's words, he spoke in so low a tone. To judge by the smile on Aline's face, they were anything but unpleasant. The general followed, bending over Aline's hand, and a moment later they were gone.

There ensued immediately a scramble; you might have thought it was a race to see who could get away first from their charming hostess, who knew perfectly well that every one had been bored to death.

"My dear," said the Countess Potacci, "was it kind to ignore us so utterly? If it had been for anyone but the prince—"

"If you are walking," Jules Chavot was saying to Stetton, "I'm your man. I go to the Place, you know."

"Thanks," Stetton replied; "I don't think I'll leave just now."

The other looked at him in surprise, but said nothing as he turned to say good night to Mlle. Solini. Czean announced the Potacci car, and that of Mrs. and Miss Ford; in another minute they had departed, and Chavot followed them, with a last curious glance at Stetton, who was standing under the electric light in the hall with a gloomy and determined air.

The door closed. Vivi had gone to the library, and Aline and Stetton were alone. She turned to him, smiling:

"Well, was it not a success?"

Stetton grunted something unintelligible, and stood regarding her for a full minute in silence. Then he turned without a word and began to mount the stairs to the floor above. Aline, still smiling, watched him until he had nearly reached the top, then she called:

"But M. Stetton! Where are you going?"

He stood at the top of the stairs, looking down at her, as he said roughly:

"Come up here. I want to talk to you."

As these words, and the tone in which they were uttered, reached Aline's ears, a sudden and dangerous flash shot from her eyes. She said:

"But why up there? You know very well I will not do that. We can talk in the library."

Stetton replied calmly:

"I would rather not—Vivi is there. I will wait for you in your room."

Before Aline could say anything in reply he turned and disappeared in the hall above, and she heard a door open and close.

Aline stood for a minute without moving, while her eyes narrowed to a thin slit and her face grew pale with anger. She opened her mouth to call to Czean, but checked herself abruptly.

"I am not through with him yet; I must be cautious," she thought, and she smiled.

She walked to the door of the library and told Vivi that she was going to her room and did not wish to be disturbed, and they kissed each other good night. Then she returned and mounted the stairs and entered her room, closing the door softly behind her.

Stetton sat in a chair by the side of a table near the center of the room. He had lighted the reading-lamp and picked up a book from the table, but he was not reading.

As Mlle. Solini entered he raised his head slowly and met her eyes with what was meant to be an expression of grim resolve. But as he saw the anger on her face and met her fiery glance he turned his gaze away.

Aline stood before him saying:

"M. Stetton, you will be good enough to tell me what you mean by this."

The young man replied doggedly:

"I want to talk to you."

"Well?"

Suddenly, fired into anger by the coolness of her tone and her air of contempt, Stetton sprang to his feet and shook his fist at her, shouting:

"I want you to understand that this is my house! I'm tired of having you treat me like a dog!"

Aline, still perfectly cool, interrupted him:

"M. Stetton!"

Something in her tone quieted him; he sank back into his chair while she continued:

"Do not talk so loud—the servants will hear you! That is better. Let me tell you, you are mistaken. In the first place, you are ridiculous to complain; have you not my promise? And this house—no, this house is not yours, and you know it. You turned everything over to me and put it in my name. That was gracious, I know; but it is not generous for you continually to remind me of what I owe you."

Stetton exclaimed:

"So that's it, is it? You get your hands on what you want and then tell me to go to the devil!"

"*Monsieur,* you are offensive."

"I hope so; I intend to be." The young man rose to his feet, facing her. "You think you can make a fool of me! Don't you think I see what you're after?"

Aline advanced and placed her hand on his shoulder. Then she said:

"Stetton, you do not believe that."

"Believe what? I believe—"

"That I am trying to make a fool of you! Be sensible! Look at me!"

He turned and met her eyes, and as he did so she placed her other arm across his breast and caressed his cheek with her hand. "Now, tell me," she said, "you are jealous of the prince, is that it?"

"Yes," he answered simply; held by her eyes and the touch of her hand.

"Well, that is foolish, because it is impossible. You are impatient, that is all—ah, I do not blame you!" She still clung to him, brushing his cheek with her fingers. "I am not less so myself—you make it hard for me—have you forgotten that I love you? Look at me. There—there!"

Stetton had taken her in his arms and was covering her face with kisses.

A knock sounded on the door of the room and was twice repeated. Aline drew herself away, whispering to Stetton to move to one side, where he could not be seen from the door. Then she walked to the door and opened it the space of a few inches.

It was then that Kemper, Aline's maid, proved to be unfit for her position, lacking the virtue of discretion.

As Mlle. Solini opened the door in a manner surely intended to inspire caution, and showed her face in the opening, Kemper's voice was heard on the outside, in a low but perfectly distinct tone:

"He has come, *mademoiselle*!"

There she stopped abruptly, evidently at some sign from her mistress.

But too late, for Stetton had heard. And, curiously enough—for his brain was not of the quickest—he had also understood. In one bound he was at the door and had thrown it wide open, and started to brush Kemper aside as she stood just without the threshold.

Quick as he was, Aline was quicker still. She sprang past him and ran to the head of the back stairway. There she stopped and called down into the darkness the one word:

"Run!"

Just as Stetton reached her side a door was heard to open and close below. Turning with an oath he ran back to Aline's room and through it to the room behind.

Looking from the window which faced on the rear yard of the house he saw the figure of a man, made plain by the light of the moon, running to the gate which led into the neighboring yard, through which he disappeared. The man was rather less than medium size and appeared to be bareheaded, while flying coattails stretched out behind as he ran.

Stetton threw the window open and, leaning out over the casement, shouted at the top of his voice:

"General Nirzann!"

Suddenly Aline's voice sounded in the room:

"*Monsieur,* close that window, or I shall have Czean throw you out of it."

The figure of the man had disappeared. Stetton turned to face Aline. She was standing in the middle of the room, gazing at him with eyes that blazed with anger.

Outside, in the hall, the moans of Kemper, the maid, could be heard through the door; Stetton, as he thrust her aside in the rush for the stairway, had knocked her head against a corner of the wall.

If Aline was filled with rage, Stetton was no less so. For a moment he stood by the window, then he moved a step toward her, trembling from head to foot. His words, when they came, were so choked with fury as to be barely articulate.

"So," he sneered, "your cousin has taken to using the back stairs, has he? I'll show you, and I'll show him, too! You wouldn't make a fool of me, would you? No, you bet you wouldn't! You bet you won't! What have you got to say?"

Aline's voice was deadly calm as she replied:

"You are mistaken, M. Stetton. That was not General Nirzann."

"Don't lie! Don't try to lie out of it! I saw him!"

"Nevertheless, you are mistaken. It was not General Nirzann."

Stetton glared at her.

"Then who was it?"

"I refuse to tell."

Aline's voice was hard now and her eyes held a dangerous glitter. Stetton, brought up sharply by her words, stood and glared in silence, surprised out of his rage. Finally he said slowly:

"You refuse to tell?"

"I refuse to tell," Aline repeated in the same cold, hard tone.

"But, good Heavens! do you mean to tell me—you admit—"

"I admit nothing. Nor will I explain anything tonight. You are mad—you would not believe me if I told you the truth."

"Tell me who it was?"

"I will not."

"By Heaven, you shall!" cried Stetton violently, advancing with a threatening gesture. Rage again possessed his being. "I say you shall tell me!"

Aline did not move.

"If you lay a hand on me I shall call Czean," she said calmly.

"Tell me who it was?"

"I will not."

For a minute there was silence, while they glared at each other. Then Stetton spoke:

"You know what this means. I will ruin you."

Aline remained silent and he continued:

"I will run you out of Marisi. You know that I have it within my power to do it. And General Nirzann will go, too. At the same time I'll fix both of you."

Aline said:

"You will not do that."

"Won't I? Oh, won't I? I'll show you. I'll give you

till tomorrow night—twenty-four hours. You've pulled the wool over my eyes long enough. If you'll leave Marisi with me tomorrow, well and good. I'll keep my mouth shut. You know where to find me. And if you don't leave with me and agree to our immediate departure, I'll fix it so that you'll have to leave without me."

As he spoke Aline's manner had undergone a sudden change. A curious smile appeared on her face; the glitter disappeared from her eyes, and in its place was an expression almost of appeal. She appeared to hesitate a moment before she said:

"Then you would still—marry me?"

"Yes. But there would be no fooling this time," said Stetton grimly.

"And if I do not come?"

"I shall do what I have said," replied Stetton, thinking he had her. "I'll show you you can't make a fool of me! Remember, I'll run you out of Marisi!"

"How much time do you give me?"

"Twenty-four hours."

"Very well," said Aline calmly, and she held out here hand. "Good night."

"But are you coming?"

"I will tell you tomorrow. I must have time to think."

"But I must know—"

"*Monsieur,* you have given me till tomorrow—at midnight."

Stetton looked at her and started to take her hand; then, checking himself abruptly, he merely bowed. Without another word he turned and disappeared into the hall.

Aline stood still in the middle of the room. When she had heard him descend the stairs and leave the house she went into the next room and sat down at her writing-desk.

After a few minutes of thought she took out a piece of note-paper and wrote on it as follows:

DEAR M. CHAVOT:

You told me the other day that if ever I needed you I could make you happy by telling you so. It was a pretty speech; if it was more than that, you may call on me tomorrow morning at eleven. That is all I will say now, except to tell you an old motto of mine: No one should ask for favors who is unwilling to bestow them. Therefore, if I ask one of you—

ALINE SOLINI.

Aline read the note over, sealed, addressed, and stamped it. Then she rang for Czean.

CHAPTER IX.

M. CHAVOT DISLIKES AMERICANS.

Jules Chavot, some time of Munich, has already been marked as a man of taste. This in what he considered the essentials of life. No. 1 in this list was women.

No one ever knew whether he lived on an income or by his wits, and he generally succeeded in making himself so well liked that no one ever stopped to inquire.

Indeed, nothing whatever was known of him in Marisi, where he had made his home for the past two years, except that he had been forced to leave Munich on account of the death of a young infantry officer who had rashly taken it upon himself to cross rapiers with M. Chavot, merely because he had offered himself as a substitute—and been accepted—in the affections of a certain young lady.

This was all of the reputation of M. Chavot that had preceded him to Marisi, and those who know Marisi will appreciate the fact that it gave him a certain independence of action.

But M. Chavot had really been bored to extinction in Marisi until the afternoon when he first saw Mlle. Solini in her carriage on the Drive. He got an introduction to her and within a week was her devoted slave.

At first he had received no encouragement whatever; then suddenly, as though she had all at once perceived his attractions, Mlle. Solini's attitude toward him had completely changed. Perhaps, in the tangle of intrigue which she was creating in Marisi, she foresaw, even at that distance, her need for M. Chavot; at any rate—to discard speculation—he received her smile.

Her favors so far had been meager, though graciously given, and M. Chavot was preparing himself for a long and delightful siege. Then came the dinner-party for the prince and the sudden shock to the young Frenchman's aspirations.

"The game's up," he said sorrowfully to himself, as, after leaving Mlle. Solini's, he made his way to the establishment of Mosnovin, back of the old Russian House.

There he emptied his pockets completely in two hours at roulette—at the end of the first hour he had been winner by six thousand francs—and returned to his room at two o'clock in the morning in search of sleep.

Seven hours later he awoke, yawned, stretched himself luxuriously, and called for his mail and a glass of vichy. When the mail arrived, a few minutes later, it proved—oh, frailty of woman!—to consist of five delicately tinted, daintily scented notes. There were probably some tradesmen's bills and letters also, but we shall pay as little attention to them as he did.

Four of these notes he glanced at indifferently and threw aside; but when he read the fifth he jumped in one bound from his bed to the middle of the room, calling for his valet.

In forty-five minutes he had shaved, dressed, and breakfasted, and was on his way to No. 341 the Drive.

Czean showed him into the drawing-room, and, after a short wait, during which M. Chavot appeared to restrain his impatience with difficulty, Aline entered. He rose to his feet and bowed, and she crossed to him, holding out her hand. The lucky man was permitted to kiss it.

As he did so the clock in the library struck eleven.

"You are punctual," said Aline, smiling at him.

M. Chavot bowed again. "As a money-lender."

"I did not know that punctuality was a characteristic of money-lenders."

"Ah, *mademoiselle,*" said the Frenchman, assuming a sorrowful air, "then it is evident that you have never given one your note. I speak from sad experience."

Aline laughed and, seating herself on a divan, invited him with a gesture to sit beside her. When he had done so she said:

"No; to make a bad pun, I send my notes only to my friends."

"Then I am happy; I received one this morning."

"So I supposed, *monsieur,* and you make me happy by acknowledging it so promptly. I know that what you had said gave me sufficient reason to believe in your friendship, but Frenchmen are great talkers."

"Yet we have been known to act—at times."

"At all times."

"I assure you, you libel us!" cried M. Chavot with a smile. "But we ought not to object to being made a target for wit, since we use it so freely ourselves. In what I said to you, *mademoiselle,* there was neither wit nor dullness—it was simply the truth."

"Then you are my friend?"

"You know it—I am devoted to you."

"It is so easy to say that, M. Chavot."

"And still easier to prove it, when it is true. Try

me. You said in your note that you had need of me. Here I am. Try me."

Aline appeared to hesitate, while a little frown gathered on her brow. Finally she said:

"I begin to be sorry that I sent you that note. Do not misunderstand me"—the young man had opened his mouth in protest—"I believe in your sincerity. I would not hesitate to ask a favor of you, but this can scarcely be called that; it requires a greater degree of devotion than I have any right to expect."

"*Mademoiselle,* you wound me and insult yourself."

"No; do not be angry; I mean to be kind, and I am right." Aline paused a moment before she continued: "And now I have made up my mind. We will forget all about that note. It is best."

"But it is impossible!" cried poor Chavot, feeling that he had somehow made a misstep, but unable to imagine how. Then, struck by a sudden thought, he added: "It must be this, that you no longer have need of me."

"No, it is not that," replied Aline. "I will be quite frank, *monsieur.* I need a man who loves me well enough to risk his life for me—a husband, a brother—I could not expect—"

Chavot interrupted her:

"*Mademoiselle,* I beg of you! You say you need a man who loves you well enough to risk his life for you?"

"Yes."

Chavot rose to his feet and stood before her.

"Here I am."

"But, *monsieur*—"

"Here I am," the young man repeated.

"Then—you love me?"

"As well as you could wish."

"Ah!"

Aline's eyes grew suddenly tender and she extended

her hand. Chavot took it, dropping to his knees, and covered it with kisses.

"You know it!" he cried passionately. "You know it well!"

"Perhaps," Aline smiled. "At least, I hoped for it."

Her tone and glance caused the young man to tremble with joy. Suddenly he arose, saying:

"But I do not wish to discount my happiness. Tell me how I can serve you."

"Are you so anxious to risk your happiness?"

"No. I am desirous of earning it."

Aline looked at him.

"After all, you may decide that it is not worth it. If you do so you will not offend me."

Chavot repeated impatiently:

"Tell me."

Again Aline hesitated, then she said, without taking her eyes from his face:

"To begin with, a man has insulted me."

The Frenchman shrugged his shoulders. "I will fight him and, if you wish, kill him. What else?"

"That is all."

"That is all?" This incredulously.

"Yes."

Chavot laughed.

"But, *mademoiselle,* I thought you were going to ask me to risk my life. That is absurd; no one in Marisi can stand before me for five minutes."

"So much the better; my revenge is sure."

"This man—do you wish me to kill him?"

Aline allowed the light of hatred to to appear in her eyes as she replied: "Yes."

In spite of himself, M. Chavot started in surprise. He had no false notions of women; he knew very well that they usually contain quite as much of the devil as of the angel; but he had not expected this cold and laconic sentence of death. There could be no doubt of

Aline's sincerity; she wished the man to die. Chavot looked at her curiously.

"He has insulted you mortally then?"

"Yes. I cannot tell you, *monsieur;* but if I did you would agree with me." But Chavot's start of surprise had not escaped her, and she added: "There is yet time—I have not told you his name—"

"You will tell me now."

"You are sure?"

"Tell me."

"His name is Richard Stetton."

Chavot looked at her quickly.

"Stetton! The American who was here last night?"

"Yes. It was last night—he stayed behind—"

"I remember," Chavot interrupted. "I saw him. I wondered then what the deuce the fellow wanted."

"Some day," said Aline, "I will tell you what he did. He not only insulted me; he threatened me, and—I admit it—I fear him. That is why there must be no delay."

"There shall be none."

"It must be done tonight."

"It shall be."

Aline took the young man's hand and raised it to her lips.

"Ah," she murmured; "if I do not love you. M. Chavot, it is only because I have not dared. What can I say, except to again remind you of my motto?"

"I insist on nothing," the young man exclaimed, his brain fired with rapture. "Only—now, as I look at you—every moment that I wait is a year."

He seized both her hands and gazed into her face with burning eyes.

Aline suddenly drew her hands away and her eyes gleamed coldly.

"Well, your love will receive its reward when it has earned it. Come to me tomorrow and say, 'M. Stetton is dead,' and then—you will see."

In the midst of his passion Chavot felt himself shudder at her words. For one instant he doubted her and feared her. The indifference of her tone as she spoke of the death of a man, the glitter of hatred that had twice appeared, unmistakably, in her eyes—these were not reassuring and almost gave the lie to her tenderness. Chavot felt a momentary thrill of revulsion in the height of his fascination, curiously intermingled.

Something in her eyes, in her very attitude, appeared tigerish to him and seemed to warn him to beware. But he laughed at himself for his weakness, thinking, "I am no baby; I can take care of myself; I have risked more to gain less," and said aloud:

"*Mademoiselle,* you are right; I shall expect my happiness only when I have deserved it. There is only one thing to be said. If I kill this morning—and I shall—it may be necessary for me to leave Marisi immediately."

"In that case I shall come to you."

"You swear it?"

Aline pressed his hand. "I swear it!"

And five minutes later M. Chavot departed, feeling that for the first time since he had come to Marisi he really began to live.

In the meantime the intended victim of this pleasant little plot was going about preparations of his own, wholly unlike a man who has only a few hours to live. The preparations appeared to be of some importance and seemed to point to a journey, since luggage was being packed and several little articles of comfort for travel were being purchased.

The fact was, Mr. Richard Stetton had fully persuaded himself that he was at last to have his own way with Mlle. Solini. After leaving her house the night before he had lain awake in bed for two hours considering his position, which he had found completely satisfactory. He felt sure that Aline would never allow herself to be exposed to the sneers and insults of Marisi; rather than that, she would meet almost any demand he might make.

The next morning he rose in better spirits than he had known for a month, and after a cold plunge and a hearty breakfast began to make preparations for the journey to Paris. He had decided on Paris for several reasons, of which the chief was that he wished to be seen in the restaurants and on the boulevards with his beautiful wife to be.

Aline would absolutely create a sensation; all Paris would smile at him, whereas previously, on two or three occasions which he would have preferred to forget, Paris had laughed at him. He closed his account at the bank, packed his luggage, and gave notice at the hotel. It is astounding how easily a man can delude himself into regarding a remote possibility as an apodictic certainty.

Toward noon Stetton started out in search of his friend Naumann, and ended by finding him, much to his surprise, at the legation, seated before a desk heaped with paper.

"Not working, I hope?" said Stetton incredulously.

"My dear fellow," said the rising young diplomat, "you insult my profession. I never come in this office but to work."

"Which explains, I suppose, why you come only once a month. I've been looking for you for a solid hour. I came here last."

"That comes of your lack of appreciation of my colossal industry. But what's up?"

"I'm leaving Marisi."

Naumann glanced at his visitor in surprise. "Leaving Marisi. When?"

"Tonight."

"No! But I thought—what of Mlle. Solini?"

"She is going with me."

"Indeed! And the other—Mlle. Janvour—"

Stetton frowned; the thought of Vivi had been the only disturbing element in his roseate plans. He replied:

"I don't know. I suppose she will come, too."

It was evident that the young diplomat was considerably affected by this news. He rose to his feet and walked to a window, where he stood for some moments in silence. Then he turned, regarding Stetton with the air of a man who wishes to say something but cannot find the words, and ended by asking:

"Where are you going?"

"To Paris." Stetton glanced at his watch and added, rising to go: "I must get back to the hotel; I'm expecting a message at any moment. What I wanted to say was, will you dine with me tonight?"

"Why—that is—yes."

"All right." Stetton hesitated a moment before he continued: "I don't know—it is just possible that we won't be alone. You won't mind?"

"You mean—"

"Aline and Vivi may be with us."

After a short silence Naumann said with abrupt decision:

"I'll come."

"All right; that's settled, then. At seven sharp."

Stetton returned to his hotel, some dozen blocks away, at a rapid gait, and asked the clerk if any messages had come for him. Being told that there were none, he was plainly disappointed. It was already nearly two o'clock in the afternoon; he had expected to hear from Aline long before this. He went up to his room, not caring to exhibit his impatience in the lobby and corridors.

There he remained for an hour, having left instructions that any message that came should be delivered immediately. None arrived. He thought of reading, but his books were packed away. For a long time he sat waiting—the most distressful of all occupations.

He took to pacing the floor, and finally, unable to

remain inactive longer, he snatched up his coat and hat and sought the street. A minute later he was seated in a cab, on his way to No. 341, the Drive.

Czean opened the door. Stetton pushed his way inside without saying anything, but was halted by the voice of the butler:

"Mlle. Solini is out, *monsieur.*"

Stetton turned abruptly, and after a moments' hesitation asked for Mlle. Janvour. She, too, was out, said Czean.

"Where did they go?"

The butler did not know, and Stetton left, more impatient than ever. He reentered the cab, instructing the driver to join the line of carriages and automobiles farther down the drive. For an hour they followed the stream up and down, but the carriage of Mlle. Solini was not to be seen.

Stetton finally gave it up and returned to the hotel. He rushed to the desk. There were no messages.

Now, for the first time, the young man began to fear that Aline was going to allow him to do his worst, and oppose her word to his. Then he was struck by another thought: what if she had decided to leave Marisi without him?

He would go to No. 341 and force the truth from Czean's burly throat; he would go to the palace and get satisfaction from General Nirzann. A dozen grim resolutions entered his brain, only to disappear as rapidly as they came. All of which had the effect of forcing him to admit to himself that Mlle. Solini had fascinated him beyond all hope of resistance; he was being driven mad by the thought of losing her.

Gradually he compelled himself to become calm. After all, there remained nearly seven hours till midnight, and he had given her until then to come to him. It was inconceivable that she would discard a man who was in the habit of making presents to the amount of one hundred thousand francs in cash.

This reflection restored his ease of mind completely. He sat down at a table in his room and wrote a letter to his father, and one to a friend in Paris, after which he shaved and bathed himself, having nothing better to do, and dressed for dinner. By then it was nearly time to expect Naumann, and he left his room and descended to the lobby to wait for him.

In a quarter of an hour the young diplomat appeared, and they went in to dinner at Stetton's table in the main dining-room, before a window which looked out on the night throng in Walderin Place. The room, a large one, was crowded with stylishly dressed women and men in evening attire, for this was the most fashionable restaurant in Marisi.

As the two young men passed through, Stetton bowed to an acquaintance here and there, and Naumann appeared to know every one; it took them ten minutes to get to their table.

"We eat alone, then?' said Naumann as they took their seats.

"Yes. Aline was too busy to come," Stetton replied, not caring to explain the true state of affairs to his friend. "Why the deuce it should take a woman all day to pack a trunk I don't know."

"My dear fellow, I fail to understand you," said Naumann in a quizzical tone. "If Mlle. Solini was unable to come, why is she here?"

Stetton looked up from the menu.

"What do you mean?"

Naumann replied:

"Turn around and see for yourself. Fourth table to the right, just this side of the fountain. I thought you saw them as we came in."

Stetton turned and looked. What he saw caused him to rise half out of his chair with an exclamation of surprise.

It was Mlle. Solini, with Vivi at her side, sitting at a table with M. and Mme. Chébe and two or three others. At the same moment he saw, at the next table beyond, Jules Chavot with a party of young men, including M. Framinard, of the French legation, and General Paul Nirzann.

"Don't stare so," Naumann was saying. "They're looking at you."

"But what—" Stetton began, and then stopped, too astonished for words.

Immediately his astonishment gave way to anger. So Aline defied him! She came there to dine, knowing he would see her! He had not been mistaken; he understood perfectly the contemptuous and hostile glance with which she had returned his gaze. What the deuce could she mean? How did she possibly hope to escape exposure?

Why, he could ruin her with two words, and by Heaven, he would! All these thoughts were pictured on his face as he turned it toward Naumann, who began to rally him on his deficiencies as a host.

"It's no joke," said Stetton grimly. "Naumann, you were right about that woman. And listen here: I'm going to run her out of Marisi by tomorrow morning."

Naturally, their dinner was spoiled as a dinner. Conversation lagged; Stetton did not see fit to elaborate on his prophecy of dire misfortune for Mlle. Solini, and the other evidently had thoughts of his own, as he sat in full view of Vivi's youthful and animated face. Once he turned to Stetton to observe that he supposed the contemplated journey to Paris was abandoned, but he received in answer nothing but an unintelligible grunt.

The room round them became more noisy than ever as the diners grew jolly with food and wine: but no laughter was heard at the table of Mr. Richard Stetton, of New York.

Suddenly Stetton saw by the expression on the face of Naumann that someone was approaching from behind. He turned. Jules Chavot was standing at his elbow.

"You seem to have stuck all the young birds into one cage," Naumann was saying by way of greeting, with a nod toward the table which Chavot had just quitted.

The newcomer bowed.

"Yes. All but yourself and your friend Stetton. Which is as it should be."

Stetton had turned again to his place after a curt nod of greeting, not feeling in the humor for talk with this particular bird.

"And why are we so arbitrarily excluded?" said Naumann with a good-natured smile.

M. Chavot shrugged his shoulders.

"Perhaps I should have differentiated," he admitted. "To yourself there would, of course, be no objection, but there is beginning to be some feeling on the subject of rich young fools with no brains and less breeding."

As he said this the speaker glanced at Stetton with something of a sneer on his lips.

Stetton appeared not to have heard, but Naumann stopped abruptly in the act of raising a glass of wine to his lips and stared at the Frenchman in surprise.

"Chavot! What the deuce—"

Chavot interrupted him:

"Come, Naumann, what's the use pretending? I don't like to see you friendly with the fellow, that's all. You feel the same way about these hanged Americans, you know you do. It's sickening. Cads and cowards, every one of 'em, and it's time we told them so."

During this speech Naumann, guessing instantly at the other's purpose, had tried once or twice to stop him, but without success. Now, feeling that it was too late for his interference, he looked at Stetton and found him gazing at M. Chavot as though he only half understood what was being said.

"You're a fool to do this in here," said Naumann in a rapid undertone to the Frenchman; and, indeed, the diners at near-by tables were already looking at them. "If there is any difference, you can settle—"

At that moment Stetton found his voice:

"Let him alone, Naumann. It's the same old stuff—dog in the manger. Let him talk."

Chavot turned to him instantly:

"If by that remark, M. Stetton, you mean that I have a desire to possess anything which you possess—"

"That's what I mean," Stetton broke in roughly.

"Then, *monsieur,* you lie."

These words, uttered in a loud voice, were heard over half the dining-room, which had suddenly become still. The smothered cry of a woman came from the next table.

Naumann rose half-way out of his chair to intercept the blow that might be expected, with a face suddenly grown white.

Chavot was looking with a sneer straight into the face of Stetton, who alone appeared to be unmoved by what had been said. He muttered aloud:

"Sit down. Let him talk. Let the fool alone. He's a liar himself."

But though Stetton had graciously given his permission for the Frenchman to talk, it appeared that the Frenchman was not inclined to be so generous.

There was a chorus of cries from all parts of the room, Naumann sprang to his feet and forward, and a dozen waiters came running toward them as Stetton sank back in his chair from a blow delivered on his face with the palm of M. Chavot's hand.

Instantly all was confusion. Half the diners left their tables to crowd toward the scene of excitement. Six or seven waiters grasped the arms of M. Chavot, and as many more were pulling at Stetton, who was choking and sputtering with wrath in his efforts to get loose.

Voices were raised all over the room; the woman who takes advantage of every fairly exciting occasion by going off in a faint was being carried to a parlor. Marisi was enjoying itself.

Naumann, who had grasped Stetton's arm so tightly that he ceased his efforts to get at the Frenchman, was saying in a voice that commanded attention:

"Come, old man, you're making a show of yourself. For Heaven's sake, be quiet. Be quiet."

Then the young diplomat turned to Chavot and said calmly:

"*Monsieur,* what you want is quite evident. I shall call on you in behalf of my friend, M. Stetton, whom you have insulted."

At this the waiters released M. Chavot, who bowed and walked back to his own table without looking at anyone, though the eyes of every one were upon him. The crowd fell back and began to seek their tables. The waiters, grinning delightedly at this pleasing interruption in a monotonous existence, were picking up their scattered napkins and hurrying to their places.

"Come; let's get out of here," said Naumann, starting to thread his way through the maze of tables and chairs to the door.

Stetton, wondering in a dazed sort of manner what had happened, followed him.

CHAPTER X.

AT MARISI GARDENS.

Thirty minutes later Richard Stetton was sitting on the edge of the bed in his own room, with his brain still whirling in inextricable confusion concerning the cause and meaning of the scene in the dining-room of the Walderin.

His friend Naumann had just left him, after a twenty-minutes' conversation consisting mainly of a most amazing series of instructions and inquiries.

In the first place, what had happened?

Stetton pressed his hand to his brow in bewilderment and tried to bring order to his thoughts. M. Chavot had for no apparent reason called him a liar. He had instantly returned the epithet to the giver, which, according to his way of thinking, made the score a tie. Then Chavot had struck him—Stetton's face grew red at the memory—and then—

Well, then Naumann had led Stetton to his room and begun to ask him the most absurd questions.

First, he had offered to "act" for his friend. To this proposition Stetton had assented vaguely without understanding at all what it meant.

Then the young diplomat had asked if he was a good pistol shot. The answer was, rotten. How about rapiers? Stetton replied that he had fenced some. At that point Stetton lost the sense of things entirely and began to think that his friend Naumann was going crazy.

Finally he managed dimly to grasp the idea that he was expected to fight somebody with swords or something; but, by the time he opened his mouth to disclaim utterly any such intention, Naumann had departed. His last words had been something about returning in the morning as soon as he had completed "negotiations."

The combination of unusual and exciting events left no definite impression on Stetton's mind. There was too much to think about. He said something aloud to himself and realized, in a sort of surprise, that he had pronounced the word "duel." That was a starting-point; his thoughts assumed a degree of clearness.

Then his gaze shifted to his trunks, standing in the middle of the floor, and his mind shifted to the query, "What is that for? Where was I going?"

That in turn brought the thought of Aline, the scenes of the night before at her house, his threat to expose her, and the message that had not come. Then he had seen her in the dining-room, and there was M. Chavot, who had done something or other, and he would avenge himself on Aline tomorrow morning, and he might as well unpack the trunks.

He rose to his feet with a muttered oath, undressed himself mechanically, and went to bed and to sleep.

In the morning everything was different. He awoke early, with a depressing sense of impending misfortune and a feeling that the face of the world had changed entirely in the past twenty-four hours. A cold plunge revivified his body and cleared his mind.

All that had the night before been chaos and confusion now resolved itself into two or three definite facts which suddenly presented themselves with staggering force.

There was the contemplated trip to Paris; that must be abandoned—at least, for the present. He unpacked his trunks and returned the clothing and other articles to their places in the room. By the time he had completed this task, which took a full hour, he felt that he was hungry, and telephoned for breakfast to be sent to his room.

Over his fruit and coffee he reflected on the second problem: the fulfilment of his threat to Mlle. Solini. After all, now that he came to consider the details, it presented some little difficulty. He could not very well make a round of the drawing-rooms of Marisi to carry the information that Mlle. Solini was an impostor and a liar; he still stopped a little short of belief in Naumann's story of her.

He settled it finally with a decision to go to the Prince of Marisi with his wondrous tale, and by one stroke destroy both Aline and General Nirzann.

There remained the matter of the little unpleasantness with M. Chavot. He made short shrift of that. He simply dismissed the whole thing as an outlandish absurdity.

Granting that duels were considered good form in Marisi, they were not so in New York, and he, for one, had the common sense and the courage to stick to the customs of his native land. This phase of the matter he thought important enough to be argued out in detail.

Why, he said to himself, if we believe that when in Rome we should do as the Romans do, it amounts to this, that when we find ourselves among cannibals we should eat each other. Which is manifestly absurd. *Quod erat demonstrandum.*

Nevertheless, he somehow felt himself in this instance to be treading on dangerous and delicate ground, and he vetoed his first impulse, which was to go in search of his friend Naumann and end the thing in two words. Instead, he decided that he had better remain in his room and wait for Naumann to come to him, as he had promised to do.

It was a long wait, for it was then only nine o'clock, and Naumann did not appear until eleven. Exactly at that hour a message came over the telephone to say that M. Frederick Naumann was asking at the hotel desk for Mr. Richard Stetton. Stetton instructed that the visitor be shown up to his room.

The young diplomat entered breezily, yet with a certain air of seriousness which he seemed to consider suitable to the gravity of the occasion. His response to Stetton's slightly embarrassed greeting was a profound bow and a warm shake of the hand.

He wanted to know how Stetton felt, and congratulated him on his appearance of having had a good night's sleep. Then he sat down on a chair with the air of one about to begin an important and lengthy conversation, and said abruptly:

"Well, everything is settled."

Stetton glanced up quickly, with an expression on his face that plainly indicated relief.

"Ah," he exclaimed, "then M. Chavot—"

"M. Chavot had little to do with it," the other interrupted, "though in that little he behaved admirably. M. Framinard, a friend of mine attached to the French legation, acted for him."

Stetton rose from his chair and grasped the hand of his friend Naumann.

"I owe you a world of thanks," he said with some emotion.

"Not at all," declared the young diplomat. "I did my best, of course, and the arrangements are about as advantageous to us as they could possibly be. M. Framinard, who was in a position to make demands, graciously granted all my requests."

This speech appeared a little strange to Stetton; he could not understand why M. Framinard was "in a position to make demands." Had not he himself been the recipient of the blow? A feeling that he must uphold his rights in the matter showed in his voice as he said:

"Of course, M. Chavot will apologize?"

Naumann appeared astonished at this observation.

"Apologize!" he exclaimed.

"Certainly," said Stetton in a firmer tone. "I know you said that everything is settled, but I insist on an apology. Unless," he added, "he sends one through you."

"I don't know what you mean," said Naumann, apparently mystified. "M. Chavot has not apologized, and there is no reason why he should. He is willing to give you satisfaction."

"But you said everything was settled!"

"So it is, and as satisfactorily as possible. You are to fight M. Chavot with infantry swords tomorrow morning at six o'clock behind the old Marisi Gardens on the Tsevor Road."

Stetton dropped back into his chair with a sudden feeling that he needed fresh air.

He was completely taken aback.

So that was what Naumann had meant when he said that everything was settled! Great Heavens! Everything was the exact opposite of settled! He wanted to say something, he wanted to cry, "Impossible!"—he wanted to inform Naumann, who appeared to be as much of a barbarian as Chavot himself, that he (Stetton) possessed the common sense and the courage to stick to the customs of his native land.

He actually opened his mouth to speak, but somehow there seemed to be no words anywhere.

Naumann, in the meanwhile, was talking at some length. He said that M. Framinard had been inclined to choose pistols, but that he had been overborne by his (Naumann's) strategy. He explained that the selection of weapons was in the nature of a triumph, as the heavy infantry sword would be much less dangerous in the hands of the expert, Chavot, than the agile rapier would have been.

It thus became a matter of strength rather than agility, though, of course, they would use only the points. Despite Chavot's marvelous excellence as a swordsman—Stetton shuddered—it really placed the combatants nearly on a par. The young diplomat ended by questioning his principal concerning the nature and extent of his experience in fencing.

Stetton found his tongue.

"Is this thing necessary?" he blurted out.

The other looked at him.

"What do you mean by that?"

"I mean—all this—all this—it's silly. Rank nonsense. I won't do it."

Naumann, beginning to understand, gazed at him oddly.

Then he said slowly: "That's ridiculous, Stetton. You have challenged M. Chavot. You must meet him. It is not only necessary; it is inevitable."

Stetton exclaimed:

"I tell you I won't do it! It's rank nonsense!"

The young diplomat rose sharply to his feet, and when he spoke his voice was clear as the ring of steel.

"M. Stetton, it was with your sanction I carried your challenge to M. Chavot. My own honor is implicated. If you do not fight him as I have arranged, I will be compelled to go to his second and apologize for having acted on behalf of a coward.''

There was a silence. Naumann stood motionless, tense, gazing straight at Stetton, who again was beginning to feel bewildered and helpless as he had the night before. The word ''coward'' was ringing in his ears like the sound of an alarm of fire, and confusing his thoughts.

He managed to stammer something which carried no sense to his own ears, but which seemed to mean something to Naumann, who said, without relaxing his attitude of stern inquiry:

''Then you will fight?''

Somehow feeling that he was speaking against his will, Stetton uttered the word:

''Yes.''

Instantly Naumann's manner changed. He resumed his seat, and in a cordial and friendly tone repeated all the details of the arrangements. Stetton understood not a word of it; his brain was engaged in a little civil war of its own.

Then, caught by some phrase, his ear gave attention. Naumann was talking of a man, by name Donici, and by profession master of fencing.

''He has rooms just above mine,'' the young diplomat was saying. ''You'd better spend an hour or two with him this afternoon and freshen up a bit. I'll go over and see him now. Then I must go to the office for an hour or two, after which I'll come after you.

''I shouldn't advise you to go out, unless you want every one to stare at you. Lie around and take it easy— read a book or something. *Au revoir.*''

And on the word he departed.

As the door closed behind him, Stetton rose to his feet. He was glad to be alone—that was his first thought; then, the next instant, he felt that he wanted someone to talk to. He crossed over and sat on the edge of the bed.

Then he jumped to his feet and began to pace rapidly up and down the room. An overwhelming thought, which is only faintly conveyed in the words, "I am going to fight a duel," was hammering at his temples with sickening force and regularity.

He became possessed of a sudden, insane anger—at Chavot, at Aline, at himself, at everybody! "Fool!" he cried aloud, without any idea as to whom he meant to apply the epithet. He crossed to the mirror in the door of the wardrobe and looked at himself, his face, his hands, his clothing, as though the object had never met his gaze before.

He felt himself seized by a sullen lethargy, an irresistible torpor of mind and body; he believed that he was about to faint. He threw himself across the bed and lay there, without moving, for two hours.

He was roused by the ringing of the telephone bell; a few minutes later Naumann entered. He started slightly at sight of Stetton's pale face and rumpled clothing, then announced that he had made arrangements with Signor Donici, who was at that moment waiting for them.

Stetton never forgot that afternoon in the room of the Italian fencing-master, with its two large windows overlooking Walderin Place, and its walls covered with foils, rapiers, masks, and daggers. The bloodthirsty appearance of the room was in direct contrast with that of Signor Donici himself—a little, round man of most astonishing grace and agility, and a face that would have reminded you of the face of a cherub but for the little turned-up mustache.

While the instruction was in progress, Naumann sat on a chair at a side of the room, smoking cigarettes, and now and then offering a suggestion, for he was no mean swordsman himself. He was surprised and considerably encouraged at sight of Stetton's ability with the foils, for, though he was plainly an amateur, he showed that he was acquainted with the principles of the game.

All his tricks, however—those little twists in variation of the four chief movements—were absurdly antiquated, and Signor Donici, noticing this, turned his attention to teaching him new ones.

For two hours, resting at intervals, Stetton lunged and parried, and leaped and slid till he finally threw down his weapon from sheer exhaustion. Sweat was pouring down his face and neck, and he was panting heavily.

"That's enough," he declared. "Gad, I was never so hot in my life!"

Naumann went with him back to the hotel and left him in his room, saying that he would return at dinner time, and Stetton found himself again alone. But the fatigue of his body had communicated itself to the brain; he was too tired even to think. He took a cold plunge, wrapped himself in a dressing-gown, and sat down in an easy chair to rest.

That evening at dinner the table in the main dining-room of the Walderin which was occupied by Mr. Richard Stetton and M. Frederick Naumann was the center of every gaze. Gossip had been busy with the scene of the night before and the one that was expected to follow as its natural sequel, and fancy was flying high.

Many stories were being whispered about; it is unnecessary to pay any attention to them further than to say that the name of Mlle. Solini was mentioned in none of them. Rumor, therefore, was running true to form.

Though the two young men furnished plenty of matter for pleasing conversation at other tables, there was very little of it at their own. To be sure, Naumann talked enough, but his companion found it anything but pleasing.

The young diplomat had somehow got started on a recital of the details of the half dozen or so duels he

had witnessed—in one of which he had been a principal—and his descriptions of some of the fancy thrusts
and cuts were so just and vivid that Stetton would have
sworn he could see the blood flow.

With this difference, that the wounds and gashes appeared to him to be on his own body instead of those
of the combatants in Naumann's little tales. By the time
they reached the roast he felt like a dead man! He had
long before wished to be one.

The dinner ended, and the two young men left the
room, followed by a hundred pairs of eyes, and Stetton
felt the gaze of every pair. They separated in the lobby;
Naumann's last words were, "Don't bother to leave a
call—I'll be around in time to get you up." Just as
though they were going to spend a pleasant day in
the country.

Stetton started for the elevator, realizing that the eyes
of everyone in the lobby were turned upon him in open
curiosity, perhaps even—he shuddered—in pity. The
elevator-boy, too, regarded him as though he were
some unusually interesting animal.

Again he found himself alone in his room, this time
with a long night before him. He undressed himself
and put on a bathrobe and slippers, feeling vaguely that
to make his body easy and comfortable might have a
similar effect on his mind. In this expectation he was
grievously disappointed.

For upward of an hour he alternately lay on the bed
and paced the floor; then he walked to the writing-
table, took out a sheet of paper and a pen, and began
a letter to his father and mother.

The letter was a most curious document, and it is to
be regretted that there is not space to give it in full.
Never before in all his life had Stetton felt that he had
so much to say. He wrote with feverish rapidity, covering page after page, feeling that in the midst of a
horrible nightmare he was talking to some one who
knew and loved him, and would sympathize with him.

The letter was for the most part tender, reminiscent, and sentimental, though there was in it no touch of philosophy save that of egoism. For three full hours he wrote, and when he finally rose from the table, after placing the letter in an envelope and sealing it, he had worked himself into a frenzy of self-pity that was little short of sublime.

Most of the long night yet remained.

What to do?

He felt that sleep was impossible. Thoughts—plain thoughts, that brought plain pictures—returned in their keenness to torture him. He sat down with a book and gritted his teeth in the effort to bury his mind in it, but the effort was useless.

He got up and walked to the window, which he opened; the cold air rushed across his face. But the sight of the city with its twinkling lights seemed to madden him; he shook his fist furiously at the unoffending night.

Then he closed the window and walked to a chair and sat down, burying his face in his hands.

At half past five the following morning Stetton, accompanied by his friend Naumann, entered a big, gray touring-car in front of the Hotel Walderin.

The morning was cold—so cold that the wet snow which had fallen during the night was turned into frosty ice on the pavements and sidewalks.

The two young men were dressed warmly in fur coats and caps, and had just gulped down two hot cups of coffee.

As they seated themselves in the tonneau and the car started forward, Stetton's gaze was riveted on the back of a man, dressed likewise in fur, who was seated beside the chauffeur. He turned to Naumann and inquired with a whisper:

"Who is that?"

"The doctor."

Stetton looked away.

The car sped swiftly down the drive nearly to its end, then turned to the left on the Tsevor Road. The streets were deserted and silent, and there was that odd, splotchy appearance of the atmosphere as though daylight were arriving only in spots. Everything seemed to be covered by a cloak of gray solemnity.

Stetton no longer felt or thought; he sat as one in a dream; but he was being gradually roused by the cold air entering his lungs; he breathed deeply, feeling a pleasure in the sharp twang in his breast and at his nostrils. He knew that the time was not long now; Naumann had told him that the car would carry them to the rendezvous in twenty minutes.

Struck by a sudden thought, he leaned forward to look over the seat in front, then began feeling about on the floor of the tonneau with his feet.

"What is it?" asked Naumann.

Stetton replied:

"I don't see—where are the swords?"

"Framinard is bringing them."

Again silence. They had reached the country now, and the car sped swiftly onward past rows of gaunt, bare trees with layers of icy snow on their black branches, and now and then a farmhouse or a peasant's hut.

The cold seemed to increase; the men buried their chins deeper in the fur collars of their coats. The car crossed a bridge and just beyond turned sharply to the left; ahead was a long, level road, at one side of which, about a mile away, appeared a large, sprawling frame structure that looked like a deserted sheep-barn. As the car neared this building Naumann leaned forward and touched the arm of the chauffeur, who nodded and brought the car to a stop.

The men sprang out and started down a narrow, winding path which led to the rear of the building. Naumann was in front, followed by Stetton; the doctor, who was carrying a black leather satchel, brought up the rear.

They found the others already there in one of the numerous outlying sheds warming their hands over a fire they had made of old boards. As the newcomers entered they straightened up and bowed stiffly.

Stetton noticed a long, black, wooden box lying on the ground at the feet of M. Chavot, and gazed at it in a sort of fascination.

Naumann and M. Framinard moved together to a corner of the shed and began to converse in low tones. The doctor placed his satchel on the ground and sat down on it. M. Chavot remained standing by the fire and assumed an attitude of amazing unconcern.

Presently the two seconds returned from their corner to announce their decision that it was not light enough within the shed; upon which the whole party moved outside. Framinard and Naumann carried the wooden box, which they placed on the ground and opened, displaying to view two swords unsheathed.

"Remove your coats, *messieurs,*" said M. Framinard, who, as the elder of the two seconds, was entitled to the office of spokesman. He added in an undertone to Chavot: "Hurry up, man, we'll freeze to death."

The adversaries removed their coats and hats. Chavot appeared in a tight-fitting woolen jacket, while Stetton wore a heavy-knit jersey.

Stetton, for his part, was acting purely mechanically; a piece of advice from Signor Donici, the finishing touch for one of his tricks, was repeating itself over and over in his head:

"Twist under with the point—twist under with the point."

Stetton closed his lips tight to keep from saying it aloud: "Twist under with the point."

"M. Chavot, you have the choice," M. Framinard was saying. As he spoke he lifted the wooden box and stood it on one end.

Chavot approached and put out his hand to take one of the swords. As he did so M. Framinard slipped on the icy snow and fell.

The box overturned and Chavot grabbed at it to keep it from falling.

His hand came in contact with the point of one of the swords, and he drew it back hastily with an oath.

"What is it?" asked Naumann, stepping forward.

"Nothing. A mere prick," said M. Chavot indifferently while picking up his sword.

"But if you are wounded—"

"I tell you it is nothing!"

Framinard had by this time recovered his feet, murmuring apologies, and handed the other sword to Stetton. He insisted on examining Chavot's hand, but, seeing that it was the merest scratch, motioned the adversaries to their places.

Stetton was biting his lip to keep his teeth from chattering, and found himself, to his own profound surprise, wishing quite naturally that it were not so cold. He was startled by Framinard's voice:

"Messieurs, en garde!"

A quick salute, and there followed the ring of steel. Almost with the first meeting of the weapons Stetton felt his heart sink within him.

The firmness of Chavot's eye was equaled only by that of his wrist, and Stetton felt both of them at once. It was impossible to conquer this man—and yet—and yet—he felt the blood tingle in his veins—perhaps—

They were trying each other out.

Chavot fenced with easy caution, keeping in mind the treacherous ice they had for a footing; Stetton was putting all his brains in his wrist and letting his body take care of itself. Chavot, observing this, pressed closer, advancing the hilt.

There was a sudden flash of steel, a quick turn, and Chavot, bending low, leaped forward like a panther. The point of his sword tore through the jersey of his adversary, who, in leaping aside to avoid the thrust, slipped on the ice and fell to his knees; but he regained his feet as the Frenchman turned to renew the attack.

Naumann had stepped forward with an anxious question, but as Stetton shook his head and remained on guard he stepped back again.

Then, all of a sudden, Stetton felt his adversary's wrist lose half its firmness and cunning, and at the same instant saw an expression of distress and wonder in his face.

"A trick," thought Stetton to himself, and he became more cautious than ever.

But Chavot's sword had inexplicably lost all its fire; once, essaying a mild attack with feint, he quite uncovered himself, and Stetton could have easily run him through but for his own excessive caution.

A look of puzzlement appeared on the Frenchman's face, and an anxiety that amounted to desperation. His arm grew so weak that he was barely able to hold his sword.

Then, so suddenly that no one knew just how it happened, M. Chavot sank helplessly to the ground, while his weapon fell from his hand and slid twenty feet away on the frozen snow.

Stetton, utterly bewildered, stepped back and rested the point of his sword on the toe of his boot. The two seconds and the doctor rushed forward and knelt over the prostrate figure and began feeling all over his body and asking where he was hurt. But Chavot knew no more than they.

He kept turning his eyes from one to the other and saying, in a puzzled tone: "What is it, what is it? He didn't touch me."

Framinard turned to Stetton:

"Did you touch him?"

Stetton shook his head emphatically.

"No."

They were opening Chavot's clothing to see for

themselves when suddenly he made a quick movement and uttered an exclamation as though he had discovered something. His body was twisting and quivering now with the little involuntary movements of a man in great pain, and his eyes were rolling from side to side.

He raised his hand—the one that had been accidentally scratched by the point of his sword—and examined it closely, muttering to himself: "Ah—ah—ah!" in the tone of one who understands everything.

With great effort he said calmly:

"*Messieurs,* I am poisoned."

An exclamation of incredulous horror burst from the lips of the onlookers. Chavot silenced them with a terrible glance and continued, speaking with difficulty:

"It was on the point of my sword, with which I scratched myself.

"I am not to blame, but you would not understand. I must speak to M. Stetton. I have only a few minutes." As no one moved, he exclaimed in a tone of furious impatience: "I tell you I must speak to M. Stetton—alone! Leave me!"

The others fell back at the look of command and agonized entreaty in his eyes, and Stetton approached and stood by his late opponent.

"Kneel down," said Chavot. "they must not hear."

As Stetton obeyed the body of the Frenchman writhed and twisted on the ground like one in torture, and a horrible grimace of pain parted his lips. When he spoke again it was in a whisper, and he appeared to force the words from his burning throat with a terrible exertion of the will.

"Listen," he said, and the word sounded like the hissing of a snake. "You heard—my sword was poisoned."

He paused for an instant, trembling violently, and grasped Stetton's arm in a grip of steel in an endeavor to steady himself.

"It was Mlle. Solini—curse her for a demon of hell!—beware—beware—"

Stetton felt the dying man's fingers sink into the flesh of his arm.

"She wanted to kiss my sword—and I—idiot!—I took it to her last night—mine—a string of red silk—I am dying—romance—romance—"

A tremendous shudder ran over the form of the Frenchman, after which he lay still with closed lips. Stetton glanced round at the others, and they ran forward.

The doctor knelt down and placed his ear against Chavot's breast.

After a long minute he looked up and said in a tone of horror:

"He is dead."

They had to pry his fingers loose from Stetton's arm, one by one.

CHAPTER XI.

A ROYAL CALLER.

When Richard Stetton found himself again entering his room at the Hotel Walderin, it was with the most curiously mingled emotions his breast had ever entertained.

Relief at his escape from the sword of his adversary and horror at the manner of the Frenchman's death were uppermost, but all was penetrated with the thought of Aline and Chavot's dying words.

He hardly dared to doubt them, for he had a bit of corroborative and convincing evidence of their truth. On picking up Chavot's sword from where it had fallen on the ground, he had seen, just where the blade joined the hilt, a tiny string of red silk thread. He had torn it off and thrust it in his pocket before returning the sword to M. Framinard.

He had said nothing to any of the others concerning the purport of the Frenchman's last words.

In the first place, he himself was not sure of their truth; and even granting that, what good end would it serve to spread the story? If Aline was guilty, nothing could be more certain than that she had so managed that no evidence could possibly be found against her. And Chavot's story was so fantastic, so practically improbable, that it might easily be set down as the delirium of a brain, writhing in agony and burdened with its own crime.

But what of Aline?

He had sworn to be revenged on her—as he phrased it, to "run her out of Marisi." Somehow his desire for revenge was not so keen as it had been two days before. This thought made him uneasy, he did not know why, and he raised his voice aloud in a new vow for vengeance.

First, however, he must see her. Why? Merely to find out if Chavot's story were true. Of course, that would make no difference. In any event, he would ruin her fine plans in Marisi before the sun set.

These reflections occupied his mind as he changed his clothing and ate a hearty breakfast. By then it was ten o'clock, and he got into a cab in front of the hotel and gave the driver the address of Mlle. Solini's house.

Certain of his doubts might have been set at rest if he could have seen the expression on Mlle. Solini's face when she was informed by Czean that Mr. Richard Stetton was in the library. A gleam of surprise and anger leaped into her eyes as she instructed Czean to ask the visitor to wait.

"Chavot has failed me," she murmured to herself; "so much the worse for him."

She hesitated, asking herself whether she should see Stetton. She rose and walked to her writing-desk and unlocked one of the drawers and counted the money it contained—thirty-two thousand francs, all that was left of the American's hundred thousand.

"That is not much," she said aloud, with a smile. Then she closed and locked the drawer and, after a leisurely glance at herself in a mirror, left to meet the visitor.

As she entered the library, where Stetton was waiting, he rose to his feet and bowed stiffly. He had, in truth, a difficult task before him, for never had Aline appeared more beautiful and bewitching. She wore a blue dress that clung to her form as though affectionately caressing her warm body; her golden hair and blue eyes and white skin had the intoxicating effect of white snow and blue sky and the golden radiance of sunshine.

The young man's heart beat faster as he looked at her; he stilled it with an effort as he said coldly:

"You are perhaps surprised to see me, *mademoiselle*."

Aline crossed to a chair by the fireplace and invited him by a gesture to resume his seat before she replied:

"A little, I confess. After what happened three nights ago, that is natural."

"I do not refer to what happened three nights ago."

"No? To what, then?"

"To my—to what happened this morning."

"Ah! You mean—"

"My affair with M. Chavot."

"But why should I be surprised to see you on that account?"

Stetton looked into her eyes as he replied:

"You know of no reason?"

"None."

"M. Chavot was an excellent swordsman."

Aline gave a start of surprise.

"You say 'was'? But then—what—"

"M. Chavot is dead," said Stetton calmly.

A quick gleam—was it of remorse or hatred?—came and went in Aline's eyes.

"You killed him?" she said, rather a declaration of fact than a question.

"No."

She exclaimed impatiently:

"What then? Why do you not tell me? Is it a riddle?"

Without replying, Stetton rose to his feet and, thrusting his hand in his waistcoat pocket, took forth a little piece of red silk thread.

"Do you recognize that, *mademoiselle*?" he asked, handing it to Aline.

She started the barest trifle, then, after a moment's hesitation, took the piece of thread and looked at it curiously.

"What do you mean?" she said finally. "How could I recognize an ordinary piece of silk thread?"

"I thought you might," said Stetton, looking at her with what he meant to be a searching gaze, "since it is the one you tied on M. Chavot's sword."

Aline returned his gaze with a perfect assumption of astonishment.

"The one I tied on M. Chavot's sword!" she exclaimed. "Are you by any chance gone crazy, Stetton?"

He persisted:

"Do you deny it?"

"It is too silly to deny."

Stetton resumed his seat.

"Perhaps you will change that opinion," he said, "when I have told you what I know. I may as well begin at the beginning."

And he told her the story of the duel, including a detailed description of the death of M. Chavot. At this Aline shuddered; and when he told her of the Frenchman's dying words and his curses for Mlle. Solini, her face blazed with an appearance of honest anger and indignation.

Then Stetton told of finding the corroborative bit of thread on the hilt of the sword, and ended by asking Aline sternly if she still thought his accusation silly. She replied:

"It is not only silly; it is insulting and horrible. I cannot think that you believed it, Stetton. Also, it is impossible; how could M. Chavot have brought his sword to me?"

"Easy enough, in this case. M. Framinard has told me that the swords were left at Chavot's rooms overnight. There was nothing wrong in that."

Aline rose to her feet, saying with an air of dignity:

"Enough, M. Stetton. If you believe that I have done this thing—if you believe that I could do it—"

"I do not say that I believe it," cried Stetton, also rising.

"You have certainly intimated your belief."

"Not at all; I merely asked you to deny it."

"I did so."

"It is not true?"

"No."

"You did not see M. Chavot last night, nor go to his rooms?"

"No. Wait a moment." Aline hesitated an instant, then added: "Yes, I did see him—I had forgotten. He was here only a short time."

"And you did not—not—"

"No." Again Aline hesitated, appearing to reflect, then she said slowly: "M. Stetton, there is something else which I should perhaps tell you. You will understand some things better when you know. You remember three nights ago, when you stayed behind after the dinner party?"

Stetton nodded; as though he could forget!

"Well," Aline continued, "that man whom you thought was General Nirzann was really M. Chavot.

No—do not interrupt. He had handed me a note in the dining-room, saying that he wished to see me alone as soon as possible. He did not explain the request, except to say that his reasons were urgent. I told him to come back after the others were gone, and instructed Kemper to show him to my room when he came.''

Stetton was silent, drinking in her words. She resumed:

''I had told him to use the rear stairway, because I did not wish any one to see him return. Then, when he came, you were there, and—you know the rest. Since then I have thought that perhaps that was why he sought a quarrel with you, unless—were there any other differences between you?''

''None.''

''Then that explains everything.''

It would be unfair to Stetton to say that he swallowed this story whole, but there were several points of it that strongly appealed to him.

It disposed of General Nirzann entirely in the matter, it explained Chavot's eagerness for a fight, and it gave a reason why the Frenchman should try to cover Mlle. Solini with obloquy. He wanted to believe it, and he ended by doing so, though not without drawing enormously on his plentiful stock of credulity and vanity.

He looked at Aline. How beautiful she was, and how utterly desirable! After all, if she loved him, even a little—

''But why did you not tell me all this before?'' he asked in a tone which suggested that he would withdraw the question if it offended her.

Aline smiled.

''You gave me no chance.''

His memory was that he had given her a dozen chances; had, in fact, begged her to tell him who the man was and what he was doing there; but he forbore to press the matter. The real reason, he told himself, was Aline's spirit of independence; he had been too high-handed with her. He said:

"Aline, I am going to tell you this, that I believe you. Perhaps I'm a fool, but it seems to me that the whole trouble has been that you want to have your own way and I want mine. We can't both have it, that's certain. But you ought to do this much for me: marry me and leave Marisi. Come to Paris, Vienna, anywhere. We've made a mess here of everything. Come, will you go?"

Aline cried:

"But what of Vivi?"

"We can take her with us."

There was a silence, then Aline said:

"No, I will not do that. My dear Stetton, you are so impatient! Give me but a little more time. Two of the wealthiest young men in town are already nibbling at the bait; another month and we can go. Really, you must be patient; it would be ridiculous to waste all that I have done here."

"But, hang it all, I have waited so long already."

"It will be only a little longer. Be patient. You think, perhaps, that this delay means nothing to me. I do not choose to show it, that is all. Only, my dear friend, you should know better. A woman such as I am does not promise herself to a man unless—unless—"

"Well," said Stetton eagerly, "unless—"

"Unless she loves him."

Stetton moved swiftly to her side and enfolded her in his arms.

"Say it," he murmured, kissing her.

"I love you," said Aline in a low and sweet voice.

"Again," commanded Stetton.

"I love you."

"Ah," cried the young man, trembling with joy, "and I love you! Great Heavens! It drives me mad just to look at you, and to hold you like this, in my arms—

146

ah!'' His voice suddenly became rough: ''And you ask me to wait! How can I?''

''That is easy, if you love me.''

''You are wrong; that is what makes it difficult. What is easy is for you to make me do anything you want me to.''

''Well, am I not worth it?'' smiled Aline, sure of herself with his arms round her.

''A thousand times!'' cried the infatuated young man in a tone of ecstasy. In sober truth her caresses maddened him.

When she was in such a mood, or when she chose to make herself so, there was an irresistible voluptuousness in her every movement, in the mere touch of her finger. And her wonderful blue eyes, when she allowed them to glow with tenderness and the promise of love, set his veins on fire with every glance.

They talked a while longer—talk that consisted mostly of frenzied ejaculations on the part of Stetton, and little tender words from Aline.

Gradually, having thus in a way settled the future, she brought him round to a consideration of the present. And suddenly—he could not for the life of him have told how it came about—he found himself asking her if she were in need of money.

''What a question to ask a woman!'' cried Aline, laughing. ''Silly! You ought to know''—she tapped him on the cheek—''that every woman—'' she tapped him on the other cheek—''always needs money.''

They laughed together, and Stetton took her in his arms.

''Extravagant is no name for it,'' he declared, kissing her. ''But there—I shall go to the bank this afternoon, and if there's any left, I'll send it to you.''

Soon after that Vivi entered the room and Stetton made ready to depart, after greeting her with a bow. The girl had been out to the hills south of the city with a party of the younger set of Marisi society, skating and tobogganing, and her cheeks and eyes glowed and glistened with youth and health.

Even Stetton was conscious of a feeling of admiration as he looked at her. He lingered a moment in conversation before he went away.

The moment the door closed behind him Aline sprang to her feet with an exclamation of relief.

"Come, Vivi," she cried, "you must help me. It is noon already—I have only an hour—I thought he would never go."

"Still, if you are going to marry him—" said Vivi with a smile.

"Good Heavens! I'll get enough of him then. But come, I must not wait another minute."

She dragged the girl off upstairs.

Judging by the carefulness of her toilet. Aline was preparing for an occasion somewhat out of the ordinary. Vivi and Corri, the new maid, struggled with the great mass of golden hair for thirty minutes before its owner was satisfied.

The gown she was to wear, which had been selected the day before, lay on the bed, a creation of Monsard in black chiffon and velvet, with simple Grecian lines that yet could not hide the air of modishness that clings to some women's clothing as it does to their personality. The hair done, Aline sent Vivi downstairs to ask Czean if her instructions had been carried out to the letter regarding luncheon.

"Tell him if anything is short of perfection he loses his head," said Mlle. Solini.

When Vivi returned fifteen minutes later the toilet had been completed.

"How do I look?" asked Aline, rising from her chair for inspection.

The answer was already in the eyes of the girl, who had halted on the threshold. For a full minute she gazed, quite soberly. Then, "You are the most beautiful woman in the world," she said, with the seriousness of one profoundly and frankly impressed.

Aline laughed, and, crossing the room, passed her arm around Vivi's waist.

"Let us hope others will think so," she said. "It is really important, for both of us."

She began to ask the girl of her morning's sport, and the names of those who had composed the party. Vivi named two or three, and then Aline asked abruptly:

"Was the young Potacci there?"

Vivi glanced at her quickly, and then away, replying simply:

"Yes."

Aline smiled. "You do not like him?"

"Not at all."

"He is the best match in Marisi."

"But he would not look at me! Besides, I am afraid of him."

"Well," said Aline, "we shall see."

After a moment's pause she started to speak again, but was interrupted by the ringing of the doorbell downstairs. The next instant they heard Czean open the door, and his respectful tones, and then another voice sounded in the hall, low and pleasant. A minute later steps were heard on the stairway, and Czean appeared at the open door of the boudoir to say:

"The Prince of Marisi is in the drawing-room, *mademoiselle*."

It will be understood at once that Aline had wasted not a minute of her time at the dinner party three nights before. A *tête-à-tête* lunch with the Prince of Marisi was something that any woman in town would have given her eyes for, though in some cases it would have necessitated a considerable amount of discretion.

Aline herself had felt that she should perhaps have tactfully declined the honor, or postponed it, and she had made no mention of it even to her good friend the

Countess Potacci. A long ride and a hard chase make the best game.

As Mlle. Solini entered the drawing-room the prince rose with a profound bow. The greeting smacked of formality, and Aline responded to it in like manner. The prince approached.

"You see I am punctual," said he, taking her hand, with his lips parted in the smile that made women forget he was a prince.

"In my country that is not considered a compliment," said Mlle. Solini. "We Russians have a saying, 'The sooner started the sooner over.'"

"And like most sayings," retorted the prince, "it fails to apply in the present instance. If I wish a thing over I never begin it. Punctuality with me is born of desire."

"Your highness's kindness is ably supported by your wit," said Aline, leading him to a seat. "But I warn you to be careful—the more I get of pretty speeches, the more I want."

The prince had seated himself beside her on a divan, and was regarding her with a gaze that was almost a stare.

"It is impossible to make pretty speeches to you, *mademoiselle*," he declared abruptly. "One doesn't know where to begin."

Aline laughed—a little, musical, rippling laugh.

"Still, if you look long enough—" she said, with an assumption of hopefulness.

"That is hardly possible," said the prince firmly.

"What, to find matter for a pretty speech?"

"No; to look long enough."

Aline, perceiving that the prince was a hard rider, decided to draw away into safety by the old ruse of doubling back.

"But this is absurd!" she cried. "In another minute your highness will be making love to me, and you have not yet had your lunch!"

As though called from some magic domain by the word, Czean at that moment appeared in the doorway.

"Luncheon is served, *mademoiselle,*" he announced.

Aline rose.

"Shall we go?" Then, as the prince stood beside her and offered his arm, she added: "We lunch in the dining-room. You know the way, I believe."

As soon as they were seated at the table, Aline took the conversation in hand herself. To tell the truth, this woman who had managed so many men had at last found one who she was afraid was going to manage her.

The tone of the prince's voice and the glance of his eye, the very way in which his head moved on his shoulders, conveyed a suggestion of power which, when he cared to use it, would sweep away all obstacles.

"He is dangerous," Aline was thinking; "I must look out for myself."

She began to talk of houses—houses in general, and the house of M. Henri Duroy in particular, which she declared was much too small even for a family of two.

"It is annoying," she said, "to be compelled to lunch in your dining-room. It is too—what shall I say?—formal. The library is dingy. And from what I have seen, I would say that all Marisi houses are about the same."

"It is different, I suppose, in Russia," said the prince, without displaying any enthusiasm for the subject.

"Yes, but there everything is different. We seem to have more room everywhere, more air, more space. The fact is, Europe is stifling."

"Still, I would hesitate to condemn a continent," said the prince, with a smile.

"That is because it is your own."

"Perhaps. But others seem to find it amusing."

"In which number I beg to be included. It is not

that I find it dull. But in Warsaw, for instance, there is a sureness about life that is unknown here. It is as though—but there—I am afraid I am too deep for myself.''

Mlle. Solini laughed, but with a sweet seriousness in her eyes.

Changing the subject abruptly, she began to ask the prince of his travels. She said that she had heard that he had visited America, and confessed to a lifelong curiosity concerning that country. The prince sighed, but graciously proceeded to tell her all about the land of freedom.

From that they arrived somehow at a discussion of the alliance with the Turks; the prince professed himself astonished at Mlle. Solini's knowledge of politics. Time flew swiftly; they were both surprised to find themselves sipping coffee, and to hear the clock in the library strike three.

The prince declared it was impossible to believe that two hours had passed so quickly.

''At that rate,'' he said, ''a year with you, *mademoiselle,* would seem but a day. It is not idleness, but pleasure, that is the thief of time.''

''An afternoon, then, would be hardly worthwhile,'' said Aline, looking at him over her cup. ''Otherwise I would offer you one—this one.''

''Do not!'' cried the prince, as though in alarm. ''I would not be able to refuse, and I must meet a delegation of petitioners at the palace in an hour. They were to have come at two o'clock; I postponed it—for this.''

''You see!'' cried Aline, laughing. ''I not only understand politics, your highness; I am an influence.''

''You are, indeed.''

At something in the prince's tone Aline glanced up quickly. He was looking at her in a manner that was not new to her, and yet, in his case, there was a difference.

He spoke again, looking into her eyes:

''You are an influence, *mademoiselle.*''

"In politics?"

"No. I am not talking of politics. That is for old men and fools, certainly not for a beautiful woman like you. I have a habit of frankness. Shall I tell you something?"

He appeared really to mean it as a question, requiring an answer, as he stopped and looked at Aline inquiringly. She replied:

"If you need my permission, you have it."

"It is this," he said quietly: "you interest me more than any other woman I have ever known. With me, that is saying a great deal."

"Your highness is pleased to be kind."

"I have said I am frank."

"Then if it is true, I am gratified and honored."

Aline felt the stiffness of her words, but she also felt herself, for once, genuinely embarrassed. This was not the road she had mapped out for the Prince of Marisi to follow; how could she get him out of it? She said:

"No doubt your highness has been interested in many women."

"A few. It has been my chief amusement in life. You see, *mademoiselle,* I am frank."

Princely this, indeed! Aline had had enough of it. She did not regard herself as an amusement; nor, to do her justice, was she; but the prince did not know that. She pushed back her chair abruptly and rose to her feet. The luncheon was ended.

They returned to the drawing-room. The prince evidently felt that he had received a rebuff; his manner, courteous and amiable to an extreme, nevertheless held a tinge of dissatisfaction.

Aline was smiling and perfectly at ease; she felt that she had begun to take things in her own hand. They had talked but a few minutes when the prince rose to take his departure. His car was waiting in front.

"I need not tell you," said Aline—they were in the

reception-room, by the door—"of my gratitude for your highness's kindness."

"It is not gratitude I want," said the prince. "Indeed, there can be no question of gratitude between you and me, *mademoiselle*. I have to thank you for a most pleasant afternoon. *Au revoir.*"

Aline watched him through the glass of the door as he descended the stoop and entered his limousine, the door of which was held open by a footman in green and yellow livery. The car started forward with a jerk and disappeared down the drive.

"If he is piqued," said Aline to herself as she turned away from the door, "so much the better."

Then she murmured aloud, the unconscious voicing of a thought: "The Princess of Marisi."

She moved to the library and, seating herself before the fireplace, was soon buried in thought.

There was a quick patter of steps on the stairs, and Vivi's voice came from the doorway:

"Aline, have you been in my work-basket?"

Mlle. Solini looked round:

"What is it?"

"My red silk thread," said Vivi. "I can't find it anywhere."

Aline hesitated a moment before she replied:

"It is in my room. I was using it last night. You will find it on my dressing-table."

"Thank you," called Vivi, as the quick patter of her feet was again heard on the stairs; and again Mlle. Solini buried herself in thought.

CHAPTER XII.

A DANGEROUS MAN.

It would seem that the city of Marisi was determined to give Richard Stettin a merry time during every minute that he spent within its limits. It was not even sufficiently hospitable to allow him a good night's rest, no sooner did he dispose of one source of danger and anxiety than another appeared to take its place.

Leaving Mlle. Solini's house shortly after noon, he had walked up the drive toward the offices of the German legation, smiling at the world as he went along.

He did not exactly believe everything that Aline had told him, but neither did he have strong doubt concerning any one point of her story. Nothing that she had said was impossible, and nothing was certain.

He decided that it was the duty of a gentleman to give her the benefit of the doubt, especially when the gentleman had just left her embrace. Besides, had she not declared that he would not have to wait much longer for their marriage.

At the legation, where the clerks eyed him with frank interest, as though he had been a personage, he was told that M. Naumann had not appeared that day and was not expected till the morrow. He continued his walk down the drive and stopped at Naumann's rooms, but found that he had missed him by half an hour. Then he went to his bank for some funds and performed two or three other little errands, arriving at the Hotel Walderin for lunch a little before three o'clock.

As soon as he stepped inside the lobby he was hailed by the desk clerk, who came hurrying to his side with an important and mysterious air.

His message, which he conveyed in a low tone of secrecy, was to the effect that the chief of police had called twice at the hotel to see M. Stetton, and had left word to communicate with him immediately on his return.

"But what did he want?"

"I do not know, *monsieur*; that was all he said."

Stetton took the elevator to his room. He was thinking to himself that somehow Naumann and Framinard had bungled their plans, which had been arranged with the help of the doctor, and that the police were investigating the death of M. Chavot.

This new trouble promised to be considerably more unpleasant, though less dangerous, than the one he had just escaped. Scandal, publicity, perhaps even a scene in court, would be the result.

"Hang it all," he muttered, "what have the idiots done?"

He went to the telephone and called up the office of the chief of police. After fussing and wrangling for ten minutes, and receiving three wrong numbers—without which incidentals no European telephone call is complete—he finally got connected with the office.

"Hello!"

"Hello! This is Richard Stetton. I wish to speak to the chief of police."

"What do you wish to speak about?"

"I don't know. He called to see me while I was out, and left word for me to communicate with him."

"What is your name?"

"Richard Stetton."

"Spell it."

Stetton did so.

"What is your address?"

"Hotel Walderin."

There had been a pause of some length between the questions; the clerk at the other end was evidently carefully writing down the answers. His voice came:

"Wait a minute, please. I will let you know."

Stetton waited not one minute, but twenty. He fumed

with impatience; he stood first on one foot, then the other; he swore under his breath; he worked the receiver-hook violently up and down, and he ended by leaning wearily against the wall. As he did so the voice that he had heard before sounded at the other end:

"M. Stetton?"

"Yes."

"Are you the M. Stetton who was present at the death of M. Jules Chavot this morning?"

"Yes."

"Very well. The chief of police instructs me to say that just at present he does not care to talk to you. You will probably hear from him later."

"But what does he—"

There was a sharp click as the man at the other end hung up the receiver. With an exclamation of anger Stetton began to move the receiver-hook up and down; but, as he continued this operation steadily for five minutes without getting any attention from the operator or any one else, he gave it up and placed the receiver on the hook with a vicious bang.

"Idiots!" he muttered to himself, meaning no one in particular.

He snatched up his coat and hat and left the hotel in search of Naumann.

The search lasted three hours, and was unsuccessful. The young diplomat appeared to have suddenly disappeared from the face of the earth. Nor was M. Framinard to be found either at the French legation or at his rooms. At seven o'clock Stetton returned to the hotel, cold, tired, and hungry. He had not eaten anything since breakfast.

After dinner he went out again to continue his search, but with no better success. He finally gave it up as hopeless, and, finding himself not far from No. 341, thought of going to see Aline; but a glance at his watch showed him that it was past ten o'clock, and he returned to the hotel and went to bed and to sleep.

He was awakened in the morning by the telephone. M. Frederick Naumann was asking for him at the desk.

When Naumann entered a minute later he found Stetton sitting on the edge of the bed, dressed in white crepe pajamas and smoking a cigarette. His reception, though not cordial, was warm.

M. Stetton desired to know where in the name of the seven saints the rising young diplomat had been keeping himself for the ten years immediately preceding.

"In two words," said Naumann, when he got a chance to speak, "I have been saving your precious neck from the noose of the hangman. Never in all my life have I worked as I worked yesterday. I am waiting for you to thank me."

"Thanks awfully," said Stetton with irony. "Now, go on. What do the police want with me?"

Naumann smiled broadly.

"Was the old nut here, too?"

"If by the 'old nut' you mean the chief of police, my answer is, twice," said Stetton. "Kindly explain. I thought you and Framinard and the doctor had it all fixed up."

"So we did," replied Naumann, helping himself to a cigarette and taking a seat. "We had our report carefully written out, signed by all three of us as witnesses, and presented it in due order to Duchesne. He's the chief.

"The whole trouble started in the notorious fact that Duchesne hates Germany and all Germans. He tried to make it warm for me, and nearly succeeded, despite the fact that I had the words of Framinard and the doctor to support mine. I spent seven hours yesterday afternoon and night hunting for General Nirzann under guard. When I finally found him and got him to go with me to the prince I received my liberty and Duchesne received a reprimand."

"But what did Duchesne want? What did he say?"

"He accused me of assisting you to poison Chavot."

Stetton shuddered, murmuring: "What an awful mess it might have been!"

Naumann blew a cloud of smoke thoughtfully toward the ceiling, then said:

"It's none too pretty as it is. Listen here, Stetton; you know more about this thing than you've told. Of course, I'm not ass enough to think you had anything to do with it, but why wouldn't you tell us what Chavot said?"

"Because it would have done no good." Stetton paused a moment before he added: "It wouldn't hurt perhaps to tell you. But it doesn't alter anything. Chavot died of his own dirty trick!"

"But what was it he said to you?" Naumann insisted.

The other looked at him with an air of calculation.

"If I tell you," he said finally, "it must go no further. You will understand why."

"I shall not repeat it."

"Swear it."

"On my word."

And once more Stetton repeated the story that had been conveyed to him in the disconnected and painful phrases of the dying Frenchman. He did not, however, for some reason unknown to himself, make any mention of the piece of silk thread.

As the tale was finished Naumann sprang to his feet in excitement.

"But that explains everything!" he cried. "I was sure of it. Chavot may have had his faults, but he was a man of honor. It explains everything!"

"It would," agreed Stetton imperturbably, "if it were true."

Naumann exclaimed:

"True? Why, man, of course it's true! Nothing could be more certain! It all fits in perfectly. Chavot was just the sort of romantic fool to carry his sword round to some woman to let her kiss it, but he was a brave man and no murderer. Of course it's true!"

"I happen to know that it isn't," declared Stetton with the air of a man who knows a great deal more than he has told. "Chavot lied! Mlle. Solini had nothing whatever to do with it."

Naumann looked at him quickly.

"How do you know that?"

"She told me so."

"Told you— How? When?"

"Yesterday. I asked her. She denied absolutely any knowledge whatever of the whole affair."

"You asked her—good Lord!" Naumann sank helplessly into a chair.

Then he again sprang to his feet.

"Stetton," he said slowly, "you positively need some one to look after you. It's amazing! It's incredible! I suppose you went up to Mlle. Solini with a polite bow and said: '*Mademoiselle,* kindly tell me if you are a murderess.' And when she answered no, you believed her. Stetton, you're worse than a baby. You're an imbecile! If any—"

"Hold on!" the other interrupted. "Perhaps I'm not such a fool as you think. I did not, as you amusingly suppose, bow to the lady and ask if she were a murderess. I questioned her for a quarter of an hour before she even knew what I was driving at."

"Well, there's no use arguing about it," said Naumann in a sudden tone of determination. "This is a matter for the police."

"It is nothing of the sort," said Stetton firmly, "and you know it."

Naumann looked at him incredulously.

"Do you mean to tell me you are going to say nothing whatever about it?"

"I am not."

"Then I shall."

"No, you won't. You gave me your word you'd mention it to no one."

"But, hang it all, it's infamous! Why, if we—"

Stetton interrupted him:

"Wait a minute. Even granting that Aline is guilty, how would it do any good to inform the police? Where's your evidence? Chavot is dead. You couldn't possibly connect her with it in any way."

"But he told you—"

"The ravings of delirium. No one would believe it against her word, with no evidence to support it."

The truth of this was so apparent that Naumann was forced to admit it. Still he argued, saying that they owed it to Chavot to clear his name of the odious blot that had been placed upon it; but he could do nothing with Stetton, who continued to affirm his belief in Mlle. Solini's innocence.

As Naumann's impatience increased, the American became more obstinate; at one point of the controversy it began to appear as though Stetton would soon have another duel on his hands. But they gradually calmed down, and when the young diplomat rose to go an hour later the two young men shook hands warmly and parted in friendship.

Naumann left the hotel to go directly to the legation, where he expected, and received, a severe reprimand for having become involved in so unsavory an episode as that of M. Chavot's death.

"It is unfortunate for me," said Baron von Krantz, with a look of disapproval from under his heavy eyebrows, "that you possess so small a share of discretion. You are very well aware that we are already regarded with disfavor in Marisi, and you should take every precaution to avoid giving it anything to feed upon. I have not yet decided whether I shall make a report to Berlin."

Naumann sought his desk and began an assault on the pile of papers that had accumulated during his absence of two days. It was not a very successful assault, for his mind was elsewhere, as indeed it had been now for something over a month.

He was thinking of a sweet, girlish face with laughing black eyes and a crown of lustrous black hair; and by the side of this picture there came, unbidden, another—that of a wondrously beautiful woman whose eyes, to Naumann's fancy, had no laughter in them, but the cunning of a devil and the infamy of one.

His interest in Vivi, he had often told himself, was purely romantic; he had merely felt pity for her at her helplessness in the clutches of Mlle. Solini. But of late he had not been quite able to persuade himself that his interest was limited to this.

He was conscious of an increasing desire to see her, to touch her; more than once he had found himself wondering what it would be like to hold her in his arms, to kiss her—

At such times he would shake himself impatiently and ask himself, with furious indignation, why he should take the trouble to theorize concerning a sensation which he had so often experienced. As though he had never held a woman in his arms!

"But not Vivi," something would whisper within him; "not Vivi, with the laughing eyes and lustrous hair—'' Then he would swear at himself aloud and go out for a walk.

Today he was frankly and increasingly worried for Vivi's welfare—even, he told himself, for her life. He was firmly convinced, in his own mind, that Mlle. Solini, as she called herself, was responsible for the death of M. Chavot, with the poison intended by herself for Stetton.

As he thought over that dreadful scene he was amazed at the woman's fiendish cleverness. For if her scheme had been successful; if Chavot had wounded Stetton instead of himself with the poisoned sword, the result would have been that the Frenchman would probably have been condemned and executed as a murderer, and she would have been rid of both of them.

Whatever accusations Chavot might have made, she would have so arranged it that no slightest proof could be found against her, and the Frenchman would simply have earned the additional odium of having attempted to place the blame for his own crime on the shoulders of a woman.

And Vivi was in the power of this creature—more, she even loved her! And who knows where Aline would strike next?

Naumann shuddered.

Suddenly the face of Vivi, trusting, innocent, with smiling lips, appeared before his eyes as plainly as though she herself were standing there in front of him. Beside it, as always, there was slowly outlined that other face, fair indeed and beautiful, but which appeared to him to lose all its beauty in its wickedness.

A sudden, swift resolve entered his brain. He set to work feverishly, and in less than an hour had cleared away the mass of papers on his desk, dictated a score of letters, and filled a pad with memoranda and recommendations for Baron von Krantz.

Then he snatched up his coat and hat, and, finding a cab outside the legation, got in and gave the driver the address: "No. 341 the Drive."

As the cab rolled smoothly along Naumann tried to formulate some plan of action. A dozen ideas offered themselves, only to be rejected all.

"There is one thing that would frighten her," he said to himself, "and that is an encounter with Vasili Petrovich. She is afraid of him, and well she might be. If I could only find him! I know of nothing else."

He was undecided what to do when the cab stopped in front of No. 341.

He wondered curiously how he would be received by Mlle. Solini, or if he would be received at all.

When she came to him in the drawing-room with

outstretched hand and a smile on her lips he took the hand and bowed over it without returning the smile. If Aline was surprised to see him, she betrayed no sign of it, as she motioned him to a chair and took one for herself.

"We have not seen you for a long time," she began in a tone of friendliness. "Though, to tell the truth, we have hardly had reason to expect you."

But Naumann was in no humor for preliminary courtesies. He said abruptly, looking straight into Aline's eyes:

"I do not come as a friend, *madame,* and you know it."

"Ah!" said Aline quietly, with a flash of her eyes. "I admire you for that, M. Naumann—it is frankness, and that is what I like. For what have you come?"

"I don't know."

A smile of real amusement appeared on Mlle. Solini's face.

"You don't know?"

"No. That is, I do know, and yet I wonder why. I come to warn you."

"To warn me?" Aline's eyebrows were lifted.

"Yes."

"Are you so interested in my welfare?"

The young diplomat made a gesture of impatience.

"At least, I did not come to play with words," he said. "Let us not pretend, *madame.* You know very well what I know and why I came. Let us both be frank."

"Well, then, frankly, I do not understand you. You say that I know what you know. What is that?"

Naumann looked straight at her as he replied:

"I know, for instance, that you are responsible for the death of M. Chavot. No—do not start with indignation and surprise—you do it very well, but it is quite useless. I am not telling you what I guess at, but what

I know. I repeat, it was you who poisoned the sword of Jules Chavot.''

Suddenly, as he spoke, a change appeared on the face of Mlle. Solini. It was as though she had lowered a curtain from before her eyes, as she returned the gaze of M. Naumann with a frank expression and mocking. She said, in the tone of one uttering a challenge for amusement:

"If it is as you say, *monsieur*—and I will not presume to contradict you—what then?''

For an instant Naumann was taken aback, then he recovered himself and said quietly:

"I expected that. I knew you were capable of it. Perhaps you are right in your insolent security; perhaps it is impossible to fasten this particular crime on your shoulders, where it belongs. But that is not all I know. I know also that you are the wife of Vasili Petrovich, and that you betrayed him and tried to kill him.''

"Well—for the sake of argument, I will grant that also—and what then?'' Aline smiled sweetly.

"Merely this, that you are in danger of overreaching yourself. And now I will tell you why I came. I came for Mlle. Janvour. Depraved and wicked as you are— you asked me to be frank, *madame*—you know that as long as she remains with you she is approaching her ruin.

"I want to take her away from you. I will have a guardian appointed for her; I will see that her welfare and happiness are assured. I have no ulterior motive, *madame;* you who read men so easily can see that for yourself. I do not—'' He hesitated for an instant, then continued: "I do not pretend to love her, but I am sorry for her. That is all.''

There was a long silence, while Aline sat looking into the young man's eyes, without a trace of emotion in her own. Then suddenly she rose and walked to the door and pressed a button on the wall. In a moment a servant appeared, and she said:

"Tell Mlle. Janvour to come to the drawing-room."

Then she returned to her chair to wait. They heard the heavy footsteps of the servant on the stairs, and shortly the quick patter of Vivi's little feet.

As the girl entered the room, Naumann rose and bowed. Vivi's rather effusive greeting came to a halt when she observed the profound seriousness on both their faces.

Aline said abruptly:

"Vivi, I sent for you to ask you a question. M. Naumann and I have been talking of you. There is no need to repeat what he says about me, since you have heard it before from his lips—and in my absence.

"He now says that I am unfit to take care of you—that I am depraved and wicked—that he wishes to find a home for you among his people—that he wishes you to leave me. I will add that he does not pretend to love you, but declares that he is sorry for you. I called you to let you decide for yourself."

Vivi was looking first at Naumann, then at Aline, with a face suddenly grown pale. Her lips quivered as though she wanted to speak, but could not find the words, and the expression in her eyes told of the struggle that was going on within her breast.

As for Naumann, he, too, found himself without words when he felt that he most needed them. "He does not pretend to love you—" It sounded harsh and somehow false.

Did he love her, then? But before he could crystallize his tumbling thoughts he heard Vivi's voice:

"*Monsieur,* you have no reason to be sorry for me." The voice trembled and was very low. "You know that I love Mlle. Solini; you are wrong to say such things of her. But I—I assure you—I appreciate your kindness—your interest—"

Suddenly her voice broke and stopped, and, covering her face with her hands, she turned and ran from the room.

There was a silence. Then Naumann turned to Aline, and his voice also was trembling as he said:

"*Madame,* you have taken advantage of me. You will regret it. You did not wait for me to tell you all that I know; I will now tell you the rest. This morning I received a letter from Vasili Petrovich. I shall answer it tomorrow. I shall expect to hear from you before then."

And then, while Mlle. Solini remained standing motionless and silent in the middle of the room, for once in her life startled out of speech, the young diplomat walked to the hall, took up his coat and hat, and left the house without another word.

For a long minute Aline stood still where he had left her. Then she moved slowly to the door and down the hall to the library, where she seated herself in her favorite chair in front of the fire.

She remained thus a long time, buried in thought; then, glancing at the clock, she rose and started for her room to dress for dinner.

"Decidedly," she murmured aloud, as she began to ascend the stairs, "this M. Naumann is a dangerous man."

CHAPTER XIII.

THE GENERAL RUNS ON AN ERRAND.

If anyone in Marisi had been asked what was the most interesting room in the palace of their prince, the answer would have been: "The one at the rear of the main corridor on the left, on the second floor." And if they had been further questioned why, they would have replied, "Because no one is ever allowed to enter it."

In this room, which the prince permitted no one to enter, he was seated alone on the morning of the day of the events narrated in the preceding chapter. There appeared to be nothing in the room or about it that would justify the mysterious exclusion of the curious; nor, in fact, was there.

On three of its sides were shelves of books, above which hung paintings and etchings, distributed in a somewhat haphazard fashion. On the fourth side, which faced the drive, were three double windows and a wide-open fireplace. A large table was in the center, heaped with books and papers.

The fact was that the prince, who found himself in a position considerably more public than he would naturally have wished, had simply chosen this den as a retreat from the importunities of subjects and sycophants.

The prince was half sitting, half reclining, in a big easy chair placed between the table and the fireplace. His eyes were closed and his chest moved regularly up and down with his breathing; it might have been thought that he was in reality asleep.

But young De Mide, his secretary, would at once have noticed the two little lines of wrinkles extending across the high white forehead, and would have known from that sign that his master was engaged in deep and profound consideration of some weighty and important subject.

Suddenly the prince opened his eyes, sat up, and rose to his feet with a short laugh greatly resembling a grunt—certain indications, De Mide would have said, that he had reached a decision. He left the room, walked down the corridor to its farther end, and mounted a flight of stairs on the left. In the corridor above he halted before a door at about its middle, and knocked on it sharply. A voice sounded:

''Come in.''

The prince entered.

As he did so General Paul Nirzann jumped up from

a chair he had been occupying near the window and bowed half-way to the ground.

"Ah! Your highness, I am honored."

"You usually are," said the prince dryly. "As, for instance, last evening."

The general looked at him with a deprecatory air, saying:

The decision was left with your highness."

"I know, but you had already decided for me."

"Is that possible? I beg your highness's pardon; I simply made a request."

"Yes, and it led to another offense for poor old Duchesne, whom you hate, but who nevertheless loves me as well as you do."

The face of the little general grew red with indignation.

"You will pardon me, your highness," he cried, "but that pig of a Duchesne has never—"

The prince interrupted him:

"That will do, Nirzann. You are hardly to blame, after all, for I really believe that young Naumann was in the right. But that is not what I came to discuss; let us forget it."

General Nirzann remained standing while the prince walked to a chair and seated himself. Then the general resumed his own chair and sat in respectful silence, waiting. Presently the prince spoke abruptly:

"Some time ago, Nirzann, you introduced me to a Mlle. Solini, who you said was your cousin."

The general looked at him quickly.

"Yes, your highness."

"She came, you said, from Russia. She herself has since informed me that she selected Marisi for this season on your recommendation. One or two things have led me to believe that this recommendation was owing to—well, let us say, for my benefit."

"But that—your highness knows—" The general halted in confusion.

"You need not deny it," said the prince with a smile. "I shall not make it a matter for reproach; indeed, I owe you a debt of gratitude. Mlle. Solini interests me."

"I am not surprised at it," said General Nirzann, who had recovered himself instantly at hearing the word "gratitude."

Disregarding this slightly impertinent observation, the prince continued:

"Yes, I admit it, I am interested in her." He paused for a moment, then asked abruptly:

"Is she really your cousin?"

But the general, who had been expecting just this question, had an answer ready:

"Certainly, your highness. Why do you ask that? If you doubt me—"

"No, I do not doubt you; I am merely seeking information. She is your cousin, then?"

"Yes."

"From—"

"Warsaw."

"She is Russian?"

"Yes. That is, on her father's side. Her mother was German—it is through her that we are connected."

"I see. Her estates, then, are near Warsaw?"

Again confusion appeared on the face of the general. He started twice to speak, without saying anything, and ended by declaring abruptly, in the tone of a man who has determined to speak the truth:

"They would be, your highness, if she had any."

"Ah!" The prince lifted his eyebrows. "But I expected that. This little tale of her fabulous wealth is a child of your brain, Nirzann?"

The prince's tone was friendly, and the general grinned as he replied:

"Yes, your highness. For the—let us say— amusement of Marisi. Otherwise she would have been ignored."

"Quite right. I applaud your acumen. She is not of noble birth?"

"No."

The prince frowned slightly at this answer, and walked to a window, where he remained for some minutes looking down into the street. The general sat silent, knowing perfectly well what was going on within the other's mind, and well satisfied with his knowledge. Suddenly the prince turned:

"I repeat, Nirzann, I am interested in her."

The general said:

"And I repeat, your highness, that it is not at all surprising."

"But she is your cousin?"

"A distant one."

"Then you think—"

"I think exactly as your highness does on all subjects."

"And Mlle. Solini?"

"I cannot answer for her. You have, no doubt, already discovered that she has a mind of her own. Most of her life she spent in a convent, but in the past two or three years she has been from one end of Europe to the other."

"When do you expect to see her?" the prince asked abruptly.

"I don't know. Perhaps this evening."

"Could you see her this evening?"

"Yes, your highness."

"Alone?"

"Certainly."

"And ask her—"

"Whatever your highness wishes."

"Then do so. I need not tell you what to say. I would advise you to use as much strategy and delicacy as possible. And if you are successful, in the end, there is a vacant Cross of Buta that I should know how to make use of."

171

The general fell on one knee, his face pale with joy.

"Your highness—I am overwhelmed—it has always been my desire—"

"I know," the prince smiled. "That will do, Nirzann. Earn it, and it is yours."

And, adding that he would expect the general to ride beside him at three o'clock as usual, the prince departed.

All of which goes to explain the expression of mingled hesitation and resolve on the face of General Paul Nirzann as, a little after eight o'clock that same evening, he rang the bell at the door of 341 the Drive.

All afternoon he had been impatiently awaiting this hour; now that it had arrived, he found that he had not yet decided what to do with it. At one instant his thought was that everything would be plain sailing; the next, remembering Aline's ambitious schemes both for herself and Vivi, the chance of success appeared slim.

He had indeed chosen an unfortunate time for his strategic assault on the fortress of the fair. Only two hours before his arrival Aline had heard from Naumann's lips the words, "I will write to Vasili Petrovich tomorrow," which had caused her to pay M. Naumann the compliment of declaring that he was a dangerous man. A doubtful one, indeed, not without its conjectural effect on his future—which he should have foreseen.

But General Nirzann, who was not skilled in the detection of subtle shades of expression on faces, saw nothing out of the common on that of Mlle. Solini as she welcomed him in the library.

There was restlessness and impatience in her manner, but he had been noticing that for some time now. For the rest, he was too absorbed in the difficulties of his own mission to give much study to its object.

They talked for an hour on various subjects. A dozen times the general began cautiously feeling the ground to lead up to the purpose of his visit, but invariably was taken away from it by Aline, until he began to think she had guessed it and was consciously avoiding it—in which supposition, of course, he flattered himself.

At length, having discussed the details of Aline's successful campaign in Marisi and offered one or two tentative suggestions for the future, he approached the subject of money.

"There is no want of that," said Aline, replying to his question. "I have over a hundred and twenty thousand francs in cash."

The general whistled in surprise.

"What the deuce!" he exclaimed. "Is this American made of gold?"

"So it would seem. But have you nothing to say of my dexterity at getting it from him?"

The general looked at her quizzically.

"That depends. You know what I have said before. It seems to me impossible that the man is fool enough to give up so much for nothing."

Aline laughed. "He has expectations—of marrying me."

Nirzann snorted.

"To be frank," he said, "I wish to know whether he is going to be in a position to interfere."

"Interfere? In what way?"

"With—certain plans."

Aline looked at him with quick suspicion. "But we have discussed all this before."

"I know. But if it becomes necessary to get rid of him, what then?"

"I have told you I will do so whenever you are ready."

"Whenever I am ready to leave Marisi with you, yes. But what if we abandon that intention?"

Aline regarded the general for a moment with a quizzical air, then said dryly:

"My dear Paul, you are trying to find out something. Have I not told you twenty times that your attempts at subtlety are ridiculous? Come—what is it you want? Out with it."

"Shall I be frank, then?" asked the general in the tone of one who is willing to come out in the open rather than take any unfair advantage.

"Yes," Aline smiled. "I beg of you, general, do not deceive me."

He was saying to himself, "I must use strategy; I must be tactful."

After a moment of thought he said aloud, impressively:

"Aline, this morning the prince came to see me in my room at the palace." General Nirzann never pronounced the words "my room" without adding "at the palace."

"Indeed!" said Aline, glancing at him.

"Yes; and he came to talk of you. Actually. He pretended that the object of his visit was to discuss that unfortunate affair of M. Chavot's death, but I saw through him. He came to talk of you."

"Indeed!" Aline repeated. "His highness is very kind."

"But it was not kindness. I assure you, he was thinking only of himself. *Mademoiselle,* you have said that you love me. I have been compelled to believe myself secure in your heart. But what if I have the Prince of Marisi for a rival?"

Aline looked at the general, and so faint and subtle was the mockery in her eyes and on her lips that she safely dared his blunt observation.

"My dear Paul," she said, "the only reason I repeat that I love you is that it gives me pleasure to say it. You know it well. Not even the prince himself can displace you—in my heart."

For the first time in two months the general neglected to fall on his knees before her in rapture at words of love from her lips. The fact was that he was being torn cruelly by conflicting emotions.

In so far as he could love a woman, he loved Aline, but his capacity in that direction was limited. The true passion raged not within his valorous breast. Stronger than his love for any woman, for all women, was his attachment to his prince and the desire to stand first in his graces—and, besides, there was that little matter (not little, however, in its importance to the general) of the Cross of Buta.

These thoughts being uppermost in his mind, Aline's protestations of love merely brought a smile to his lips—a smile that, on the face of a common man instead of a general, might have been called a simper. He said, attempting a sigh:

"Nevertheless, dearest, I begin to fear. The prince is irresistible."

"Not against you, Paul."

"Alas! I fear so—even against me."

"Do you not hear what I say? I love you."

"But if the prince should attempt—"

"He would be unsuccessful."

"I cannot believe it."

"I swear it."

"I do not believe it." The general was getting desperate.

Aline laughed outright.

"My dear Paul, you say that very much as though you do not want to believe it."

But against this insinuation the general protested warmly.

"How can you say that? Good Heavens! Have I not risked my reputation—my very existence—for your sake?"

"Still, it is plain that you are willing to give me up."

General Nirzann was getting a little bewildered, seeing that he was going round in a vicious circle and getting nowhere. Decidedly, he must admit something or give it up. Between the two alternatives there was but one choice. He cleared his throat. How to say it?

He opened his mouth and closed it again. Then he plunged forth recklessly:

"No, I am not willing to give you up. But, *mademoiselle*, I am the servant of my prince. Everything that I have—my purse, my honor, my life—belongs to him. And even what is dearer than all else—"

Aline interrupted him sharply:

"Stop, general!"

He continued with increasing firmness:

"You must understand me, dearest Aline. You know that I love you; but where my prince would enter I must step aside. That is what I came to tell you. Not as an emissary, I assure you—not that—but his wishes are plain. What can I do? Unhappily I have nothing but a choice of two evils."

"And to lose me is the lesser one?" She was enjoying herself immensely.

"No—that is—you must understand—" The general wondered why the deuce she should think it necessary to put things in so unpleasant a manner.

"I do understand," said Aline dryly. "And this is my answer: I love you!"

"Of course, of course; and I love you," replied the general, beginning to show signs of impatience. "But do you not see? It is impossible to refuse the prince."

Aline said calmly:

"Then I shall accomplish the impossible."

At this plain statement of intention the general rose to his feet in excitement.

"I know what it is!" he exclaimed. "It's that American! I have suspected this all along. You won't give him up—that's what it amounts to."

"Do you mean M. Stetton?"

"Yes, I do; and it's true!" cried the general, getting more excited every minute.

Aline said sharply:

"It is absurd, and you know it."

"It is true! You love him!"

"Ridiculous."

"You love him! You have been deceiving me!"

Aline shrugged her shoulders contemptuously; then, after a moment's reflection, looked at General Nirzann with a sudden air of decision.

"Listen to me, Paul. The American is a fool. I care not that for him," snapping her fingers. "No—let me finish! Or, rather, answer a question. You came here to-day as an emissary from the prince. Am I not right?"

The general began to protest; but, seeing the uselessness of it, ended by admitting that it was as she said.

"And what does the prince want?"

The general, seeing that she knew everything, anyway, replied simply:

"He wants to displace me in a position which he does not know I possess."

"You are sure of that?"

"Of what?"

"That he does not know."

"How is that possible, *mademoiselle*?"

Aline sighed with something like relief.

"Very well. I am glad to know that if you have ceased to love me, you at least have not betrayed me. As for the prince's desire, this is my answer: a fortress worthy the name neither invites a siege nor surrenders without one. You are a man of war, general; you will understand me."

"But—"

"No; do not say anything more; I will not listen to you."

Aline inserted a tremor into her voice.

"As for you, Paul, I will not say that you have broken my heart; but you have made me unhappy. Ah—Paul—no—do not speak—"

Aline sank back into her chair and covered her face with her hands.

General Nirzann, delighted and confused and dissatisfied all at once, after endeavoring vainly for ten minutes to get her to listen to him, turned reluctantly and left to go with his somewhat cryptic message to the Prince of Marisi.

CHAPTER XIV.

A PEACE OFFERING.

At the hour that General Nirzann left No. 341 to return to the palace, which was a little after ten o'clock in the evening, M. Frederick Naumann was seated in his furnished rooms on Walderin Place, gazing moodily at the wallpaper and confessing to himself that he was in the very deuce of a quandary. He had been seated thus for two hours, and he remained two hours more. Then he rose wearily and undressed himself and got into bed.

It was another hour before sleep reached him, and when it came it was accompanied by unpleasant dreams and frequent awakenings. All night he tossed about like one in a fever, and when the first ray of the light of morning entered at the window he rose, feeling that to lie still another instant would drive him mad.

Dressing hurriedly, he went for a walk in the cold morning air in search—Heaven help him!—of peace of mind.

He had ceased asking himself if he loved Vivi Janvour. He had no sooner left Mlle. Solini's house the night before than that question had met with a decided and desperate affirmative. But that only made matters worse.

In the first place, he had no reason to believe that his love was returned. Secondly, he was a man of considerable wealth and social position, of whom much was expected, both matrimonially and otherwise—and who was she?

He groaned. She was Vivi, and that was enough for him, he told himself furiously. But there was Mlle. Solini. He groaned again.

He had turned east, toward the poorer residential portion of the city, and was walking rapidly along the silent streets, neither knowing nor caring where he went. After an hour of this he felt that he was hungry, for he had eaten no dinner the evening before, and he entered a cheap lunch-room for some eggs and coffee, not noticing the chipped, stained dishes and soiled oilcloth.

Then he resumed his walk, still with his back turned to the heart of Marisi. In another half-hour he found himself approaching the country. Still he kept on; the turmoil and restlessness of his brain had communicated itself to the body.

Vivi, offered her choice between him and Mlle. Solini, had turned her back on him. That was his thought; it was followed immediately by this, that he was not being fair to himself. Considering the way in which Mlle. Solini had presented the alternative, what else could Vivi have done?

The words, "He does not pretend to love you," were ringing in his ears, in the voice of Mlle. Solini. He exclaimed aloud in a sort of puzzled fury: "How the devil did I happen to be idiot enough to say that?"

Then, carried away by a sudden bewildering burst of anger, he had threatened Aline, saying that he would communicate with Vasili Petrovich.

Would to Heaven he could! Of course, he thought, Mlle. Solini was too clever not to have seen that his threat was a mere empty bluff. He would not have been surprised to know that she knew much more of where Vasili Petrovich might be found than he did.

It was next to certain that Vasili, with his energy and furious desire for revenge, had found her long before this, and a meeting between them could have resulted only in her death or his. And she was very much alive.

Naumann was brought suddenly to a halt at finding that he had reached the end of the narrow, winding lane he had been following. Thus reminded of his surroundings, he looked about him in some surprise. He seemed to have got far out into the country.

On all sides nothing was to be seen but barren fields and gaunt, skeleton-like trees. He looked at his watch; it was nine o'clock. With an exclamation of wonder at the distance he had walked, and feeling himself a little tired, he turned about and began to retrace his steps toward the city.

Three hours later he arrived at his rooms all but exhausted in body and with his mind more unsettled and restless even than before. He had decided on nothing; indeed, he asked himself, what was there to decide?

He loved Vivi; well, what of that, since she did not love him? Even if Mlle. Solini, moved by his threat, should renounce her claims on the girl, what good would that do if Vivi was unwilling to leave her?

He sat down in a chair by the window of his reading-room, looking out across the place at the buildings on the opposite side without seeing them.

Clearly, the only sensible thing to do was to forget all about it. Surely that was simple enough. As though he had never been in love before! Dozens of times! Something whispered within him: "But Vivi is different." Bah! How different?

Was a man of the world like Frederick Naumann to succumb to the old trick of an innocent face and baby eyes? What a fool he had been! That was the thing to do, of course—forget all about it. He would begin at once—let us see, exactly how does one begin to forget?

There was a knock on the door. Naumann, startled,

jumped in his chair, then called out an invitation to enter.

The door opened, disclosing the form of old Schantin, the *concierge*. He entered, closing the door behind him, and bowed awkwardly. In his hands he held a parcel wrapped in brown paper, about the size of a cigar-box.

Naumann's impatience at the interruption showed in his tone as he said:

"What is it?"

"A package, *monsieur*. Left by a messenger. You were out. He said it was to be delivered to you personally, and you know, *monsieur,* I am always—"

Naumann interrupted him.

"All right. Lay it on the table and get out. I'm busy."

When the *concierge* had left, with an expression of utter amazement on his stupid old face—for never before had he left the room of M. Naumann without having received a kind word and a substantial tip—Naumann sat back in his chair to begin again to forget. He flattered himself that the matter promised to be quite simple.

"Bah!" he thought. "Why the deuce did I work myself into such a stew? In a week I won't even remember her name."

Then, realizing suddenly that it was well past noon and that a considerable amount of work was awaiting him at the legation, he rose to change his clothing, which had become soiled during his tramp in the country. He had tied his scarf and was crossing to the wardrobe to take out a coat and waistcoat when his eye happened to fall on the parcel left on the table by the concierge.

"What can it be, anyway?" he muttered, lifting it curiously and taking out his knife to cut the string.

Inside the paper was a gray pasteboard box. Removing the lid, his astonished eyes beheld a tiny, pink-tinted envelope resting on what appeared to be the product of some Marisi bakery shop.

The envelope was inscribed in a small round hand: "M. Frederick Naumann."

He tore it open and took out a small sheet of notepaper, on which was written the following:

Dear M. Naumann:

If I offended you last night I am sorry, but what could I do? You will say, perhaps, that I acted with foolish pride, and you will be telling the truth.

Do not think that I undervalue your friendship, or that it is not dear to me. Of course, I cannot ask you to come again to the house of Mlle. Solini—you must not come here, I beg of you—it makes me unhappy.

But here is a peace offering, *monsieur*—you see I have not forgotten a happy hour you gave me once. I shall always be your friend.

Vivi Janvour.

Naumann read the note three times and pressed it passionately to his lips as many dozen. How like Vivi it was! His Vivi! For she should be his—he swore it. He forgot all about his vows to forget.

And evidently, though it was too much to say that she loved him, she did actually think of him and care for his friendship. To be sure, she told him plainly not to come to see her; but that was only natural, considering the hostile relations existing between himself and Mlle. Solini.

He turned his attention to her peace offering. It consisted of half a dozen apricot tarts, exactly like the ones they had eaten together the day he had taken tea with her, which she declared she had made herself.

This, he said to himself with a smile, was even more like Vivi than the note. He could see her little white hands dabbling daintily in the flour—her brow, he decided, would be puckered up in a little serious frown.

The tarts, with their delicate brown crust and reddish amber fruit, lay side by side in two neat rows. Naumann had not eaten anything since his hasty breakfast in the cheap lunch-room early in the morning. He took up one of the tarts in his fingers, feeling as he did so that he was performing a rite of love.

The tart was half-way to his mouth when a loud knock sounded on the door. The rite of love was interrupted in mid air. Naumann turned, calling out "Come in," and hastily returned the tart to the box.

It was Richard Stetton, who was dropping in, as he said with his first words, in the expectation of being amused. At sight of Naumann in his shirt-sleeves he demanded to know if it was fitting for a hard-working young diplomat to stay in bed till the middle of the afternoon.

"My dear fellow," said Naumann, motioning the visitor to a chair, "it gives me pleasure to inform you that I rose this morning exactly at six o'clock. Kindly apologize."

Stetton helped himself to a cigarette from a box on the table and settled himself comfortably in the easiest chair in the room.

"Apologize?" he asked scornfully. "Never. In the first place, I don't believe you. Secondly, if you really did get up at six o'clock in the morning, it merely proves that you are insane. What the deuce did you mean by it?"

"Oh, nothing. I went for a walk."

"For a walk?" This incredulously.

"Of course. My dear fellow, it is the most pleasant hour of the day."

"Yes—for sleeping. However, I find the subject tiresome. How about our friend Duchesne? Is he still trying to make trouble?"

"Not since his little interview with the prince," replied Naumann over his shoulder. He was standing in front of a mirror, buttoning his waistcoat. "Don't worry about that any more; it's all settled."

"Chavot's funeral is tomorrow morning."

"Yes? Are you going?"

"I haven't decided. Hardly know whether I ought to go or not."

Stetton rose from his chair and walked to the table, depositing the stub of his cigarette in a tray and taking a fresh one from the box.

"Hello!" he exclaimed suddenly. "What's this? Fixing up for a bachelor tea?"

Naumann turned to find his friend gazing curiously at the box of apricot tarts.

"Oh—that," he said with a touch of confusion; "why—it's just a sort of present."

"Made especially for your consumption by the fair hands of some fair lady, I presume," observed Stetton. "Who is she?"

Naumann replied:

"Mlle. Janvour. Not that it's any of your business, you know."

"The deuce you say!" Stetton looked at him in some surprise. "Vivi, eh? Guess I'll take one."

"I guess you won't," the other retorted, springing across the room and snatching the box away.

Stetton shrugged his shoulders and walked back to his easy chair. "All right, keep your old tarts—I've eaten 'em by the hundred, anyway." After a second's pause he continued with a grin: "By Jove, I know what it is. I know why you're so careful of 'em. Naumann, you're an ass."

"What are you talking about?"

"You. You and your fertile imagination. Don't blame you a bit. Can't be too cautious. You're perfectly right. Since the tarts come from No. 341 they're probably poisoned."

The tone was that of heavy sarcasm. He exclaimed in mock terror, as Naumann took one of the tarts from the box and started it for his mouth: "Look out there, man—don't eat that! It'll kill you!"

"Don't be so funny," replied Naumann dryly; but, nevertheless, his hand stopped half-way to his mouth, as it had before at the sound of Stetton's knock.

For a moment he gazed at Stetton in silence, then he slowly returned the tart to the box, which he placed on a shelf in the wardrobe.

Stetton was laughing in high glee.

"By Jove, he believes it!" he exclaimed. "I'll be hanged if the man doesn't actually believe it!"

There was no answer from Naumann, who remained standing by the door of the wardrobe, gazing at his visitor with the expression of one who has just discovered something to think about. For a full minute he stood thus while Stetton continued his ejaculations of gleeful amusement, and ended by demanding:

"You don't mean to say you seriously believe it possible? Come; don't be an ass. I was joking, of course."

"Maybe it isn't a joke," replied Naumann slowly. "I don't know whether I believe it or not. You don't understand; you don't know all the circumstances."

He stood again considering for a time, then suddenly took forth a pink envelope and, drawing forth the note, handed it to Stetton, asking:

"Do you happen to know Mlle. Janvour's handwriting?"

Stetton took the note and read it through, still with a grin on his face. Then he returned it, saying:

"It looks like it, but I can't tell for sure. Haven't seen anything but her signature. But say—better be careful—the note may be poisoned, too, you know."

Naumann paid no attention to this observation.

"It isn't possible," he muttered to himself, frowning. "It isn't possible."

For a minute he stood looking at the note, while the frown deepened. Then, with a quick gesture of decision, he walked to the table, took up the telephone, and asked the operator to give him the number of Mlle. Solini's house.

Stetton, who began to see that his friend, for some reason or other, was really treating the matter seriously, sat in his chair and listened in silence. Naumann quarreled with three or four operators, trying to get the number he wanted. At length he was successful; he heard a voice on the wire which he thought he recognized, saying:

"Yes, this is Mlle. Solini's residence. What is it, please?"

Naumann replied:

"Please let me speak to Mlle. Janvour."

"This is Mlle. Janvour."

"Oh!" For a moment Naumann was confused. Then: "This is Frederick Naumann."

"M. Naumann?" There was a flutter in the voice at the other end. "I did not recognize your voice."

"No? I recognized yours. I called you up, *mademoiselle,* to thank you."

"To thank me?" The voice held a puzzled tone.

"Yes; to thank you for the note you sent me this morning."

"The note I sent you?" This in a tone of amazement.

"Yes. I received it an hour ago, when I returned to my rooms."

There was a slight pause before the response came:

"But, M. Naumann, there must be some mistake. I have not sent you any note. What did it say?"

"Pardon me—then you didn't send it?"

"No."

"Nor a box—a sort of—er—parcel, containing a peace-offering?"

"No. Really, I don't know what you are talking about. What was in the box? What did the note say? Where did they come from? Are you making fun of me, *monsieur?*"

Naumann replied soberly:

"No, *mademoiselle;* please do not think that I would ever try to make fun of you. But this—I am afraid this is serious. I can't explain now. Perhaps later. I'll call you up again."

Vivi's voice sounded vaguely and inaudibly at the other end; she was evidently talking to someone standing near her. This for perhaps a minute; then suddenly her voice sounded clearly over the wire: "*Au revoir,* M. Naumann."

Instantly there was a click in his ear; she had hung up the receiver.

Naumann turned about, facing Stetton.

There was a short pause, then he said abruptly: "Your joke isn't a joke, after all. She didn't send it."

Stetton exclaimed: "Rot! That doesn't prove anything."

"No, but something else will," said Naumann grimly. He took his overcoat from the back of a chair and put it on, then took up his hat. "Come on."

"Where are you going?"

"You'll see. Come on."

Stetton began to protest: "Not if you're going out on a wild-goose chase with your imagination for a guide. I'm no detective."

"This is no wild-goose chase. I've got an idea, and I want to use it. Come on. I need you."

Stetton rose, still grumbling, and took up his coat and hat. A minute later the two men were in the street together; Naumann, who appeared to know exactly where he was going, halted a cab and, getting in after Stetton, gave the driver an address in the eastern part of the city.

"The reason I want you," the young diplomat explained as they were carried rapidly along, "is that our errand has to do with the police, and since my quarrel with Duchesne over the Chavot affair I prefer not to ask them for anything."

Stetton looked at him in amazement.

"You don't mean to say you're going to the police with this! Are you crazy?"

"Not exactly. I'm not going to the police—at least, not in the way you mean. Our errand is at the city pound. The police are in charge of it."

"The city pound!" Stetton's amazement increased. "My dear fellow, I really believe we'd better go to the insane asylum instead."

Naumann vouchsafed no reply to this, but sat gazing steadily ahead as the cab jolted steadily over the rough paving stones. The ride lasted for something like half an hour, and was ended when the driver stopped in front of a low, red-brick building with barred windows and an iron padlocked gate for a door.

Naumann glanced up in surprise to find that they had reached their destination, and began to tell Stetton in as few words as possible what he wanted him to do. Stetton appeared to be both amused and astonished at what he heard, but, seeing his friend's seriousness, promised to obey orders.

Stetton jumped from the cab, advanced to the iron gate, and rang for admittance. After a wait of a minute or so the gate was opened the space of a few inches and someone from the inside questioned him. His answers appeared to be satisfactory—the gate was opened further and he passed within.

There followed an interval of ten minutes or more, while Naumann, seated in the cab, eyed the gate with increasing impatience. At length it again swung open and Stetton reappeared, carrying in his arms a small black and tan dog, evidently of the breed commonly known as "cur."

"Good!" cried Naumann as Stetton walked to the cab and handed in the dog. "Did you have much trouble?"

"None whatever," Stetton replied, entering the cab and brushing off his hands. "They have fifty or more in there. You ought to see 'em. They gave me my pick for five francs.''

"He'll do. Go ahead, driver. Back where we came from—No. 5 Walderin Place.''

During the return journey Stetton, having performed his mission, gave his opinion of it in no uncertain terms. It was absurd—a huge joke—a ripping, roaring farce—blessed if he wouldn't tell everybody in Marisi he knew. The town would be too hot to hold M. Frederick Naumann, who was making a profound ass of himself. The whole thing was ridiculous.

To all this Naumann made no reply whatever. He sat sunk in meditation, so far as circumstances would permit—for the black and tan dog, which he was holding on his lap, appeared strongly to disapprove of riding in a cab, judging by his struggles to get free. Naumann clutched him tightly in his arms, nor paid any attention to Stetton's unfeeling observations concerning the absurdity of the performance.

Arrived at No. 5 Walderin Place, they dismissed the cab and mounted the stairs together to Naumann's rooms, carrying the dog with them. As soon as he was put down on the floor of the reading-room the animal began to scamper about, barking furiously.

Stetton threw himself into a chair, still calling Heaven to witness that his friend Naumann had gone completely crazy, and ironically commiserating the dog on the dire misfortune about to befall him.

Naumann opened the wardrobe, took forth the pasteboard box and took out one of the tarts.

"Here, doggie!" he called, and began to chase the animal round the room. "Here, doggie! Nice doggie! Here, doggie!''

Stetton was exploding with laughter.

The dog stopped, approached cautiously and sniffed at the tart. Then he backed off, shaking his head as though in grave doubt.

"Wise pup!" yelled Stetton in glee. "He's as crazy

as you are, Naumann—those tarts are the best stuff in Marisi. I know—I've eaten hundreds of 'em.''

The dog approached again, sniffed more eagerly than before, snatched the tart suddenly and gulped it down. Then he stood looking up at Naumann, wagging his tail, which in dog language is usually taken to mean, ''I want more.''

Naumann stood regarding him with intense gravity, quite as though he expected him suddenly to blow up.

''Ladies and gentlemen,'' called Stetton in stentorian tones, ''we will now present the last act of the soul-stirring drama, 'The Modern Borgia.' Look at him, ladies and gentlemen! Observe him well!

''He is perhaps the cruelest man now living. He eats 'em alive. At his present rate of activity it is estimated that he will destroy the entire population of Marisi within the space of one year and two months. Note the viciousness of his eye! See the blood-lust in his—''

''For Heaven's sake, stop it!'' cried Naumann. ''Perhaps you won't feel quite so funny in a few minutes. I have a reason for all this, Stetton, and a good one. Watch the dog.''

''He seems to be all right, so far,'' replied Stetton, grinning. ''In fact, he's a good, sensible pup. Why don't you give him another one—don't you see he's asking for it?''

''That might be a good idea,'' said Naumann, taking the suggestion seriously.

He went to the wardrobe and came back with another of the tarts, which the dog gobbled with apparent relish. Immediately Stetton started off again on his oration:

''Ladies and gentlemen, we will now present the last act of the soul-stirring drama, 'The Modern Borgia.' Look at him—''

He kept this up for five minutes, warming up to his topic as he went along. Then suddenly his tones lost their vehemence, he lost the thread of his discourse, and his voice stopped.

Indubitably something was happening to the dog.

The animal had ceased wagging its tail for more. Instead, it was looking up at Naumann with a pitiful expression in its eyes and a hanging lip.

Suddenly it turned and walked toward the door, whining dismally, then changed its course and went through an open arch into the bedroom. The two men following it heard a low whine coming from under the bed.

"What the deuce does it mean?" asked Stetton, suddenly become serious. Naumann did not answer.

For several minutes they stood silent, while the whine became continuous and louder. Suddenly Naumann bent down and, reaching under the bed, seized the dog by the hind leg and pulled him forth.

Involuntarily he started back at sight of the misery and agony in the beast's eyes.

It was frothing at the mouth, and its head was rolling from side to side; the whine had become a low, heart-rending moan. The little body was quivering and trembling all over.

"This is horrible," said Naumann with a white face. "I was a brute to do this. It's horrible!"

It was soon over.

The moan became more and more feeble, and the head scarcely moved. The expression in the dog's eyes as he turned them up to the two men standing over him was horrible, indeed, and seemed to Naumann to hold an accusation; he turned his own eyes away.

Suddenly there was a violent twitching of the animal's legs; the moan ceased, and the body became still. Naumann looked round again when he heard Stetton say in a low tone:

"He's dead!"

"Poor devil!" said Naumann with deep feeling. He added: "But the Lord knows I'm glad it wasn't me!"

"And the question now is," said Stetton with an attempt at facetiousness that did not hide the tremor in his voice, "Who made the tarts?"

CHAPTER XV.

LOVE AND STUBBORNNESS.

Perhaps the most difficult thing you can ask of a man is that he either forgive or forget a deliberate and premeditated attempt on the part of another to take his life.

Life gives value to everything and holds all values in itself; it is, of course, trite to say that a lover loves it better than his mistress and a miser more than his gold. Otherwise they would both starve to death.

Frederick Naumann liked life as well as the next man; you can imagine his feelings when he discovered that the woman he already hated had tried to take it away from him. His hate increased tenfold and was seasoned with fear.

He swore revenge on Mlle. Solini; and when Stetton took occasion to observe that there was no proof that Mlle. Solini was the author of the attempt on his life, Naumann gave his friend the lie direct, but apologized immediately after.

He set out at once, however, to find the proof, and went about it in a manner which indicated that he meant business. He took the paper in which the box had been wrapped and the box itself, containing the four remaining tarts, and locked them in his wardrobe. This done, he went below in search of the concierge to obtain information concerning the messenger who had delivered the parcel.

But old Schantin, whose eyesight and hearing were none too good anyway, remembered very little.

Was the messenger a man or a woman? A man.

Was he in uniform? Schantin didn't know.

A man or a boy? He wasn't sure.

What did he look like? The concierge was completely at sea on that point; he only knew that it was some sort of a man.

Which way did he go after delivering the parcel? Out of the door. At this answer, the only definite one he received, Naumann lost patience entirely and left Schantin blinking helplessly on his chair near the door of the outer hall.

It was then three o'clock in the afternoon, and Naumann hastened to his desk at the legation for the first time that day. His duties were performed in a perfunctory and hasty manner, but still there was enough to keep him busy till after six o'clock. Then he went to the Hotel Walderin to dine with Stetton.

That night in his room he considered the question that confronted him from every possible angle. One thing he had decided at once—he would not report the affair to the police.

For one thing, they probably could not help him; for another, they certainly would not, so long as Duchesne was in command; and for still another, if he became thus associated with another unsavory episode it would in all likelihood result in his being recalled to Berlin. If he succeeded in finding proof of Mlle. Solini's guilt, that would be a different matter; he would see that she was punished for it, if he had to move heaven and earth.

But how to obtain the proof? As for tracing the messenger, that appeared to be utterly hopeless, since Schantin had no recollection of him whatever. The tarts could be chemically analyzed and the sale of the poison traced; but that was a long chance, and besides, only the police could make such an investigation with any promise of success.

There remained the parcel and the box itself and the note. If only he dared to ask the assistance of the police! Surely Mlle. Solini, clever as she was, had not succeeded in covering every track.

In his own mind Naumann was as thoroughly convinced of her guilt as though he had seen the act with his own eyes. Also, he was just as certain that Mlle. Janvour had had nothing whatever to do with it, and he was more than ever resolved to get the girl away. How, was another matter.

Evidently Mlle. Solini had not thought so lightly of his threat after all, since it had led her to the daring and all but successful attempt on his life. But the bluff would no longer serve; she had declared war, and his only chance was to fight back.

In his bed that night a thousand schemes and surmises raced back and forth through his brain until he finally fell asleep through sheer weariness.

The one clear thought that he possessed when he awoke the following morning was that he must save Vivi. He felt that if he could only see her and talk to her she must perforce listen and believe.

He started to the telephone, to ask her to meet him at a restaurant for lunch; then, on second thought, decided to take a more open course. He waited till eleven o'clock; then, unable to restrain his impatience longer, took a cab for 341 the Drive.

He half expected that Mlle. Solini would refuse to allow him to see the girl; perhaps would see him herself, feeling her position impregnable, to ask him with her mocking smile if he had written to Vasili Petrovich. In that case he could do nothing but swallow her defiance, and then—well, and then he would see.

No doubt in this expectation he was correct; but luckily Mlle. Solini was out. So said Czean, at the door.

"And Mlle. Janvour?"

"I will see, *monsieur*. Step into the drawing-room, please."

In a few minutes Czean returned to say that Mlle. Janvour was in her room and would be down shortly. Naumann sighed with relief. He had no sooner composed himself to wait than the door opened and Vivi appeared on the threshold.

She was dressed in a loose house gown of gray, caught together at the waist with a rope girdle; Naumann thought he had never seen her look so charming.

"I am glad to see you, *monsieur*," said Vivi, approaching with outstretched hand. In her manner was ill-concealed curiosity, mingled with an air of reserve.

"And surprised, of course," said Naumann, bowing over her hand.

"Perhaps—a little," the girl confessed, smiling at him. "I see you so seldom that it is something of an event. Won't you be seated?"

"And usually an unpleasant one," said Naumann, finding a chair for her and taking one himself. "As the day before yesterday, for instance. I know it was unpardonable of me, *mademoiselle*—I should have come to you first—"

"Not at all," Vivi protested, recovering in a degree her natural ease of manner. "You were most kind and thoughtful, M. Naumann; if I did not thank you I do so now. Only, it was impossible."

"Impossible for you to accept my offer, you mean?"

"Yes."

"And why?"

"Is it necessary for me to repeat my reasons?"

"No. I do not know why I asked. I know I have no right to annoy you as I do."

"You do not annoy me, *monsieur*."

"It is evident that I do."

"Pardon me—it is not so—you must not say that." Vivi's eyes were looking earnestly into his. After a short pause she added, as though involuntarily: "You know very well you are the only friend I have in Marisi."

Naumann smiled:

"It is hard to believe that."

"Nevertheless, it is true."

"You do not treat me as though I were."

"Do I not?" cried Vivi warmly. "You are wrong, *monsieur*; it is you who treat me badly. You never come to see me, and what can I do? One day—do you remember it?—I thought we were really going to be friends. The day you promised not to say anything more of Aline. It is true you kept your promise, but by saying nothing."

"Am I not here now?"

"Yes, but with some terribly serious purpose; I can see it in your eyes. You come to tell me something; I would much rather you came to tell me nothing. Is it about that mysterious note you received the other day?"

"Yes. Yesterday."

"Well, I admit I am curious about that. I've been waiting for the explanation you promised me. You have discovered, of course, that it was written by someone else. What was in it? How was it signed?"

For reply Naumann reached in the breast-pocket of his coat and took out a pink-tinted envelope, from which he extracted a sheet of paper. Then he said:

"I received this day before yesterday morning, *mademoiselle*, in a box of apricot tarts. It is signed with your name." He handed the note to the girl.

At the first glance Vivi exclaimed in wonder: "Why, this is my handwriting!" Then, examining the note closely, she continued: "No, I believe not, but it looks like it. Exactly. All except the T's; I make very funny T's."

She read the note over twice; then, looking up at Naumann, added: "It is precisely my signature. And it is on my note-paper. Where did it come from?"

"I have told you; it came in a box of apricot tarts— the peace offering."

"Apricot tarts!"

"Yes. Exactly like the ones you gave me once at tea. Do you remember? You said you made them yourself."

"Yes—so I did."

Vivi stared at him a moment in silence, then continued:

"But where could they come from? Who could have sent them? And why?"

"I can answer the last question. There is one thing I haven't told you. The tarts were poisoned."

A look of horror came into Vivi's eyes. She cried:

"Poisoned!"

"Yes, *mademoiselle*. When I telephoned you and discovered the note was a forgery, I grew suspicious. I fed one of the tarts to a dog. He was dead in ten minutes."

"But that is horrible!" said Vivi in a low tone, gazing at him as though half in doubt of what she had heard. "It is impossible. Who could have done anything so dreadful as that? And who could know my handwriting, and get my note-paper, and know about the tarts—"

The girl paused abruptly, while her eyes began to fill with a new expression of dread and fear.

"*Monsieur*, what is this you are telling me?" she cried half angrily.

"The truth, *mademoiselle*," replied Naumann earnestly. "It is unnecessary for me to say more; you are beginning to draw your own conclusions, and you are right."

"You mean—it was someone in this house?"

"Yes, and someone who hates me."

There was a long silence. On the face of the girl appeared an expression of understanding and doubt and fear. Naumann sat silent, waiting for her to speak. Finally she said:

"I know. I know what you are thinking, M. Naumann. You think it was Aline who—who did this. You have come here to tell me so. I can't believe it—I can't—I can't!"

"But it is true. Think, *mademoiselle*; how is it possible that it could have been any one else?"

"I do not believe it!" cried the girl.

And to that assertion she held steadfast, despite everything Naumann could say. A dozen times he recapitulated the proof, which was overwhelming, but Vivi remained loyal.

He ended by becoming impatient and declaring that no one in their senses could doubt such a chain of evidence. Vivi, up in arms instantly, retorted that he had better go to the police if he felt so sure of his knowledge, and accused him of bias and malice.

"But I don't understand!" cried Naumann in despair. "I don't see how you can possibly doubt! And I am not prompted by malice—you wrong me when you say that."

"I know; forgive me," said the girl, softening instantly. After a short pause she added: "M. Naumann, I want to ask you a question; then perhaps you will understand. Would you believe this thing of your mother on this evidence? Would you believe her a murderess?"

"Great Heavens," cried Naumann, "of course not! You do not know my mother."

Vivi replied earnestly:

"But Aline has been a mother to me, and more. Do you not see? I love her. *Monsieur*, you are mistaken—I feel it—I am sure of it!"

Naumann perceived at length that his case was hopeless. To argue with a woman against a genuine and deep affection is the business of a fool.

Still he did not despair. Vivi had not been angry with him; that was surely a sign of something. She had said that he was her only friend in Marisi. He looked at her, and began where he should have begun in the first place. He said:

"Then, *mademoiselle*, if you look upon Mlle. Solini as a mother, I will talk no more of her."

"That is what I asked of you two months ago," said Vivi with a sudden smile.

"I know; I should have obeyed you. You think, perhaps, that I can talk of nothing else."

The girl protested that that was exactly what she did not think.

"Do you not remember that day in the library? You were charming. There! Is not that a confession for me to make when I ought to be angry with you?"

"I like you to be angry," declared Naumann irrelevantly. "It makes your eyes flash. If the truth were known, it might be that that is why I say things you do not like."

"I hope not," said Vivi, suddenly serious, "for it hurts me. To have to be angry with you, I mean. And the worst of it is, you can be so pleasant. Quite the pleasantest man I know."

Naumann laughed at her tone of a critical woman of the world, and at the little serious twist of her lips.

"It is not much to be champion of Marisi," he declared. "Wait till you get to Paris. I should be doing well if allowed to call your carriage at the Sigognac."

"Paris!" cried Vivi, forgetting everything else at sound of this, to her; magic name. "Oh, I can hardly wait! We are going in the spring."

"With—"

"With Aline."

Naumann frowned, and there followed an awkward silence. He knew very well what he wanted to say, and was only trying to decide how to say it. He ended by observing lamely:

"I should like to show you Paris myself. And Berlin, and London—don't you think we could have a good time together?"

"Hardly," laughed Vivi mischievously. "I wouldn't go without Aline, and fear you wouldn't be very gay."

"But I don't mean with Aline. I mean alone—just you and me."

"Oh! That would be very pleasant if it were possible."

"But why is it not possible?"

Vivi looked at him quickly. Yes, his face was like his tone—quite serious. She felt somehow that she had given herself away, or was going to, and she said with a touch of dignity:

"Do not let me think you are in earnest, M. Naumann."

"But I am in earnest!"

"Then, do you mean to insult me?"

"Insult you!" Naumann stared at her in amazement. Then, slowly, his face filled with the light of understanding, and at the same time grew eloquent with denial and protest.

"*Mademoiselle*! Surely you could not think that I meant— You could not! How could I insult you when I love you?"

"*Monsieur*!" cried Vivi, her face blazing.

But Naumann, having pronounced the word, felt himself well started and plunged recklessly on.

"I love you!" he repeated. "You know it. I have loved you ever since the first time I saw you. Great Heavens! Insult you? I worship you, Vivi! Let me call you that! Vivi, don't turn away from me—let me look at you! Dearest!"

Then, struck suddenly with the thought that what he was saying was of some importance and deserved a measure of dignity, he rose to his feet and said distinctly:

"Mlle. Janvour, will you marry me?"

Vivi's face had gone from white to pink, and from pink back to white. Her eyes refused to meet his, and when she finally spoke her voice trembled and was so low he could scarcely hear the words.

"But M. Naumann—you know me so little—it is impossible—that you—you—"

"Vivi, look at me! I love you!" His voice, too, was trembling.

"*Monsieur*—I do not know—"

"Do you love me?"

"*Monsieur*—"

"Do you love me?"

There was a sudden tense silence. And then, before either of them quite knew what was happening, his arms were round her, holding her close, while he knelt beside her chair. She struggled—a little; their lips met; her arms were round his neck.

"Ah—ah—ah—" she breathed, sighing like a breeze of spring.

"Vivi, darling—you do love me—look at me—"

Again their lips met.

"Do you love me, Vivi?"

He repeated the question over and over, and finally there came from somewhere near his shoulder, in a voice muffled and scarcely audible with emotion, the word:

"Yes."

He held her tighter. Presently he spoke again:

"Will you marry me, Vivi?"

At this question, uttered in a tone which, though tender, was not without insistence, Vivi drew away as though in sudden fright.

"I don't know—I must think—" she stammered.

Naumann cried, as though astonished:

"But you love me!"

"Yes," said Vivi simply, recovering herself. "Yes, *monsieur*, I love you. I think I have always loved you. But when you ask me to marry you, that means a great deal, doesn't it? Perhaps you don't realize—are you sure you want me?"

"Want you!" Naumann encircled her again with his arms. But she held him off.

"You know, *monsieur*, there are many things to consider—your family—your position—"

"I know," replied Naumann, a little sobered by her tone. "I have thought of everything, Vivi. But nothing else matters. Will you marry me?"

"Then—yes."

Again she submitted to his embrace, but with a curious hesitancy. It was not that she was cold; her eyes, eloquent with love, spoke of the sweetness of her surrender; but still she was troubled with some secret thought. After they had remained silent for a long time she gave it voice.

"Of course," she said abruptly, "you will ask Mlle. Solini."

It was like a bombshell thrown into the midst of a peaceful camp, though it lay smoldering for some time before it burst.

Naumann, to begin with, allowed himself an expression of surprise, saying that he did not think it at all necessary to ask Mlle. Solini for the hand of Mlle. Janvour. Vivi protested that she could not marry without Aline's consent, and added:

"I told you she has been a mother to me."

"But surely you see that it is impossible for me to ask anything of Mlle. Solini!" cried Naumann.

Thus the argument began. Vivi, warm with loyalty, declared that she owed everything to Aline, and that to disregard her in this most important question of her life was unthinkable. Naumann retorted that he could not see how Mlle. Solini was in any way concerned in the matter.

Vivi replied that Aline was concerned in anything that concerned her, and wanted to know if Naumann would prefer the girl he would marry to be entirely without protection or connection—a thoroughly indiscreet question, since it led the young man to declare that he would certainly wish his intended wife to be anything rather than the protégée of a murderess.

202

The bomb exploded at this point with a deafening roar. Vivi said coldly:

"I have told you that you wrong Aline. You must not insult her, *monsieur*, if you wish me to think well of you."

"But what has she to do with us?" cried Naumann. "You ask me an impossibility. I would not speak to Mlle. Solini; I would not ask a favor of her if it were to gain the world."

"Then, I am sorry."

The girl's face was white.

"Do you admit that you are unreasonable?" Naumann demanded.

"How can I? There is no use in discussing it, M. Naumann. It is you who are unreasonable."

"Child!" cried the young man angrily. "You are stubborn, that is what it is, and you know it."

Vivi said, trying to smile:

"I would not make a very good wife, if I am stubborn and unreasonable. That is enough, *monsieur*."

"You mean—"

"We need not quarrel longer."

"Then you send me away?"

"Yes," she replied bravely.

"You want me to leave you?"

Incredulity, astonishment, despair—all were in his voice and eyes.

"Yes," Vivi repeated.

There was a silence, while they stood gazing at each other. Naumann's face went red and white by turns; he was trembling with emotion; once or twice he essayed to speak, while a look of entreaty and appeal appeared to fight with the anger in his eyes, but found not their way to his tongue.

Suddenly a voice sounded from the doorway:

"Vivi! Ah, M. Naumann!"

They turned. It was Mlle. Solini, wearing a toque and furs; evidently she had just entered by the street-door. For a moment there was silence, while she stood looking keenly from the girl to the young man and back again; then Naumann, bowing deeply to Vivi, proceeded to the hall without uttering a word, took up his hat and coat and left the house.

Mlle. Solini watched the door close behind him, then turned to Vivi, who had sunk back in her chair and covered her face with her hands. In the woman's eyes was an expression of compassion and genuine affection; an expression that no one else had ever seen there or ever would. She crossed to the girl's side and, bending over her chair, took her in her arms and laid her cold cheek against the girl's warm one, wet with tears.

"Vivi, what is it?" asked Mlle. Solini tenderly. "Tell me, dear, what is it?"

"Nothing," replied Vivi, raising her head and trying to smile through her tears. "Nothing is the matter— nothing whatever. Only—oh, Aline, my heart is broken!"

CHAPTER XVI.

THE PRINCE MAKES LOVE.

On leaving the house of Mlle. Solini, Naumann returned directly to his rooms at No. 5 Walderin Place, in a state of mind not easily to be described.

There could be no more nonsense about forgetting Vivi Janvour—that he knew. He loved her, and he would always love her. He wanted her as he wanted nothing else in the world.

He called himself a fool, an idiot, a thundering imbecile. After all, had she asked him anything unreasonable? Was not her attitude toward Mlle. Solini perfectly understandable—more, was it not commendable? Should she be condemned for her loyalty?

Still, if she loved him, could she not make concessions to his prejudices and beliefs—beliefs well founded on knowledge?

One thing was certain—he could do nothing about the poisoned tarts. The note might possibly be proved a forgery, but Vivi herself had been nearly deceived by it. It was written on her own paper.

Any activity of his in the matter would probably result in more trouble for her than for the one he knew to be guilty. Aline Solini possessed the cleverness of the devil himself. So thought Naumann as he took the box containing the four remaining tarts and threw it on the fire.

Then he sat down to watch it burn, railing at Fate, as many another man has done with less reason before and since.

There we will leave him, to return to No. 341 the Drive, after passing over an afternoon and a night. You may be sure Mlle. Solini was wasting no time in railing at Fate; she was not in the habit of leaving her affairs to the management of that dame's capricious hands.

Nevertheless, her great campaign was not prospering. Her ship of intrigue was caught in a dead calm. Her subtle and powerful attack appeared to have been repulsed not only with ease, but also with contempt.

In plain English, she had received no message nor hint of one from the Prince of Marisi since General Nirzann's diplomatic mission of two days before. True, she had seen the general several times, but all he would say of the prince was that Aline's message had been delivered, and that there was no reply.

So much being explained, you will understand the light that flashed in the eyes of Mlle. Solini when, on the day following that on which Naumann had won and lost his love, she was informed by Czean, as she sat at her writing-desk in her boudoir, that the Prince of Marisi was awaiting her in the drawing-room.

"Tell him I will be down shortly," said Aline, while her eyes flashed with joy. Fifteen minutes later she descended, having made a hasty but by no means ineffective toilet.

In the first minute, after greeting the royal visitor, she saw that the message carried by General Nirzann had had its effect. The prince had descended from the attitude of a man who takes what he wants to that of one who takes what he can get.

It was not exactly that he treated her with increased respect, for he had never been lacking in that; it was something subtle and indefinable in his manner of looking at her and speaking to her that seemed to say, "You make the rules; I will follow them."

They conversed for an hour, amiably but quite impersonally, on every conceivable topic. The prince made no mention whatever of the message he had sent by General Nirzann, or the one that had been returned to him.

He appeared to think it quite natural to drop in for a little chat with Mlle. Solini, though Aline knew that no one else in Marisi had ever been similarly honored. As he rose to go the prince said:

"No doubt you received a card from De Mide?"

Aline answered in the negative. The prince continued:

"Perhaps he hasn't sent them out yet. I am giving a dinner at the palace tomorrow evening, and I have placed your name on the list. I shall see you there?"

"Is it not a command?" smiled Aline carelessly, concealing the elation that rose within her. Had not the Countess Potacci tried to console her the day before because she had not been invited to this dinner?

"I would not have you consider it so," the prince was saying in answer to her question. "When we are willing to ask a favor of anyone we do not presume to command them.''

''If it is a command, I obey.''

''And if it is a favor?''

''I grant it.''

A minute later the prince departed. The door had no sooner closed behind him than Aline rushed to her room to send a note to the dear countess.

When the card of invitation arrived that evening it was found to contain the name of Mlle. Janvour as well as that of Mlle. Solini. This struck Aline as a little curious; nevertheless, she went with it at once to Vivi's room to acquaint her with the news and consider what dress she should wear.

But Vivi declined flatly to go at all. She was lying on the bed with a damp cloth tied round her head; her eyes were red and swollen and her face white.

''Come,'' said Aline, ''this is absurd! And all for that little fool of a Naumann! Dear child, he isn't worth a single tear. You must go; an invitation from the prince is a command.''

Vivi said stubbornly:

''I can't help it. I won't go! Say I'm sick; say anything you want. I won't go!''

Aline was forced to give it up.

Accordingly, the following evening, at a little before seven o'clock, Mlle. Solini departed for the palace alone in her limousine. Strictly speaking, of course, it was Stetton's limousine; but no one knew that.

It was her first glimpse within the palace, and the truth was that she was more than a little uneasy at her lack of knowledge of the proprieties and ceremonies to be observed. Once inside the great bronze gates at the entrance, she was conducted by a servant down the shining marble corridor to an apartment at its farther end. She had no sooner stepped on the threshold than she heard the voice of General Paul Nirzann:

''Ah! We have been expecting you, cousin.''

In another instant he was at her side, and they crossed the room together, surrounded by a low murmur of admiration from the assembled company at the appearance of Mlle. Solini. Aline was at home.

Three hours later she returned to No. 341 flushed with triumph. She had outshone every other woman in the room—that much she could see with her own eyes, even if she had not seen it in the eyes of the men.

At dinner she had sat at the right hand of the prince, and throughout the evening he had paid her marked attention, to the exclusion of everyone else. This, of course, had not pleased the ladies present; the old Countess Larchini had been moved to the point where she administered a direct snub to Aline loud enough for all to hear. Shortly afterward Aline had heard Mme. Chébe ask the countess the cause of her quarrel with "the beautiful Russian."

"I have no quarrel with her," Larchini had replied. "She is an upstart, and must be shown her place."

To which Mme. Chébe had retorted:

"Take care, countess; you are indiscreet; what if her place turns out to be the palace?"

At the recollection of which Aline was still smiling as she mounted the stairs to her room after returning home; the smile was a scornful one.

"Bah! They are of no importance one way or the other," she said to herself as she rang the bell for her maid. "Well, we will see."

Whatever were the prince's thoughts, it soon became evident to all of Marisi that they were concerned with the beautiful Russian. On the afternoon of the day following the dinner-party his limousine was seen standing for two hours in front of No. 341. The next day it was the same, and the next, and many days thereafter.

Marisi began to talk. What was worse, Marisi began to whisper; and some slight echoes reached the ears of Mlle. Solini. At each succeeding report, carried to her by her faithful friend, the Countess Potacci, she frowned and said nothing.

Receptions and entertainments were now being given at the palace almost daily, and the beautiful Russian was always present, and the place of honor was always hers. She no longer accepted any invitations save those of the Countess Potacci and Mme. Chébe, who—as she was perfectly well aware—were engaged with the others in tearing her to pieces behind her back. Aline smiled at them, biding her time in patience.

It soon began to appear that she would need all the patience she possessed, and more: She had given up her afternoon drives, for the prince called every day. But when that is said, everything is said.

He did not speak the words that Mlle. Solini wanted to hear; he did not assume the attitude she expected and desired. He had attempted once or twice in his masterful way to make love to her; but Mlle. Solini, whose quick ear had detected at once the fact that he was pitched in the wrong key, had repulsed without offending him.

Each time he had responded to her desire with the most perfect good nature.

At length Mlle. Solini grew impatient. One evening after the prince had gone she sat for two hours alone in the library, meditating on her tactics and trying to discover the error in her strategy. There could be no doubt, she told herself, that the prince was fascinated by her.

He spent several hours of every day with her; he humored her slightest whim, when she thought it advisable to have any; twice, to try her power, she had actually dictated his policy on affairs of state, one of which had been of some importance.

What was it, then, that held him back? The mere fact that she was not of royal birth? She turned that suggestion aside with scorn; she knew the prince; he was not a man to be hindered in his desires by ordinary or conventional obstacles.

It must be—and this thought had occurred to Mlle. Solini many times within the month—it must be that General Nirzann had betrayed her by revealing to the prince the truth of his own connection with her. Ah, if he had! Aline's eyes blazed dangerously.

"At any rate," she said to herself as she arose to dress for dinner, "I shall know tomorrow. I shall risk all, and I shall either win or lose. We shall see."

The following afternoon the prince called at a little after two o'clock, as usual. Aline received him in the library quite informally, for they had come to know each other very well indeed, and had long since dispensed with all ceremony. On this occasion, however, there was a certain constraint, an air of aloofness, in her manner, and the prince observed it at once, glancing at her curiously. The glance did not escape Mlle. Solini; she had resolved that on that afternoon nothing should escape her.

"I am moved once more to observe," said the prince, drawing up an easy chair before the fire, "that this is easily the pleasantest spot in all Marisi. And if you knew how I love my study, *mademoiselle*, you would appreciate the compliment."

Aline, who was seated in a chair by the table, merely smiled for reply.

"And all it needs for perfection," continued the prince, "is for you to be reading aloud. Poor De Mide! I have grown to detest the very sound of the man's voice. Yesterday morning, if you will believe me, I came nearly throwing a book at him. What shall it be today? Turgenef?"

Aline replied:

"I don't believe I shall read today, your highness. I don't feel inclined that way."

"No?" The prince turned around in his chair to look at her. "Not the headache, I hope?"

"No, I have not a headache today." (The reader will understand that Mlle. Solini's headaches had occurred on those rare occasions when she had been unable to refuse an afternoon to Mr. Richard Stetton, of New York.) "I don't feel like reading; that is all."

"I am sorry; I had really counted on something of Turgenef today," said the prince in the tone of a man who has been unjustly deprived of a privilege. "Well, then we shall talk. You will be glad to hear that young Aschovin has been pardoned."

"Your highness is most kind."

"Come, now!" Again the prince turned around in his chair. "That is not a tone for you to use to me, *mademoiselle*. You know it."

"Nevertheless, I use it, your highness."

The prince rose to his feet, facing her, and said abruptly:

"Something is wrong. What is it?"

"Nothing, your highness."

"Have I offended you?"

Aline did not reply. She sat for a moment, returning his gaze in silence; then she also rose to her feet and stood facing him, with eyes that were clear with the light of a sudden resolve. Finally she spoke:

"Your highness is right; there is something wrong. I have something to say—something unpleasant—unpleasant, that is, for me."

The prince frowned; when there was anything unpleasant to be said he much preferred to say it himself. As he did not speak, Aline continued:

"It is possible that your highness will be offended, and that is why it is unpleasant. Still, you ought not to be; you have told me often to be frank with you. It is this, that your highness must not come to see me anymore."

The prince gazed at her as though he had not understood.

"Not come to see you anymore?" he repeated blankly.

"No. You will understand. Do you not know that all Marisi is talking about me? Perhaps your highness does not hear these things; then I will tell you that every one is saying that I am your mistress. There, you see I am quite frank. It is absurd, of course; but I must preserve the shred of reputation that is left to me."

Certainly the prince could understand that. He did so, and was instantly on his guard, though he could not quite conceal his astonishment as he looked at the beautiful Russian with a gaze that tried to force its way into her heart. There was a long silence.

Aline resumed her chair; the racing of her pulse was not betrayed by any expression of her face. The prince walked to the fireplace and stood for a long time looking down on the red coals. When he turned it was with a gesture of determination. He spoke abruptly:

"You say it is absurd for Marisi to suppose that you are my mistress. Why? You are playing with me, *mademoiselle*, and that is a dangerous game."

Aline interrupted him with a voice quite as firm as his own:

"Pardon me; your highness is mistaken."

"*Mademoiselle*, it is hard to believe you."

"Believe it or not, your highness, it is the truth."

"Then, if that is so," demanded the prince, taking a step toward her, "tell me why you have given your time to me. You have made me love you—you have made yourself necessary for my happiness—and now you send me away! *Mademoiselle*, there is something behind all this!"

"Nothing more, your highness, than a desire to preserve my honor."

The prince glanced at her with quick suspicion. "And what do you mean by that?"

"I mean that whatever my own happiness might require, I would not take it with a burden of shame."

212

"Ah," said the prince slowly, while the light of understanding appeared on his face, "I see!"

"I expected nothing," Aline interrupted. "Or if I did, I do so no longer."

Her voice was tremulous with emotion.

"Do you not see that you are being cruel to me? That what you say is more painful to me than death? It seems I expected the impossible. I am paying for it now."

Her voice trembled so that she seemed scarcely able to go on.

"Yes, I admit it. I expected—everything. Now leave me—go—go!"

She leaned forward in her chair and buried her face in her arms on the table.

For a moment the prince stood looking down at her uncertainly; then suddenly he bent over and placed his arm across her shoulder. Her sleeve, flowing open, exposed her arm; his hand rested on her delicious white skin; his head was so close to hers that her hair was against his cheek and about his eyes. He said in an uneven voice:

"Aline—I did not think—it is impossible—come— you must love me—look at me—you must—"

Aline's shoulders were shaking under his touch, and when her voice came it was mingled with sobs.

"Go!" she cried. "Leave me—please—you are brutal—go—go—"

He pulled at her; she would not move, but kept begging him to go. Then, feeling perhaps that a prince cannot afford to make himself ridiculous, he straightened up abruptly and turned away.

With a last, lingering glance at Aline's shaking figure from the door of the library, he left the house without another word.

Aline waited till she had heard the outer door close behind him.

Then she jumped up from her chair and ran to the

window in front in time to see him enter his limousine and drive away. When she turned there was a smile on her face—a smile of joy and triumph.

She said to herself aloud:

"He is mine!"

CHAPTER XVII.

STETTON MAKES A PROPOSAL.

When the Prince of Marisi returned to the palace he went at once to his study, as he called it—that room at the end of the corridor on the second floor about which all Marisi was curious, because no one was ever allowed to enter it. Arrived there, he threw himself into a chair and buried himself in meditation.

In that, however, he could find no relief. He rose to his feet and began to pace up and down the room, with his forehead wrinkled in a deep frown. It had been many years since the prince had been moved so profoundly as he was at that moment.

He stopped before the fireplace and stood looking up at a portrait that hung over it—the portrait of a woman about thirty years of age, with dark hair and large, serious eyes.

"Sasoné," the prince murmured aloud, "Sasoné, it is not you who can help me, but you can forgive."

For a long time he stood looking at the portrait in silence; then, with a sudden gesture of decision, he turned and rang a bell on the table. When a servant appeared an instant later, the prince asked if General Nirzann was in the palace.

"Yes, your highness; the general is in his room."

"And De Mide?"

"He went out, your highness, saying that he would

be here before your highness returned. He did not expect you—"

"Very well; that is all."

As soon as the servant had disappeared the prince also left, to make his way to the room of General Nirzann on the floor above.

It was evident that General Nirzann, like De Mide, had not expected his prince to return at so early an hour. He was seated in an armchair, dressed in a pink dressing-gown, reading a book. As the prince entered he jumped up with an exclamation of surprise, threw down his book, and bowed half-way to the floor.

"Remain seated," said the prince with a wave of his hand, crossing to a chair.

The general, with a merry twinkle in his eye, wanted to know if his cousin Aline had lost her charm or was merely indisposed.

"It is of her I came to speak," said the prince, with so serious an expression on his face that the general instantly altered his own to agree with it.

"What the deuce has she done now?" thought he with an inward frown.

As usual, the prince plunged immediately into the heart of the matter. He began abruptly:

"General, there are some things about Mlle. Solini that I wish to know, and to know positively. If you can tell me, so much the better. If not, I shall send De Mide to Warsaw to find out."

The effect of these words on General Nirzann may be easily understood. Send De Mide to Warsaw! That would mean the discovery of the general's deception; it would mean his ruin, his banishment from Marisi; the end of everything. The general, trembling inwardly, took a firm grip on himself. He said, in as calm a tone as possible:

"I cannot understand why you say that, your highness. If you doubt me—"

The prince interrupted:

"No, Nirzann, I do not. I have never entertained a very glowing opinion of your abilities, but your fidelity is beyond question. That is why I come to you. I do not need to explain why, but this has become a serious matter. In the first place, Mlle. Aline Solini is your cousin?"

"She is, your highness."

The general's tone was calm and firm; it would appear that he was capable of both courage and resolution in a crisis.

"She has estates near Warsaw?"

"She has had, your highness. They are no longer even in her name."

"Has she an equity in them?"

"No. She has nothing."

The prince looked at him sharply:

"She is spending a great deal of money in Marisi. Where does she get it?"

The general was prepared for this question; he and Aline had long before decided what answer should be given to it. He replied:

"She has told me, your highness, that she has a balance of cash left from the disposal of her estates."

"I see." There was a short pause, then the prince continued: "Now be frank with me, Nirzann. What do you know of your cousin?"

"Very little, your highness. I have often told you so. Most of her life was spent in a convent. At one time she even considered taking the veil, and I believe she has not yet entirely abandoned the idea."

"Has she any relatives besides yourself?"

"None."

"Absolutely none?"

"Absolutely. I have often told your highness that my family has its last male representative in me. We are doomed, it seems, to extinction."

The general actually achieved a tone of mournfulness.

"That is right; you have often told me that." The prince paused; he appeared to be thinking. Then he said abruptly: "I have sometimes wondered, general, why you do not marry your cousin."

General Nirzann smiled.

"Surely that is not a matter of wonder, your highness. In the first place, she has but little money, and I have none. Secondly, she won't have me."

"Ah!" The prince's eyebrows were lifted. "You have asked her, then?"

"Many times, your highness. Would it be possible to see such a prize without making an effort to possess it?"

The prince smiled; he was pleased to hear this sentiment, which had been his own echoed by other lips, even those of General Nirzann.

"You are right," he declared; "you are positively right, Nirzann. She is indeed a prize."

"A prize for princes," said the general, beginning to feel more sure of himself.

"Yes, a prize for princes." The ruler of Marisi frowned. "But one for which even a prince must pay the full price. That is why I came to talk with you, Nirzann. I know I can depend on what you tell me.

"I shall not send De Mide to Warsaw—it would be useless; I know everything that can be known. I shall see you tonight at dinner. *Au revoir!*"

And he departed as abruptly and unceremoniously as he had entered.

As soon as he had left, General Nirzann sprang to his feet in swift and uncontrollable agitation. At that last speech of the prince's he had had all he could do to contain himself. Great Heavens! What had he done?

"One for which even a prince must pay the full price." That could mean but one thing. But it was unthinkable! A prince of Marisi to marry an adventuress, a peasant courtezan? General Nirzann sank back in his chair, groaning in dismay and despair.

To this had he been brought by that demon in the form of a woman! He felt bewildered and crushed by the sudden rush of misfortune. What could he do?

To allow the prince to accomplish his design was impossible. Rather anything than that; for the prince had judged correctly of General Nirzann; if he was nothing else, he was loyal. He had meant to toss Mlle. Solini to him as a plaything—and now this!

The little general swore that he would cut her throat and his own into the bargain before he would allow her to become Princess of Marisi; and he meant it.

Something had to be done, and at once. His first thought, of course, was to go to Mlle. Solini; but a moment's reflection showed him the uselessness of it. He knew very well what would happen.

He would threaten her with exposure; she, knowing that in betraying her he would also betray himself, would defy him to do his worst. Next he thought of going to the prince and telling him the truth. But that held the extreme of danger.

If the prince really contemplated marrying Mlle. Solini in spite of her comparatively humble birth, he must indeed be infatuated with her, and he would not deal lightly with the man who, by his own confession, had so deceived him.

For an hour the general remained irresolute, while a thousand schemes raced in and out of his brain. Now he would throw himself into a chair in despair; again he would spring to his feet and pace rapidly up and down the room.

Was there no way out of it? That devil of a woman! He would like to wring her neck! What was to be done? The general tore his hair and called to the heavens.

Suddenly, struck with an idea, he stopped short. Ah, Perhaps—perhaps— He considered for a moment; then, suddenly making up his mind, snatched up his coat and hat and ran through the hall and down the stairs to the *porte-cochère* of the palace.

A limousine was standing at the foot of the steps. The general sprang in, calling to the driver:

"The Hotel Walderin—and hurry."

Ten minutes later he was asking at the desk of the Walderin for Richard Stetton.

"M. Stetton?" said the polite clerk. "I will see if he is in, general."

A wait of five minutes, which to the general seemed an hour, and a message came from M. Stetton to show the visitor up immediately.

To say that Stetton was surprised to receive a call from General Nirzann would be to put it mildly. But he was usually content to take things as they came, and he merely allowed himself to wonder, "What can that fellow want with me?" However, his surprise showed on his face as the general entered the room.

The two men bowed politely and looked at each other with an expression which, though not exactly hostile, was certainly not overcordial. As for the general, he was in no mood to humor petty antagonisms. This was a matter of life and death to him, and he came straight to the point.

"M. Stetton," he began abruptly, "no doubt you are surprised to see me."

The young man admitted that the call was somewhat unexpected in its nature.

"I have come to you," continued the general, "concerning a matter which is equally important to both of us, and—"

Stetton interrupted him to ask him to be seated. The general, moving in quick little jerks, placed his hat on one chair and himself on another and resumed:

"My errand has to do with Mlle. Solini. I believe that you are interested in her."

Stetton, wondering what on earth would come next, admitted that this surmise was not incorrect.

"What I have to say will surprise you," continued the general, "perhaps as much as it surprised me. As

219

you know, I have been—er—more or less intimate with Mlle. Solini, and I am perfectly aware of the relations that exist between you and her.

"Well, she is playing you double. She is betraying you. *Monsieur*—" The general halted for a moment; then continued impressively: "Unless you or I do something to interfere, Mlle. Solini will marry the Prince of Marisi within a month."

Stetton did not appear so surprised, after all. Instead, he smiled as one who possesses superior knowledge and said:

"You are mistaken, general."

Then, when the general began to insist that he knew only too well what he was talking about, Stetton continued, interrupting him:

"Pardon me—just a moment. It is no wonder that you have been deceived, with all the rest of Marisi. Indeed, for a time I was deceived myself, when I saw that the prince was spending every afternoon at Aline's house. I demanded an explanation, as my right, and she explained everything in two words. It is Mlle. Janvour the prince goes to see—if he marries anyone, it will be she."

"Rot!" cried the general. "I tell you it is Mlle. Solini herself!"

"Mlle. Solini says otherwise," smiled Stetton, unmoved.

"Then she is deceiving you."

"It is hardly likely. She would not dare."

"But it is! *Monsieur*, I see I shall be forced to tell you the source of my information." The general paused a moment, then continued: "It is the Prince of Marisi himself."

This made its impression. A look of doubt and astonishment appeared on Stetton's face.

"The prince!" he exclaimed.

"Yes. Perhaps now you will believe. Mlle. Solini has been lying to you, which is not surprising. She intends to marry the prince; it has been her game all along. What is worse, the prince intends to marry her."

Stetton leaped to his feet with an oath, advancing toward the general.

"This is the truth?" he demanded.

"It is the truth, *monsieur*." The idea of resenting the implication did not enter the general's head.

"The Prince of Marisi told you that he is going to marry Mlle. Solini?"

"Not in so many words. No. But his meaning was unmistakable."

There was a silence. Stetton resumed his chair. The general regarded him anxiously. What was he going to do? The question was soon answered, when the American again rose to his feet, walked rapidly to the wardrobe, and took down his coat and hat. Then he turned:

"General, I thank you. It is true we are not friends, but you were perfectly right to come to me, and I thank you. We stand together in this matter. There is no time to be lost."

The general also rose. "Where are you going?"

"To see Aline. Will you come with me?"

But the general had already decided that he would allow Stetton to fight the battle alone. He had a dozen excuses ready, and he recited them glibly as the two men left the room together and descended in the elevator.

Stetton did not insist; he was glad, indeed, of the other's refusal. They parted in front of the Walderin; General Nirzann to return to the palace in the limousine, and Stetton to take a cab to 341 the Drive.

The truth was that Stetton by no means held implicit belief in the general's story. With him Aline had done her work well, playing on his vanity with the expertness of a master musician fingering the keys of a piano-forte.

She had allowed him just enough encouragement to lead him to believe that she longed for their wedding as much as he. She had explained all her activities with perfect logic. Still, the tale of the general was enough to cause even him to doubt, and he was consumed with impatience as he sat waiting for Mlle. Solini in her—or his—library.

Entering, she crossed to his side and offered him her lips to kiss. Stetton accepted the offer with alacrity, but with a lack of warmth that did not escape her attention. Her thought was: "A few days more, M. Stetton, and I shall say good-by to you forever." She said aloud:

"My dear boy, you have something on your mind. See how easily I can read you! That is a proof of love. But come, out with it."

Stetton had long before given up all attempts at finesse with Mlle. Solini. He replied simply:

"It is not pleasant."

"Good Heavens! It never is."

"It will require a great deal of explanation."

"It always does."

"It amounts to this, Aline, that you have been lying to me."

"*Monsieur!*"

"Now, don't fly into a rage. You have found out by this time that I am plain-spoken. I say what I believe. I repeat, you have been lying to me."

"What do you mean?"

Stetton eyed her for a moment in silence, with a look that was meant to be searching and disconcerting.

"I'll tell you what I mean," he said finally. "Sit down!"

When Aline had obeyed this command he told her word for word what he had just heard from the lips of General Nirzann.

Aline heard him through in silence. When he had finished she observed calmly:

"Well, what of it?"

"It is true, then!" cried Stetton, suddenly enraged,

for he had expected an immediate and vociferous denial. "You admit it!"

"I admit nothing. I simply say, if it is true, what then?"

"Answer me! Is it true?"

There was a silence, while he stood looking down at her with blazing eyes. He repeated his question a dozen times, in varying tones of insistence and anger; she sat motionless and silent, with lowered eyes. Suddenly she spoke, and there was something in her tone that compelled attention:

"M. Stetton, I will answer your question, but in my own way. Will you listen to me?"

"You can answer yes or no," he insisted, "and talk afterward. Is it true?"

But she persisted, and he was forced to give way. He took a chair across the table, saying with a frown:

"Go on. But to begin with, you know what I know, and what I will do."

"I know," said Aline. "I know only too well. That is why I want to talk to you. I am going to appeal to your generosity, and that is something I have never done before with any man."

"I have not too great a stock of it left," said Stetton dryly.

Aline replied:

"No, and that is why I do not count on success. But I feel that I owe myself the chance, if there is one. *Monsieur*, it amounts to this, that it rests with you to save me."

"That is exactly what I am trying to do."

"I do not mean that. I mean to save me from yourself. I am at your mercy; I admit it. I am asking you to be generous."

Stetton grew impatient.

"But what do you mean? What do you want? What are you talking about? It occurs to me that I have been fairly generous already."

And indeed, so he had; was there not at that moment over two hundred thousand francs in cash locked away in Mlle. Solini's desk upstairs?

"You have been generous," agreed Aline, "more so than I had any right to expect. But that is not what I mean. I do not want money, *monsieur*; I want my freedom."

"Your freedom?" This suspiciously.

"Yes. Do you not see? *Monsieur*, three months ago—it seems as many years—I promised to marry you. I understood at the time very well what I was doing. I made that bargain willingly; indeed, what else was there to do? I was in great danger—I was alone—I had to think of Vivi as well as myself. But since then I have grown to detest and hate myself for it. You are a gentleman, *monsieur*. I ask you to release me."

"What! What! You—"

"Wait—let me finish. Despising myself as I did, I yet had every intention of living up to my word, desiring only first to dispose Vivi safely in marriage. I had that intention till yesterday. But yesterday"—here Mlle. Solini's voice faltered—she appeared to be overcome with emotion—"yesterday, *monsieur*, an honorable man—a gentleman—asked for my hand in marriage."

"The prince!" cried Stetton furiously.

"I do not say who it was, *monsieur*. It would not be fair to him. But now you know what I want. His offer is honorable. I ask you to permit me to accept it."

She stopped, looking at Stetton through lowered lids. He appeared to be really touched, as he gazed at her in silence. He said finally:

"But it is impossible! I love you!"

"*Monsieur*, you cannot refuse me. I beg of you—I plead for your mercy—"

He replied more firmly, in a tone of finality:

"It is impossible. I cannot give you up."

Aline's manner suddenly changed. She raised her

head with an air of defiance and looked straight into his eyes as she said:

"You will not give me my freedom—you will not release me from my bargain?"

"I will not."

"What if I do as I please?"

"You dare not."

"You would betray me?"

"If you force me, yes."

There was a silence. Again Aline's eyes were lowered. Then she looked up again and said in a tone of hopelessness:

"Very well, *monsieur*. But of one thing rest assured—I will not allow you to cover me with shame. My bargain with you is ended."

Stetton gazed at her in astonishment. "But what are you going to do?"

Aline replied in the same tone of hopelessness and despair:

"What can I do? There is but one thing left to me—a life of resignation and piety. You found me in a convent, *monsieur*. I shall leave you to go to one."

Instantly Stetton was jumping up and down in frantic protest. She should not go! He would not permit it! He loved her—he could not give her up! He would follow her to the door of the convent—he would prohibit her entrance!

Stetton stormed, threatened, and pleaded by turns. She had made the bargain—she should live up to it! Did she not love him? He would not give her up—he could not! He would do anything—he would go anywhere—he would give her anything in the world she wanted.

But she would not move from her decision.

Her eyes were wet with tears, and, seeing them so for the first time, he thought them ravishingly beautiful. He felt an irresistible desire to kiss the tears away. But she would not let him touch her.

"Never," she cried, "never, never."

He exclaimed in despair:

"But you must—you must! I can't live without you! To lose you now? It would drive me mad! Aline—my darling—listen, Aline—you must marry me!"

"Ah, *monsieur*, it is too late! No—no—do not tempt me—I have decided—"

Instantly he was on his knees, begging and pleading with her to marry him. Suddenly she murmured something—he protested violently—it appeared that she doubted his sincerity. He swore by everything sacred that he had never been more in earnest in his life.

She looked up and asked abruptly:

"Would you marry me now—tonight?"

"Why—that—I don't see—" he stammered, completely taken aback.

"But I do see, *monsieur*. Forgive me, but I have reason to doubt you."

"What can I do?" cried Stetton. "To marry you tonight is impossible. There are arrangements to make—it would appear strange— Anything I can do I will do."

"You are willing, then, to bind yourself?"

"Utterly! You mean a contract? Gladly!"

"No, I do not mean that. I would not ask that. But why—I wish to feel assured—will you write to me tonight?"

"Write to you?" He appeared not to understand.

"Yes," she answered. "Write what you have said."

This was a close game she was playing now. She risked a smile—a little tantalizing smile that softened her words.

It was unnecessary. Stetton could see no reason why he should not write a proposal of marriage to the woman he seriously intended to marry. He said as much, and expressed a willingness to execute the document at once on the table in the library.

Aline thought quickly. There was no paper in the house except her own and Vivi's, tinted and scented, and that, she decided, would be dangerous for her purpose. She replied that it was unnecessary to do as he suggested; it would be sufficient for him to send his formal proposal from the hotel.

Stetton replied in the tone of one who intends to make good his words, "You will receive it tomorrow morning," and went his way.

CHAPTER XVIII.

PROPOSAL NUMBER TWO.

"Czean!"

"Yes, *mademoiselle*."

"Has the mail arrived?"

"Yes, *mademoiselle*; I am bringing it."

It was ten o'clock in the morning.

Mlle. Solini was in the library, reading aloud to Vivi, who sat by the window with some embroidery. In the earlier mail Mlle. Solini had been disappointed; there had been many letters, but not the one she was looking for.

As she took this which had just arrived from the tray, which Czean held out before her, there was an expression of expectation that approached anxiety on her face. She ran through the little bundle eagerly—ah! There it was—"Hotel Walderin."

She opened the envelope and quickly glanced over the letter. Then, laying her book on the table and telling Vivi she would return in a moment, she went upstairs, opened a drawer of her writing-desk, placed the letter inside, closed the drawer, and locked it.

"There!" she breathed with a sigh of satisfaction. "So much for him!"

Then she returned to the library and resumed her reading—a play of Molière's—for Vivi's instruction and her own amusement.

The morning passed. Noon arrived. Then one

o'clock, and luncheon. By the time that was over it was nearly two, and Mlle. Solini began to exhibit signs of restlessness.

She told herself that she had no reason to be uneasy—had not General Nirzann told Stetton that the prince had signified his intention of marrying her? Nevertheless, her restlessness increased.

She walked to a window of the drawing-room and stood there, looking out on the street, for half an hour. She went to her room and quarreled with her maid about nothing at all. The afternoon wore away.

Four o'clock found Mlle. Solini again in the library, reading; only by a conscious effort of the will could she force her mind to follow the words in their sequence. Dinnertime came, and with it the end of hope. The Prince of Marisi had not appeared.

In the evening Stetton called, and Mlle. Solini was compelled to humor him for three weary hours, in order not to rouse his suspicion. As an alternative, he must be preserved.

This was difficult; the young man was burning with love, and appeared to expect his affianced to be similarly afire. She managed somehow to satisfy him, and when he left quite late she threw herself on her bed, thoroughly exhausted in mind and body. Waiting was a dreary performance for Mlle. Solini; she preferred to act.

The following day she waited till half past three o'clock; then, as the sky was sunny and the air warm and pleasant, she ordered the open carriage and went with Vivi for a ride.

It was her first appearance on the drive in nearly a month, and it created a small sensation. Wherever she passed people could be observed whispering to one another, but none failed to greet her with the utmost politeness. All that they said of Mlle. Solini might be true; in the meantime they preferred to practice caution.

They had just made the last turn at Savaron Square,

and Aline had ordered the coachman to drive home, when, on swinging again into the drive, she found herself looking directly into the eyes of the Prince of Marisi, seated by the side of General Nirzann in the royal carriage.

He was looking straight at Aline. In spite of herself, the color mounted to her face; she inclined her head in a dignified bow, and the prince returned it, she thought, somewhat coldly.

That was all. The two carriages rolled on in opposite directions. Aline bit her lip in vexation, and failed to recognize Stetton, who passed them soon afterward in a touring-car.

On the following day Mlle. Solini did not leave the house. Through a window of the drawing-room she watched the afternoon promenade for an hour; several times she saw the royal carriage containing the prince and General Nirzann. Again the thought occurred that the general had betrayed her.

"But," she argued to herself, "the prince would never forgive him. No; he is mine; I must be patient."

Despite this, she was uneasy; and when Stetton called in the evening she was as gracious and kind to him as she had ever been. He would talk of nothing but the happiness that was soon to be his, and was so insistent in his demand for a definite date for its consummation that Aline finally named a day early in June.

M. Stetton also had a little project on foot for her amusement. He had happened to hear that morning at the hotel of an old French château some miles out of Marisi on the Tsevor Road, which had been turned into an inn. He wanted to know if Mlle. Solini would drive out there with him the following day in his motor-car. He hastened to add that he would, of course, expect Vivi to accompany them; upon which, after a moment's reflection, Aline accepted his invitation and said they would be ready to start at ten o'clock.

The day proved to be a happy one for Vivi and Stetton, and, to all appearances, for Aline also, save for one little incident that occurred as the car sped swiftly through the pleasant hilly country to the west of the city.

They had just passed a little wooden bridge and turned to the left down a long stretch of straight, level road, at the right of which, some distance ahead, appeared a cluster of low, rambling sheds.

Stetton glanced at the spot with a start of recognition, and then, he scarcely knew why, turned to Aline and observed:

"That is where I fought Chavot."

She glanced up quickly, and he fancied that she shuddered, but she said nothing.

The château was about fifty miles from Marisi, and they reached it a little after noon. Everything was delightful. They had luncheon on an enclosed terrace, into which the sun shone brightly; off to the right the mountains rose, a majestic line of purple.

For an hour or more they lingered over their coffee, served in little earthen cups, while Stetton and Vivi chatted pleasantly about nothing at all, and Aline gazed toward Marisi, thinking of a great deal. Then they made ready to return.

It was nearly five o'clock when Aline and Vivi were set down by Stetton at the door of No. 341. Vivi ran upstairs to her room; Aline went to the library and rang for Czean.

"Has any one called?" she asked when he appeared.

"Yes, *mademoiselle*. The prince was here at two o'clock, and again at four."

"Did he leave a note, a message?"

"Nothing, *mademoiselle*."

Aline's eyes sparkled. At last! She did not regret her absence; on the contrary, she considered it a lucky stroke. Still, she must contrive that the prince should see her, and as soon as possible; she knew where her strength lay.

After a few minutes' thought she went to the telephone and called up the Countess Potacci. The countess was delighted to hear from her dear Aline; she complained of having been neglected.

What was that? Mlle. Solini wished to invite herself to occupy a seat in the countess's box at the opera that evening? Certainly! The countess would be glad to have her.

They would stop at 341 for her on their way. Aline said that was unnecessary, as she could go in her own car; but the countess insisted. They would call for her at eight o'clock.

Aline hung up the receiver, calling for Czean to serve dinner half an hour earlier than usual. Then she ran lightly up the stairs to her room. All her fatigue from the day's long ride was forgotten; she was in the best of humor and spirits, and spoke so kindly to her maid that she lost a considerable portion of the reputation she had acquired in that quarter.

When she went down to dinner two hours later Vivi ran up and threw her arms round her, exclaiming impulsively:

"I can't help it! You are so beautiful!"

Aline laughed and kissed her. The truth was that she enjoyed no one else's praise so much as Vivi's.

She received enough that night, though most of it was not for her own ears.

No sooner had she entered the Potacci box at the opera on the arm of the count than every glass in the house was leveled in their direction. But it was not for this that Aline had come, and a hasty glance at the royal box across the auditorium showed her that it was empty. It was yet early, however, and the prince was always late.

The lights grew dim and a hush fell over the house, while the orchestra commenced the overture. Then—

the opera was "Rigoletto"—the curtain arose on the scene of much color and little music in the palace of the Duke of Mantua, and the hunchbacked jester began the antics that were to lead him into the path of grief and death.

But Aline had not taken her eyes from the royal box; and soon she was rewarded by seeing the curtains slowly open and the prince appear, followed by General Nirzann and one or two other members of the household. Aline turned her eyes to the stage.

The curtain fell; the auditorium was again lighted; the hum of conversation was heard on every side. Half a dozen of the young sparks of Marisi appeared in the box of the Count Potacci, attracted thither by the presence of the beautiful Russian.

Aline received them graciously and chatted pleasantly; all the time, however, she was watching the royal box out of the corner of her eye.

The visitors disappeared; the curtain again rose; all was again darkness and silence, save on the stage, where the *Duke* and *Gilda* soon began their amazingly amiable duet.

At the end of the second act the Potacci box became crowded; it would seem that Marisi fancied it could read the thoughts of the beautiful Russian by looking into her eyes, and no one is so interested to discover the truth or falsity of a piece of gossip as those who have started it.

General Nirzann appeared to pay his respects to the countess and Mlle. Solini; evidently he had been apprised by Stetton of the success of his mission three days before, for he greeted his cousin Aline with warmth and effusion.

Aline was listening to him and a dozen others who were trying to talk all at once, when suddenly she heard a new voice behind her greeting the Countess Potacci. It was that of the prince.

As he came toward the front of the box the others

fell back before his imperious glance, looking at each other significantly. Aline kept her gaze steadfastly ahead. Suddenly she heard his voice quite close to her, low and musical:

"Good evening, *mademoiselle*."

She replied calmly, without turning round:

"Good evening, your highness."

Again his voice sounded, this time lower still and full of significance. He uttered the one word:

"Tomorrow."

Then he fell back to the side of the Countess Potacci, who would have given her eyes to know what that whispered word had been, and the others again crowded round the beautiful Russian.

The face of one, however, was filled with something besides admiration; General Nirzann was trying to guess at what the prince had said. To be sure, Stetton had told him that he himself had Mlle. Solini's promise of her hand, but the general was beginning to appreciate Aline's capacity for intrigue, and he feared her.

During the last act Aline watched the stage without seeing it; what did she care for murdered maids or betrayed jesters? She allowed herself, however, a feeling of contempt for poor *Rigoletto*—the weak fool, to entrust his vengeance to the hands of another. Assuredly that would not have been the way of Mlle. Solini.

On the way home in the Potacci carriage she paid no heed to the comments of the count and countess; she kept repeating to herself the word: "Tomorrow."

An hour later, alone in her own room, she surveyed herself in the mirror with satisfaction and approval.

"Tomorrow," was her thought, "tomorrow."

The following morning she awoke late. Stretching herself luxuriously, she rang for her maid; then followed her chocolate and mail, after which Vivi came in to say good morning. She was sitting on the edge of the bed, playing with Aline's golden tresses, when there came a sudden knock on the door. In response to Aline's invitation to enter, Czean appeared.

"M. Stetton is in the library, *mademoiselle*."

Aline appeared to reflect for a moment. Then she said in the tone of one who has made sudden decision:

"I am not at home."

Czean stammered:

"But, *mademoiselle*—he already knows—I have told him—"

"I am not at home," Aline repeated sharply. "Tell him so."

Czean disappeared to give the lie to Stetton. As for Vivi, although she was greatly surprised at this sudden change in the fortunes of M. Stetton, she made no observation on the matter. She had long before learned that the more inexplicable a thing appeared to be the less likely was Mlle. Solini to explain it.

The burning of bridges is a pastime that only the sure-footed should allow themselves; this Mlle. Solini knew, and yet she had applied the match. The prince's "tomorrow" had arrived.

This should be her day of triumph; everything was well in hand. She had the confidence of her genius; and when, at a little after two o'clock in the afternoon, she heard the outer door open and the voice of the Prince of Marisi in the hall, her pulse remained as steady and composed as her face. Czean, who had received his orders, escorted the royal visitor at once to the library, where Aline was sitting alone.

As soon as Aline looked into the prince's eyes as he crossed the room to take her hand, she saw that the battle was over and the victory won. He had come to claim his prize, and to pay the price that was demanded for it.

Aline resolved that it should not be too easy for him; she remembered that scene in the same room three days before, when he had left her in the midst of her humiliation. True, it had been assumed, but he did not know that. Today he should answer to her pride.

The prince appeared, in fact, to be a little ill at ease. He began with some conventional remark concerning his disappointment of the day before. Aline, delighted to have the cue, replied with a long and circumstantial account of their trip into the country, and ended by observing that she and Vivi had about decided to go by automobile to Paris, for which place they intended to depart in the course of a week or so.

"You are going to Paris?" asked the prince in a tone which implied that no one ever went there.

"Yes. Does that surprise your highness?"

"I thought you intended to stay in Marisi."

"So we did, for a while. We have changed our plans."

Aline said this, not as one who expresses an intention for the sake of evoking a protest, but quite naturally as a matter of fact. It had its effect on the prince. He regarded her for a moment in silence, then said abruptly:

"You are less acute than I thought, *mademoiselle*. Did you not understand what I said last night?"

Aline smiled.

"Was it so cryptic, your highness? I took it to mean that you would honor me with a visit today." She glanced at him, as much as to say, "And here you are."

"A quite natural deduction," said the prince dryly. "But had you no idea of the nature of my visit?"

"I am not good at guessing riddles, your highness."

"But you are an adept—do not deny it—at reading the hearts of men."

"Perhaps—of men. But not of a prince."

"It is all the same."

"Your highness will forgive me; experience has taught me the difference."

The prince's face suddenly became quite grave. He gazed toward Mlle. Solini as though he were looking not at her, but through her; his thoughts, serious ones, appeared to be elsewhere. Suddenly he said:

"If there is a difference, you must admit that it is not a fictitious one. Let us be frank, *mademoiselle*. I did not come here today to play with words, though you do it so delightfully." He paused; as Mlle. Solini did not speak, he continued:

"The other day I said something that angered and offended you. I am not going to apologize, though I hope for your forgiveness—and more. You know, *mademoiselle*, that my life does not belong to myself; and perhaps you are right, for therein lies the difference between a prince and a man.

"My family has ruled in Marisi for two hundred years. We have not the ostentation of the larger thrones, but our pride is equal to theirs. Behind the familiarity and democracy of our relations with our people there exists a tradition stronger even than that of the family of your own Czar."

The prince paused, regarding Mlle. Solini expectantly, but she said nothing. He resumed:

"I do not need to explain why I am saying all this to you, *mademoiselle*. You know very well. You know that I love you, for you are able to read the hearts of men, and to play with them. I speak calmly and gravely, because it affects others than myself when I ask you to become my wife and share with me the throne of Marisi."

Aline drew a sharp breath. She felt the eyes of the prince upon her, with their sternness and gravity. To tell the truth, she was not a little embarrassed. Quick, hot, passionate words—these she could command at will; but to dissemble in the face of this deep and calm sincerity was not easy. She finally murmured:

"I do not know—I have not sought this honor, your highness—if it is a sacrifice, I will not accept it."

"It is a willing sacrifice, *mademoiselle*. Do not misunderstand me. For myself"—and here, for the first time, the prince's voice held a note of passion—"for myself, I would hesitate at nothing. I love you; that is enough. It is of others I am thinking when I speak of sacrifice. But they will make it willingly for me. Do you accept, *mademoiselle*?"

"I—I—" Aline faltered and stopped.

A note of eagerness crept into the prince's voice.

"Tell me. Do you accept?"

Aline extended her hand. The prince took it in his own and pressed the fingers to his lips quite gravely.

"I accept, your highness," said Mlle. Solini in a low voice, moved, in spite of herself, by his manner.

The prince straightened up, drawing a long breath.

"Ah!" he said in a new tone.

It was more than an exclamation; it was a prayer. Then, in a sudden burst of passion, long restrained, he made a quick step forward and took her roughly in his arms. He held her close, and sought her lips with his own.

"This—this is what I wanted!" He was breathing heavily. "I love you—you witch—you witch—I love you!"

"No—no—" Aline pushed him away. "Your highness must not—your highness—"

The prince half released her, still keeping an arm around her shoulders.

"Not that any more," he said, in the voice of love. "My name is Michael. Say it."

"But—your highness—"

"No! Say it!"

Again he drew her to him, this time with firm tenderness; still he was trembling from head to foot.

"Say it," he repeated.

She whispered in his ear: "Michael."

"You love me?"

"Yes."

"Say it."

"Michael, I love you."

After that, silence. A long silence, broken here and there by soft murmurings and little electric words. At length the prince released her from his embrace and began to talk to arrangements—it appeared that a great deal of ceremony was connected with the betrothal of a prince.

When he announced that he would send General Nirzann with a formal proposal, in writing, on the following morning, Aline turned her head quickly to hide the smile that appeared on her lips. She could guess how General Nirzann would relish that mission.

The prince went on to say that he had selected the general for that office as being peculiarly fitted for it on account of his relationship with Mlle. Solini. He added that everything must be kept strictly secret until the time came for a formal announcement from the palace.

To all his suggestions Aline listened respectfully and assented as a matter of course. The prince made ready to leave. They had been together over three hours; night was beginning to fall, and the library was dim with the ghostly and melancholy light of dusk.

"I shall see you tomorrow," said the prince, holding her in his arms and kissing her. "Tell me again that you love me."

"Michael, I love you."

A moment later he was gone.

Aline rang for lights.

But not the brilliance of all the lamps in the world, nor of the sun itself, could have equaled that in her own eyes.

CHAPTER XIX.

THE GENERAL ON GUARD.

IMAGINE a man—for we are nothing if not modern—imagine a man in a thoroughly tested and guaranteed aeroplane, with a warranted stabilizer, sailing along peacefully—and not too swiftly—through the warm and pleasing air of a spring in Arcadia.

Below, not at too great a distance, appear smiling green valleys and silvery winding streams; from a grove of trees, a little to the right, arises the song of thrushes and nightingales. Above, the blue sky, with the glare of the sun softened deliciously by a few light, fleecy clouds.

Imagine all this; and then think that suddenly, almost without warning, the sky is overcast, great clouds of rain begin to fall, the wind howls and sweeps in a whirlwind of fury, all grows dark, and the aeroplane, trembling violently, breaks squarely in two and goes crashing toward the earth.

Picture to yourself that man's emotions and sensations, and you will have an approximate idea of how General Paul Nirzann felt when, on meeting the prince after his return to the palace, he was greeted with the words:

"General, I am going to marry your cousin."

True, at first he was conscious of no sensation whatever. He was completely stunned. He gazed at the prince with the look of a man who has been unexpectedly knocked on the back of the head, and stammered:

"Your highness—I—what—your highness says—"

"Are you so amazed?" asked the prince, laughing. "You should not be. I surely made myself clear enough the other day."

"But it is impossible!" cried the general, beginning to find his tongue.

"Ho!" exclaimed the prince in great good humor, with a twinkle in his eye, "I see what it is! You are jealous—you admitted you wanted her for yourself. You are too late, Nirzann; besides, you yourself called her a prize for princes."

Then, more seriously: "Of course, you must not breathe a word of this—not a word to any one. Come to me tomorrow morning at ten o'clock; I have an errand for you. If you—Well, De Mide, what is it? Oh, yes, I had forgotten. Remember, general, not a word."

The prince walked off on the arm of his secretary.

The general stood like one paralyzed, feeling the world tumbling about his ears. He was unable to think. By some queer trick of the brain a phrase he himself had used and the prince had just repeated was running over and over in his head: "A prize for princes—a prize for princes."

He was not sure but what he was saying it aloud, and, observing a footman regarding him with a stare of curiosity, he somehow made his way down the great hall and up the stairs to his own room.

There he remained for two hours, pacing up and down in feverish agitation. There was a knock on the door; a servant appeared. The prince desired to know if they were not to have General Nirzann's company at dinner.

The general replied in the negative, saying that he would dine out. Again he took to pacing the floor, but he could find no loophole of escape. He sighed, and came to a sudden determination; then he stood still in the middle of the room, surveying the familiar objects about him with the air of one who says farewell; tears were in his eyes.

To do him justice, the general's decision was in the way of being heroic; let him have his due. Again sighing, he left the room and sought the street. Fifteen minutes' walk brought him to the door of 341 the Drive.

Mlle. Aline Solini fancied that she knew very well what was in store for her when Czean appeared at her door to announce that General Nirzann wished to see her. An unpleasant scene, that was all. Her first impulse was to refuse to see him.

"After all," she thought, "it must be done sometime, and as well get it over with." Then, aloud: "Tell him I will be down in a few minutes, Czean."

As the prince had said, Aline knew well how to read men's hearts, and, he might have added, their minds. With her first quick glance at the face of General Nirzann, torn with regret and despair, and at the same time firm with the strength of an unalterable resolution, she saw that her task was not to be so easy as she had expected. Nevertheless, she had no doubt of the outcome.

The general rose to his feet and approached her with a majestic strut. He wasted no time in preliminaries; he said abruptly and almost fiercely: "We are alone?"

"Yes, we are alone." Aline smiled, saying to herself with a touch of amusement: "The little general is going to be theatrical."

The general was speaking: "*Mademoiselle*, three hours ago the Prince of Marisi told me that he is going to marry you."

She replied calmly: "That is true."

"Pardon me, *mademoiselle*, it is not true; it is impossible."

"How impossible?"

"I will not allow it."

"You cannot help yourself."

"I can, and I will."

These sentences were shot forth with the rapidity and incisiveness of the reports of a Gatling-gun. At this last declaration of the general's, uttered in a tone of the utmost determination, Aline made a gesture of incredulity.

For a moment she stood still, returning the general's gaze with one quite as firm as his own; then she said, as one who is forced to argue a matter which has already been decided:

"General, listen to me. I understand your position perfectly—both its strength and its weakness. I do not deny that you have certain claims on me, and let me tell you this—that you will always possess my gratitude. I am going to marry the Prince of Marisi. I warn you not to attempt to hinder me."

"You are not going to marry the prince."

"I am."

"I will prevent it."

"How?"

"By telling him the truth about you."

"Bah! You dare not, my dear general; it would be to ruin yourself."

"I know that very well; I have resigned myself to it."

Aline looked at him quickly; the fellow had actually said that as though he meant it! Which, of course, was absurd. She said dryly:

"That is quite useless, general. You are trying to frighten me. I know you too well to believe you. You are too old and too wise a man to cut your own throat. I am willing to talk with you sensibly, but I will not listen to your foolish threats."

She stopped, expecting the general to break out into loud protestations of his sincerity and earnestness; but he did not speak. Instead, he stood regarding her in silence, with a little, forlorn smile on his lips, but with clear, determined eyes.

For the first time a tinge of foreboding crept into Aline's thoughts. Was it possible that this little man was going seriously to oppose her—that he was willing to drag her down with him to double ruin?

But why?

Did the fool really love her?

But, no—she would manage him. Bah! To carry the thing thus far and be foiled at last by the little general? Impossible!

"If you think my threats are foolish, you are mistaken, *mademoiselle*."

The general was speaking quite slowly and distinctly, as if he wished to make himself very plain. "I mean every word I say. You see, I owe everything I have in the world to the Prince of Marisi." The general's voice became plaintive in its earnestness. "Everything.

"I love him; I would die for him, as I have served him. Do you know what he said to me the other day? And we were talking about you, too. He said: 'General, your fidelity is beyond question.' That is great praise from his lips, *mademoiselle*! I can honestly say I deserved it. You tell me I am too old and too wise a man to cut my own throat. I would cut my own throat—literally—rather than betray my prince."

"Betray him!" cried Aline. "My dear general, who is asking you to betray him? Is it betraying him to permit him to marry the woman he loves?"

Mlle. Solini realized with a feeling of anger that she was descending to argument.

The general replied calmly:

"Pardon me, *mademoiselle*; when that woman is you—yes."

"Ah!" cried Aline, while a glance, furious and keen as the flash of steel, darted from her eyes. Unmoved the general continued:

"I may seem brutal; I cannot help it; I shall speak plainly. You have deceived me and tried to outwit me. You are betraying and deceiving M. Stetton, and accepting money from him. These things alone would make you unfit to become Princess of Marisi. But in addition to that, there are so many ambiguous things about you—indiscretions—shall we say—more than enough; I am determined."

"Ah, what a gentleman you are!" Aline spat out these words in one furious breath.

"I am no longer a gentleman, *mademoiselle*; I am merely the servant of my prince."

Aline was compelled to believe. Every tone of the general's voice, every glance of his eye spoke of the deepest earnestness. There was no doubt of it; these were not mere empty threats; the man would actually do as he said.

Aline looked at him, and if looks could kill the general would assuredly have dropped dead in his tracks. Her brain was working with the rapidity of lightning. There had been a time, she thought, when the general could not have spoken to her as he just had done. What a fool she had been to loosen her hold on him! If only she had not neglected him when she began to feel that he was no longer useful to her! She glanced at him swiftly, speculatively. Perhaps—

She crossed to the general's side and placed her hand on his shoulder. He appeared to take no notice of the movement, but stood in silence, as though awaiting her decision.

"Paul," she said—he had always been childishly pleased when she called him that—"Paul, I cannot believe that you will do what you say."

"Do not doubt it," replied the general grimly. She fancied that his shoulder moved slightly under her touch—a good sign, she thought. She said, allowing a note of tenderness to creep into her voice:

"But I do doubt it. You cannot be so cruel to me. Have you forgotten everything? Do you no longer love me?"

Her arm crept round his neck; she moved a little closer to him.

"Can you blame me, Paul, for wanting a home, a position, a name? You know the one I would take if I could; I do not need to tell you where my heart is. If you will not marry me yourself, Paul, why do you refuse to allow me to find happiness where it is waiting for me?"

There was a pause, while the general regarded her with an air of sadness and commiseration. But when he spoke his voice was quite firm; more, final.

"Aline, I am sorry—believe me—I am sorry, but it is impossible. I am determined." And he repeated, as though to strengthen his resolution, which, indeed, was quite strong enough already: "I am determined."

Aline thought: "He is weakening." Her other arm crept around his neck; her hands met on his shoulder.

"Paul," she murmured, looking into his eyes— "Paul, listen to me. Do you think I have ceased to love you? I could not, dear. Because I marry the prince I do not need to give him my heart. It is yours; it will always be yours. And—"

She got no further in her mistake. The general, suddenly understanding her, tore her arms from his neck and pushed her away with such violence that she would have fallen but that her outstretched hand fell on the back of a chair. Nirzann stood breathing heavily, regarding her with eyes of horror and disgust.

"My God!" he cried, choking with wrath and contempt.

Aline sank back in a chair, turning her face away. She was no longer angry; on the contrary, she was composed and deadly calm. She perceived at last that the case was desperate; that only a miracle or a stroke of genius could save her. She must think—she must have time to think! She turned to the general:

"You have made up your mind to betray me?" She asked it as one asks an ordinary question for the sake of information. For reply, the general merely nodded.

"And what you demand is that I voluntarily cancel my engagement with the prince?"

"I demand nothing. I offer you an alternative."

There was a short silence; then Aline said:

"I don't know—my brain is confused—I don't know what to say. Give me time to think—leave me and come back in an hour."

He replied roughly:

"There is no need to think; it is a simple choice—yes or no."

"But I must think—my brain is whirling—what harm can that do? You would be wise to humor me, if you expect me to consider your desires in my answer."

"I do not expect you to consider my desires, *mademoiselle*; I do not wish that you should." He paused, but she did not speak, and he continued: "I am not thinking of myself, but of the prince. And let me tell you this, I will not wait an hour, nor ten minutes. Nor will I trust your word—I will not even allow you to remain in Marisi. When I go the limit I do not stop on the way, and I fear you."

"Really, general, you flatter me." Aline, playing for time, spoke sarcastically. "You will not trust my word? What else can I give you?"

"I don't know—something—a letter—an agreement—I must have something in writing. If I do not have it when I leave this house I shall go straight to the prince and tell him all."

A letter! Aline turned her eyes away quickly, lest she betray her thought. A letter! Wait—how could it be done—oh, for a minute to think! Ah! She nearly breathed it aloud. An idea! Wait—wait—yes— Her brain was working like lightning, in swift, brilliant flashes of inspiration. She turned to the general:

"You insist on my answer now?"

"Now."

"And you say—a letter—"

"Yes. A letter to the prince. That would be best."

"And I must leave Marisi?"

"At once."

There was a silence, while Aline sat apparently reflecting. The general stood regarding her with the calmness of a man who is prepared to die, and who therefore can be moved by nothing. Suddenly Aline spoke:

"I will go."

"You will go?" the general cried, startled. He had not expected this.

"Yes. I will go. At once. Tonight—or tomorrow mornir_. And I will give you your letter. Some day, general, you shall pay for this. I do not know how nor when, but you shall pay for it." She arose.

"I expect to, *mademoiselle*." The general was unmoved by her threat; he had expected that. "But let me warn you, don't try any tricks with me. I must have the letter now, and you must be out of Marisi for good by this time tomorrow." Then, as Aline was moving toward the door leading to the hall, he called out sharply, "Where are you going?"

"To my room, to write the letter," was her answer.

He made no reply, and she disappeared.

The general sat down to wait. After all, it appeared that he was really going to escape with a whole skin. He was conscious of a certain feeling of gratitude toward Mlle. Solini, not very strong, perhaps, but still it was there; and when, after an interval of fifteen minutes, she returned, holding in her hand a pink envelope, he regarded her with somewhat less contempt than he had half an hour before. Now that it was all over, he felt, indeed, rather kindly disposed toward her.

Aline, approaching him, held the envelope out in her hand. It was unsealed. On its face was a postage-stamp; below it was addressed: "Michael, Prince of Marisi, Marisi Palace, Marisi."

The general took it and, after glancing at the address, put it in his pocket.

"That is the end of everything," Aline was saying, "of everything." Her tone was one of sorrow and resignation, not unmixed with anger. "Now, general, I am going to make some demands of you—I deserve something from you—you cannot deny it."

The general bowed and started to speak, but she interrupted him:

"I shall leave Marisi tomorrow morning. I would not stay anyway, after this. I do not want the prince to get that letter till after I have left. I do not want you yourself to read it till tomorrow morning; I need not explain why now; you will understand when you read it. You must promise me, general; you must swear to it."

"I promise, on my word," said the general, moved in spite of himself at this calmness in the face of disaster. "I promise gladly, *mademoiselle*. And if there is anything else—"

Aline appeared to think for a moment.

"Only this," she said finally, "that if M. Stetton asks you about me, tell him you know nothing. Nothing. Promise me."

"I promise, on my word," repeated the general, thinking that he was getting out of it rather cheaply.

"Remember, you are not to read the letter till tomorrow. And of course it must go through the mail— that is why I stamped it—the prince must not know you have seen it."

"Indeed not!" thought the general, and he said:

"You have my word, *mademoiselle*. I shall do exactly as you say."

There was an awkward pause. Aline drew back, as though to signify that there was nothing more to say. The general began uncertainly:

"*Mademoiselle*—Aline—I am sorry—"

She looked straight at him:

"That will do. I do not want your sympathy. Leave me—it is over. Leave me."

For a moment the general returned her gaze in silence; then, without a word, he turned and left the house.

CHAPTER XX.

THE GENERAL KEEPS HIS WORD.

General Paul Nirzann slept well that night. His aeroplane—to return to our dashing metaphor of the previous chapter—had righted itself and was again sailing peacefully along. The only cloud on the horizon was the loss of his Cross of Buta; the general really regretted that. But he had to acknowledge, though not without a sigh, that it was cheap at the price.

He was thoroughly glad that he was at length finished with Mlle. Solini. Of course, he had never really loved her, and for some time past he had feared her. In all conscience, he and Marisi were well rid of such a woman.

He did not doubt but that she would leave in the morning, as she had promised; indeed, Marisi would be the last place where she would want to remain, after the destruction of all her plans.

For his own part, he kept his word with her. He deposited her letter in a drawer of his desk without looking at it, wondering at the same time why she had placed this curious restriction upon him. For some time he lay awake; his dominant thoughts were of security and thankfulness. He slept soundly.

In the morning he rose rather late. He sang—or, to be strictly accurate, uttered noises—while he dressed, and ate a hearty breakfast in his room. He was lingering over the coffee when a glance at his watch showed him that it was twenty-five minutes past nine.

He remembered that the prince had commanded his presence at ten o'clock—for what purpose the general easily guessed—and, thinking that the matter of the letter must be attended to before then, he went to his desk and took it from the drawer.

The envelope itself held memories for him; he had himself received several exactly similar. He could see now, in his mind's eyes, that little corner of Aline's dainty writing-desk where they lay scattered about in an ebony box—two colors, pink and blue. This one was pink. The general sighed, took out the letter, and read:

To His Highness the Prince of Marisi:

What I am going to say will no doubt astonish your highness. As for me, it breaks my heart.

I shall be brief; I must either say too much or too little, and I prefer the latter.

In four words—I cannot marry you.

Your highness knows that I would not write this without a reason, and a powerful one. Forgive me if I do not tell you what it is.

By the time you read this I shall have left Marisi; I shall never see you again. Ah, Michael—I may call you that once more, may I not?—I had thought that the first letter I should write to you would be very different from this.

I can say no more—*adieu*.

ALINE SOLINI.

The general read this letter over three times, and each time the frown on his brow deepened. Not that he had any fault to find with it, considering its purpose; indeed, he thought it perfect. It had an air of finality.

But why had Aline insisted so strongly that he should not read it till this morning? He could not understand that. He read it over again. Decidedly, there was nothing in it to explain that curious request.

But—he shrugged his shoulders—what of that? There was the letter; it was sufficient; quite sufficient. He returned the letter to the envelope, moistened the mucilage on the flap with his tongue, and sealed it.

Then he pressed a button on the wall beside his desk.

"But that would not do," he thought. "I must mail it myself."

When a servant appeared a moment later he dismissed him, saying that he would perform his errand himself. He rose, put on his coat and hat, and sought the street, and, walking some distance down the drive, deposited the letter in a mailbox.

As he heard it fall to the bottom of the box he breathed a sigh of satisfaction, and turned to retrace his steps.

By the time he reached his room it lacked but a minute till ten o'clock, and; stopping only to deposit his hat and coat on the back of a chair, he left it again to hasten to his appointment with the prince, in that room on the floor below, at the end of the corridor, which we have seen twice before. The general, being of the household, had the privilege of entering its sacred precincts; and he never did so without a little straightening of the shoulders at the thought of that privilege.

The prince, as it appeared, was in great good humor. When the general entered he was engaged with De Mide, his secretary, but their business was soon ended, and De Mide prepared to leave.

General Nirzann moved ostentatiously out of his path to the door. He did not like De Mide, and took advantage of every occasion to show it.

"You are punctual, I see, Nirzann," said the prince, as the door closed behind the departing secretary.

"Am I not always so, your highness?"

"I suppose so. The fact is, my dear general, you have so many virtues it is difficult to remember all of them."

The general smiled politely at his prince's little joke. "Your highness is kind to remember even one of them," he declared, quite as though he meant it.

"That will do, Nirzann; you will never be a courtier; you are too clumsy," laughed the prince, seating himself in a chair and motioning the general to one on the other side of the table. "But come; we must get down to business. Of course you know what I want you for?"

"I can guess."

"To be sure. You are to carry my formal proposal to your cousin." The prince arranged some papers on the desk before him. "I have been working at it with De Mide. I think we have it in proper form, but there are some gaps to be filled in. To begin with, what was her father's name?"

The general called on his wits, realizing that the farce must be played through. After a moment's hesitation he replied:

"Nicholas—Nicholas Solini."

The prince wrote something on the paper. "And her mother?"

"I—really, I do not know," stammered the general. "That is, I forget the name of her family. Her given name was the same as that of my cousin—Aline."

Again the prince wrote on the paper. Then he looked up with a frown:

"Now, about those estates in Warsaw. You say they are no longer in her name?"

"No, your highness."

"Then I suppose her residence could hardly be said to be there," observed the prince. "Let us see; I think this will do." He looked at the paper for a minute in silence, then began to read aloud from it:

"To Mlle. Aline Solini, of Marisi, daughter of Nicholas Solini, of Warsaw, and his wife, Aline, greeting from Michael William Feodor Albert Keff, Prince of Marisi, Duke of Gernannt, Chevalier of the Order of Mestaniz. His highness, by these presents—"

The general sat listening respectfully while the prince read the somewhat lengthy document from beginning to end.

Once before the general had heard such a paper read in this same room—many years before.

As this thought crossed his mind he glanced up involuntarily at the portrait over the fireplace—the portrait of a woman of about thirty years, with dark hair and serious eyes.

She would have thanked him, the general thought, if she could; it was well that Mlle. Solini was not to take her place.

"You will take this to Mlle. Solini at once," the prince was saying. "I want all preliminaries arranged without delay so that we can make the public announcement as soon as possible. You will conduct the affair, of course, with due formality. You will understand, Nirzann, that I am eager for haste in this matter."

The general managed a smile.

"I can well understand that, your highness."

"Yes. Since you are Mlle. Solini's only living relative, you will be expected to officiate in that capacity at the wedding. And before I forget it, I have a little present for you."

The prince opened a drawer of the table and took out a little ivory box, which he opened, displaying to view a cross of gold, with yellow and green ribbons.

"Your Cross of Buta, general. Here, let me— What is it? What's the matter?"

"I—I—nothing, your highness." A swift spasm as of pain had distorted the general's face. "That is—I felt something—it has passed now."

"That is what comes of dining out," said the prince with a smile. "You know your weakness, general."

"It has passed," said the general, who was looking relieved. "Your highness will forgive me—I should not—in your presence—"

"Good Heavens, man," the prince interrupted, laughing, "don't apologize! Indigestion has no respect for princes."

"Your highness is always kind." The general rose. "I am ready to go with your—er—proposal whenever your highness pleases. If there are any—"

The general's voice stopped suddenly, while his features were again distorted with a spasm of pain. This time it continued twice as long as before.

"What is it?" again cried the prince, looking at him in quick sympathy.

The general sank back weakly in his chair, while his eyes grew wide and staring and his lips twitched convulsively.

The prince crossed hastily to his side with an exclamation of alarm.

"What is it, Nirzann? Are you ill? What is the matter?"

"I don't know, your highness." The general appeared to be speaking with difficulty. He tried to struggle to his feet, but fell back again into the chair. "Perhaps—if I—if I—"

Then, quite suddenly, there came from his lips a great cry of pain—the cry of one who is being tortured with insupportable agony.

"Help!" he cried, again trying to rise. "For God's sake, help me!"

The thing had come so suddenly that for an instant the prince stood as one paralyzed. The next he was ringing the bell on the table and calling to the footman without. Then he sprang back to the general, who was slowly slipping from the chair onto the floor, and supported him in his arms.

In another moment two or three servants rushed into the room, attracted by the prince's cries. One he sent for water; another for the doctor, who was in the palace; and still another helped him support the general.

They had all they could do to hold him; he was struggling in their grasp like a crazy man, uttering screams of agony that sounded throughout the palace and reached even into the street. Other servants and members of the household rushed in, crying out in startled tones; all was confusion and uproar; they had thought the prince was being murdered.

De Mide, arriving breathless, offered to take the place of the prince beside Nirzann; but the prince shook his head, crying:

"The doctor—get the doctor!"

At that moment the doctor arrived—a man of sixty or more, wise and competent, who had served the prince's father before him. He pushed his way through the throng to the side of General Nirzann, who was a terrible sight to behold as he struggled in the arms of the prince and the footman.

His eyes were rolling wildly about, his face was red and distorted, and froth was coming from his mouth. The old doctor gave him but one glance before he turned to the De Mide and said sharply:

"Clear the room!"

Then the doctor turned and gave some swift instructions to a servant who had entered with him and who now disappeared at a run. De Mide ordered every one from the room; it was cleared in three seconds. No one remained but the prince, the doctor, and De Mide.

General Nirzann had slipped to the floor. The doctor knelt beside him, holding him down with both arms. The general's movements were more feeble now; his body was moving from side to side with little convulsive twitches. A low, continuous moan came from his lips.

The servant who had taken the doctor's instructions entered, carrying a case of instruments and bottles. De Mide hurried him forward, crying:

"Here, doctor—here you are!"

There was a silence, broken only by the moans of the general, now so feeble they were scarcely heard. The doctor raised his head and said gravely:

"Send him away. It is too late. Send him from the room."

"But what is it?" cried the prince. "This is horrible! In Heaven's name, what is it?"

The doctor did not reply. He was gazing at General Nirzann, whose body was trembling with spasmodic shudders that ran from his head to his feet. But his eyes were steady and seemed once more to hold the light of reason. The doctor leaned forward and spoke distinctly:

"Look at me, general. Do you know me?"

The eyes shifted, and the general's voice came, painful and gasping, as though every word were torn from his throat by force:

"Yes—Anchevin—yes." Again the eyes shifted toward the prince. "Your highness—listen—before—I am dying—Aline—Aline—"

He stopped; more would not come. The doctor took a pitcher of water and poured some over his mouth; then he leaned forward and spoke:

"Answer me if you can, general. Use all your strength. You have been poisoned. Do you know who did it?"

A sudden light flashed into the general's eyes—the light of comprehension. Then their expression changed as quickly to one of the most intense fury and hatred— so plain, so fiercely malignant, that De Mide and the prince recoiled involuntarily.

And again words came from the general's lips, but this time in a whisper, barely audible, though he was plainly making a terrible effort to speak intelligibly.

"Poison!" he gasped. "Yes—I know—yes— mucilage—mucilage—"

That was all. Several times more he opened his lips; it could be seen that he was exerting himself tremendously to speak; but no words came. His fingers were plucking convulsively at the edge of his coat; his eyes closed, then opened again; a tremor passed all over his body, and he lay quite still.

The doctor rose to his feet, turning to the others; they saw by the expression on his face that all was over. Their own faces were filled with a question—a question of horror; the doctor answered it without waiting for them to speak. His voice was very grave.

"Your highness, the general was poisoned. And with some quick poison—something that he has taken within the hour. Do you know—"

The prince interrupted him in a voice of agitation:

"I know nothing, Anchevin. He was sitting there, talking to me; the attack came suddenly and without warning. Why—I can't believe—it was only ten minutes ago—"

He stopped abruptly and stood looking down at the body of the general as though he were just beginning to understand what had happened. This for a long time; then he murmured gently: "Poor old Nirzann—a faithful servant and a true friend."

No one will deny that the little general deserved the epitaph.

Then the prince, suddenly rousing himself, turned to the others:

"Anchevin, you must repeat to no one what you have just said. Call it anything you like; there must be no mention of poison. De Mide, you will do what is necessary. Get Duchesne on the telephone and let him confer with Anchevin, but let him understand that whatever investigations he makes must be kept strictly secret. We owe it—to him."

The doctor began:

"Your highness, there must be an autopsy—"

"Good Heavens!" cried the prince. "Anchevin, you are ghoulish. Do what is necessary, but don't talk about it. De Mide, the general must be removed to his own room."

"Yes, your highness."

"And don't forget to impress Duchesne with the necessity for secrecy. If there is any—"

He was interrupted by the ringing of a bell. It was the telephone on the prince's desk. De Mide crossed to it and took up the receiver. The others heard him speak, and, after a short pause, say:

"Yes, the prince is here."

Another pause, then De Mide asked:

"Who is it?"

Then:

"One moment, please." De Mide placed his hand over the mouth of the transmitter and then turned to the prince.

"Mlle. Solini wishes to speak to you."

With an exclamation of surprise the prince hastened to take the receiver from his secretary, at the same time saying:

"You may go—both of you. Return in five minutes."

Then, when the doctor and De Mide had disappeared, he spoke into the telephone:

"Aline! Is this you, Aline?"

"Yes, your highness."

"Ah! I recognize your voice."

"And I recognize yours." A short pause. "I wanted to ask your highness—I wanted to know if you have received a letter from me this morning?"

"A letter? No."

"Oh! Then it hasn't been delivered. I am glad of that. I mailed it this morning, and then, half an hour afterward, found it on my desk."

"You found it on your desk?" repeated the prince, puzzled.

"Yes. I had placed a letter to someone else in the envelope addressed to you." There was a little silvery laugh in her voice. "And it is a letter which I would much rather you didn't read. That is why I telephoned you—I don't want you even to open it." Again the laugh. "Your highness knows that all women have their strictly private secrets."

"I know," said the prince, and began to return her laugh; but his eye rested on the body of General Nirzann, lying on the floor almost at his feet, and the laugh stuck in his throat.

"I will return your letter unopened, Aline. I shall speak to De Mide about it at once."

"That is what I was afraid of—that someone else might read it."

"I'll see that they don't. I'll guard your secret for you; I have the right, haven't I?"

"Yes, your highness."

"Not that!"

"Then—yes, Michael."

The prince was wondering if he ought to tell her of the death of her cousin, and how, but decided that it would be too rude a shock, coming thus suddenly over the telephone. But neither should she learn it through the cries of newsboys or the headlines of a newspaper.

He asked if he might call on her at her home in half an hour, saying that he had something of importance to tell her that could not be entrusted to the telephone. That arranged, he hung up the receiver and turned just as a knock sounded on the door.

It was De Mide, come to say that servants were preparing the general's room and would soon arrive to carry him there. The prince nodded gravely, without speaking.

Then, when the secretary had gone, he walked over to the body of the little general and stood looking down at him in silence.

His thoughts reverted to the general's dying words. They had been of Aline and of the prince himself, perhaps—so thought the prince—the only persons he had ever loved. But then—at the very end—

The prince's brow was wrinkled in a puzzled frown. He muttered aloud:

" 'Mucilage!' Now what the devil could he have meant by that word mucilage?"

Which was one of those questions that never find an answer.

CHAPTER XXI.

STETTON GOES HUNTING.

The young are always with us."

The man who wrote that called himself a philosopher; but he would have shown clearer claim to the title if he had written instead: "The young are always with themselves."

Youth is the age of conceit, arrogance, vanity and egoism. It was the age of Richard Stetton. Thus much given, you can guess at the young man's feelings when, upon calling four different times at the house of Mlle. Solini—twice a day—he was told each time that she was not at home.

At the first call he believed it. The next he wondered. The third he doubted. The fourth he pushed his way past Czean at the door and went stalking through the drawing-room, library, dining-room and kitchen. The place was empty, except for the servants, who tittered behind his back.

What to do? He had not quite worked himself up to the point of daring to mount the stairs to her room and force an entrance. Besides, he felt that he was making himself ridiculous. He left the house with a threatening glance at Czean, who had followed at his heels throughout the search.

On his way back to the hotel he bought a newspaper. The first thing in it that met his eye was an account of the death of General Paul Nirzann.

The following morning, feeling that the situation was getting a little beyond him, Stetton went to his friend Frederick Naumann for advice; and then, for the first time, he told the whole story of his relations with Mlle. Solini, even to that burning proposal of marriage on which he had exercised all his epistolary genius a few nights previous. When he had finished Naumann was staring at him in incredulous amazement.

"You don't mean to say you were ass enough to propose to her in a letter!" cried the young diplomat.

Stetton saw no reason why he should be considered an ass.

Naumann groaned.

"My dear fellow, it was bad enough to propose to her at all! And to put it in writing! Of course, the worst trick she could play you would be to marry you, but the Lord knows what she'll do.

"Don't ask me for advice. The only thing I can say is, get that letter, burn it, take the ashes to San Francisco and drop them in the Pacific Ocean. She's too much for me; I've washed my hands of her."

With which Stetton was perforce contented.

After that he stayed away from No. 341 for two whole days. On the morning of the third day he attended the funeral of General Nirzann at the Church of Montrosine, in the company of Naumann. The service was public, and the church was crowded; but in all the throng Stetton had eyes for only one figure—that of a slender woman, dressed in black and heavily veiled, who sat far to the front on the right, by the side of the Prince of Marisi.

It was Aline, who, as cousin of the general, was of course the chief mourner.

As he sat listening to the chant of the priest, Stetton conceived an idea. Perhaps, after all, he thought—for seeing Aline dressed in the garb of grief, hypocritical though he knew it to be, disposed him to generous thoughts—perhaps, after all, she had really not been at home when he had called.

He had been too impatient. He should have done—well, he should have done what he was going to do now, that very day.

At the conclusion of the ceremony at church Stetton accompanied his friend Naumann back to his rooms. There they chatted till noon. Stetton calculated that it would take two hours for the funeral procession to go to the cemetery and return; at one o'clock, therefore, he left Naumann and went afoot down the Drive to a point nearly opposite No. 341.

After a wait of fifteen minutes he saw the royal carriage drive up and halt in front of that number. Aline and Vivi got out, assisted by the prince, who took them to the door, and then returned and reentered the carriage, which resumed its way to the palace.

Stetton waited five minutes by his watch, then crossed the street, ascended the stoop and rang the bell.

"I'll know this time," he muttered grimly to himself. "I'll show this smart *mademoiselle* a thing or two."

He stood close to the door in order to be in a position to push his way in as soon as it was opened.

But the door did not open. After a minute's wait he again rang the bell. Another minute, and still there was no sign from within.

He pressed his finger against the bell-button and kept it there; then he began punching it with little vicious stabs. Still there was no sign.

He put his face against the glass of the door and tried to look within; he could see nothing, but he knew that anyone standing at the farther end of the hall could see him plainly. For five minutes he stood alternately ringing the bell and pounding on the door, which was locked; then, muttering a string of oaths, he gave it up and returned to the street.

It was now quite evident, even to him, that Mlle. Solini neither desired nor intended to see him. He perceived the fact, but he could not understand it. Why, he was going to marry her—he, Richard Stetton, of New York, rated—or soon to be rated—at ten million dollars!

Was the woman crazy? Aline Solini, a nobody, penniless, an outcast—it was absurd! In all America there were not ten girls who would not have jumped at the chance! Positively, she was out of her senses!

But out of her senses or not, it was perfectly plain that she would not see him. That, in short, he had been cut dead. Refused the house! The house for which he himself had paid the rent! By the time Stetton reached his room at the hotel he had worked himself into a raging fury.

He forced himself to calmness and began to consider possibilities. He could not very well break in the door. He thought of waylaying her on the street, but decided that it was beneath his dignity. As for an appeal to the agent of M. Duroy, owner of the house, that was impossible, for the simple reason that it had been taken in Aline's name.

He ended by deciding to leave Marisi for good, charge his expenditures, of something like half a million francs, to the account of experience, and forget Mlle. Solini finally and forever. He even leaped to his feet with an oath and began to pack his trunks. He stopped almost before he had started. The face of Aline was before him.

The lips, with their inviting curve, the white, soft skin, the glorious eyes, filled with promise—and with this, the memory of her arms about his neck, her delicious breath against his cheek, her soft words of love whispered in his ear. No—another oath—he could not give her up—he would not! He sat down at his desk and wrote her a letter of nine pages.

After that he waited for three days. No answer came to his letter. He sent another, longer than before—one that was surely calculated to move a heart of stone.

To this he confidently expected an answer, and it was with a feeling of despair that he found none on the following morning. He wandered dejectedly into the reading-room of the hotel and picked up a newspaper. The first thing that met his eyes was the following, in bold headlines:

THE PRINCE TO WED

Announcement Made of His Engagement to Mlle. Aline Solini of Marisi

No Surprise to Society, Which Has Admired and Courted the Beautiful Russian Since Her Arrival

Betrothal Approved by Council—Wedding to Take Place Late in July

Stetton stared at these headlines for five minutes without moving, while his face slowly assumed the expression of a man who is reading his death sentence. Then, mechanically, as one in a dream, he read the article from beginning to end.

Many details were given of Mlle. Solini—her parentage, the date of her birth, *et cetera*. It was called a genuine love-match. The wedding would have been set for an earlier day but for the fact that Mlle. Solini was in mourning for the recent death of her cousin, General Paul Nirzann.

Messages of congratulation had been received from all over the world. *Et cetera, et cetera*.

Stetton rose and walked out into the street. He was dazed; he knew not whither to go or what to do. He started rapidly down the Drive, then halted, cursing aloud.

What was the use? He would not be admitted.

Another thought came—he would go to the Prince

of Marisi and tell him the truth about Mlle. Solini. He was filled with savage fury; he wanted to strike her, to crush her. He started off down the Drive toward the palace, in long, rapid strides; he could not get there soon enough.

Suddenly a hand fell on his arm and a voice sounded in his ear:

"Hello! What's up? You look as though you were marching in the face of a thousand cannon!"

It was Naumann. Stetton halted.

"Aline is going to marry the prince," he said, as though he were announcing the end of the world.

"I know it," said Naumann dryly. "It's the talk of the town. You're well rid of her, old chap. But won't the prince have a merry time of it!"

"He will, indeed," Stetton replied grimly. "And he won't have to wait long, either. I'm on my way to the palace now."

The other looked at him sharply.

"What's that? What are you going to do?"

"I'm going to cook Aline's goose for her. I'm going to tell the prince all about her."

The face of the young diplomat suddenly became serious—very serious. He said emphatically, grasping Stetton by the arm:

"My dear fellow, you are going to do nothing of the sort."

"No? Watch me!"

"But it's folly—madness—suicide!"

"I don't see why. Anyway, I'm going to do it."

There was a pause, during which the two young men glared at each other. Finally Naumann spoke:

"Stetton, you can be more different kinds of an ass than any ten men I've ever seen. Listen to me a minute! Do you realize how serious this is? Have you any idea what it means to go to the Prince of Marisi and tell tales of the woman he has publicly announced he is going to marry? Unless you have proof—double-riveted, apodictic, instantaneous proof—of every word you utter, you'll find yourself in jail in two minutes."

Hesitation and doubt replaced the determination in Stetton's eye; the strength of these words was impressive. He said:

"But what can I do? Hang it all, don't you see I've got to do something?"

"Come over to my rooms," said Naumann, placing his arm through that of Stetton. "We'll talk this thing over."

Half reluctantly Stetton allowed himself to be led back along the Drive. Here and there they met boys with papers, shouting the news of the prince's engagement to Mlle. Solini, the beautiful Russian. On the street corners groups of people were gathered, talking; it was easy to guess of what. Everywhere they saw smiles and beaming faces.

"Why the deuce are they all so happy about it?" demanded Stetton.

Naumann replied:

"On account of the future heir."

At which the American grunted as though such a sentiment were beyond his comprehension.

Arrived in Naumann's rooms they began, as the young diplomat had said, to "talk it over." At first Stetton refused to be impressed. He declared with an air of bravado that the Prince of Marisi was the same to him as any other man, and that nothing and no one in the world should balk him of vengeance on Mlle. Solini, the perfidious, the treacherous, the odious.

"I agree with you," retorted Naumann, "that she is all that and more. But what can you do about it? Come; get down to cases; what specific charge can you make against her?

"When you get your audience with the prince, what are you going to say?"

"I—I—why, a dozen things."

"What, for instance?"

"In the first place, I'll tell him that she is not General Nirzann's cousin. It was that lie that got her in."

"How are you going to prove it?"

By the look on Stetton's face when he heard this question, you might have thought he had been asked how he was going to prove that the world was round. He repeated:

How am I going to prove it? Why, you know it yourself! She's no more General Nirzann's cousin than I am!"

"Quite true," said Naumann patiently; "but you must remember that the general is dead. You must have proof."

Stetton ended by admitting that he had none.

"But," he cried impatiently, "what does that amount to? That is the least of what I have to tell. How I found her in the convent in Fasilica, how she bargained to marry me, how she shot the man that saved us—the one you think was her husband—how she poisoned Chavot—"

Naumann interrupted wearily.

"But, I repeat, of all these things you have no proof—absolutely none. You yourself don't believe she poisoned Chavot."

"Yes, I do now. And also, how I've given her four hundred thousand francs since she came to Marisi."

"Good Lord!" Naumann looked at him in amazement. "You don't mean to say you've given her that amount of money! How? In checks? An account?"

"No. Mostly in cash and jewels. There were no checks."

Naumann shrugged his shoulders and spread out his hands.

"There you are again. Where's your proof?"

"But I paid the rent for the house personally; gave it to Duroy himself. That's something."

"Not much. Couldn't she say you were acting as her agent? Stetton, you haven't a leg to stand on. The worst of it is that only a week ago you sent her a written proposal of marriage; it is the most powerful weapon she could have against anything you might say. You can't go to the prince with more accusations; believe me, if you do you'll regret it."

In the end Stetton was forced to admit that his friend was right. If General Nirzann were alive it would have been a different matter—so said Stetton grimly, and Naumann agreed with him. As it was, nothing could be done. Nothing.

But still Stetton could not smother his desire for revenge. He brought his hand down on the table with a bang, crying with an oath:

"I'll tell you what, Naumann, I'd give one million dollars in cash to get even with her! I mean it!"

Naumann was standing in front of a window with his hands in his pockets, looking out with a frown across Walderin Place.

As Stetton spoke he turned and said abruptly:

"Well, there's a chance."

"A chance? What do you mean?"

"A chance to get even with her, as you say."

"In Heaven's name, how?"

"Find Vasili Petrovich."

Then, as the other stood gazing at him in slow comprehension, the young diplomat continued:

"You have told me that he was only wounded that day in Fasilica—that you saved his life. Then depend on it, he is still very much alive and searching for the woman who injured him. If you can find him he will soon see to it that she doesn't marry the Prince of Marisi or anyone else. You'll have all the revenge you want."

"But where is he?"

"That's the question. He isn't at Warsaw; that much I know, for I've written there several times. But he's somewhere. Find him. Advertise all over Europe; go yourself if you find a clue anywhere. It's just possible he's still in Fasilica. Find Vasili Petrovich, and he'll do the rest."

"By Heaven," cried Stetton, "I will!"

In another minute they were discussing details and plans for the search. There was plenty of time; according to the announcement, the wedding was to occur late in July, and this was early in April.

Now that something had been decided upon— something that bade fair to be productive of results— Naumann laid bare a corner of his heart to admit his own vital interest in the proceedings, on account of his love for Mlle. Janvour. Stetton had no time to waste on thoughts of Vivi or Naumann; his head was filled with one exclusive, overmastering idea.

In the first place, they prepared an advertisement which Naumann was to insert in every newspaper of any importance in Europe and Russia. It read as follows:

Vasili Petrovich, of Warsaw, will please communicate at once with Frederick Naumann either at Berlin or Marisi.

Secondly, Naumann gave Stetton all the assistance and information possible for his search, regretting that he could not assist personally.

He gave him letters to his father in Berlin, acquaintances in Warsaw, St. Petersburg, and Paris, and a dozen men in the diplomatic service stationed in different cities. Stetton had suggested asking the aid of the police, but Naumann had vetoed the idea, explaining:

"It would be dangerous on account of what will follow if we find him. We may use them as a last resort."

Finally, after a discussion lasting four hours, everything was arranged, and it was decided that Stetton should leave Marisi without delay.

On the following morning the Tsevor Express had

for one of its passengers Mr. Richard Stetton, of New York. His destination was Fasilica.

It was three months before Stetton saw Marisi again, and in that time he traversed all of Europe and most of Russia.

He began, as they had decided, with Fasilica. There he found nothing.

He went on to Warsaw, where the manager of Vasili Petrovich's estates, upon reading the letter of Frederick Naumann, received him with open arms. But of his master he could tell him nothing—absolutely nothing—he had not heard from him for a year. Still, he did have a clue, a very slight one.

On the strength of that clue Stetton proceeded to St. Petersburg. Still no trace.

Next he journeyed to Berlin and sought out Naumann's father, who gave him suggestions, but nothing more, and they led nowhere. Thenceforth it became a mere wild-goose chase, and nearly attained to the dignity of a mania.

He visited Paris, Rome, Budapest, Vienna, Moscow, Marseilles, Athens; and the first of July found him back at Warsaw. Time then was short; and Stetton, worn out in body and mind, headed himself for Marisi and the advice of his friend Naumann, from whom he had heard but once or twice in the entire three months.

He arrived at Marisi at eight o'clock in the evening and went directly to the Hotel Walderin for a bath, a change of linen, and dinner. That done, he went to Naumann's rooms at 5 Walderin Place.

Naumann was delighted to see him, but in despair at his lack of success. Stetton, however, refused to lose heart, saying that they still had nearly a month before the date of the wedding, and that by procuring the aid of the police they might yet be successful. He was stopped in the middle of this speech by the look of surprise that appeared on Naumann's face.

"Haven't you heard?" cried the young diplomat.

"Have you been out of the world altogether? Haven't you got any of the dozen or so letters I've written you in the past few weeks? Don't you ever look at a newspaper?

"My dear fellow, the Prince of Marisi and Mlle. Solini were married two weeks ago!"

CHAPTER XXII.

BACK AGAIN.

That night Stetton and Naumann sat together in the latter's room until well past twelve o'clock. Many things were said.

Naumann told of his repeated efforts to see Vivi and his final success, only to be interrupted by Mlle. Solini and ordered from the house. Also, that since the prince's marriage it had been delicately hinted to the German minister that his secretary, Herr Frederick Naumann, was *persona non grata* in Marisi, as a result of which hint Naumann was to be transferred to Vienna within the month. He had even been denied entrance to the palace when he had called there in a final desperate attempt to see Vivi.

These, and many other occurrences, were related by Naumann; but when Stetton finally left to return to his hotel he remembered none of them. His mind was occupied with the attempt to realize that Aline was lost to him irrevocably; that Aline, the woman who had promised to marry him, who had given him her kisses and embraces and words of love, was now Princess of Marisi.

It was only now, for the first time, that he fully realized the extent of his infatuation for her. When he reached the room and once more found himself alone, he gave himself up to a very delirium of despair. He did not sleep that night.

The morning brought no relief. A thousand times during the night he had tried to tell himself that all was over; that he might as well say farewell to Marisi forever, and the sooner the better. But he could not bring himself to the point of a decision to go.

He was constantly haunted by the face of Aline; it was ever before his eyes. He did not know whether he loved or hated her; he only felt he could never forget her.

Then suddenly his humor would change, and he would curse her with every oath in his vocabulary. He would drive her to ruin, to death itself; above all, he would have his revenge.

As for Vasili Petrovich, he had given up all hope of finding him. He was certain in his own mind that Aline's bullet, on that never-to-be-forgotten morning in Fasilica, had, after all, been fatal. Vasili Petrovich was dead—so he told himself—revenge would come from his own hand or not at all. He swore that it should come.

It was in this mood that he sought the street, after a late and unsatisfactory breakfast. Having no place to go in particular, he proceeded in desultory fashion to 5 Walderin Place and ascended the stairs to Naumann's rooms.

The young diplomat was not in. He returned to the street and wandered down the Drive to the German legation. There he remained for an hour, chatting with Naumann, whom he found in almost as low spirits as his own.

At eleven o'clock he was again on the Drive, strolling along at random, wondering where to go and what to do. Suddenly he halted, turned, and found himself directly in front of the white marble palace of the Prince of Marisi. He had, in fact, been carried there by his own mind and will, though quite subconsciously.

As he stood there, gazing at the great bronze portals not a dozen paces away, he was possessed of a sudden, overwhelming desire, which was, in fact, nothing but the crystallization of a thought that had entered his mind many times during the night and morning. Now it grasped him fiercely, so that he did not hesitate even to argue the matter with himself.

He walked down the marble flagging, entered the bronze gates, and handed his card to the servant at the door, saying that he desired an immediate audience with the prince.

He was led down the broad corridor to a reception-room and left there to wait. There were four or five other people in the room, evidently likewise waiting for an audience with the prince. In a few minutes a servant appeared and beckoned one of them to follow him. Another ten minutes and Stetton heard his own name from the door:

"M. Stetton, the prince will see you now."

Stetton followed the servant for some distance down the corridor, up a flight of stairs, and into a large room of state, hung with rick tapestries and old savars, with an air of formality and ceremony even in the rugs that covered the polished floor.

Before a table, in a great armchair of ebony, was the Prince of Marisi; at a smaller table nearby a young man sat, writing. As Stetton entered, the servant at the door called out his name in a loud voice. He crossed the room, stopping a few paces in front of the prince.

The prince extended no greeting to him, though they had dined at the same table three or four times not long before. Instead, he looked up and said abruptly:

"You wished to see me?"

"Yes, your highness."

"What is it?"

Stetton hesitated, then said in a low voice:

"Your highness would prefer—that is, what I have to say is for your highness's ears alone."

"You are sure of that *monsieur*?"

"I am sure of it."

The prince turned to the young man writing at the table.

"De Mide, leave us. Return when M. Stetton is gone."

De Mide rose without a word and departed.

"And now," said the prince, "be brief, M. Stetton. There are others waiting."

"I will try to, your highness." Stetton was calling on his courage. "What I have to say will both surprise and displease your highness, but you must believe that my only motive is to serve you. It is of Mlle.—the princess that I want to speak."

"The princess?" The prince frowned and looked at him sharply.

"Yes, your highness. There are certain things about her which you ought to know, and which I am sure you do not know. Things that are unpleasant, but are unhappily true. Your highness will be offended to hear them, but in the end you will thank me."

The prince's frown was deepened.

"Do you mean to say that you have accusations to make against the princess?"

Again Stetton gathered his courage together. He replied in a firm tone:

"Yes, your highness."

"Of what nature?"

"I can only answer that by relating them in detail."

"They are grave?"

"Yes."

The prince rang a bell on the table. When a servant appeared he said:

"Tell the princess that we request her presence."

The servant disappeared.

"But, your highness—" began Stetton in a voice of protest.

The prince interrupted him:

"That will do. I manage things my own way, *monsieur*."

274

There was a wait of five minutes. Stetton consumed it in speculation, as to what was going to happen; the prince looked through some papers on the table.

Then the door opened softly, and Aline entered. Evidently she had questioned the servant who had summoned her, since she gave no sign of surprise or any other emotion on beholding Stetton. She crossed the room and stood beside the prince, who was the first to speak.

"*Madame*," he said, "I have sent for you to hear what M. Stetton has to say. He wishes to speak of you. Now, *monsieur*, you may proceed. Be brief."

M. Stetton suddenly became conscious of a great desire to sink through the floor. He realized that Naumann had been right—eminently right. There was nothing he could say; nothing he dared to say.

He saw very plainly in the prince's eye what would happen to the man who tried to bring odium on the woman who bore his illustrious name without—as Naumann had said—indubitable and instantaneous proof. Several times he opened his mouth to speak, but could find no words. He was seized by an ignominious but overwhelming desire to cut and run.

The prince spoke with brusk impatience:

"Well, *monsieur*?"

Then, as Stetton remained silent, the princess's voice suddenly sounded:

"Your highness, I can understand M. Stetton's embarrassment and reluctance. I know very well what he wishes to say, and it is quite natural that he should hesitate to speak before me. I am sorry that he finds it necessary to speak at all, but your highness is already aware that I am not perfect,"

Judging by the little smile that appeared on the prince's face at this observation, his highness was aware of nothing of the sort. The princess turned to Stetton:

"Monsieur, if you wish me to explain for you, I shall be glad to do so."

Stetton nodded, and the expression on his face was one of gratitude.

"Your highness will be surprised and displeased at what I have to say," began the princess, unconsciously repeating almost the very words that Stetton had used a few minutes before; "but I hope for your forgiveness, though I have been unable to forgive myself. I shall be brief.

"Your highness will remember a day when you left me—I thought forever—unhappy, miserable, in tears. On the very next day M. Stetton asked me to be his wife, and I accepted. Indeed"—the princess glanced at Stetton, then continued, without noticing the prince's start of surprise—"I still have the letter he sent me, which I assure him I shall always treasure.

"Three days later your highness came to me at the opera and gave me reason to believe—that is, told me you would call on me the following day. That same night I canceled my engagement with M. Stetton. I am to blame; I do not deny it; it was a perfidious action, and M. Stetton is perfectly right to feel that he has a grievance against me."

The princess paused, looking first at the prince, then at Stetton, her lovely face filled with humble and touching appeal. The prince appeared to be somewhat astonished. He looked at the young man, saying sternly:

"What is this, M. Stetton? Do you consider it a grave accusation against a woman to say that she has changed her mind?"

As for M. Stetton, he stood speechless. Rage at his helplessness, wonder at Aline's devilish cunning and ready wit, and withal a certain gratitude at being lifted out of his dilemma—all these mingled emotions left him confused and silent.

In the meantime the prince was eyeing him steadily, waiting for him to speak. He wanted to break out in bitter denunciation of this woman who was Princess of Marisi, but he dared not and could not. He ended by not speaking at all.

He made a deep bow to the prince and princess, turned without a word and made for the door.

As he reached it he heard Aline's voice behind him, saying: "Let him go, Michael."

Another minute and he was on the street.

Well, this was the end of everything. So ran his thoughts. Not only was Aline lost to him forever, but all hope of vengeance was also gone. The adventure, which at one time had appeared certain to lead him to the altar of happiness, had landed him nowhere, empty-handed. The chapter was closed. For his part, he would waste no time crying over spilled milk; he reached this philosophical conclusion as he entered the door of his room at the Walderin.

He ate lunch without any appetite for it, wandered about the streets for an hour, and chatted another hour with an acquaintance he met in Walderin Place.

Three o'clock in the afternoon found him seated in the reading-room of the hotel with a book in his hand, though his crowded thoughts would not permit him to read.

Suddenly feeling a hand on his shoulder, he looked around to find Frederick Naumann standing at his elbow. Naumann was saying:

"I've been looking for you for two hours. What the deuce have you been doing with yourself?"

Stetton, seeing no reason for taking his friend into his confidence concerning his brilliant performance at the palace, replied that he had been nowhere in particular.

Said Naumann:

"I want to talk with you. Come up to the room."

Stetton, who didn't want to talk with Naumann or any one else, reluctantly led the way to the elevator and to his room. It was true that the young diplomat had the air of a man who brings news; but what news could interest him now?

When they had lit cigarettes and found seats, Naumann began abruptly:

"I got a letter this morning."

This did not appear to Stetton to be exactly catastrophic, and he said nothing.

"A letter from Mlle. Janvour," continued the young diplomat in a tone of elation. "What do you think of that?"

"I can't say that I think much of anything."

Naumann snorted:

"No? Well, I do. In the last two months I've written her a dozen times and spent a small fortune in bribes, and this is the first word I've had from her."

"What does she have to say?" This in complete indifference.

"Not much. But it's something. Stetton, I'm going to marry her. I can't live without her. But the princess has forbidden her to have anything to do with me—and she won't. She says so in this letter."

"Then how the deuce do you expect to marry her?"

"But that isn't all she says," continued Naumann, disregarding the other's question. "She says she still loves me; that she can never love anyone else, in the same sentence that she tells me not to send her any more letters. This decides me. I'm going to write to Berlin tonight. Within two days the police of all the world will be looking for Vasili Petrovich."

"They won't find him."

"And why?"

"Because he's dead."

Naumann glanced at him sharply:

"What do you mean by that? How do you know—"

"I don't know it. At least, I have no knowledge of it. But I am perfectly certain that he is dead. Good Lord! Haven't I myself looked into every corner of Europe big enough to hold a microbe? It's useless."

"You talk as though you didn't care whether we find

him or not," said Naumann with some heat. "What has happened?"

"Nothing. I'm through, that's all. Through with the whole business. I'm sick of it. Let me tell you something, Naumann—the man never lived that could hand Aline Solini anything she didn't want to take. She's too much for me, and she's too much for you. I've given it up. I leave for New York tomorrow morning."

"Ho!" cried Naumann. He insisted: "Something has happened. You weren't talking this way last night. What is it?"

In the end Stetton gave a detailed account of his visit to the palace.

When he had finished Naumann protested that he could not see why the occurrence, humiliating as it was, should decide Stetton suddenly to renounce all his plans; indeed, it should naturally have increased his eagerness and energy in their performance.

But Stetton, not to be moved, persisted in his determination to leave Marisi the following morning. When Naumann rose to go, three hours later, they shook hands and told each other good-by. Naumann was dining out that evening, and Stetton expected to leave the following morning too early to see him.

After all, he did not go. He had made all preparations; there was nothing to detain him; he simply didn't go. He seemed to the unable to bring himself to the point of departure.

Naumann hinted, not without a touch of malice, that he was probably waiting for the Carnival of Perli, which was to begin in a week or two. The Carnival of Perli, he explained, was an annual midsummer event in Marisi, and the street pageant of the opening day would be led by the prince and princess in a golden chariot. No doubt, said Naumann, Stetton would want to see that.

"I would," Stetton answered, "if I could have Vasili Petrovich at my side. I think the prince would return to the palace in his golden chariot alone."

Three days passed, and the morning of the fourth found Stetton still in Marisi. A dozen times he had decided to leave on the next train for the west; each time he had failed to do so, for no apparent reason whatever. He had met Aline once with Vivi on the Drive; she had bowed to him politely and amiably, and he had felt a savage satisfaction in pointedly turning his back.

But on the fourth day he finally made the jump. At one o'clock in the afternoon he called on Naumann at the legation to say farewell. Naumann shook hands with a laugh.

"If I thought you were really going," he declared, "I'd remonstrate. The carnival is on next week, and, really, you shouldn't miss it. It's no end of fun. But you'll be here, all right."

"You'll see," was Stetton's retort. "This is final. Goodby, old chap. I'll see you some day somewhere, perhaps."

And three hours later found him actually seated in a compartment on the Berlin express as it roared through the valleys at the rate of sixty miles an hour.

He told himself that he had seen the last not only of Marisi, but of Europe. The place sickened him. He wanted to get back to America. New York! Everything would be different. He would forget all about Aline Solini in a week. And he would get to work. The Lord knew it was time, anyway. Marisi! He hated the very name.

He stopped for a day in Berlin to pay farewell calls to friends and acquaintances, and two days in Paris, for the same purpose. Then he went on to London, where he transacted some business with the branch office of his father's manufacturing company, and lingered three days more, in the meanwhile having secured passage on the Lavonia, which was to sail from Liverpool in a few days.

That night he attended the theater and had supper at the Savoy with an old acquaintance—a Harvard classmate who had come to England as agent for an American automobile.

What with his manner of talk and string of reminiscences, it seemed to Stetton that he was already breathing the air of the States. How good it sounded! How good it would be to set foot once more on Manhattan pavements!

But the following morning, though this feeling had not departed, it was accompanied by one of sadness and regret. There was nothing definite about it, and by the time he boarded the train for Liverpool it had left him free to enjoy happier thoughts.

He told himself that he had not realized, until he was actually ready to begin the last lap of his journey home, how much he had wanted to be there. The faces of his father and mother were before him; he was surprised to find himself actually longing to see them. He could hardly wait for the train to reach Liverpool.

He was the first to descend at the station, which was crowded.

It was three o'clock in the afternoon. Cabbies were shouting themselves hoarse, men and women were running hither and thither in every direction, the station announcers and agents of the steamship companies were bumping into each other with true British clumsiness, and newsboys were completing the din by crying out an extra edition of an afternoon paper.

Stetton beckoned for a cab and gave directions to take him to the pier, and at the same time tossed a boy a penny for a paper.

He handed his bag to the cabbie, told him where to go, and entered the cab. Once inside, he opened his newspaper.

In the upper left-hand corner, in big black letters, was the word ''Extra''; and just below, in letters quite as black but not so big, was something that made Stetton's face turn suddenly white.

For a long while, as the cab rattled over the rough cobblestones of Liverpool toward the steamship pier, he sat gazing at the headlines like one paralyzed; then he read the short article printed below:

MARISI, July 19.—The Prince of Marisi was shot and killed by an anarchist today while leading the pageant of the Carnival of Perli with the princess.

The princess narrowly escaped, and is prostrated by the shock. The assassin was captured.

Below this meager account were the words:

More will follow in a later edition.

The cab stopped; the door flew open; they had arrived at the pier, Stetton was startled by the voice of the cabby:

"We're here, sir!"

Stetton looked up with a face as pale as though he had just seen a ghost, and said:

"I've decided not to go. Drive back to the railroad station, and drive like the devil."

In another thirty minutes he was again on a train, headed for Marisi.

CHAPTER XXIII.

PRICE—TWO MILLION DOLLARS.

There are many kinds of power in the world, and though some of them are able to stand alone, most are rendered useless without money to develop or uphold them. Political power certainly belongs to this latter and larger class, though in some instances it manages to live by what it feeds on. When this fails, destruction follows.

Thus, roughly, might be summarized the thoughts of Aline, Princess of Marisi, as she sat alone one afternoon in her boudoir in Marisi palace.

It was three days after the final obsequies had been performed over the body of the prince; a week had passed since his assassination. The princess had secluded herself in the palace and refused to see any but one or two of her most intimate friends.

She had, indeed, plenty to think about. During the life of Prince Michael she had known little or nothing either of state affairs or his personal ones; she had just begun to make her influence felt in little matters of detail, and that was all. But with his death she had become in fact the ruler of Marisi; on the very day following she had sat on the throne at a meeting of council.

Since then she had learned many things; among them being this from the lips of De Mide, that the state coffers were sadly depleted and those of the dead prince empty; worse, somewhat in debt.

For the coffers of the state the princess felt little concern; they could be made to attend to themselves. But those of the prince—that is to say, her own—were a different matter. According to De Mide, it was difficult to procure cash even for the household expenses.

There was six hundred thousand francs due Latorne, of Paris, for the magnificent diamond cross which the prince had given Aline for a wedding present. As much more was owed in Marisi.

Since the death of Prince Michael the creditors were clamoring for their money; what was worse, they refused to advance more. The princess was already in debt to the state treasury, and, besides, it also was practically empty. It was impossible, De Mide had said, to get cash even to pay the servants of the palace.

Not a very pleasant situation, surely, for a newly bereaved princess. So thought Aline; but, true to her character, instead of wasting time in bewailing the difficulties of her situation, she set about finding a way to remove them.

Her first thought was increased taxes. When she pronounced that word De Mide smiled.

"Very little of the revenue is derived from taxes," he asserted, "and that little goes to the state. The funds of the ruler of Marisi come from Paris and St. Petersburg, in recognition of certain services rendered those governments in connection with the Balkan States and the Turks. France pays two hundred thousand francs a year, Russia two hundred and fifty thousand. Prince Michael collected these sums three years in advance; nothing can be expected there.''

Thus Aline found herself confronting a real problem. And by dint of thinking a great deal of money she came, by a natural chain of association, to Richard Stetton, of New York. With her to think was to act; she went to the telephone and called up the Hotel Walderin.

At the first sound of Stetton's voice, eager and joyful when he discovered to whom he was talking, the princess knew that he was still hers. That was all she wanted to know. She asked him to come to see her at the palace the following morning at eleven o'clock.

When Stetton arrived, twenty minutes ahead of time, he was shown at once to the apartments of the princess on the second floor, and into a little reception-room, daintily and tastefully furnished. He had waited but a moment when he heard the rustle of a curtain behind him.

He turned and saw the princess.

Aline expected little difficulty in this interview; nevertheless she came prepared for the battle. Never, thought Stetton, had she been so beautiful, so desirable.

Dressed in mourning purple from head to foot, her white skin and golden hair possessed almost a supernatural loveliness, while her gray-blue eyes glowed—with what, Stetton wondered—with welcome?

For his part, he was plainly embarrassed and ill at ease. He bent over her hand as of old, but dared not kiss it. Truth was, he was more than a little afraid of her. In addition to everything else, was she not a princess?

''I cannot say how glad I was to find you were still

in Marisi," Aline was saying. "I had feared you would have returned to America."

"I did," said Stetton, looking at her as though he were trying to fill his eyes. "That is, I started. At Liverpool I read of the prince's death and returned."

"Ah!" Aline smiled. "Then you knew, after all."

Stetton looked at her, puzzled.

"I mean, you knew I would expect you," Aline explained.

"I do not understand that."

"But, *monsieur*—then why did you return?"

"I don't know. Yes, I do know. To see you."

"There!" said Aline, as though he had admitted something. "You see, I am right."

"Perhaps," Stetton agreed, "but I don't know what you are talking about."

Aline laughed.

"You knew I would send for you."

"How could I know that? I hoped, perhaps."

"And why, *monsieur*? I thought you hated me."

"And so I do."

"Then why did you hope I would send for you?"

"Because when I do not hate you I love you."

Aline glanced at him approvingly.

"My dear Stetton, you are developing a tongue. That is well. You are going to need all the accomplishments you can muster."

"For what purpose?"

"That is the secret, to be divulged later. Now, let us be frank—the preliminary skirmish is over. Tell me exactly what you think of me, and tell me the truth."

"You know very well what I think of you."

"Nevertheless, tell me."

"I cannot tell you."

It was easy enough to tell what the young man meant by the expression of his eyes.

Aline smiled as she said boldly:

"Then show me."

The next instant Stetton had her in his arms, pulling her against him roughly, passionately, and raining kisses on her cheeks and eyes and lips.

"That is what I think," he cried in a voice hoarse with feeling.

What he was doing then he had been dreaming of for months. Her breath against his face maddened him; her lips, though they did not respond to his pressure, were soft and yielding.

"This is what I think," he cried again, intoxicated.

"But, Stetton, you must remember," Aline began, trying to free herself.

"I remember nothing—nothing but this, that I love you! You would tell me that you are a princess, that I must respect the memory of the prince. I respect nothing. I love you!"

"But you should not tell me—now," Aline protested in a voice that was an invitation to tell her again.

"I should not tell you at all," said Stetton grimly. "I know it very well. I am a fool to love you, and a still bigger fool to tell you so. You see, Aline, I am beginning to know you. You have never loved anyone, and never will. You never loved me; you merely played with me, got what you wanted, and then threw me over. And still I love you, in spite of your—"

The princess interrupted him.

"You are wrong."

"Wrong to love you?"

"No."

The princess paused for a moment, then with a sudden air of decision continued:

"Stetton, you are wrong; I repeat it." She looked at the young man with tender eyes. "Why should you say I do not love you? Because I married the prince? Surely you do not think I loved him? Can you not understand that a woman's ambition may be stronger than her love? Well, my ambition is satisfied"—she looked at him meaningly—"my love is not."

286

"You mean—" cried the young man, trembling with joy, not so much at her words as at the expression of her face.

"I mean, Stetton, that I still have your proposal, and that I am willing to accept it."

This was a little sobering. A sudden frown appeared on Stetton's brow.

"Ah, that—" he began, and stopped.

"Do you hesitate?" asked Aline, fixing him with her eyes.

The truth was, he did. He could not understand it. A month ago—nay, a day—two hours ago—he would have asked nothing better for happiness than this which was now offered to him.

In all conscience, had he not had enough of this woman and her wiles? Did he not know her to be treacherous, perfidious, dangerous? Still, to have her for his own—to realize in actuality the desires that had possessed him for so many months—was it not worth any price?

And was she not a princess? Another thought, fed by his vanity, and therefore growing rapidly, entered his mind. Aline had everything she wanted—position, wealth, everything. If she still desired him, it must mean that she really loved him. Besides, for what had he returned to Marisi, if not for this?

"Do you hesitate?" Aline repeated.

For all reply he took her again in his arms. Again his lips sought hers, and this time met with a response as ardent as his own. For a long time they stood, holding each other close; then Aline gently disengaged herself and held him off with her two hands on his shoulders.

"You see, Stetton," she said, looking into his eyes, "we are going to be happy after all. We will forget everything, will we not? Except each other. Now, do you not see that I love you—that I have always loved you?"

The only reply came from his burning eyes. He was too filled with the rapture of her presence to speak.

Soon after she told him he must leave. For the present, she said, they must practice extreme caution; they must give no basis for rumors so soon after the death of Prince Michael. The event that had opened the way for their happiness would at the same time defer its consummation.

But if Stetton was impatient, she declared that he was no more so than she. He need fear nothing more than the temporary delay; she was his—his forever.

Stetton departed with a lighter heart than he had known for many months.

When he had gone Aline stood looking at the door which had just closed behind him for a full minute.

"For the purpose," she said finally to herself, "I could not do better in all the world. Easily managed, vain, passionate, ignorant—in short, a perfect fool. And with his fifty millions, which, by the way, must be investigated—"

She turned and rang a bell, to send for De Mide.

A week passed. Stetton called at the palace daily and had long conferences with Aline; it began to appear that it was not so easy a matter to become the consort of a princess.

Aline had not yet broached the subject in council, but she had sounded two or three of its members privately, and she reported that their final approval was almost certain. The difficulties of the matter were presented to Stetton in so strong a light that he declared his inability to comprehend how they had any chance whatever of success.

"We would not have," said Aline, "but for one thing."

"And that is?"

"An heir to the throne is expected in six months."

Stetton's face reddened, and he abruptly changed the subject.

A week later Aline informed him that two of the council members who remained obstinate could be won by bribes.

Old Duplann, she felt sure, could be had for fifty thousand francs. As for Cinni, a shrewd young Italian who had conducted the late prince's negotiations with the French and Russian governments, that was a different matter. It would require twice that amount with him. A mere hundred and fifty thousand francs in cash—which she did not happen to possess—would turn the scale in their favor.

Stetton provided it, without a murmur. Indeed, he had not expected to get off so cheaply.

The day of the council meeting arrived. Stetton remained in his room at the Walderin, awaiting a message from the palace. The meeting was scheduled for twelve o'clock; an hour before that time he was fuming with impatience. He thought the time would never pass. Noon came; he could scarcely contain himself.

Then one o'clock; and exactly on the hour the telephone-bell rang, and he received word that the princess desired to see him at once. He rushed from the room and to the street, where he had kept an automobile waiting all day. In five minutes he was at the palace.

His first glance at Aline's face, as she met him in her reception-room, told him that all was over. It was eloquent with disappointment, rage, and despair. He cried out without waiting for her to speak:

"What is it? What have they done?"

"Ah, Stetton!" sighed the princess, taking his hand and looking sorrowfully into his eyes.

"They have refused!" cried the young man, feeling his heart sink to his boots.

"No." Aline shook her head.

"They have not refused? What then?"

Aline did not reply at once. Still holding Stetton's hand, she drew him down beside her on a divan. Then she said, seeming to have difficulty to find the words:

"No, they have not refused. But they might as well have done so, for they have imposed conditions that are utterly impossible. They are stubborn, impudent, detestable—I hate them!"

"But the conditions! What are they?"

"It would do no good to tell you." Aline was holding his hand in both her own.

"Tell me!" he insisted frantically. "What are they?"

"No; indeed, I cannot."

But he insisted so earnestly that she was finally forced to yield. She began:

"In the first place, they demand that you be given no power whatever in Marisi politics, either domestic or foreign."

"Bah! What do I care for their politics? What else?"

"They ask that you sign away all claims of whatsoever kind on the State of Marisi for your—our children, if we have any. Under certain conditions this clause may be abrogated later, but only by their will."

"Well, that is not impossible. Is that all?"

"No. The last is the worst. They demand that you furnish ten million francs to the state, to be used in the treasury of the throne."

Stetton jumped to his feet in amazement.

"Ten million francs! Two million dollars!"

"Yes. Of course, it is merely another way of refusing. They knew very well that you would be unable to furnish that amount. It was Cinni who did it—and he took our money! The greasy wretch!"

Stetton kept repeating: "Two million dollars!"

"They would listen to nothing," Aline went on. "I pleaded with them, threatened, stormed; you may be sure I did not let them off easily. But they were immovable. They would not reduce the amount by a single sou."

"Two million dollars!" said Stetton.

Aline pressed his hand. The expression in her eyes was one of sadness and despair.

"Ah, Stetton!" she sighed. "This, then, is the end.

You must know this, my disappointment is as bitter as your own. To have so nearly approached happiness, and then to lose it!''

Stetton sighed. "Two million dollars!"

"Yes. It is monstrous. 'Twas Cinni who did it—the oily, wily Italian. I hate him! Some day, Stetton, you may be sure we shall be revenged. They pretend—well, it makes no difference what they pretend. We shall be revenged; I shall make it the task of my life.

"If only I dared defy them! But no—the people are with them—I would lose everything. I thought that to-day we would be betrothed; instead, we must say farewell!'' Her voice trembled. "You will not forget me, Stetton? You will think of me, as I shall think of you? And to know—''

She was interrupted by a quick movement from the young man. He had risen to his feet and stood facing her, his face lit up by a sudden resolve. He said abruptly, in the tone of one who has made a momentous decision:

"Aline, I will get that ten million francs."

She also rose to her feet, with an appearance of astonishment. "Stetton," she cried, "you cannot! It is impossible!''

"I will," he replied firmly.

She doubted it, and said so. He stuck to his assertion, and finally persuaded her. She applauded his sublime resolution and threw herself into his arms, crying that after all they would be happy, their love would receive its reward.

She declared that she hated to give in to Cinni and the others, but if Stetton thought her worth it she would see that he did not regret his bargain. Besides, she added somewhat ingenuously, would he not have a ruling princess for a wife?

So much decided, they entered into a discussion of details. It would be necessary, of course, for Stetton to go to America to see his father.

As a matter of fact, he did not expect much opposition in that quarter. His father certainly would not be overjoyed at the prospect of handing over two million dollars, but how his mother would jump at the chance of having the Princess of Marisi for a daughter-in-law! She would consider such an acquisition cheap at double the price. No, there would be no opposition there.

He did not explain all this to Aline; he merely told her that he would have no difficulty to procure the necessary amount, but that he would have to go to New York to get it.

"I did not imagine," said Aline playfully, running her fingers through his hair—they were again seated on the divan—"that you carried that much money around in your pocket."

It was decided that Stetton should leave for New York the very next day; they were both anxious, though for very different reasons, to have the matter settled as speedily as possible. It was thought that he would be able to return to Marisi within a month.

"And then," said Aline, "we shall not have long to wait. The wedding must not take place until a year after Prince Michael's death, but we shall be assured of our happiness, we shall be together, and the time will fly swiftly. We shall be a happy family, Stetton—you, Vivi, and I."

"That reminds me. I had almost forgotten. I saw Naumann last night—Frederick Naumann. He wants to marry Vivi."

Aline frowned. "I know it."

"Well, why not?"

She replied dryly:

"For a dozen reasons. I think you are acquainted with most of them."

"But all the same, Naumann is a good fellow, and he is a good friend of mine. Can't you forgive him for my sake? If we are going to be happy we ought to be willing to extend our happiness to others. You see what your love does for me; I am beginning to be unselfish. Indulge me in this, won't you?"

Aline laughed.

"So you are beginning to be unselfish? Well, it would be a pity to hinder you. We shall see about it when you return; if you are successful no doubt I shall be ready to forgive anybody anything.

"And now"—she glanced at her watch—"you must leave me. I must have a talk with De Mide before dinner, when I shall see Cinni and one or two others. If you see your friend Naumann tonight, tell him not to despair."

Stetton rose to go.

"There is no question about my seeing him. He is probably waiting at the hotel now."

"All right. Tell him. And, of course, come in the morning before you go, and say good-by."

Stetton kissed her hand and left.

CHAPTER XXIV.

AT THE GARE DU NORD.

After all, Stetton did not get away from Marisi on the following morning. When he called on Aline at the palace, quite early, to say good-by, he found her engaged with De Mide and Cinni, and was forced to cool his heels in an antechamber for three hours. By the time he finally obtained an audience it was long past his train-time, and he postponed his departure till the afternoon.

He had intended to go straight to Hamburg and sail from there, but altered his route at the request of the princess, who had errands for him to perform in Paris. She had discharged Cinni from her service that morning, though not without a struggle; and at De Mide's suggestion had decided to entrust Stetton with a message to the French government.

He canceled his booking from Hamburg, and procured a passage on a steamer sailing from Cherbourg four days later.

With the feel of Aline's parting kisses still on his lips, and after a hearty hand-shake with Naumann, who went to see him off, he boarded a west-bound train at Marisi station at five o'clock in the afternoon.

His thoughts during the two days' journey were somewhat confused and not entirely pleasant. True, he was at last sure of having Aline for his own; on the other hand, he did not relish the task of confronting his father with a request for two million dollars in cash. Indeed, long before he reached the French border he had decided to leave that part to his mother.

Arriving in Paris late at night, he went to the Continental Hotel. By noon the following day he had delivered the princess's message to the French premier and, since his sailing time was still thirty-six hours away, decided to remain in the city on the Seine another night.

He passed it somewhat hilariously with Mountain-Richards, of the American embassy. They traveled the usual route, from the Café de Paris to Montmartre; Stetton returned to his hotel and bed at seven o'clock in the morning.

At four o'clock he rose, broke his fast, and ordered a cab to take him to the Gare du Nord, having arranged the matter of luggage on the day previous.

At the railway station he bought a book or two and some magazines, which he stuffed in the traveling bag he was carrying. As he straightened up and started toward the doors leading to the trackway, he felt a heavy hand on his arm and a gruff voice sounded in his ear in French:

"Young man, I want to talk with you."

Stetton turned, startled, and found himself looking into a pair of piercing black eyes.

Their owner, a giant of a man with a black beard

that covered all the lower part of his face, was holding Stetton's arm in a grip of steel.

Recognition flashed into the young man's brain with that first glance, and left him speechless.

It was the man of Fasilica, whom he had last seen, many months before, lying prostrate with Aline's bullet in his body!

"I want to talk with you," the man repeated, in a tone that meant much more than the words. He added, gazing into Stetton's eyes:

"I see you recognize me."

Stetton tried to free himself from the other's grasp.

"Really, *monsieur*," he stammered in a voice that he tried to keep calm, while his face turned suddenly pale, "you have the advantage of me. Take your hand from my arm."

The other did not move as he said in a hard voice:

"Don't try to lie to me. You recognized me at once. Come. It is useless to try to escape me. I want to talk with you."

Stetton's brain was whirling in confusion. He glanced round. The room was crowded. People were rushing about in all directions. Not ten feet away a *sergent de ville* stood against a pillar, his eye roving idly over the throng.

People who passed were beginning to glance curiously at the two men, one holding the arm of the other, who was struggling feebly to release himself. Stetton opened his mouth to call to the *sergent de ville*. He was stopped by the voice of the man with the beard:

"Don't do that."

His tone, and the look of his eye, showed Stetton the futility of his intention. This man could not be shaken off in that way. He would follow him to America, around the world, anywhere above or below the earth, before he would forego his purpose.

He must do something—say something—what? He

looked at the man whose fingers were still around his arm, and said with an effort at impatience:

"Well, what is it you want?"

"Come with me. We can't talk here; people are beginning to notice. I have some questions to ask you."

Stetton protested:

"But my train leaves in three minutes. If you have a question to ask, ask it. I am listening."

A sudden gleam appeared in the eyes of the man with the beard—a cold gleam and menacing.

"*Monsieur*," he said, and it was evident that he was forcing himself to speak calmly, "if you knew me better you would not argue with me. When I become angry I neither know nor care what I do. I would advise you to do as I request."

Stetton did not risk another protest. He was struck with a sudden thought—that is, sudden for him—to the effect that his wisest course was to make friends with this man; to deceive him, since he was unable to combat him. He said in a tone of conciliation:

"I do not wish to argue with you, *monsieur*; I am merely anxious to make my train. But there is one two hours later; I suppose I can take that. What is it you want?"

For reply the man with the beard uttered the one word "Come."

Then, with his hand still on Stetton's arm, he guided him to the door of the railway station and across the street to a cheap café on the corner. They entered and seated themselves at a table on one side of the room, which was half filled with cab-drivers, clerks, and railway employees.

A waiter approached. The man with the beard ordered a bottle of wine and laid a five-franc piece on the table to pay for it. He remained silent until the waiter had brought the wine and filled the glasses, then he looked at Stetton and began abruptly:

"In the first place, *monsieur*, I wish to know if you have recognized me?"

Stetton, who had made up his mind what to do, replied promptly in the affirmative, and added:

"You are the man who saved us that night in Fasilica. The night of the siege."

The man with the beard nodded.

"I am. And in addition to that, I am the man whom you left to die."

Stetton tried to smile.

"You seem to be very much alive, *monsieur*." Then, at the light that leaped into the other's eyes, he added hastily: "But what else could I do, under the circumstances? My first duty was elsewhere."

"That is not my opinion," said the man with the beard dryly. "It was a base action, and you know it. But let it pass. It is unimportant; as you say, I am alive. The truth is, I do not know whether I owe you anything or not. That is what I want to find out. You entered my house that night with a woman."

"With two women," put in Stetton.

"You know the one I mean. The other—the girl—I do not know her. I mean Marie Nikolaevna. How came you to know her? What was she to you?"

Stetton frowned.

"By what right do you ask me that?" Then, as the other leaned forward in his chair, he added quickly, "But there is no reason why I should not tell you. She was nothing to me, *monsieur*. I did not know her. I met her quite by accident."

Stetton went on to explain how he had found the two women in the convent and helped them to escape, up to the point where they had entered the house of the man with the beard.

"That is all," he finished. "You know the rest, *monsieur*."

The Russian was eying him steadily.

"You had never seen her before?"

"Never."

"Then why did you leave me to die? You did not know how badly I was wounded. I had saved your life. Why did you attempt to take mine?"

"But I did not!" cried Stetton hotly. "In fact, I saved it. When you moved on the floor she pressed the revolver to your head and would have pulled the trigger if I had not snatched it from her hand."

His sincerity was so apparent that there was no room for doubt. Still the man with the beard insisted:

"But why did you leave me helpless, and, for all you knew, fatally wounded?"

Stetton replied: "That would be a long story. She told me—but does it matter what she told me? I was made to believe that you were a monster, a rogue, unfit to live."

The man with the beard nodded.

"That was like her. That is what she would do. I see, *monsieur*, that you were not to blame. It is not strange that Marie Nikolaevna was able to fool you— she who fooled me so easily. It is not easy to fool Vasili Petrovich. We are quits when you tell me one thing. Where is she?"

As he asked this question the Russian's voice trembled with expectation and his hand grasped the edge of the table.

Stetton tried to meet the piercing black eyes, but could not, as he replied promptly and in a tone of firmness:

"I do not know."

There was a silence. Stetton forced himself to meet the other's eyes, but quickly turned away, unable to withstand that searching gaze.

The man with the beard spoke in a grim voice:

"*Monsieur*, I want the truth. Where is Marie Nikolaevna?"

Stetton merely repeated: "I do not know."

Then, suddenly furious with himself for allowing this man to address him thus, he exclaimed angrily:

"Are you trying to quarrel with me, *monsieur*? Why should I tell you anything but the truth? Of what interest is this woman to me? I have not seen her since that morning in Fasilica."

The Russian laid a hand on his arm and said:

"I do not say I do not believe you. I want to know. You say you have not seen Marie Nikolaevna since that morning?"

"No."

"Where did you leave her?"

"In Fasilica."

"Where in Fasilica?"

"In—" Stetton hesitated; he had no time to think—"in the convent, where I found her."

The Russian's glance was like a flash of lightning.

"The convent was destroyed."

"I know—" Stetton stammered—"I know—that is, part of it. There was a room—some rooms—she said friends would take care of her—"

There was a pause. Stetton was cursing himself for a fool, and trying to think of a way to repair his blunder when suddenly and inexplicably the Russian's manner changed. He lowered his eyes, then raised them again to look at the young man with an expression of confidence and friendliness. He said:

"*Monsieur*—pardon me, but this is a vital matter to me—you are telling me the truth?"

Stetton replied with all the firmness he could muster:

"I am. Why should I tell you other than the truth?"

Another silence. Stetton glanced nervously at his watch. The waiter approached to see if the gentlemen required another bottle of wine, but found that they had not touched the first one. Then suddenly the man with the beard rose to his feet and said:

"I thank you, *monsieur*, and beg your pardon for having detained you. *Adieu*."

And with the word he departed, so rapidly that by the

time Stetton turned round in his chair he had already disappeared into the street.

Stetton sank back in his chair.

His first thought was: "So Aline's name is Marie Nikolaevna!"

A hundred others followed, of more importance and infinitely more disturbing. This was Vasili Petrovich, Aline's husband, for whom he had searched all over Europe; and now that he no longer wished to find him—

Aline, then, could not marry him. That, in a way, brought its consolation; there would be no need for that two million dollars. But to lose her! After all his struggles, all his attempts, all his disappointments—to lose her!

Then came a most vivid picture of the man who had just left—his piercing, stern eyes, his grim, significant tone, his grip of steel, his massive, muscular frame. No, it would not do to risk crossing the path of Vasili Petrovich.

As for Aline, she was doomed; it was certain that he would find her sooner or later. And as for Richard Stetton, the best thing he could do was to go on to America as he had intended, and stay there.

But to lose her! It was impossible. Her face appeared before his eyes, as he had seen it three days before. To lose her! It was more than he could ask of himself, now that success was in his grasp, to relinquish it.

Did she not love him? Possessed of everything that her heart could possibly desire, had she still not desired him? And for the man who warned her that Vasili Petrovich was alive and searching for her, there would be in addition unbounded gratitude.

Stetton sat in his chair in the café for two hours, while these thoughts surged back and forth in his brain. The thought of giving up all hope of possessing Aline was unbearable; the thought of the certain revenge of Vasili Petrovich was terrifying.

But it was not for nothing that he had come and gone at the snap of Aline's fingers for many months.

At the end of the two hours he rose, left the café, hurried across the street to the Gare du Nord and found a train for the east then on the track. When it pulled out, ten minutes later, he was on it.

Having once decided, and finding himself actually headed for Marisi, he was filled with burning impatience to reach his destination.

The train, rushing across the Continent at the rate of fifty miles an hour, appeared to him barely to move. He could not sit still for five minutes at a time; he kept walking up and down the aisle between the compartments with his watch in his hand; each village that they passed brought its measure of relief—he was that much nearer. When the train stopped at a station he would leave the car and stand on the platform, fuming with impatience till they were again under way.

What would Aline do? Would she yield to him? Would she start a search for Vasili Petrovich? He knew she was capable of it, and of a great deal more if she found him. Clearly, it would be an ugly business, but he could not help that.

He must have her at any cost; it was impossible to give her up. Good Heavens! How the train crawled along like a decrepit old man with a cane! Would he never get there?

They had reached Berlin; the train was slowing down as it entered the outskirts of the city. There would be a wait of forty minutes there; Stetton wondered how he could make it bearable. He wandered into the next car to the rear, and, as he entered from the platform, found himself looking directly into the face of Vasili Petrovich!

Stetton stood for one moment as one struck dumb; Vasili Petrovich did not move.

Then the young man turned and bolted precipitately into his own car and compartment, closing the door after him, and sank back on the seat. His face was pale, and he was trembling from head to foot.

His first thought, when he had recovered sufficiently

to have any, was to leave the train at Berlin and return to Paris—in short, to give it up. This, he told himself, could be no coincidence; Vasili Petrovich was following him—a black nemesis.

He shuddered as he reached for his bag on the rack above. Why should this giant Russian suspect him? But it was enough that he did.

Then, suddenly, he was seized with blind rage at the fate which was tearing the prize from his grasp just as he had his fingers on it. It should not be!

He burst out into a string of oaths. He would show this Vasili Petrovich! He would outwit him—this burly giant with the piercing black eyes and the brain of a child. He forced himself into calmness in order to be able to think.

By the time the train halted at the station in Berlin, a few minutes later, he had conceived a plan and prepared to act on it. He knew Berlin well, and with that knowledge had perfected his plan.

The train had barely stopped when he dashed from the steps and into the station. A quick glance over his shoulder showed him the man with the beard leaping from the car behind; he bounded forward. He rushed through the gates, waving his certificate of passage in the face of the official who stood there, out into the street, and to the right.

A short block down, a turn to the left, and there, as he had expected, was a group of motor-cars, standing for rental. He rushed up to the man in charge:

"Which is the fastest car here? Quick!"

The man gave him a glance which indicated that he strongly disapproved of such indecent haste, and slowly pointed to a big, gray touring-car on the other side. Stetton leaped in; the chauffeur was on his seat.

"To Augburg!" he called; and he added, as the car started smoothly forward, "a thousand francs if you make it in two hours."

The car leaped ahead; in ten seconds it had disappeared

down the street. The man whom Stetton had first accosted turned to make an observation on mad foreigners to another of the chauffeurs, and was surprised to find himself confronted by a man about twice his own size, with glowing black eyes and a black beard.

The man with the beard was speaking:

"That man who just rented a car—where is he going? What directions did he give?"

The car-starter looked at him superciliously and informed the questioner politely that it was none of his business.

The man with the beard thrust his hand in his pocket; when he brought it forth there was a flash of gold. He drew the car-starter aside; their hands touched; there was a single whispered word:

"Augburg."

The man with the beard turned and ran back to the railroad station. Entering, he approached the clerk at the information desk.

"Does this train for Marisi stop at Augburg?"

"Yes."

"At what time?"

"Two thirty-nine."

A gleam of satisfaction appeared in the Russian's eyes as he turned, walked back to the trackway and boarded the train he had left less than five minutes before.

In the meantime, Stetton, in the gray touring-car, was threading the streets of Berlin. Slow work, that; but after thirty minutes of it they reached the city limits and the car leaped forward. During that wild ride Stetton had no time to think; he was too busy holding himself in his seat.

As they reached the railway station at Augburg, eighty-five miles from Berlin, he glanced at his watch; it was twenty-five minutes to three. He shoved ten one-hundred-franc notes into the grinning chauffeur's hands and leaped from the tonneau into the station.

"Has the Marisi express passed?"

"No; due in three minutes."

"It stops here?"

"Yes."

And five minutes later found Stetton back in the same compartment he had left in Berlin.

He was certain that Vasili Petrovich had been left behind. He had seen him rush after him into the station at Berlin; no doubt he was at that moment searching that city high and low. No, he need no longer fear Vasili Petrovich. The wily Russian had found his match.

Stetton thought of searching the train for him, to make assurance doubly sure, and did in fact start to explore the car to the rear. But the doors to most of the compartments were closed; the attempt was fruitless. He returned to his own compartment and sat down, as easy in mind as possible under the circumstances.

It would be hard to say which was the clearer picture in the eye of his mind: that of Aline or the man with the beard.

The nearer he approached his destination the more nervous he became, the greater his impatience and anxiety.

What would Aline say? What would she do?

He worked himself up to a point where each second made the next more intolerable. The meeting with Vasili Petrovich had thrown him completely off his balance; he was little better than a man guided solely by the impulse of a mania.

When the train finally reached Marisi, at eight o'clock in the evening of the following day, he rushed through the station like one possessed, leaped into a cab, and shouted to the driver:

"To the palace!"

CHAPTER XXV.

ON THE BALCONY.

On that side of Marisi palace which faces the east, shut off from view of the drive by the trees and shrubbery of the grounds and garden, there is a broad marble balcony running from one end of the wing to the other.

This balcony, which is some twenty feet above the ground, is reached from the palace through a series of French windows, those in the front leading to the apartments of the prince and those in the rear to the rooms of the princess.

Over its marble balustrade the branches of century-old trees wave majestically, and, in the summer, stir softly about the thousand scents rising from the garden below. On a hot summer night it is the most comfortable spot in the city, as well as the most pleasant.

On this balcony sat the Princess Aline and Mlle. Janvour, at a little after eight in the evening. They had left the dinner-table only a few minutes before, and Aline had brought Vivi with her partly to escape the intrusion of other members of the household, and partly because she wished to inform her of a certain decision which she had that day resolved upon, to the effect that if she still wished to marry Herr Frederick Naumann the princess would give her consent and blessing.

The woman and the girl sat for a long time without speaking.

The evening was soft and mild, and sweet with the fragrance of the garden. The noises of the city sounded at a distance; its clamor was reduced to a soothing and pleasing hum.

All was quiet and peaceful, even in the breast of the princess; for not only were her plans in a fair way of completion according to her desires, but she was about to confer happiness on her Vivi, the only creature in the world for whom she had ever felt any genuine affection.

She pressed Vivi's hand and opened her mouth to speak, but was interrupted by the entrance of a servant through one of the windows leading onto the balcony.

The princess turned impatiently:

"What is it? I was not to be disturbed."

The servant approached apologetically:

"I know, your highness, but M. Stetton insisted. He is—"

"M. Stetton!" cried the princess.

"Yes, your highness. He is below. He would not be refused. He says it is of the utmost importance that he see you at once."

The princess had recovered herself. She said calmly:

"Show him up. I will see him here."

Then, when the servant had disappeared, she turned to Vivi:

"You had better go, dear. I had something to tell you—it must wait. Kiss me."

Vivi kissed her, not once, but many times, then turned to go. As she passed through the window to the hall within she met Stetton. He was making for the balcony almost at a run and gave her the merest nod in passing.

His pale face and excited manner roused the girl's curiosity, but she said nothing as she continued on her way down the hall to her own rooms.

Stetton stepped through the window. The balcony was comparatively dark, and coming as he did from the brilliantly lighted palace, he could see nothing.

He heard Aline's voice:

"Here, Stetton, I am here. What is it? Why have you returned?"

He made his way to her side, where she stood against the marble balustrade, and took her in his arms and

306

kissed her. She endured his embrace with ill-concealed impatience, repeating:

"Why have you returned?"

Stetton began:

"I got as far as Paris—"

"Did you see M. Candalet?"

"Yes."

"His answer?"

"Was favorable. But—" Stetton hesitated, then said abruptly:

"Aline, Vasili Petrovich is alive. I have seen him."

The face of the princess turned suddenly pale; so pale that Stetton observed it in the dim light from the windows. She put out a hand and grasped his arm.

"Vasili! You have seen Vasili Petrovich? Where? When?"

"In Paris. At the Gare du Nord."

"But he did not see you?"

"Yes, and followed me to Berlin. I shook him off there."

Then, while the princess stood looking at him in amazement, he related his experiences of the past two days, from the interview with Vasili Petrovich in the Paris café to his arrival at the palace a few minutes before. Never had he seen Aline so moved; her eyes flashed fire; her whole body was tense.

"Fool!" she cried, when he had finished. "You should not have returned to Marisi at all! Why did you not remain in Paris and write to me? Why did you not—but there!" Her tone was one of furious scorn. "An eagle does not catch flies; nor should we expect a fly to catch an eagle."

Stetton did not exactly understand this observation, but the tone was enough. He protested hotly that he had done the best thing possible; at least, he had not gone on to America and left her in ignorance of her danger.

"*Mon Dieu*! What a man!" said Aline with increasing scorn. "But that would have been much better than to lead him straight to me!"

"I tell you I ditched him in Berlin!" cried poor Stetton, who had expected the most profound gratitude for his heroism.

"Perhaps," said the princess, forcing herself to be calm. "But you are no match for Vasili Petrovich, my dear Stetton. I have no doubt that he is in Marisi—perhaps in the street, in the garden there, now."

The princess glanced about uneasily, then suddenly crossed to the windows through which the light shone from the hall, and drew the curtains across the glass, leaving the balcony in darkness. Then she made her way back to Stetton's side and continued:

"You do not know this Vasili Petrovich. He is capable of anything. He is the one person in the world that I fear. You acted for the best—I know that—but you have plunged us in danger. I shall send for Duchesne in the morning, and have the entire city watched for him. Ah, if I once get him in my hands—"

Aline's eyes glittered so brightly that Stetton saw them in the darkness. After a pause she began again abruptly:

"But, after all, why did you return? Why did you not go on to America, and write me of this meeting?"

Stetton stammered something about coming back to find out what to do.

"Do?" cried the princess. "We shall do as we intended, of course!" Then, at a movement from the young man, she moved close to him and put an arm around his shoulders. "Do you think, Stetton, that I will let this Vasili cheat me of you?"

"But he is your husband!"

"Bah!" Aline snapped her fingers. "That only makes it the more imperative to get rid of him."

She moved closer to the young man and put her other hand on his shoulder.

"It will not be necessary to make any change in our

plans. Go to America—start tomorrow—and by the time you return there will be no Vasili Petrovich."

Stetton shuddered at the calmness of her tone. For the thousandth time he tried to tell himself of the danger he was putting his head into, and for the thousandth time he forgot everything else in the promise of her eyes and the sweetness of her kisses.

Her arms were round his neck; she was breathing words of love in his ear; he held her against him roughly, feeling the beating of her heart on his breast, filled with a mad fire.

"Aline," he whispered, "Aline! You know I love you—I love you—I love you—"

Suddenly the princess started and turned about quickly.

"What was that?" she whispered in a tone of alarm, but without removing her arms from the young man's neck.

"What? I heard nothing."

"That tree—that branch there—it moved—see, that one over the balustrade—"

"It was the wind."

"But there is no wind. Stetton, let us go in. I confess it, I am alarmed."

"Bah! You are fanciful. It was nothing." He held her again in his arms and pressed his lips to hers. "Come, Aline—I shall leave tomorrow, then—be kind to me tonight! I love you so! As for Vasili Petrovich, you are right; we will not let him rob us—"

The sentence was never finished.

Stetton suddenly felt his throat gripped in fingers of steel, and at the same moment saw an arm stretched round him toward Aline.

She started back with a cry of terror as she saw herself confronted by a man with a black beard and piercing black eyes, that were brilliant even in the darkness of the balcony.

But she was not quick enough; the fingers of the man's free hand closed about her own throat, slender and white, and sank into the flesh.

After that there was not a sound. The man with the beard stood towering above them, holding them at arm's length; against his great strength they were as babes.

They grasped the sleeves of his coat and tried to pull themselves free; they tore frantically at his fingers, which closed ever tighter about their throats; all was futile.

"Marie"—the voice of Vasili Petrovich came, merciless and terrible—"Marie, demon of hell! Look at me—ah—look in my eyes—what do you see there, Marie Nikolaevna? It is the wrath of God!"

They struggled more feebly. The man with the beard laughed aloud.

"No, no—it is useless—it is the hand of fate around your throat—and yours, you lying dog. I have waited—I have waited—"

Slowly, inexorably, they were pressed to the floor by his overpowering weight and strength—to their knees—down—down—they lay on their backs on the marble pavement; the fingers of steel sank ever deeper in their throats.

Vasili Petrovich was on his knees between them; his arms moved up and down; there was a dull, sickening thud.

A second time, a third, a fourth; then, without releasing his hold, he bent over closely and examined first the face of Stetton, then that of the princess. This for a long time; but what he saw was death.

Vasili Petrovich rose to his feet and stood looking down at the body of the woman.

"Marie." he muttered, and repeated it several times. "Marie—Marie."

He turned abruptly, walked to the balustrade and swung himself onto the branch of a tree that hung over the balcony, and disappeared in its dense foliage.

There was the sound of bending limbs, and, a moment later, the muffled noise of his feet landing on the grass of the garden below.

The branch swayed gently back and forth over the marble balustrade.

Its movements became slower and slower, until the trembling of the leaves finally ceased entirely and became still.

All was night and silence on the balcony.

Somewhere in southern France—exactly where does not matter—perhaps at Nice—on the white sand of the beach, under a large multicolored parasol, sat a young man and a girl.

They were dressed for bathing, but their costumes were dry; it was perhaps not the first time that they had found something on the beach more interesting than the waters of the Mediterranean. They had been silent for a long time, gazing steadfastly into each other's eyes; between them, on the sand, their hands were clasped tightly together.

Suddenly the girl spoke:

"And yet—I believe—my sadness makes me happier." She smiled soberly. "So you should not be jealous of it."

The man looked at her. That is, he would have looked at her if he had not been doing so already.

"I am jealous of anything and anyone that gets the smallest fraction of your smallest thought," he declared emphatically.

"No; I am serious," replied the girl. "You must not expect me ever to forget Aline, and if I want to talk of her it must be with you, for there is no one else. How could I forget? How horrible it was!"

The girl covered her face with her hands.

"Vivi! Vivi dearest!" The man tried to pull her hands away. "You must not think of that—you positively must not. To please me, dear. As for Aline, I shall not ask you to forget her, and I shall talk of her with you whenever you want me to. Dear, you must not—the doctor has forbidden it and you must take heed. Come, talk of me a while—you know what I want you to say."

Evidently the young man knew what he was about, for at this request the girl suddenly uncovered her face and looked at him.

"M. Naumann," she said emphatically, "if you begin that again you will regret it."

"But Vivi! To wait a year is impossible! Six months at most—make it six months. You know very well what mother thinks—"

Vivi interrupted him:

"Your mother agrees with me, young man, and you know it."

"But, hang it all, I tell you I can't wait a year! I won't! In the autumn I go to Rome and you will stay at Berlin—what the deuce do you expect me to do?"

The girl sprang to her feet.

"As you please, *monsieur*," she cried gaily. "Always do as you please; that is my motto, as it was that of the Abbey of Saint Thélème. And now farewell, *monsieur*."

Waving her hand at him mockingly, she raced down the beach toward the surf. In an instant he was on his feet and after her, and they entered the water together with a tremendous splash.

And thus, finally, it happened that Vivi Janvour, who was distinctly French from the tip of her toes to the top of her head, changed her nationality as well as her name and became a German *frau*.

No one will say that she didn't deserve her happiness or reproach her for remaining loyal to the only friend her early years had known. Content in a convent and modest in a palace, she made the best and most obedient of wives; and yet—this should be whispered—if you wish to procure a favor from Herr Frederick Naumann, who has become somewhat of a power in politics and diplomacy, it would not be a bad idea first to gain the approval of the mistress of the house.

Still, Naumann had his way in the matter of a certain date.